Hollywood is a place where they'll pay you a thousand dollars for a kiss and fifty cents for your soul.

I know, because I turned down the first offer often enough and settled for the fifty cents.

Marilyn Monroe

In the sleek and driven world of Los Angeles—where celebrity, sex, and love are optioned to the highest bidder—two famous sisters are locked in a dangerous duel.

One is a bestselling novelist.
The other is a renowned actress.

One is very good.
The other is very, very bad.

They are divided by a corrosive hatred.
And united by a shocking secret....

Once again, the author of the international bestseller *Palm Beach* has created a rich and stylish tale of glamor, decadence, and revenge—Hollywood style.

THE
SISTERS
PAT BOOTH

BALLANTINE BOOKS • NEW YORK

**To Nat Wartels and the
company he founded.**

Library of Congress Catalog Card Number: 86-29303

ISBN 0-345-34789-7

This edition published by arrangement with Crown Publishers, Inc.

Manufactured in the United States of America

First International Edition: December 1987
First Ballantine Books Edition: May 1988

PROLOGUE

AT TARA IT WAS TOMORROW, AND FOR SCARLETT O'Hara it was another day. She stood still on the polished mahogany floor of the old porch, beaten but unbowed, and the sigh of her sadness billowed through the intricate folds of her ivory lace dress. She was home at last, home at Tara, where the fields and the trees and the dear red earth had endured to comfort her in the midst of heartbreak.

Scarlett breathed in deeply to capture the honeysuckle-scented breeze, and she wiped away the beginnings of tears in the eyes that had seen so much sorrow: her beloved Georgia burning as Sherman marched malevolently through Atlanta to the sea; little Bonnie's pale face relaxed in the death that so many of her friends had found; and Rhett . . . Rhett, who gave not a damn for her feelings or her future.

She walked slowly across the columned portico and her fan waved gently at the heavy heat as the sun knifed down on the sleepy county. How many days had there been like this? Lazy, mint-julep, Ashley afternoons with strong ponies in the dogwoods, yapping hounds among the cotton bolls, and swift swallows against the royal-blue sky. So many things were the same, but it was the differences that fathered the glistening tears. Everything she cared about had gone, gone forever, with the heartless wind.

Jane was lost, deep in the role of Scarlett. She had never had an acting lesson in her life, and she had never heard of Stanislavsky and his Method, but she knew instinctively how to do this. To be believed you had to feel, to be real you had to suffer, and right now her heart was breaking, as Scarlett O'Hara's had done.

She was oblivious to the crane, hovering vulturelike above the set, where Pete Rivkin, the director, sat. She had no idea where the camera angles were, and still less the chalk marks on the wooden floor which told her where to stand. But it didn't matter. It simply couldn't matter less because the emotion that was flowing from her was almost tangible, and because her spectacular, mind-melting beauty was burning onto the film and filling it with a vision that would drive America mad. It was the first day of principal photography for the television maxi-series *Tomorrow is Another Day*, the breathlessly awaited sequel to *Gone With the Wind* and there wasn't a person on the set who didn't know that they were present at the birth of a legend. The scent of a blockbuster triumph was everywhere: in the shining eyes of the humble grips, in the manic glow that surrounded Pete Rivkin, in the energizing electricity that sparkled and crackled in the San Fernando Valley air. But most of all it was in the haunting, beguiling eyes of the star: in the lilt of her heart-stopping voice, in the delicate anguish of the make-believe broken heart that hid shyly beneath the perfect geometry of her magnolia brushed breasts.

Jane reached down into the reservoir of feeling: a child dead, a lover lost, a civilization in ruins. She could *feel* the pain—Scarlett's pain, *her* pain. Jane, too, had clawed her way back from the brink of tragedy and disgrace, and although she was only twenty-two, she, like Scarlett, had been tested by the fire. Poor Scarlett was racked by love. Well, so was she. Scarlett had been destitute and far from home. So had she. Scarlett had fought and battled and finally triumphed over her enemies. And by *God*, she had, too. She had wandered into the Hollywood fast lane—an innocent on the fearful freeway, high on life and low on street smarts, and the crash course in the rules of the road had all but destroyed her. But now she was the conquering queen, and out there in the crowd, watching her success, was the sister who had tried so desperately to wreck her life. The delicious thought flew around the edges of Jane's consciousness, and behind the tears her mind smiled as she thought of the bundle of impotent fury that would be seething somewhere at the back of the set. Scarlett would have appreciated that—the sharp sweetness of revenge, enemies cast down, rivals vanquished.

Above Jane, Rivkin's hand was raised in a Strangelove salute. Like a cobra preparing to strike he waited for the moment. Then his arm arced down, and, at the signal, the camera and its crew zoomed along greased tracks for the close-up.

Jane turned her face toward it, allowing the angled sunlight to catch her tear-stained profile. Once again she sought the emotion that would make the words live. What did Scarlett feel for Rhett? It was easy. It was all there, tucked up loosely in the folds of memory. He own lover, locked in her arms beneath hot, wet sheets on the steamy canyon nights while Los Angeles slept. The man she worshipped, who had left her, as Rhett had left Scarlett. . . . The camera hovered closer to catch her trembling upper lip, her stricken face, the mask of her sorrow.

"Rhett," she whispered, her voice quiveirng with the despair of the deserted lover, "Rhett, find it in your heart to forgive me, as I forgive you."

From the back of the set—her eyes small with her vast hatred—Julie Bennett watched her sister. A force field of malice clung to her, a vibrating aura of desperate aggression, and all around her, despite the denseness of the crowd, there was space as the busy film crew subconsciously separated themselves from her evil. In the middle of her private hate cocoon Julie's teeth were grinding in her head, and the blood boiled in her veins as her pinpoint pupils contracted even further, their needle lasers of malice streaking out toward the target.

Jane. Always Jane. Jane who was the living reminder of the mother she loathed and of the father she worshiped. Jane, who had hijacked her childhood, forced her into exile, who had so effortlessly stolen the only two men she had ever loved. Through her steaming mind the litany of grievance rolled round and round, and her pudgy fingers clasped tight and the sweat sprang from her palms as she contemplated her dreadful failure to achieve the vengeance she had always sought. What did it matter that she was the bestselling authoress in the world? What was money, fame, success without the power to harm the one person in the universe she had vowed to destroy? At every turn Jane had slithered away from her fury. Julie had baited the traps, laid out the poison, and her fertile, Machiavellian mind had dreamed up exotic hells for the sister she despised, but despite all the lies, the cheating, and the scheming Jane had escaped. Now she was almost beyond harm. *Tomorrow* was already a triumph, and the reason was plain for all to see. Jane. Jane, bringing tears to the eyes of the seen-it-all movie makers. Jane, conjuring up emotions in the hard-bitten professionals like spirits from some vasty deep. Jane. Jane. Always Jane, riding on a magic cloud to the stars where Julie's hatred would be unable to touch her.

There was one chance left. The ultimate option. But to gain her terrible objective Julie would have to sacrifice herself. The deed she was about to do would mean the end of everything for her—of her career, of her reputation, of her phenomenal income. She smiled grimly to herself, her florid features twisted and turned by her wrath. It would be worth it, because Jane would not survive the holocaust she was about to unleash. Like Samson, she herself would perish as she destroyed her sister, and the sacrifice would be a small price to play for the glory of her vengeance.

‡She clutched the heavy manila envelope to her heaving breast, and the breath hissed between her teeth as she prepared to use its horrible contents—the fearsome weapon of her retribution. Soon, so soon it would be all over. All would end in the maelstrom of revenge as the hurt and betrayal were finally washed away in the flood tide that would drown them all.

So she muttered to herself the promise, her thin, tight lips mouthing the mantra of her diamond-hard purpose, as she elbowed her way through the set toward Jane.

"I will never forgive you, little sister. For what you are, for what you were, for what you have done to me. Any minute now, I promise, you will understand the meaning of pain."

* * *

Twenty feet from Julie, and sixty feet from Jane, Billy Bingham's finger was on the trigger of the gun. Like some beautiful scarecrow, hunched and bent in his tattered blue jeans, he stood awkwardly amidst the chaos of cameras, electric gables, and boom microphones. He was gaunt, haggard, and pale as death, but he still looked like an angel, the sweet innocence of his face giving no hint of the vengeance he was about to unleash. Billy's eyes swam in and out of focus, and in the quiet of the crowded set he tried hard not to faint. The pain was crashing in against his mind, mighty waves of agony showering their frothy crescendoes into the depths of his being. In a way he was grateful for it, because it reminded him of why he was there. He had never murdered anyone before. It would be a first time, almost certainly a one-off, and he wanted to do it right. But unconsciousness was threatening the deed he wanted so desperately to perform. He needed only a little bit longer. In a few seconds the slate would be clean at last.

He bent down, and his black curly hair fell forward as he wiped the sweat from his forehead on his bandaged hand. The scrambled nerve endings jangled in his screaming brain as he fought to concentrate. This would be his ultimate work of art. No painting, no sculpture could compare with what he was about to do now. It would be perfect, beyond mere beauty, a good deed in an appallingly naughty world.

He had never felt so finished. He was over. He had stopped.

The pain said so. The dreadful injury that caused the pain howled the message from the rooftop of his mind. Never again would he paint the pictures that had given meaning to his life. So life must end. At twenty-five the handsome whip-cord body, the moody, sensitive eyes, the remarkable vision that turned the commonplace into beauty were merely the discarded props of last year's play. The curtain was about to fall on the angry, angst filled drama of his life, and the one who had lowered it was close . . . close . . . so close.

Through the swirling mists he could see her, and the thought of the bullet and what it would do strengthened his tired body. So he stiffened his shaky grip on the butt of the hidden revolver as he staggered through the packed set toward the one he would kill.

Robert Foley ran as if the hounds of hell were snapping at his feet. The parking lot at the studio was about a quarter of a mile from the *Tomorrow* set, and a fiendish arrangement of impenetrable wire fences had prevented him driving straight to his destination. His lungs were like bellows in his chest and the red hot San Fernando Valley air burned in his flared nostrils as he tried to make his body do the things it wasn't used to doing. He was lean and fit, but doing a 400 meter dash fully clothed in a 90 degree sauna was asking a lot. So the sweat ran from him, and his muscles howled their protest as he ran on in the super-heat to prevent the tragedy that must not be.

In his mind the ghostly music played, the funeral dirge merging with up-tempo discords of alarm and fear. A wicked, evil thing was about to happen, and he was the only person in the universe who could prevent it. A few minutes before he had learned the secret that he should have known all along. All through the years, without realizing it, he had possessed the key that could unlock the mystery, and now it was his duty and his Fate to open wide the Pandora's box that alone would stop the crime.

He could see the edge of the crowd now, see the silent chaos of spider web wires, floodlights, and tracking cameras, and still he ran, his heart crashing in his chest as his pounding legs powered him toward the set. On the portico of the vast mock Tara he could see Jane, small, still, infinitely vulnerable, communing with the camera that loved her. The relief exploded within him. The filming had not been interrupted. Yet. He was not too late.

But too late for what? His terrible dilemma was still not resolved, and Robert Foley's racing brain tried once more, at this late stage, to decide what he would do. To save what he loved, he would have to betray what once he had loved more. Even at this moment, as his body rushed headlong toward the revelation, a portion of his mind howled "no." Part of him forbade what the other part willed. Which would win—the future or the past?

The dreadful thing was that he didn't really know.

He had arrived. At the edge of the set a few of the less busy turned disinterestedly to watch the stranger. At the back, a camera platform was raised a foot or two above the action. Robert Foley didn't hesitate. He leaped onto it, and his wild, straining eyes scanned the ant-heap of activity that unfolded below him. At once he saw her. Through the set, parting the movie makers like the Red Sea, surged the menacing figure of Julie Bennett. In her hand, held high like some talisman of doom, was the manila envelope with the power to make Robert Foley's steam heated blood run cold. Like an arrow to its taret, Julie Bennett was flying toward the porch of Tara. Flying toward Jane.

"Wait," he screamed at the top of his voice. "Wait!"

It was as if someone had shouted in church. One hundred heads snapped around to find the heretic who had dared to mock the ritual of filming.

In the pregnant silence Robert Foley heard his own voice. It didn't sound like his. It was loud and clear and shaking with transcendent conviction. To all who heard it, to Robert himself, it sounded like a voice from another world, and his words cut through to the very core of his spellbound audience.

"Stop! Julie Bennett, in the name of God, stop now! Before you do the thing that will break your heart."

PART ONE

CHILD WOMAN

"It's a wonderful day when a child becomes a woman," said Mary, staring out dreamily over the mist-shrouded Cotswolds.

"It's a frightening one when a woman becomes a child," said Frederick.

Julie Bennett, *Child Woman*

ONE

"Rude am I in my speech. . . .
And therefore little shall I grace my cause
In speaking for myself. Yet, by your gracious patience
I will a round unvarnish'd tale deliver
Of my whole course of love."

THE VOICE FLOATED OUT FROM THE STAGE LIKE A tangible thing. Beaming, echoing, swimming on the waves of air, it caressed the walls of the all but empty theater, insinuated its silky presence into dark, desolate corners, and rode proud and free down the deserted aisles—glorying in its magic, in its power to loosen the shackles of trapped imagination.

Sophie sat stock-still in the thrall of her husband's extraordinary stage presence. She hardly dared to breathe, to move, in case she disturbed the beauty as his words communed with her soul and set free her thoughts on the wild wings of fantasy. He was like a god up there. His face blackened, his aquiline features sharp, his eyes darting, standing upright, honest, and true, he *was* the Moor. He had *become* Othello.

"Rude am I in my speech": It was a mighty lie, but, strangely it was also the purest truth. No voice had ever given more eloquent meaning to Shakespeare's words here at Stratford, the home of the poet; but like Othello, the brave soldier, Richard Bennett always spoke his mind in terms that anyone could understand. And his accent was definitely "not quite right," at least in the supercharged world of haute bohemian café society in which Sophie mixed. But that was light-years away. This was reality. This was Richard's domain. The one in which he was the mightiest of princes, and she no longer Sophie, social high priestess of the 1960s and princess of Rumania, but the lowliest peasant girl fit only to bathe the feet of her master.

She felt the thrill rush through her as the years melted away. He had done this to her then, and he was doing it again now. She was literally ecstatic as she lost herself in the drama of desire for the man she had once dreamed of owning—the god who was now her husband. Richard Bennett, the outsider. The working-class boy who had conquered the world of stage, who had dragged his way out of the artistic desert of his humble origins to electrify the world with his brilliance, who even now was scorned for the effrontery with which he had dared to defile the blood of a European princess with his peasant genes. Othello, the blackamoor, the brilliant soldier who was good enough to fight the battles of the noble Venetians he served, but was not thought worthy of the aristocratic and fair-skinned Desdemona.

> *"She loved me for the dangers I had pass'd,*
> *And I loved her that she did pity them."*

It was true. She had loved him for the things he had achieved and the horrendous odds he had fought to get them. He had been her hero, and at moments like this he was her hero once again.

The sharp, high-pitched voice cut into the dream. "Richard, that's superb. Really, very fine, but a little too slow." The excitement in the voice of director Trevor Phillips was barely controlled. This *Othello* would be a critical *rave*. He had never heard Richard Bennett in such good voice during a rehearsal. Richard was giving it everything he'd got—reaching down into the reservoirs of feeling to dredge up the glorious emotion. It was all so *believable*. The agonies and the passion of 1604 alive and well in the here and now. Was it something to do with the fact that Richard had insisted on full stage makeup for the run-through of his major monologues? But Phillips knew there was another, infinitely more powerful reason, and it sat a few rows in front of him in the otherwise deserted auditorium. Sophie was doing this to Richard. He was acting his heart out for her.

Phillips vowed to make absolutely sure she would be there on the opening night.

"Okay, if it's all right with you, we'll go straight on to the 'I had been happy if the general camp . . . had tasted her sweet body' speech."

Sophie twisted in her seat, irritated. How dare Phillips interrupt? How dare he criticize a genius he could never understand? Her fierce eyes pierced the gloom, targeting the small, round figure of Trevor Phillips sitting alone at the back of the theater.

An insistent whisper at her side intervened. "Mother. Mother! Don't *say* anything. It's a rehearsal, and he's the director. The whole point of the thing is that he criticize the performance. That's why Dad is here today. For him, not for us."

"Oh *shut* up, Julie." Sophie almost bit off her tongue as she tried to draw back the words. She sighed and leaned back on her seat as she mentally prepared for her daughter's onslaught. Why had the Lord sent her an impossible daughter? All day long Sophie had tried to avoid the conflict simmering constantly beneath the surface, and now a knee-jerk response to her daughter's priggish bossiness had brought it to a boil. The plot of the little play never varied: Sophie, selfish/hard/unthinking, was trying to sabotage Richard's self-respect/art/happiness, while Julie, selfless/righteous/kind, was trying to save him from destruction.

"*You* shut up, you selfish cow. For God's sake, don't try to ruin Daddy's Othello. You've ruined the rest of his life." Julie hissed the abuse through clenched teeth.

Sophie had long since given up such standard parental phrases as "Don't you dare speak to your mother like that." They had no effect at all on Julie.

"Does Dad think I've ruined his life?"

Julie lapsed into silence. That of course was the problem. Dad didn't realize that Sophie was destroying him, because he worshiped her. And if he ever *did* realize it, then he was more than prepared to let it happen. Like the offers from Hollywood: He would never accept them, but in his heart Julie knew that he wanted to. He would turn down the chance to become the greatest film star the world had ever known because Sophie, her mother, wanted to keep him in the dark, damp English prison where her toffee-nosed English friends could patronize the great peasant-actor for their private amusement. Time and again Julie had seen it happen, and it drove her into an impotent fury. At night in her bed she would dream of Hollywood and the swaying palm trees, and of warm-breezed canyon nights, and the Bennett name in neon on the marquees and in poster-paint pastels on the billboards of the Strip. She saw herself alone with her father in the brave new world beyond the green and the rain, and the hypocrisy; far from the pomp and the circumstance and the desperate reality-defying pretense.

"You won't let him go to America."

"Your father is quite able to make up his mind what he does with his life."

"Would you come and live with us if we went to Hollywood?"

Sophie felt the irritation rise within her. Julie had a way of getting to the heart of things. Right now, this minute, she would follow her stunning husband to the gates of hell and back, but she was damned if she was going to say so to her infuriating daughter. "Probably not."

"Why not?" There was triumph in Julie's voice.

"Because this is my home, and I don't want to leave it."

"*My* home is where Daddy is, or wherever he wants to be." Somehow Julie knew that was the wife's line.

"And I think you'll find that where Daddy wants to be is right here with *me*." She stole a sideways glance at her daughter to see if the knock-out punch had landed. It had. Tears glistened in Julie's eyes.

Richard's voice drew them away from their battle.

> *". . . then must you speak*
> *Of one that loved not wisely but too well;*
> *Of one not easily jealous . . ."*

Julie's tears were for herself no longer. They were for her father, for Othello and the deed he had just performed. Desdemona, his wife, was dead, but by some cruel trick of fate the real wife was alive and well, beside her in the darkened auditorium. The guilty lived, and the innocent perished in the topsy-turvy grown-up world. Julie closed her eyes tight and squeezed out the tears, as her father's remarkable art merged fantasy with reality. He was about to die, to take his life, because he could not bear what he had done. Because he had loved not wisely but far too well. She opened her eyes to see the dagger rise, its blade shining in the light. "Please God, protect him forever, from everything, from my mother, from himself," murmured Julie's trembling lips. And she vowed as she prayed that if God would not protect him, then *she* would be his champion. From this day forth, forever more . . .

But her hand flew to her mouth as the foreboding took her. Dear Lord in Heaven, it wasn't, surely, a *real* knife.

> *". . . Set you down this;*
> *And say besides, that in Aleppo once . . ."*

Trevor Phillips had stopped breathing. In all his years with the Royal Shakespeare company he had never experienced anything like this. The bemused jealousy of the simple man lost in love and driven mad by the cruel subtlety of a world he couldn't understand. It seemed that Richard Bennett had invented the emotion, real, throbbing emotion springing directly from harrowing experience, and needing only the presence of a catalyst to give it terrible birth—a catalyst like the enigmatic Sophie, princess of Rumania, who watched him in the dark. Was he acting out the pain, the hurt, the destruction for her? Was he about to wreak a poetic vengeance on himself, and on the woman who would watch him die? Phillips rose up in his seat, his hand held high, his mouth opening to stop the tragedy.

High, so high, the spotlight caught the knife as it gleamed dreadfully at the outer point of its promised downward arc.

Sophie understood him now, as before she had known the young, unsure boy, the Hamlet she had fallen in love with. She was one with him in the numbing pain—its cause, and its result—living in his mind as he prepared to die for his passion. She was a part of this, as much the creator of what was happening as Richard. Her body was alive, crawling with his words, on fire with the visions that flickered and flamed in her mind. His strong body, blackened by the genes of the Moor, wonderfully unnatural, with its hint of wild strangeness and alien delight. The violent man of war, as strong and straight in love as locked in combat with the turban'd Turk. She shuddered as the feeling took her, melting her skin and dissolving the reason of her brain as the hard rain of desire soaked her straining body. She leaned forward in her seat, oblivious to her surroundings, and her nervous tongue tried in vain to moisten parchment lips. The wave of lust was breaking over her now, and a part of her was already on the stage, tearing at him, loving him, screaming for the oneness of terminal ecstasy. She had to have him. Now. This instant. To worship his glory with the poor gift of her body.

> *"I took by the throat the circumcised dog,*
> *And smote him,* thus."

Down, down came the dagger to Othello's heart. Slow, slow to do the thing it had to do.

And Sophie heard the piercing scream, her scream, merging with another from behind.

"Richard . . . *don't!*"

"Stop it. *Stop it!*" was Trevor Phillip's desperate command.

But the point of the knife had disappeared, visible no longer, deep in the chest of the man who had died for love. Richard Bennett twisted as the terrible blow shook him. He collapsed to his knees, both hands on the hilt of the weapon of his destruction. For a second he was still, lost in the enormity of his deed; then, suddenly, he toppled sideways, one arm outstretched, racing for some touch he would never feel, and the breath rattled out of him as the blood came, at the corner of his lips, and from the chest wound, burbling, bubbling from around the point of the dagger's entry, staining crimson the gold-braid tunic of the Moor.

Julie Bennett's scream was last. High pitched with a child's dread it crashed through the shaken, shocked air. "Daddy. *Daddy!*"

The audience of three were all standing now, still, rooted there, like trees in the forest of the dead.

Now the body moved, with the dreadful effort of the dying, and the beloved face raised itself once more.

> *"I kiss'd thee 'ere I kill'd thee: no way but this;*
> *Killing myself, to die upon a kiss."*

"Richard?" Sophie's voice was small with its question.

"Daddy?" echoed Julie by her side.

"Richard!" said Trevor Phillips loudly from the back of the auditorium.

Then Julie was running, headlong down the aisle, and Sophie was running after her, and Trevor Phillips was shaking his head as he emerged from the dream that had become a nightmare.

SOPHIE OPENED THE DOOR OF THE DRESSING ROOM SLOWLY, quietly. There was a reverence about her as she acted out the steps in the new drama she had written for herself. He was waiting for her, as she knew he would be. Standing still in the middle of the small green room with its peeling paint, its cheap furniture, its ugly fluorescent light, Sophie avoided his eyes, watching him instead through the chipped makeup mirror, his regal presence framed by a score of bulbs. The blood that still appeared so real lay everywhere: smeared across the wet tunic, daubed across the charcoal that covered every exposed piece of his skin. He turned to watch her watch him, secondhand, in the mirror, and his eyes caught hers as he played the role that, unspoken, she was asking him to play.

At his side now, and still he didn't look at her, still his arms did not reach for her. His black arms. His black face. She was white and pure, a European princess who now chose to lay her body before the rough soldier from a distant land.

She knelt before him, as if in church, and she reached for him as if for the sacrament, holding his hard body to her, clasping him tight as she pressed her head against him. But his arms were at his sides, and that was what she wanted: to do it all. To give herself as a gift to this man she loved, the man who had carried her already to the very frontiers of feeling.

Sophie lifted the bloodstained smock and then he was in her hand, hard, magnificent, strong, and certain—all the things Richard's Othello had been. She bent down, to give and to receive, took him in her mouth, and felt him rear and buck as the divine stimulation touched him. He was her prisoner, trapped deliciously in her warm mouth, caressed by teeth, loved by her tongue. At first Sophie scarcely moved at all. It was enough that he was there, pleasing her with his pleasure.

His low moan was her reward. "Take off your clothes," he whispered.

Her eyes lowered, Sophie did as she was told. But still she didn't let him go. With her mouth around him, she unbuttoned her shirt and her black leather miniskirt and pushed the silk Dior panties down below her buttocks. She wore no bra, no stockings, nothing except the long black boots.

Now she looked up at him through her fine brown hair, her strong shoulders and upper arms a milk-white contrast to his stained black skin. Still holding his eyes with hers, she bore downward on him, taking him deep, deeper into her.

Richard bowed his head. It was too good. He wanted to talk to her, but words were liars. Words were nothing in the wild inferno of touch. He forced himself to concentrate. There could be no forgetting. He would use the memory as a talisman to protect him from the evil spirits of the black mornings, and the sad, bad evenings, when Sophie belonged to the world but not to him—when he had to watch as she received the homage of those drawn to the beauty of her spirit and the perfection of her body.

Quite still herself, Sophie moved around the invader she

had ambushed, taking it farther into her mouth, as she encouraged him to press at her and to have no thought of her comfort or her pain. In a way it was an atonement, a blissful penance for having taken him from the world that was his, the one in which he was a king, and for precipitating him into the world that was hers, where he ruled no more.

Sophie's mind was numb as she looked up at the black face of the Moor, the rude soldier who used her so shamefully, so deliciously. On and on he went, colliding cruelly with her throat, oblivious to the shock of his sudden thrust, as he punished her long white neck and made love to her wide-open mouth. She held her breath and willed herself to withstand the agony of his onslaught as pleasure and pain merged into one and thought stood still.

Richard watched her as he pushed at her, and savored the triumph that was such a vital part of this ecstasy. Her eyes were closed again now as she fought to live with his fearful invasion. On her high forehead lay the fine film of passion, and her broad shoulders were rigid and tense.

But Sophie wanted it all. It was time for the drama to move on. She let him go and knelt at his feet, waiting, expectant.

For an age Richard looked at her, lost in admiration for the beauty of her abandonment. She was magnificent. A warrior of the Amazon—her nipples tense and nervous, almost visibly throbbing with her terrible lust. Brown and tight, they were two perfect triangles of desperate need, screaming out for the touch of hand or lip, as they lay on the gently curving, snowy slopes of her breasts.

He reached out to her—tender now—and smoothed away the damp hair from her face. He knelt before her.

And then his dark face was on her body, and his mouth was on her smooth skin, tasting the heat and the need.

Sophie moaned her acquiescence, leaned back on the floor, and steadied herself for him. She held his head, guiding it gently.

She closed her eyes at the touch of his tongue, and her legs quivered open, wide open, as she gave him the freedom of her body. His lips were on her now, on her breasts, on her stomach, moving deliciously lower, but he delayed at the brink—

holding back from the ultimate commitment, and within her the pleasure crisis built, as his tongue, a hummingbird at the petals of a wide-open flower, built her panic.

In desperation she reached for him, arching her strong back upward from the floor, forcing his head down, down into the depths of her. "Yes, please. Oh, Richard. Yes, please."

And now his tongue reached into her and milked her joy, far inside in the steam heat of the rain forest. But still it was not enough. The tolerance to infinite pleasure racked her body and she tore at him, to make it stronger, more sublime, more frightening in its savage intensity. The rivers roared inside her, and her booted legs snaked up behind his neck to hold him in a vicelike grip, as they willed him to drown in her ecstasy. Sophie thrashed from side to side. Inside her the clarion call of a single trumpet sounded—a clean, clear note of wonderful prediction, and then one by one the instruments of the orchestra joined in. Her heart raced in her chest, and her frantic fingers clutched and clasped at the air as she thrust herself toward the timeless moment. He was at the essence of her now, the knowing tongue moving softly, rhythmically as it conducted her toward the sweet conclusion. And then it was upon her—and she was falling apart, diving, crashing down, as the shower burst soaked her world. Through the jangling, jerking orgasm she held on to him, her legs clamped tight on his neck, her love lips owning his dark face as she sprayed him cruelly with her longing. At last, it was finished and the coil spring was unwound, as her muscles freed him, and the long harsh sighs of her breathing signaled that she was spent.

She smiled up at him as he knelt between her wide-open legs, marveling at his beauty, at the beautiful thing he had made happen to her, and she reached up and touched the lips that had pleased her, the lips still wet with her love.

"Now," she said.

As he entered her Richard knew that she would have his baby. It was with an absolute and indestructible certainty that he knew that. So quietly now he rode her, lost in a world that transcended desire. This was love. The gentle movement, the easy motion of two souls in harmony working together toward creation's act. With my body I thee worship. This was what it meant. He had never known it before.

"Sophie, I love you," he said. "I love you so much."

She didn't answer but she pushed insistently against him, and moved from side to side—wide, wide open as she called out for union. It was time. The oneness of meant-to-be lovers. Richard closed his eyes as he felt God within him, the power, the ultimate meaning, and the tears ran down his cheeks as he gave himself up to the mystical experience. On and on it went, impossibly long, as his soul flowed and his magic gift transferred itself to Sophie, her soft cries and shuddering acquiescence the honor guard of welcome.

Then, the deed done, he rested his head down on her flat stomach and loved her soft sobbing as he held her tight to comfort her in the aftermath of creation.

Their happiness was a palpable thing in the unlikely room. It radiated through the dusty air, danced joyfully through the neon shadows, and reflected cheerfully from the garish green gloss paint. But there was one small area where it couldn't go, one walled-off space where the force field of an alien emotion held it at bay. By the open doorway, an oasis of pain and misery among the surrounding bliss, stood a young girl.

Julie Bennett leaned against the frame of the door, and the silent tears poured down her fifteen-year-old cheeks. She had watched it all. She had witnessed the betrayal, and it would change her life forever.

TWO

"BETTER THAN HOLLYWOOD, NO?"

Sophie of Rumania had that proud, arrogant look that said that there wasn't much she wanted, but that anything she wanted she would get. It was something to do with the triangular nature of her face, the high, haughty Slavonic cheekbones chiseling in to a pointed, definite chin. The eyes, however, said she wasn't really that kind of person at all. They were big and round and brown, and they roamed the room with enthusiasm, darting hither and thither with a naïve innocence. She was having fun, and she didn't mind who knew it.

She slipped her hand into her husband's. The Chelsea party epitomized everything that was good about the sixties. It was a hodgepodge of fun, duchesses cavorting with pop stars, cabinet ministers colluding with crimpers, models mingling with moguls. Sophie loved it all. Swinging London and Richard were the center of her life.

Richard Bennett laughed. "Don't you ever give up?"

"Not until I get my own way." She was flirting with him, and she laughed back, letting the tinkling music waft deliciously from her long and infinitely aristocratic neck.

"Better than Hollywood without you," he answered cunningly. His statement was really a question. Would he have to go to Hollywood alone?

"Oh, darling, I just can't think how you could *ever* leave

all this. I mean it's the first time in years that this has happened in England. It's all so new, and so exciting, and you're right in the middle of it. And Hollywood! I mean, really. It's so . . ." she fought for the ultimate insult, "so . . . *fifties*."

Richard paused. Was this the time? Almost certainly not. Because in a way she was right, and all around them the explosive party provided the evidence.

It was a whole new world—an exuberant, self-confident revolution of the meritocracy, and as long as he lived he had never expected to see it. For a boy from the Welsh valleys who had dragged himself up through the pre-Beatles molasses by the sheer brilliance of his acting ability, it was a gas to be in on the burning of the barricades. Shakespeare was hardly rock 'n' roll, but there was room for everyone in the sixties movable feast.

He sighed and smiled at her. "Well, we don't have to make any decisions yet. They'll hold for a bit. Probably force my price up. In Hollywood the deal's the thing." He changed the subject. "Christ, some of these people don't look very well. I think some of them could use a transfusion."

She laughed back at him. "You're just jealous, because they look 'pale and interesting.' Mind you, Keith Richard looks as if he's been in the clinches with Dracula all right. Do you think he'd shrivel up if they let the sun in at him?"

He looked at her lovingly. She was pale, too, but unlike the rock stars scattered throughout the crowd, Sophie's pallor was the product of her perfect genes. Smooth, soft, and with the beauty of a newly formed snowflake, her face glowed in the candlelight, and the twin spots of color high upon her cheekbones said that she knew what the day was like as well as the night. She was unbelievably beautiful. Broad, strong shoulders raced down to a waspish waist, the lines of symmetry enclosing a pair of breasts so amazing that very few people—men *and* women—in the room hadn't taken a moment or two to stare at them. The simple silk Ossie Clark frock gave them ample opportunity. It wasn't see-through, but the whole effect was more revealing than if she had worn nothing at all. Her breasts just stood there—the braless nipples upturned, erect, in a state of permanent arousal from constant contact with the flimsy, electric material of the dress. Impossibly long Allen Jones legs slithered from the micro-length creation that barely covered Princess Sophie of Rumania's bikini briefs.

She sipped at the glass of white wine. "Do you think that tonight might be the time to tell Julie our news?"

Richard buried his head in his hands in feigned horror. "God, must we? I was having a good time."

"We've got to soon. I mean any minute now it'll show. In fact I think it does already."

"It doesn't. Believe me. Believe anyone in the room." Sophie's stomach was pancake flat. Inside it the two-month-old baby would be wafer thin.

"We're not going to win any popularity contests, you know. She'll go spare."

"Let her!" said Sophie with a shake of her Vidal Sassoon page-boy bob. "She's going to have to get used to it."

Richard felt the pang. It was partly pity for the daughter who loved him so desperately, but also fear, at this latest demonstration of his beautiful wife's hardness of heart, her aristocratic disinterest in the fundamental happiness of others, a characteristic that had been used against him in the past, and could be used again.

"It didn't help that she was in on the conception." It was almost, but not quite, a joke, and immediately Richard felt guilty for his tone of voice. It had been thrown out as a sop to Sophie, but it was at the expense of his daughter.

"Oh, she's over that. In America she'd have been in therapy for the rest of her life."

America again. God, if he ever got there, and Sophie came too, there would be blood on the walls at the Industry parties. "Who's going to tell her?"

"If I tell her, there'll be a scene—not that anybody will care. You tell her. She's Daddy's girl." Sophie looked at him defiantly. An aggressive note had crept into her voice. She flicked a nonexistent strand of hair from her eye.

Richard groaned inside. It was just like Sophie that when she felt on the defensive she immediately moved into the attack. He peered around the room, for help and inspiration as much as to find his daughter. It occurred to him suddenly that he hadn't seen her for about half an hour. Not that he was worried. Fifteen was young to be at a party like this, but to Richard, Julie often seemed infinitely old. In the corner, the Granny-Takes-a-Trip contingent—Jane Ormsby-Gore, whose father was the ambassador in Washington, Michael Rainey, Nigel Waymouth, and other assorted upper-class ravers—had actually brought babies, one of which was sucking happily at someone's spaniel-ear breast.

Sophie helped him out. "She's over there in the corner, with one of The Scream. If he knows she's only fifteen, then clearly he's too broad-minded to care. I just hope for her sake he hasn't got halitosis."

"God, is she all right?"

"Of course she's all right, silly. I was only joking. She wouldn't let Mick Jagger get to first base. Too hung up on you." She poked playfully at Richard's ribs, and he doubled up in mock pain.

"Listen, I think I'd better have another scotch before I do this. Maybe I should go and rehearse in the loo. You could watch. It seemed to do the trick last time."

"Richard! Don't be so disgusting."

But she remembered. So well. And she put her arm around her husband's shoulders, sending the dress up three inches and turning on every man within fifteen feet as she gave them a sight of her silk Dior panties.

"Okay, here I go. Wish me well."

And he aimed himself into the packed crowd.

It was a fight to move in the Chelsea studio, as it was supposed to be. All progress through the room was a delicious battle involving spilled drinks, bodily contact with bare flesh, and eyeball-to-eyeball confrontations with the rich and famous "faces" scattered strategically throughout the room, each surrounded by its own satellite system of attentive and cheerfully subservient courtiers and jesters. He bounced off the photographer David Bailey—"Hello luv. All right, then? When's Sophie goin' to let me do 'er fer *Vogue*?"—and Justin de Villeneuve, inventor of Twiggy—"Hello, sweetheart. 'Ow's yer face?"—and slipped past a wasted Joe Cocker, a leggy, coltish Jean Shrimpton—"I so *admired* your Othello, Richard."

Julie's face lit up when she saw him. The musician's face darkened.

"Hi, Dad."

On the Sony sound system Mick Jagger was telling the world that he was unable to get any satisfaction. The rock star stared balefully at Richard as if he had just prevented him from getting his.

"Having a good time, darling?"

"Great. Do you know Vinnie? He's with The Scream."

Vinnie was dressed in black leather, tall, sharp eyed, innocent as Satan. He was also startlingly beautiful—a sort of washed-out Dorian Gray, somebody's gorgeous bouncing baby who had lost himself along the way and now, in true sixties style, was cleaning up by dirtying down. He nodded curtly toward Richard, flicking a swanlike neck and fingering a death's-head ring. "Hi, man," he said, in a flat, bored voice.

Richard eyed him doubtfully. He and Vinnie were two working-class heroes on different tracks to the honey pot. Each had much more in common with the other than either would have liked to admit. For a moment nobody spoke. It was cool to be able to endure an uncomfortable silence.

"You an actor, right?"

"Yes, I'm with the Royal Shakespeare Company."

"Oh, yeah, all that 'O' level crap."

Richard smiled but didn't answer.

Two twin points of red appeared up high on his daughter's cheeks. "Have you heard of Shakespeare?" Her voice was a whiplash.

Vinnie's sunken eyes went cunning. He smiled a dazzling smile and held up both hands, as if to avert a blow. "Okay, okay. Don't hassle me. I gotta split. Gotta split." And he sidled away into the crowd.

"Interesting guy." Richard's tone was conversational.

"Creep!" She paused. Then, "He asked me if I wanted to go to bed with him." She watched her father to see how he would react.

"Goodness! How grown-up!"

She looked as disappointed as he had intended her to be by his unimpressed response.

"I told him to forget it."

"Good for you."

He looked speculatively at his daughter. If Vinnie was into Rubens rather than Twiggy, then he would risk a prison sentence for some horizontal dancing with Julie. She was as ripe as a watermelon. Her breasts were huge—great big serious things that squirmed in the too-tight T-shirt. The rest of her was, almost literally, a supporting act. Her waist went in as waists should, but then her bottom raced out again, while well-proportioned but seriously formidable legs made good their escape from the wide denim belt that masqueraded as a skirt. Her face was full and florid, but the individual features related well to each other while the swimming-pool eyes flashed and sparkled with the quicksilver intelligence of a take-me-or-leave-me personality. All in all she would be one mighty meal, and a possibly indigestible one, to a Swiss-cheese-minded, Olive-Oyl-bodied rock star like Vinnie.

Julie snaked her arm around her father's waist. "Did you come over here to protect me from a rapacious stranger?"

"A father has to protect a beautiful daughter."

She beamed at the compliment, and again Richard felt guilty. She loved him so very much, this complicated, unlikely production of his wife's body. In a way he loved her back, but with his brain, not his heart. In his heart there was room only for the magnificent obsession that was Sophie.

He took a deep breath. "Darling, we've got some wonderful news for you." Gloom positively dripped from his words.

"What, Dad?" Julie looked at him quizzically as she read between the lines and realized that the "wonderful news" was going to contain discouraging words.

How to do this? "Mummy is pregnant." He spat it out. "You're going to have a little brother or sister."

"What? What did you say?" Julie's voice grew louder with every word.

"Isn't it great? We heard yesterday. We didn't want to get your hopes up. The doctor thinks it's about two months—"

Richard nearly bit his tongue off. Dear, oh dear, why on earth had he said *that*? Two months ago they had been in Stratford rehearsing *Othello*!

Julie stood quite still, but her face was reddening and her clenched knuckles were already white. "Who's the fucking father?" she hissed at last. "Fucking Othello?"

"Julie!"

The tears were rushing to her eyes, and the instant misery was a palpable thing. "No, really, Dad. Who *is* the father? I mean do you really *know*? Do you think it's you? I mean, Mummy is always having lunch with all those *old* friends, isn't she? Like *Lord* Buckman and Willie Partington. If I were you I'd demand a blood test."

The arrows thwacked into the target. How like Julie to turn her anger into pain, his pain. Of course it was true. Sophie's love affair with life seemed to demand that she was loved in return and not just by her husband. His obsessive adoration, overwhelming as it was, just wasn't enough. Whenever there were men around she had to have them watch her. And then, in remorseless progression they all had to like her, to fancy her, and then to love her. At which point in the game she would get bored, and somebody would have to be found to relieve the boredom—and so the dance would go on. It was an addiction of sorts, and periodically she needed her fix of masculine adoration, her hit of romantic despair, her rush of sexual stimulation. It was hell for him. Time and time again he tried to comfort himself with the belief that it was merely a harmless charade, a by-product of the high spirits and generous nature that were part of the very reason he loved her so desperately. And yet, there were the terrible moments of doubt and fear when he was sure she had betrayed him.

"Don't you dare—ever—to talk about your mother like that," he said in a faraway voice. His suddenly haunted eyes tore themselves away from his daughter and flew back across the room, to Sophie, surrounded already by a court of admirers. Vidal Sassoon, running his fingers—professionally—through her hair. Terence Donovan—master of chat—laying it on in layers. Patrick Lichfield, photographer cousin of the queen, flitting dangerously around the group, like a spider round a fly.

God how he loved her. It seemed like yesterday but it was years ago when she had burst unknown, unannounced, and uninvited into his dressing room. She had stood before him, vibrating with a magnificent enthusiasm and told him that she had fallen in love with his Hamlet. "Great art and the artist are inseparable," she had declared, "and so now I am in love with you." The brown-eyed princess of Rumania had carried his position by frontal assault, and from that day to this he had been a slave to love. Now, and for the years past, she was the reason for his life. Before, there had been his art—his mighty success on the English stage, and the cheers and the applause for the miner's son from Wales. *That* had been the fuel on which he had run. But today there was only Sophie and her beauty and her wit and, yes, her grandeur, her unconventionality, and her wild, willful freedom.

His throat dry, his face white, he stared helplessly at his daughter.

"Oh, Dad, I'm sorry. It's not your fault," Julie said, as an outsize tear rolled down her cheek.

But she knew whose "fault" it was.

Richard watched her go. She tore into the crowd and bore down on Sophie, scattering her assembled admirers like confetti at a drunken wedding.

"What makes you think you have the *right* to have another child?" she screamed at point-blank range.

Sophie had seen Julie coming and had braced herself for the worst. But somehow her daughter always managed to top that. If she ever married it had better not be to the sensitive type. Mother and daughter were alone, separated from the swinging sixties by a six-foot quarantine zone in case the loss of cool should be contagious.

"What? Sibling rivalry already? A bit early, isn't it, Julie?" Sophie felt the adrenaline hum. God, this was going to be awful. But at the same time she couldn't help having a grudging respect for her daughter. Julie knew how to fight. Thank God she was a girl, and not some boy who might have used his fists rather than his tongue.

"Not sibling rivalry, Mother. Half-sibling rivalry."

"What's that supposed to mean?"

"Do you want me to spell it out?"

"Have you been drinking, Julie?" That was for the audience. Julie never drank liquor. Sophie was playing for time.

Julie ignored the question. "Well, whose baby is it, Mum? Or don't you know? If you sit on a circular saw I imagine you never get to find out which tooth bit you."

Sophie took a deep breath and looked her daughter right in the eye. "Really, Julie, you shouldn't be so paranoid. Of course it's Daddy's baby. You should know. You were there for the conception. Or have you forgotten?"

In the age of liberation, at the birth of the permissive society, the ears were tuning in to the psychodrama. This was strong stuff even for the turned-on psychedelic group gropers of mellow yellow land who thronged around them.

Julie stood her ground for a second or two, shaking. Then, she said, quite gently, "I hate you, Mother. God, I hate you so much."

"Can't say I'm wild about you," said Sophie evenly.

"And I hate your miserable disgusting baby, too."

Julie turned quickly and disappeared into the bowels of the party.

There were tears in her eyes and despair in her heart, but there was a strange exhilaration, too—because she had a plan, a wonderful plan. A gorgeous plan that would wreak a terrible revenge on everyone—on the mother she loathed and on the father she loved—the one who had betrayed her.

Vinnie hadn't split the party. Julie found him in the place where they stacked the coats, smoking a joint into the face of a waiflike model who was clearly on something pretty heavy, probably LSD. Vinnie was saying some sexy things, but the girl just floated along on the magic carpet of her expanded consciousness.

He looked up as Julie came in, and he seemed pretty pleased to see her. It was mutual. Vinnie was part of Julie's plan. With the arrogance of his type, he assumed that she was part of his. "Hi, baby."

"Hi, Vinnie."

"You broke loose from Dad?"

"Yeah, Mum an' Dad went home."

She tried to sound like a cockney. Working class was "in."

Vinnie moved around a bit—stuck out his bony hips, licked his voluptuous mouth, and let the eyes that made the teeny boppers scream and wet their knickers do their work on Julie.

"You ever been to a Scream gig?"

"No, I'd like to."

"I'll fix you up. We're doin' the Odeon, Hammersmith, next week."

He looked at her speculatively. She was young, but he'd had the pox off younger. The trouble was that they got carried away with the excitement of it all, and when you got them home and made your move, they panicked and dropped you like a stone. Vinnie didn't need *that* after half a dozen Cuba libres at the Ad Lib or the Speak. Still, she looked good and tough. It was worth the risk.

"Listen, luv. You wanna come down the Ad Lib, then?"

"Groovy." The spaced-out model had vibed in on the invitation.

"Not you, slag."

Julie plunged in. "Great Vinnie. I'd love to. Can we go right now? I've had this scene."

"Okay, girl. Let's do it."

Blimey, Vinnie thought. Locked into a right little raver here. No sweat at all.

Vinnie was right. There would be no sweat. He would be able to lie there like a log and let it happen, because Julie knew exactly what she wanted, and it wasn't his body and it wasn't his mind. It wasn't his fame and it wasn't his fortune. No. What she wanted was him inside her, making the baby that would be the weapon of her war.

THREE

SOPHIE'S FACE HAD GONE THROUGH SEVERAL COLOR changes already. Initially it had been a ghostly white. Deep vermilion red was the shade of the moment, a fitting backdrop to her opening and closing mouth as it tried to splutter out her all-consuming rage. Julie had never seen her mother like this, and she was loving every second of it.

Her father's response had been rather different. Around the corners of his mouth and at the back of the sad eyes, some of his misery was visible, and the glass of brandy, which had appeared as if by magic in his hand, was another outward marker of his feelings. Julie was pleased about that, too. She might love him as much as it was possible to love, but he deserved this—for his infidelity, for daring to father a child that would be a rival for his attention, for loving her hated mother.

Sophie managed a sentence at last. "You'll just have to have an abortion."

Julie's face smiled the answer. "I'm five months pregnant." Everyone knew what that meant.

"How on *earth* do you know? Surely, if you've just found out you can't be . . ." Richard was clutching at straws. Somehow he knew that his daughter would not get things like this wrong.

"I've known for nearly four months now. I kept it secret because I wanted to have the baby." She still had the silly smile of satisfaction on her face, and it was that as much as anything else that was driving her mother mad—a more than sufficient raison d'être.

"How can you possibly have kept it secret?" her mother screamed.

"I just got fat, Mother. No big problem. You got fat. I got fat. You just assumed my fat was all from food."

Even through the anger Sophie couldn't let that go. "I didn't get *fat*, I'm pregnant." Immediately she regretted falling into the trap.

"Yes, isn't it nice. You're going to have Daddy's baby, and I get a nice new brother or sister. Then I have mine, and you get a brand new grandchild. We'll all be able to call you 'Granny'!"

Sophie sank down on the big chintz sofa. Like the captain on the bridge of a stricken ship, she felt messages winging in from all quarters. Cancel the Bonham-Carter dinner party. They were half an hour late for that already. Julie had chosen her moment for maximum disruption. Julie's *pregnancy* was maximum disruption. *Julie* was maximum disruption. Fifteen years old, and the father apparently some rock star called Vinnie.

It was quite clear. Julie had planned the whole thing. She was determined to have her baby, and it was an act of aggression against her parents.

Richard drank deep on the brandy. "I think I'd better phone the Bonham-Carters," he said.

"*Tele*phone the Bonham-Carters," said Sophie absentmindedly.

He didn't move. His statement of intent had been, basically, a request for guidance on what to do. He stared helplessly at his wife, beautiful as ever in the simmering John Bates evening frock. It was true. She was pregnant, but she *wasn't* fat. Julie, in contrast, was quite definitely both.

"Why did you keep it a secret, Julie? Why didn't you tell us? Why didn't you tell me? We could have helped you. Were you frightened of telling us? Surely not."

Julie couldn't give him the answer to that. He would have to work it out for himself. She tried to look inscrutable in her silence, but the smile wouldn't go away.

"She wasn't frightened of telling us," Sophie shouted. "She's not frightened of telling us now. Look at her. She's loving every minute of it. She didn't tell us because she wanted to hurt us. Why, God only knows."

"And what are you planning for the child, Julie? Are you intending to bring it up here, with us?"

"I thought I might throw it away." Julie wasn't smiling now. There was hatred in her voice, and Richard Bennett saw something in her he had never seen before. Along the nape of his neck the spiders crawled. His Julie. So quiet, so deep. So clever, so enigmatic. In the still of her waters monsters had been growing—unknown, unnoticed—and now they had surfaced to disturb their world.

"Don't say things like that, Julie. Not even as a joke," Sophie said quietly, her tone questioning, asking for reassurance.

Julie just smiled and Sophie's hot blood cooled as she saw it.

"You just didn't notice, did you, Mummy? You didn't notice how sick I was all those mornings, and you didn't care when I started eating everything in sight. You only cared that you had a fat daughter, and you didn't mind even that because *you* were putting on weight and you were worried that all the men would stop flirting with you."

"Don't talk to your mother like that."

"Richard, I think perhaps we ought to call Dr. Cameron. This isn't normal. There's something terribly wrong going on."

Julie's smile was gone now. Her face was snarled up as she spoke, her voice quivering with the pent-up anger of all the years. "You're right, Mother. There is something wrong going on, and I'll tell you what it is. It's you! You're killing my dad. Slowly but surely you're killing him. You keep him here in this miserable country, where they pay him nothing and his career has nowhere to go, and you behave like a whore and make him miserable because he's mad enough to love you. Do you know that? Don't you realize what you're doing?"

Sophie rushed at her. Julie watched her coming—proud and defiant. She took no steps to avoid the blow. Instead, she turned her face toward it, thrusting out her cheek at the arcing missile that was Sophie's hand. What the hell did pain matter when you'd won?

THE DARK GRAY CLOUDS SCUDDED ACROSS THE FURIOUS SKY, but still the rain didn't come. Julie Bennett pressed herself against the window, her knees drawn up against her tight abdomen, and wished there was someone around to irritate.

Inside she felt she had fused with nature. The depression was everywhere: in her head; dripping from the leafless boughs of the plane trees in Eaton Square; in her womb where the child she wanted to happen clung grimly to its life-support system; in the damp, sullen air in which the scrawny pigeons flew and the evening mists gathered.

Most of the day she had wandered around the room, unable to summon the energy for any kind of action—unable to light the fire, flick through *Queen* magazine, even to turn on the television. Thought was all there was, thought and the deadness of feeling—the global apathy that held her in its barnacle grip.

With a sickening thump of her heart she thought of her parents. A few miles away they would be preparing for the "joyous" event. Her mother had gone into labor at nine o'clock that morning and now the cozy childbirth scene would be unfolding in the exclusive Lindo Wing at St. Mary's. Her mother, bathed in a thin film of sweat, would be looking like a million dollars as she slotted out the baby—and every doctor in the room would already be a little in love with her, and every nurse, every midwife would be experiencing the pangs of jealousy. Outside, pacing the green linoleum, her father would be relishing the role of "worried" dad, his brow knitted in appropriate concern, his eyes questioning, his whole body hunched in concentration as he milked the moment for every last ounce of drama. If only *her* baby would come. That would do it. A frantic telephone call, a mad dash across London as the storm broke—through the wind and the rain, the lightning and the thunder—and the game of happy family would be blown to smithereens.

She looked down speculatively at her swollen abdomen. It was as quiet as the grave. Her baby was asleep. Damn it!

Once again she got up and wandered aimlessly across the drawing room David Mlinaric had designed. The room was so very Sophie, and Julie hated it: the sporting pictures, the Stubbs and the rather good Sartorius, the little tables with their framed pictures of Rumanian ancestors, and the odd signed portrait of a British royal or two.

It was all so predictable—trendy good taste. The stippled terracotta walls with their material borders, the stylish mix of Sheraton and Biedermeier furniture, the "interesting" objèts— a West Irian headhunter's dagger carved from a human thigh bone, the Elizabeth Frink sculpture of a helmeted warrior (very "now"), and one or two fun "executive toys"—silver balls suspended on string, perpetual-motion machines that showed that "one" had a sense of humor as well as a sense of style.

Julie mooched out into the corridor, purposefully avoiding her father's study, whose briar-pipe, leather-Chesterfield, brass-carriage-lamp, *Playboy* décor was the opposite end of the pole from her mother's. Instead she was drawn as if by some vile magnet to what was about to become "the nursery."

The teddy-bear wallpaper from Harrods seemed to hope for a boy, but the crib, brand new and painted with sexually neutral flowers, clearly couldn't care less. Neither could Julie. She walked toward it slowly, and something inside told her to kick it as hard as she could. The satisfying thud as her shoe connected and the paint chips flew was the nicest thing that had happened to her all day.

The diapers were already stacked in the cupboard. Box upon box of them, anxious for baby shit, terrifying in their complacent promise. Julie picked up the sterilizing unit, newborn from Mothercare. She ran greasy fingers over it and dropped it casually onto the floor. How could you hate something that wasn't there? Answer: by hating the person from whom it would come. How could you hurt the person you hated? Answer: by stealing her limelight on the day she was the star.

How nice. Somebody had thought to buy the Vaseline, and

the zinc oxide ointment, and the Johnson's baby powder. Julie reached forward for them. She squeezed the ointment on the pillow, smeared the Vaseline on the teddy-bear curtains, and sprinkled the baby powder over both. The triumphant home-coming would not be without its petty irritations. There was another question. How did you scoop the glorious moment of the mother-to-be? Easy. You started your own baby. Right now. And then you screamed blue murder until nobody was thinking about anything at all but you.

The thought struck Julie like a thunderbolt. Of course. That was it. That was the thing she had to do. But it was a danger-ous, mad thought. No, it wasn't a thought or an idea—it was a decision.

How to do it? Hot baths and gin. Old wives knew best. But she didn't like gin.

Julie walked briskly to the alcove next to the drawing room where her parents kept the drink. Champagne was something she could handle, and there was always a bottle or two in the refrigerator. She bent down, with difficulty, and opened its door: Krug for the connoisseurs, Moët for people who didn't matter, Taittinger for American visitors. Julie smiled to her-self. Which marque induced you best? They should tell you in the ads.

She picked the Moët. If her parents used it on the less important people, then it was the marque for her.

Sophie had thought the original bathroom enormous "fun" and hadn't changed it at all. The ancient tub stood on four legs, the ends of which were molded into the unlikely shapes of gargoyles. Each wore a rather surprised expression, as if it couldn't quite understand how it had come to be stranded on this vast expanse of black-and-white checkered tile. Julie, iced champagne in hand, looked around the familiar room, and the happy memories came winging in: baths with Daddy in the early days, with boats and scrubbing brushes, soaping his back and being allowed to shampoo his hair. But now even the good times made her want to cry.

She was fighting against the tears as she turned on the vast tap and watched the hot water cascade into the bath. Then she slipped out of her clothes and stepped gingerly into the scalding water. Julie tried to sit down, but she had to jump up again immediately. She rubbed her hands feverishly over the skin of her buttocks to take the pain away. At last she acclimatized and was able to sink back into the watery womb.

She reached over the side of the bath for the champagne and pressed the ice-cold neck of the bottle against her lips. She took a long, lingering swig of the fizzy, acid drink, swallowing as much as she could before the burp stopped her in her tracks. She put the bottle back on the floor and waited for the explosions to subside, but already she could feel the buzz. Her abdomen might be full, but her stomach wasn't. She'd had no food all day. The alcohol was on assisted passage into her bloodstream, and what she would be getting her child would be getting, too. This should wake him up; he'd been quiet for far too long, strangely quiet, really, now that she thought about it.

The second swig was much easier, and the third and fourth easier still. Sleepy, Julie rested her head against the enamel and the steam rose around her head and the bees buzzed in her furry mind. She was drifting now, safe and floating on a warm current, her eyes closed, all the bad feelings gone. Why on earth was she here, doing this? What an inspired choice! What a way to go! Her head lolled sideways.

Julie heard the dreadful shriek of agony and she knew it was she who was screaming. She knew, too, that there was a terrible unbearable pain, and that the clear waters of the bath were inexplicably a rusty red. About that time she became aware that she had done something incredibly stupid, that she had gone too far, and that she was sorry, but that it might be too late to be sorry. Or too late for anything at all.

FOUR

"WHAT DO WE KNOW ABOUT THIS PATIENT?"

The emergency-room registrar's tone was matter-of-fact, but the look on his face said he was worried.

"It's Julie Bennett, the actor's daughter. She'd been drinking and a neighbor heard her screaming. They had to knock down the front door, and they found her bleeding in the bath. Apparently she's only fifteen. Believe it or not, her mother's in the Lindo Wing right now—giving birth. She's a Dr. Peters patient."

The doctor jumped at that. "Is Stella Peters up there now?"

"I saw her car outside earlier." The emergency-room nurse always knew whose car was in the lot.

"Ring up there immediately. Tell her I have an emergency down here. Detached placenta, ruptured uterus. Christ knows what, but she's bleeding like a stuck pig. I need her ten minutes ago. Right?" To the room in general he said, "Okay, everyone, let's get cracking."

The team moved into action as the orders came fast and furious.

"Tip up the end of the bed, Karen." Let gravity help return the remaining blood to the starved heart.

"Nurse, telephone for six units of Group O universal-donor blood."

There was no time to match the blood to the patient's blood group.

"I'll get a line into her. Put up some normal saline till we get the blood." They had to stop the veins from collapsing with the blood loss.

"Somebody listen to the fetal heart. And wire her up to an ECG for continuous monitoring. Keep reading out the BP." Was the baby still alive?

"Sue, put some swabs into the vagina and see if you can stop the bleeding, okay?"

"Blood pressure's seventy over forty."

"Damn! Any luck, Sue?"

"No, the bleeding won't stop."

"Pulse is one twenty-five."

The nurse leaning over Julie's abdomen, listening through what looked like a toy ear trumpet, had the worst news of all. "Can't hear the fetal heart," she said.

Julie was flying up in the air now, and it was a delicious feeling of lightness, freedom, release. She could fly away like this forever. A glorious air cruise throughout eternity. Down below, far below, she could see herself—a funny, helpless thing, a bit like an old overcoat drifting on the surface of a silver sea. It was so very nice to be rid of herself at last. She had escaped, and she quite agreed with the voice from far away that said, "Where the *fuck's* Stella Peters? I think we've lost these two."

STELLA PETERS WALKED BRISKLY TOWARD RICHARD BENNETT. "Going like clockwork in there. No problems at all. I wish all mothers were like Sophie."

The consulting obstetrician smiled reassuringly as she gave the good news. Richard's face registered the relief, and his whole body seemed to relax with her words. He couldn't help it. Actors had to express what they felt. "Wonderful, wonderful. How much longer, do you think?"

"I never like to say, but not long."

God, if only every birth was like this, with the mother, brave, uncomplaining, and well exercised and pushing like a weight lifter, and the father in the right place—the corridor—

not fainting away at the foot of the bed or getting under every-one's feet.

"Well, let's hope Julie goes as smoothly."

"How is she?" Stella Peter's voice showed her concern. That was a bad business. A fifteen-year-old, eaten up with jealousy at the thought of her parents' baby, who had got herself pregnant as revenge. Dr. Peters had never known a case like it. How did a child learn to hate? How did a teenager become so cunning, so devious, so filled with malice? The psychiatrists hadn't come up with any answers at all, except to describe Julie as having a "personality disorder," whatever that meant. The term didn't even begin to do justice to what was going on in her adolescent head. The extraordinary thing was that half the time the little girl was totally charming. She was bright as a button and Dr. Peters knew that at school they thought Julie was the best thing since sliced bread, always winning prizes for her essays and her poetry. Now Julie would give birth to a little child whom she had no inten-tions of mothering, or loving, or looking after. This would be born in spite, conceived in anger, in an atmosphere devoid not only of love but of desire.

Richard splayed open his hands wide, "Julie's Julie," the gesture seemed to say.

A brave smile brightened Dr. Peters's face. "Still, let's not let it spoil *your* happy event."

"It won't." Richard meant it. Nothing could. It was as if his whole life were beginning again. He had a brand-new start with Sophie, a symbolic renewal of their marriage. He could see the future clearly now, and all the doubts and longings had faded away. The decision about Hollywood had been made, and that was a relief in itself. He wouldn't go to America. He wouldn't sell himself for money, the way Larry and Richard had. He would stay where he was with the wife he loved, in the country that had given him the ability to hone and perfect his art in the fertile ground of its mighty dramatic tradition. He would stay in England and bring up his glorious new child, watching it grow and basking in the quiet peace of family life, the demons of ambition dead at his feet.

Stella Peters knew what he was thinking. She was a good enough doctor to get close to her patients, and Sophie had told her how important this child was to both of them. Now his shining face was telling her the same thing.

"Well, I'm not leaving the building, but I've a couple of things to do, so I'll pop back later. But don't worry. Baby's fine, and mother's terrific. I've got an epidural in place so the pain's bearable, although I think that between you, me, and the gatepost Sophie *enjoys* pain. She's the toughest mum I've ever had."

"Okay, see you nearer the time." Richard half raised his hand.

Stella Peters strode toward the nursing station, and the telephone rang just before she reached it.

The nurse said, "Yes, she's right here," and held out the phone. "Dr. Peters, it's for you."

STELLA PETERS crashed into the emergency room, her face asking the questions. Already she had made the decision not to tell the parents. From what she had heard on the telephone, every single second would count.

The registrar talked fast. "I think we've lost the baby. Mother's on the edge. The blood pressure's down out of sight, and the bleeding can't be stopped from the outside. Either the placenta's totally detached, or she's torn across the uterine artery or something big." He stood back from the gurney. Whatever happened now, his ultimate responsibility was over.

Stella Peters grabbed mentally at the baton that was handed her. "What's the pressure now?" Her eyes flicked over the electrocardiograph trace. Julie's heart was showing signs of the strain at having to pump against next to nothing. Perhaps a quarter of the blood that primed it had been lost and already the atria had lost their coordination.

"I have fifty, no forty-five systolic. Diastolic pressure unrecordable."

She was all but dead, and the baby was almost certainly gone—a victim of the lack of oxygen in a womb no longer hospitable. There was only one chance and it was a slim one:

an immediate hysterectomy to stop the bleeding. For a second Stella Peters paused, and her eyes caught those of the young doctor. Both knew what had to be done, but it was a fateful decision. They were about to take the womb of a fifteen-year-old-girl who had probably just lost her baby. The sentence they were about to hand down was for a lifetime of infertility. But the alternative could be no life at all. The void of nothingness.

Stella Peters took a deep breath. In her whole career there had only been a couple of moments like this—moments when she had to play God, when she had only seconds to make a decision that would need a lifetime to resolve properly.

She knew what she would do and the perils of it. It would have to be here—unsterile, unscrubbed, no anesthetic, no theater staff, no parental consent. The precious minutes that those would take could kill the patient.

Her voice was coldly authoritarian. "We'll do an abdominal hysterectomy—right here. Right now. Somebody give me a number-two scalpel."

JULIE SOARED THROUGH THE SKIES, SUSPENDED GLORIOUSLY between heaven and earth. There was a magical lightness in her soul, and she was at one with the world—far beyond the pain and the bitterness—in harmony with the sun and the wind and the incredible beauty of nature. She was on the verge of knowing some ultimate secret, something to do with the essence of things, the beginnings of the universe, the wise and wonderful ways of the cosmos. But down there, only dimly visible, there were people clustering around the old, discarded coat—and they seemed to be shouting at her. "Come back, come back, Julie," their anguished voices urged. Julie didn't want to go back, and she fought to hold on to the glory of her dream, and to fly higher into the knowledge and the light. The voices, however, had a power over her, a force that she must learn to break. She didn't want to go back down there, to the prison of her body, to languish and despair behind the bars that were called eyes and the fetters that were skin and bone. And she was so very nearly free. It seemed as if she had only to travel a little farther and then she would be out of range of the siren voices calling her back. It was a race she had to win—by far the most important part of her life so far. And it was at that moment that Julie realized what was happening. Something to do with the sound of the word *life*, because the thing that she was so desperately trying to do was to die.

INTERLUDE

London, England. 1970.

IT WAS QUIET AS DEATH IN THE CHURCH AND THE low, flat rays of the late afternoon sun filtered through the stained glass and basked in the loneliness. But they did nothing at all to energize the fundamental stillness, the emptiness, and the cold of the fertile ground in which the love of God grew. Pale light from the flickering candles swooped and swept above the high altar and scurried and slithered around the dark polished mahogany of the pews. The priest sat, head bowed, hands folded in his lap, on the chair of the confessional box. And his was the only heart there to feel the dread.

He looked up and a shaft of gold-and-silver light caught his face, flooding in to temper the timeless gloom that would effortlessly survive it. Again he felt the shiver pass through him. It was not just the cold of the unheated church, but something else, the inescapable feeling that something was about to happen in a place and at time when nothing should happen. He smiled to himself as he recognized the power of the supernatural to move the minds of those who were attentive to heaven. He turned the pages of the missal in his lap, and his lips murmured the so-well-known prayers. Was he trying to exorcise the spirits of unease loose on the cold stone floors, spirits that flowed free from the iron gratings, and clung eerily to the intricate carving of the ancient ceiling? Or was he merely trying to calm his soul as he prepared himself for the healing ritual of forgiveness?

The clang of the opening door shocked the silence. Unseen, there was someone there now, standing in the opening of the house of God. The priest inclined his head toward the sound, and the beating of his heart told him that his premonition had been about this soul whose body had disturbed the uneasy peace. A soul in torment—far from God, and yet entering this alien place to ease the horror . . . or to revenge it.

At first the footsteps were hesitant on the floor of the aisle, then more firm. Now, as the sinner made up his mind, they began to hurry.

Inches from him they stopped. At the door of the confessional.

Once again the dread was erupting in the priest's soul, stronger and more impossibly real than before.

He saw the shadow of the penitent visible in outline through the mahogany grille, sinking down to his knees.

He held his breath and tried to slow his thumping heart. "God in heaven, strengthen me for what I am about to hear," he murmured.

The voice was strong and clear. "Forgive me, Father, for I have sinned."

It was the voice of a woman.

PART TWO

MATERIAL WORLD

"What the hell does it matter?" shouted Jake.
    "It matters because it's material," said Maggie calmly,
"and that's the stuff that the world is made of."

Julie Bennett, *Material World*

FIVE

Palm Springs, California. 1987.

"HEY, DO YOU FEEL LIKE A RIDE OUT TO PALM Springs?" Jane mouthed the words as she rapped briskly on the passenger window of the cab.

Peter Parton squinted across the front seat and, as he did so, the vision caught him full in the face. He opened his mouth to speak as he scrambled over to roll the window down. "Say that again, lady." He'd heard, but his brain was busy.

Peter had been around L.A.—he'd hung out at the beach and seen his share of women, but this one was staggering, drop-dead beautiful. Wreathed by the harsh Los Angeles airport sunlight, she was clearly a unique, fantasy girl who relegated the Christie Brinkleys, the Brooke Shieldses, and the Madonnas to sniveling also-ran status. The body was wild dreams, but it was the breasts that took the prize. She was bending over to peer in the window at him and they were hanging there—totally visible through the open neck of the expensive-looking cream silk shirt. He could see them all, except the very tips—two white, rock solid, psyche-raping sculptures.

He stared at her, a rabbit in the headlamps, mesmerized, paralyzed.

Jane stood up, and the smile lit her face as she watched the molecules reorganizing themselves in the young boy's brain. Actually, he was pretty dishy. Sort of a Don Johnson type, with a nice square jaw, cobalt-blue eyes, and a mouth full of perfect American teeth. It wasn't *entirely* by accident that she had chosen his cab. Two other black-toothed cabbies she'd passed hadn't looked as if they'd do her jet lag any good at all, and the desert was a couple of hours from LAX.

"I said, 'Could you take me out to Palm Springs?'" She feigned impatience. Hand on blue-jeaned hip, pelvis thrust forward, she arranged her legs in their most alluring geometry and pushed her bottom toward the powder-blue sky.

Peter Parton swallowed hard. "You want, I'll take you to hell and back," he managed at last.

"Well, thank you, sir, but Palm Springs will do." Her smile opened up at the compliment like the petals of a flower at the first touch of the sun.

Her extraordinary accent made him shiver, as the warm Santa Ana wind plucked at her blond hair.

"You English?"

"Yes, I am."

Peter Parton was out of the cab, and in milliseconds the girl's well-worn Louis Vuitton was disappearing into the trunk at the speed of light. He prayed she wouldn't change her mind. "How come you're riding a cab to the Springs?"

"There's a wait for the plane connection, and I'm fed up with getting in and out of things. I just want to *be* there."

"You climb right in, ma'am. You know where you wanna go. I'll make you arrive." He smiled his very best smile as he held the door open for her, the *front* passenger door. No way was he going to spend two hours rubbernecking this one in the rearview mirror. "Sixty bucks should do it." Or the price of the gas, if you're short of bread, was his unspoken thought.

"Fine." Jane stretched her long arms above her head and yawned.

"You just flown in from London?"

"Yup."

"You a model or an actress there?"

"No. What makes you think that?" The laughter exploded from her alabaster throat—a marvelous infectious sound, an invitation to conspiracy. She turned to look at him as he maneuvered the taxi into the traffic.

"You fer sure *look* like a model or an actress."

"Hey, is everyone in this city into compliments, or is it just you?"

Peter laughed. Actually everyone was. It was the L.A. thing. Love your body. Love your mind. Love your soul. You've lost weight. You're in great shape. Where'd ya get that tan? Now sex was a no-no; talking about it had taken over, and verbal foreplay was the name of the game.

"What everybody in this town is into is models and actresses." That was true for him.

"My father was an actor."

"Wow. What's his name?"

"Was. He died when I was very young. His name was Richard Bennett and he was an amazing Shakespearean actor —you know, like Olivier or Richard Burton. But he was strictly stage. He never made it to Hollywood to do the movie-star bit." The pride seemed mixed in with a tinge of regret.

"That's neat. Sounds like an interesting guy."

"I hardly knew him. Just a few scattered memories of being dangled on knees and being driven mad by boredom in endless theaters."

Jane shifted on the scuffed seat. In her Levi's, she was hot and sticky and damp. She needed a shower. "Is the air-conditioning working?"

"Just barely. I gotta get it fixed." Peter Parton felt a twinge of guilt. He really should have told her that before. In the desert the heat would be a killer. He stole a sidelong glance at her, and for a second time the vision seemed to interfere with his ability to breathe. She was draped over the front seat like some priceless tapestry, one leg cocked up beneath her, the other thrown out under the dash. Her elbow was on the worn plastic, and long, delicate fingers supported the side of her head as it turned toward him in profile. There was a thin film of moisture above the voluptuous line of her upper lip, and a large damp patch of sweat beneath her arm. In all his life Peter Parton could remember seeing nothing as beautiful.

"What brings you to America?" He tried to concentrate on

the road and to make the question sound innocent as the steamy thoughts dripped and bubbled in his mind.

"I've got a sister who lives in Palm Spings. I'm going to stay with her."

"You mean there's someone else in the world who looks like you?"

"Listen, Mr. Taxi Driver, I don't even know your name and already you're making me blush." Jane laughed as she held out her hand in mock formality. "I'm Jane Bennett."

He took it gratefully. "Peter Parton."

"And in answer to your question. No, my sister doesn't really look like me at all. Anyway, you've probably seen pictures of her. She's Julie Bennett, the author."

"*The* Julie Bennett? Who writes the best sellers? Sure I seen her. She's your *sister*?" Peter Parton had lived long enough in L.A. to be suitably impressed by fame. And Julie Bennett was a megastar—as far as it was possible to be one outside the movie business. The dream girl who had descended from heaven to ride in his cab had acquired a new dimension. Body of an angel, soul of a saint, and now related to a *star*. It was good news and bad news at the same time. It made her more interesting, if that was possible, but it also made her quite definitely less attainable.

"Yeah, she is. She's pretty big in England, but over here she's huge."

There was something about the way she said it—the slightest hint of condescension, of disapproval even—that told Peter Parton he could get away with the joke. "In more senses of the word than one." His instincts were right. Jane laughed outright, throwing back her head and letting out a peal of wicked delight.

"Hey, that's my skin and blister, Pete—as we say in London. But I suppose she is sort of, well . . . formidable looking." Again she dissolved into laughter.

"What's she like? I read one of her books once, but I can't remember much about it, except that it was pretty hot stuff. I usually catch the mini-series."

Jane thought for a second. What was Julie like? On a superficial level Jane knew her inside out. It seemed that *People* and *Us* interviewed nobody else, and so Jane was intimately acquainted with Julie's views on sex before marriage, extramarital sex, geriatric sex, and even "safe" sex, which to Jane always sounded far worse than no sex at all. She knew how Julie felt about fame, money, and the state of the Union; about Catholicism, conscience, and evangelical conservatism; about happiness, aerobics, and the meaning of life. She also knew all about her home. *Architectural Digest* featured it in the months that *House and Garden* didn't. Jane knew of Robert Mapplethorpe's haute porn on the Barcelona coffee tables, Robert Graham's seventies totem-pole sculptures out by the free-form sixty-foot pool, and Robert Rauschenberg's enraged pop paintings on the terra-cotta stucco walls of the dining room.

Then there was the business of her taste in "friends," a subject dear to the heart of the English press, who liked nothing better than peddling hypocrisy. The more daring of the magazines referred to these "friends" as "toy boys." Their faces—young, pert, wildly pretty—always different and yet endlessly the same—would stare from the glossy pages with the arrogance of those who could eat ice cream without disturbing the sleek flatness of their stomachs, who could drink all night and still be alive the next morning, who could philosophize freely without minding that it had been said and thought before.

"I don't really know her very well," Jane said. "If you've seen the chat shows you probably know her almost as well as I do."

"How come?"

"Oh, who really knows anyone?" There was a sudden irritation in her tone. The message was clear. The irresistible force of American inquisitiveness had collided with the immovable object of British reticence. It was also apparent that the beautiful, languorous cat would be able to scratch as well as purr.

In the quiet that followed, Jane stared out of the window at the L.A. motorscape: fast food for cars in the gas-pump culture, faster, greasier food for humans in the burger one. But she wasn't thinking about the promiseland; she was thinking about her sister.

Why didn't she know Julie? Why had Julie never bothered to know *her*? It was a question that seemed increasingly pressing since her spur-of-the-moment decision to land unannounced on her doorstep.

You get used to anything if you grow up with it, and Jane had lived with her sister's weird "undead" status for as long as she could remember. Her mother had refused to discuss it, and her tired and pained expression when the subject came up was more than enough to discourage further questioning. So Jane was left with only the bare facts of the story. Julie was a great writer who was obsessed with her own ambitious dreams. That was it.

Jane tossed her head, sending the Cybill Shepherd-cut hair flying in the steam heat, as she tried to rid her head of the jarring thoughts. Well, so far she had respected Julie's need for independence. And the courtesy had been returned tenfold. At the funeral six short months before, Julie's silence had matched the quiet of her mother's grave. No Julie. No telephone call. No flowers. Unreachable on a book tour in the twin cities? Forget it. Whatever was or was not possible in the New World, people like Julie Bennett could always be reached—unless they didn't want to be.

Clearly there had been some kind of a terrible family row, centered on her mother. Whatever it was, there was now only one person who could ever give the details.

The window provided distraction of sorts. The street called Century Boulevard, boxlike glass-fronted buildings and billboards, had become a dangerous, futuristic video game that went by the name of "Freeway." This particular variety seemed to require no cash to play, and it was called "San Diego." All you needed to participate was an automobile, an insurance policy, and a blind faith in God.

"This is pretty hairy."

Peter Parton had been forgiven. Jane felt the need to lighten up, and her sister was heavy in just about every sense of the word.

"You get used to it," Peter said. "The trick is to do nothing in a hurry and to expect the worst."

"I'm having no problem at all with exactly half of that."

But she wasn't frightened of course. What she was was tired, and the excitement, and the heat, and the uncertain reception that awaited her were all secondary to that.

"I think I'll try and get some sleep, and just trust in the pilot," she said, wedging her head against the chipped paint of the beat-up Chevy Impala's door.

"You do that. I'll wake you when we're just outside Palm Springs."

In seconds she was asleep.

Julie was waving to her from the balcony of the white-washed Ibizan farmhouse where Jane used to spend part of the summer with her mother. The wave was so welcoming that Jane wanted to run down the rocky path with its wild, blood-colored geraniums, and rush into the cool of the thick-walled old house with its dark oak furniture and lazy flies, and up the stairs to hug the sister she had never known. But as she came closer, she saw that what Julie was waving was a piece of the thick sackcloth that they used to wrap the goat cheese. Her big round face was scowling, and there were tears on her balloon cheeks, tears of anger and frustration and heartbreak. Jane stopped where she was, and somewhere, from the cactus field, from the old shed where the farmer kept his tools, her mother's voice called out to her.

"Don't go in, Jane. Don't go on. It's not really Julie. It's a photograph—an obscene photograph." Her mother's voice was far away, but she shouted back.

"Don't be silly, Mummy," and once again she started to run toward the house, up the gray painted stairs, to the bedroom with its cool stone flagged floor and its high wood beams.

Julie stood in the doorway to the balcony, and she turned as Jane hurried into the room. And then, quite suddenly, she became a cloud, a foul-smelling vaporish mist that rushed toward Jane and swallowed her up.

In the midst of the poisonous fog, thick and humid with its noxious fumes, Jane fought for breath. But the Julie cloud was everywhere—in her lungs, in her throat, in the heart of her being. If only she could shout—make some noise—then she would know that she hadn't died in the burning fiery furnace of vapor. She opened her mouth and tried with all her might to find the air for the scream.

"Help me!"

"Hey, you're all right. You had a bad dream."

"What? Mmmm. Oh dear." The bits and pieces of the jigsaw puzzle fell together. "Oh boy, that was horrid. Wow. How long have I been asleep?"

She sat up and inventoried her returning senses. There was no feeling in her right arm—the tingling paralysis resolving itself slowly as she massaged at her elbow.

"You've been gone about an hour or more. I was just thinking about waking you."

"Goodness, it's *hot*!"

Jane was right. The heat was everywhere. Vicious and unkind, it ruled every corner of the hurtling taxi and now the only parts of the car that were safe to touch were those that had already been bathed in human sweat. Jane felt the river pouring down between her breasts, the sticky pool that had dissolved her panties around her rock-hard buttocks, the clinging dampness of her suddenly see-through shirt.

The air-conditioning was not quite dead but it was terminally ill, and Pete had already made the fateful decision to open the windows, hoping the incoming breeze would cool things down.

It had been like opening the doors of the fort to the Apaches. The superheated desert air had cascaded in on a killing rampage, and now the temperature inside the cab was not far off the 110 degrees the radio station was claiming for the Coachella Valley.

Outside the heat was at work too. Jane could see it, shining, floating, hovering as it blanketed the earth, murdering comfort and strangling life. On either side of the tumbleweed-strewn Highway 10 the bleak desert seemed to have surrendered completely and now it was the sun's servant, laughing cravenly at its cruel jokes and waiting always for the night, when its embattled flowers and meager shrubs could be free again.

"Well, this is the desert. Whaddya think?"

Jane peered out at the low desert as it reached toward the mountains away from the San Bernadino Freeway. It was a strange, splendid place—the far side of the moon from the English hills and valleys that had been the backdrop to her life so far. There seemed nothing green nor pleasant about this grim, hard land, but shimmering on the baked surface of the barren, bleached-out scrub was a pride that mocked the easy fertility of her homeland. "I may not be pretty, but I have survived," it seemed to say. "I can endure forever, because I have lived when the elements have conspired to make me die." As if to emphasize the defiance of the eternal sun, there were occasional bursts of color in the dried-up riverbeds—intense splashes of purple, specks of white and ruby red from wild oleander, and the eerie silver of the smoke trees.

"It's . . . magnificent," Jane answered finally.

Once again she was thinking of Julie. What force had drawn her sister here? Why had Julie, whose enormous wealth allowed her to live anywhere, chosen this place? For its remoteness? For its angry rebellion against the wind and sky that tormented it? Because of its dramatic contrast to the land that had borne her?

"We'll be in the Springs in about ten minutes. You got your sister's address?"

"Yup, somewhere." Jane lifted her bottom off the slippery seat and reached with great difficulty into the soaked skin-tight jeans. Christ! She should have worn a bra. To hell with it. They looked pretty good. She pulled out the damp piece of paper. "It's off something called 'Palm Canyon.' You make a right on Las Palmas and the house is sort of tucked into the foothills of the San Jacinto Mountain. It's a pretty grand house, judging from the pictures in the magazines. Shouldn't be difficult to find."

"Palm Canyon's the main drag. And I know the Las Palmas area. No problem." Peter Parton was missing his passenger already. "You ever in L.A. with nothing to do, be sure an' look me up." He pushed a card across at her and tried not to stare too hard into the eyes that looked like the aquamarine seas off the Caribbean islands where he'd dived in the navy.

The eyes . . . and the rest of her. For him, her sleep had been a visual banquet. "I do some acting, and some scripts in my spare time. The driving's just till something hits." If she was from England it was possible she hadn't heard that one before. In the dream factory anyone could be good enough for anyone else.

But Jane was moving on. He was a sweet-looking guy, and it had been good talking to him, but she was already deep into the next scene. "Sounds really interesting. Sure I will," she managed without much conviction, as she thought about the reconciliation that was only a few minutes away. There was a part of her that worried about Julie's welcome, but it was only a small part. How people reacted to her had never been much of a problem, to put it mildly. And any bad blood between Julie and her mother would hardly have included her. She'd been only five years old when her sister had left for America. She banished the brief moment of doubt and fear, as the natural self-confidence of the astoundingly beautiful reasserted itself. Poor old Julie. All alone in a palace in paradise with wall-to-wall toy boys.

Jane felt the call of the blood. Whatever Julie had done, however badly she had behaved, she was the only close relation Jane had left, and the warm feeling of familiar affection rushed through her. She had so much energy, so much love; there would be more than enough for sad, lonely Julie cut off from life by the impossibly high walls of her fortune and fame. Jane would recharge her sister as if she were a rundown battery. She would scatter the invigorating water of her optimism all over her and make her emotional desert bloom.

"It's getting dark," said Jane.

"In a few minutes it'll *be* dark. In the desert the sun doesn't mess around. It just drops down behind the mountain, and whammo, that's it. The temperature falls about twenty degrees on the spot."

They were on the outskirts of Palm Springs now, and a while later the sun proved Peter Parton was no liar. An orange football, it dived out of sight, leaving nothing but the angry magenta of the instant Coachella Valley sunset and the creeping blackness hovering about it. As if turned on by some central switch, the car lights came on all around them, and in a minute or two they were on Palm Canyon Drive, the floodlit fan palms providing the guard of honor for Jane's arrival. Halfway down they made the right turn on Las Palmas, and soon they were heading into the blackness toward the foothills of the mountain.

"This is the old Las Palmas district," Peter told her. "All the movie crowd used to hang out here in the old days—Harlow, Gable, Monroe—even President Reagan—and singers, too. Elvis and Priscilla spent their honeymoon in his house just over there. The stars are mostly gone now. Moved up the valley to Rancho Mirage or Palm Desert—to the new country clubs."

Peter wanted to keep the conversation going. He didn't have much longer with this one, and the "promise" to call him in L.A. had hardly sounded baked in the cake.

Jane peered out into the darkness. Great banks of oleander and tamarisk trees hid the estates from the road, but there were occasional glimpses through wrought-iron gates of the palatial houses inside.

"Some of these houses are beautiful. I wonder why they all moved, and why Julie didn't."

Peter laughed. "You know how it is. One goes, they all go. Movie stars. Sheep. Only difference is the movie stars have better teeth," he said, revealing his own photogenic teeth in a typically Californian smile. "I guess it's mostly security and privacy," he continued. "They got those little buses here that show the sightseers around—just like Hollywood. You know, maps to the movie stars' homes and all that crap. Most of the old guys came to the desert to get away from all that. They just wanted to mix with one another. So they packed their bags and moved on. And the new people go to the country clubs. No way any whacked-out dope fiend or crazed biker's goin' to blast himself into one of those rich places like Thunderbird or the Vintage Club—and at least you know the guy next to you at the bar has as much as you do. Only trouble is, once you're inside you're locked up like a caged animal. I guess your sister can afford to pay for her own security."

They were on a dead-end street. At the end of the road

stood two huge stone gateposts, topped by carved white marble eagles, the head of each bird picked out by a hidden spotlight. A heavy steel gate, matte black and solid, barred the way ahead. Behind the gate the thick pebble driveway rose sharply, and Jane could see that it was lined by tall fan palms whose fronds were silhouetted against the black velvet sky by uplighters attached to their trunks. Perhaps a quarter of a mile higher up, nestling beneath the mountain, the great house shone and beckoned. This was the jewel in the Palm Springs crown. The Bob Hope estate and the Clint Eastwood home were semiprecious in comparison. Jane knew that.

At one time or another most of them had made their pitch for immortality in the media, and ordinary people could be the judges of such things. Jane had never understood the passion for the revelation of their private lives that chartacterized megamoney—a perversion that extended to the faded, jaded aristocrats of old Europe, people like the Devonshires and the Thurn und Taxis, who could buy up any movie star with the income on income on the income. They all seemed quite happy to strut their stuff for Robin Leach on *Lifestyles*, despite the fact that they had long since passed the point of needing to hype anything.

"Well, that's it, all right."

Jane felt the rush of excitement. Any minute now the great reunion. It had been a bit of a risk just taking off, but she *had* taken the precaution of telephoning the house and speaking to the butler to make sure Julie would be there—without mentioning who she was. Somehow it was better that way. A person like Julie would have endless excuses if she'd written first or called her direct. This way her sister would be presented with a fait accompli, and once she was there then Jane would soon be able to heal the wounds, whatever they were. Then there would be a new beginning for both of them. It would be the Bennett sisters against the world, and the world would lose.

"They got remote control on the gate. What shall I say, 'Jane Bennett to see Julie Bennett?'"

"No! God! What do you mean? Why do you have to say anything?"

Peter Parton turned to look at her as he picked up on the alarm in her voice. "It's a security system. Everyone in California has them. The only way they ope. the gate is if you say who you are into the intercom."

"Julie doesn't know I'm coming. I wanted it to be a surprise."

"A surprise?"

"Yeah."

"Godfathers." A sudden thought occurred to him. "Is it going to be like a *nice* surprise?"

"Of course." Jane laughed the reply, but somehow she knew she didn't sound a hundred percent sure.

"Well, okay, let's do it. Who shall we say we are?"

"Someone they'd have to let in. Oh, I don't know. What about the police?"

Peter Parton inched the cab forward until it was level with the intercom. There was apparently no need to press the red button. The voice sounded bored, matter-of-fact. "Please identify yourself and state your business."

"Palm Springs P.D. Special anticrime patrol." Peter smiled over at Jane. He was proud of the little embellishment.

A pause. "Your car doesn't carry police-department insignia."

Fucking hell. This was on video.

Jane leaned forward on her seat anxiously. She couldn't see a camera anywhere. Perhaps this had gone far enough. She touched Peter's shoulder to indicate that maybe now was the time to reveal the "joke." In answer he shook his head vehemently. It was a competition now, his native cunning against theirs. Impersonating the cops might technically be a crime, but nobody would do anything but laugh when it was revealed that the "accomplice" was the sister.

"I said this was a special unit. We're investigating reports of suspicious movements in the area. We need to check out the house." His tone was exasperated now, the let-me-in-or-else message hovering between the words.

The disembodied voice was totally unfazed. It droned on. "You have a woman in the car and Checker cab markings. Please identify yourself by name."

It was worth a try. The worst that could happen was that they would be exposed. No big deal. "Officer Tomkins and my partner . . . Mary Martin." Damn! That wasn't very good. Mary Martin, former Las Palmas resident, actress, and J.R.'s mom. But Peter was in a hurry and under pressure.

"Please wait in the car."

Jane's voice was bubbling with excitement. "Hey, this is terrific. Do you think they believed you? I feel as if I'm in a movie or something."

"We'll soon see."

It was a couple of minutes before the voice came on again. "Please proceed through the gates to the main house. Do not stop on the driveway. You will be met at the top."

"Told you I did some acting. I think I just got the nomination."

As the cab rolled to a stop, two men approached from the shadows. Each was dressed in an identical dark blue jumpsuit, black boots, and blue forage cap. And each had a gun in his hand.

"Uh oh, I think this little game just went a bit too far." Peter Parton's breezy self-confidence had vanished. He leaned out of the window. "Listen, guys, the police thing was a joke. I'm a taxi driver, and I got Julie Bennett's sister in the cab. She wanted it to be a surprise, but it looks like you fellas don't like surprises, okay?"

The flashlight played over his face. Another shone in at Jane. "Please stay exactly where you are. Please don't move at all." The voice was coldly businesslike, undramatic, and scary as hell. Then it was talking into a radio transmitter. "Better get hold of Miss Bennett. Tell her that two people— male around twenty-five, female about twenty—are being held here in the front of the house. They got in claiming to be Palm Springs police. We checked with the department; they said 'no way.' They're sending a patrol car up here right now. What should we do with these people? The girl claims to be her sister."

"What the *hell* do you means '*claims* to be her sister'?" Jane demanded. "Listen, you just take me to Julie right this *minute*. Do you *hear* me?"

Nobody took any notice at all. "Yeah, that's about it. An' tell her that the guy says he's just a cab driver, and it checks. Face fits the photo on the cab license. The girl's comin' on pretty strong. No, we weren't expectin' no sister. Didn't know Miss Bennett *had* no sister."

For what seemed like an age they waited. Presumably for Julie's instructions.

A crackling voice, blurred and indistinct, was saying something.

"I got you. Lose the guy and bring the girl up to the house. Okay? Cops should be here in five. Yeah, we got all the conversation on tape."

The swarthy head poked into the cab. "Okay, sir. You are free to go now. Just drive back the way you came. Miss Bennett has asked that the young lady accompany us to the house. Are you owed any money?"

"Forget it. I'm not goin' anywhere till this gets straightened out." Peter Parton's jaw was set.

Jane's voice was urgent. "Pete, it's best you go. I'm sorry I got you into all this. I'll be fine. Julie'll tell these guys where to get off. Really, please go. If the police arrive they may try to make trouble for you."

He looked doubtful, but it would be a disaster to blow his license. "You sure you'll be okay?"

"Sure I'm sure." She thrust a hundred-dollar bill at him. "Listen, Pete, it was great. I'll look you up in L.A. Or knock you up, as we say in England." She laughed to encourage him, but inside she was trembling—with anger, with irritation.

He waved and smiled and his tires crunched the gravel.

Jane was on her own. With a guard on either side, she was spirited upward toward the four-columned portico with its massive double doors of burnished copper. They opened soundlessly at the trio's approach and light flooded out into the darkness, silhouetting the small form of a Mexican butler, dressed in white jacket, pin-striped trousers, and highly polished lace-up walking shoes.

The huge anteroom was bigger by far than the *Interiors* piece had suggested, the size emphasized by the white Carrara marble floor. All around the room hung the trendy part of the painting collection—up-to-the-minute stuff from the Tribeca lofts and the Venice Biennale—Clemente and Schnabel, Baselitz and Hodgkin. Jane didn't have time to take it in. All eyes were now on the twin fourteen-foot double doors straight ahead, which were the only other entrance to the hallway.

Mentally Jane dusted herself down. God, what a business! Still, she mustn't let it blow the reconciliation. Right now it was enough just to *be* there, and not to be alone anymore.

The big doors crashed open.

For a second Julie Bennett stood there, framed in the entrance, her diamond Cartier leopard studs and necklace flashing, her wildcat hair flowing, and a billowing white kimono emphasizing the impression of a schooner in full sail.

She said nothing, but the look on her face curdled Jane's blood. It was as if she had been scarred by venom, hosed down by hatred. Her eyes, narrowed with anger, spiked out at Jane—lasers of malice—and by her sides her white knuckles screamed the agony of rage that gripped her.

One of the guards tried to speak. "This is the girl . . ."

Julie Bennett spat out the words that her look said were lies. "I've never seen her before in my life," she said.

SIX

"WHAT'S THE STORY ON THE LIMEY FOX IN HOLDING? She sure is a looker. Ain't never seen nothin' like her. Better 'n a movie star."

The cop collapsed into the armchair that had seen better days and stuck a grubby finger in his collar. "Smart money says she's a nut case. I got the shrink comin' in to take a look. We got her charged with impersonating an officer. She conned herself into the Julie Bennett compound, which takes some doing, and then claimed she was the sister."

"An' she ain't the sister?"

"No way. Julie Bennett says she ain't never seen her before. And for sure *she* ain't crazy. Not with all the dough she's got. That Julie Bennett's sharper than my wife's tongue. I caught her on the *Today* show. She ate Bryant Gumbel for breakfast."

"Whaddya think's wrong with the girl?"

The sarge had a reputation as an amateur mind mechanic. "Schizy, most likely. You know, grandiose delusions the shrinks talk about—thinking you're famous, or the president's daughter or somethin'."

"Well, she's still a fox. That's for sure."

"Yeah." The sarge got to the joke first. "Crazy like a fox."

The tall, thin guy with shirt and tie didn't bother to knock, and the sergeant stood up as he entered the room. So did the patrolman.

"Oh, hi, Doc. Thanks for comin' over. Got a good one for you."

The doctor allowed himself a watery smile. "They're all good. All good," he managed. Small talk wasn't his strong suit. Anyway, he had had an evening of outpatients at the Eisenhower, and there was an actor he had to see down at the Betty Ford; he'd promised to drop in later to stick some backbone into him.

"So what's the story?"

"Last night we got a call from security at the Julie Bennett estate saying some taxi driver an' a girl were tryin' to get in by pretending to be cops. They let the guy go and he hightailed it to L.A. Then she says she's Julie Bennett's sister."

"And?"

"She ain't the sister."

"We're quite sure about that?"

"Yeah. I talked to Julie Bennett myself. Said she hadn't *got* no sister."

"Great. So you got her on a felony charge pending my report. How's she been?"

"Apart from the sister business, she's fine. Seems real fed up that no one believes her. She flew in from England yesterday. Wanted to give her sister a 'surprise.' Guess she succeeded."

Dr. Carney swung his leather attaché case off the metal desk. "Okay," he said, "let's go take a look at her."

IT WAS WARMING UP IN THE GREEN ROOM OF *THE MERV GRIFFIN Special*. The temperature was a rock-solid seventy-two degrees, but anyone with an ounce of sensitivity could feel the heat.

The three stars were all sitting down, but mentally they were prowling around like sumo wrestlers, looking for openings, jockeying for positions, angling for angles that would give them an advantage when the cameras started to roll.

Mike Caine was relying on cockney *Alfie*-speak to disarm the opposition. "How can anyone do anything but like a nice unpretentious lad like me?" was his attitude. Roger Moore was playing a variation on the theme. "They cast me as a cool secret agent—the last word in public-school stiff upper lip—but I'm not ashamed to admit I'm a policeman's son who thinks the whole acting game is a bit of a lark."

Julie Bennett, sitting in the corner stroking an outsize marmalade cat, was having none of it. She'd been here before—this was her fourth Merv, the first since he had given up his regular show—and she wasn't going to let anyone sucker her with green-room politics. She narrowed her saucer eyes and made her voice soft, almost girlish. "You two couldn't do me an enormous favor and put out those cigars, could you? The smoke's making me feel sick."

The duo, who were part of the trio for Merv Griffin's "English Stars in Hollywood" special, looked up at her, startled.

The two movie stars had a weakness for Havanas. The rest of the English-speaking world called these cigars Churchills, but Caine and Moore called them Lew Grades, after the legendary British filmmaker. If they extinguished them for the "lady" then Julie would have cunningly maneuvered them into a psychologically subservient position. Later, in the desperate battle for airspace, that could and would be used against them.

For a split second each man paused, before bowing to the inevitable.

"Didn't think you had a weak stomach, Julie. Not after reading those sex scenes you write." Roger Moore laughed goodnaturedly to cover the dig, as he reached forward to stub out his huge cigar.

Julie's face registered the triumph. The victory was that she had made him do something he didn't want to do. And his crack was nothing she couldn't handle.

"Oh, Roger, you men Luisa *allows* you to read my books? I *am* surprised." Luisa Moore, Roger's beautiful Italian firecracker wife, had a reputation for keeping the star on the shortest of leashes.

She turned toward Mike Caine for the double whammy. "Does Shakira let *you* read them, Mike?" Shakira Caine, prettier by far than most movie stars, also had a well-earned reputation as an iron-willed lady. It seemed a recipe for two of Hollywood's most successful marriages.

"Listen luv—chance'd be a fine thing. I don't have time to read anything but scripts these days." The deep blue eyes stared mockingly at her. In fact, Michael Caine seemed blue all over. The baby-blue cashmere cardigan—almost certainly Scotch House—and matching sky-blue pants were a clever choice of color, tending to offset the sallowness of his skin.

"Piling up money for a triumphant return to Blighty, eh, Mike?"

It was true. Mike Caine was on a roll right now. It seemed someone had passed a law that said he must appear in every other new release. It was also true that he was spending a fortune on a farmhouse in Oxfordshire. It was a tricky subject. Hollywood liked their English to make a "commitment" to America, and Mike Caine had certainly done that. But he'd "deserted" back to England once before, only to return later to where the work was. Now it seemed he was planning a second defection. He would hope that Merv wouldn't make a big thing of it. Now Julie had sowed the seed in his mind that if Griffin didn't bring it up, she would. It was good "green room" work, and a reason why some of the real pros insisted on being kept separate from the other guests until they met onstage.

"Yeah, looking forward to spending a bit more time there. Get some bangers in, watch a bit of football." He caught a piece of the golden curly hair between thumb and forefinger and his eyes twinkled. "I was sorry to hear about yer mum," he said.

Julie Bennett's head jerked back as if she had been garroted. On her ample knee the orange animal seemed to freeze. "How did you know about my mother?" The accusation positively bristled in the words. "Knowing about my mother" was clearly an activity that ranked with strangling babies and necrophilia in the Julie Bennett scheme of things.

Mike Caine was totally unfazed by the reaction. Beneath the cheerful, joky exterior lurked a Wilkinson Sword mind and the gut instincts of a street fighter. He waved an expansive arm. "Oh, we all knew your mother, didn't we, Rog?"

Roger Moore, Mike Caine's best friend, jumped on the bandwagon. "Certainly. And your dad. Dick Bennett was a bit of a pathfinder for us all. You know, working-class boy makes good in the acting profession . . ." That said quite a bit. He was making the point, "Don't try to patronize us. Your mother might have been a princess but your old man was a peasant."

It was Mike Caine who delivered the coup de grace. "In *fact*—you won't even remember this, Julie, but *I* remember a party in Chelsea when you and your mum had a bit of barney. You couldn't have been more than fifteen at the time. Lovely lady, your mum. Great lady. Everyone fancied her like mad."

The Lew Grades were revenged. So were the "wife" cracks, and the Oxfordshire bit.

Julie Bennett had gone white. Her fingers were around the neck of the cat now, rigid, the knuckles tense, stroking no more.

"I think we've got about five minutes to go." The girl from Judy Davidson Publicity felt the urgent need to speak.

But Julie Bennett couldn't hear her. She had gone away, transported to the childhood she could never forget. So dangerous these thoughts. So vivid, so fearful, so desperately threatening. For years she had struggled to suppress them, and to some extent she had succeeded—until yesterday evening when her dreadful sister had walked into her life and torn the scabs off the wounds. The child who had lived while hers died. Jane, the living mockery of her scarred and empty pelvis. The very name was a symbol of so much pain—of her loathsome mother's fertility, of her father's callous betrayal, of the dim, distant day she had drifted away from her body, when her dead child had been ripped from her, and they had taken her womb to save her life. Julie took a deep breath.

"All made up and ready to go? I'll be taking you in in a couple of minutes, Miss Bennett." The assistant producer sounded professionally cheerful. "Ready, Miss Bennett?"

"What? Oh, yes, I suppose so." Julie stood up, the cat cascading to the floor, as she tried to pull herself together. She looked quickly into the mirror to check herself out, but she didn't see what everyone else saw. Didn't see the almost beautiful face, the great big eyes, the proud jaw, the shining hair that Vidal Sassoon was always trying to get for his advertisements. She didn't see the vast Dolly Partons that intrigued a mammary-gland-obsessed America, the piano key teeth, the Mississippi wide hips, the passable legs, the too pear-shaped ass. She didn't see the haute tart clothes—the wide-shouldered fake leopard jacket, the skin-tight black pants, the oversized wrist bangles, and the shiny gold shoes. Instead she saw a tiny, lonely little girl—brimful of love for the silver-tongued god of her childhood, chockablock full of loathing for the woman who had killed him. She saw a child who would be childless lost in the dreamscape, showered with the gifts that could fill her emptiness.

Julie watched the tears glisten in her eyes and at once she heard the hard voice of the survivor. Cold as her dead heart, the call echoed through the vast, void rooms of the ruined palace where her emotions lived. "Live, live, live," it chanted. "Win, win, win," it shouted.

She turned around, fast, decisive, in control once more, and her aura reflected the dramatic change in her internal chemistry. Mike Caine's expressive eyebrows jerked upward. Roger Moore's joined them. Julie, as the non–movie star, would go first in the number-two slot. Mike and Roger would share equal billing in the pole position, and they both knew they had better watch out. Not for Merv—he was a pussycat —but for the far more substantial feline who had just stalked from the room.

The instant applause wafted Julie onto the stage and the adrenaline rush hosed down her mental decks for action. She was a past mistress at this, but she never relaxed. That was the kiss of death to that shy, elusive animal—spontaneity. The trick was to get the nervousness just right. If there was too much, it showed. That was fine, even appealing, in a starlet fresh from central casting, but it would be a complete no-no for a hard-boiled book queen who was supposed to have seen and done it all before. To have too little anxiety was worse. The interview would deflate like a badly timed cheese soufflé amidst droning déjà vu, ennervating ennui, and bearish boredom. Luckily this Merv was a "one off," not part of the Chinese water torture known as a book tour when a typical day might include three radios, a brace of print interviews, and a live and recorded TV byte sandwiched between a flight from Chicago and another to Cleveland.

She gave Merv a kiss—such old friends—and stared fixedly into his eyes. Because of the way the camera angles played, that was the equivalent of eyeballing the audience, the people in the four million homes across America that she was really talking to.

Merv, smooth as Swiss milk chocolate, leaned over the famous glass-topped table and prepared to give great interview. "Well, Julie Bennett. How many books is it now? Thirty million. Forty million?"

"You mean just in Canada?" Julie let her eyes do the laughing, and her voice—all warm and English and mocking self-depreciation—mimicked the egotist that every watching American knew she was *not*.

Merv allowed the freckled sunburned face to relax in the grin that had turned on a generation of Middle Americans. "In fact, Julie, does anyone sell any more books than you right now?"

"Just one, Merv, just one—and he's pretty hot competition."

"Stephen King? Michener?"

"You're getting close with Michener."

"Who? I give up."

Julie gave the dimples a run. Tossed the tousled hair about, fiddled with a bangle or two, and made some breeze with her bosom.

She cocked a thumb toward the ceiling. "The man who lives upstairs."

Merv got it at last. "The Bible! Well, thank God the good book is still outselling you." He tugged at his nose, cupped his multimillionaire chin in the palm of his hand, and cuddled in—all warm and intimate—as he let the amused sincerity beam from blue eyes.

"*I* don't thank him, and are you saying my books aren't 'good' books?" She waved her finger, mock threatening, at the media superstar.

Then it was "no seriously, though" time for Merv. The

voice went reflective—sweet as honey, smooth as ice. God, what a tan! Probably just back from Palm Beach Polo after a few days with Eva. "How many years has it been since *Child Woman*? That was a *remarkable* first novel. And at the time you wrote it you were only twenty?" Merv crammed the wonder and the amazement in. He was probably thinking about something completely different, like how brilliant he'd been to sell his company to Coca-Cola.

Julie wondered whose job it was to keep the tabletop shiny. Would some guy show in the commercial break with the Windex? Merv had his fingers all over it as if it were hot chocolate fudge at the end of Lent.

Julie made herself concentrate. There were half a dozen *Child Woman* speeches, and all could be delivered fresh from the tongue with scarcely any input from the brain at all. But she was enough of a pro to recognize the slippery mind and the dangers that it posed. Nothing could stop the mighty locomotive of her book sales now, but one day, somewhere out there, the top of the mountain would be reached. Fashion would change, and the fickle fingers would reach for another author to fuel the fires of their fantasies. Then it would be the at first gentle and finally more rapid decline, until her career was racing headlong down the far side of the hill to the precipice of failure and the dreadful abyss of nonentity. For one who had cavorted in the heavens, breathing the rarefied air of superstardom, the retreat from fame would be a bitter road to travel.

So she forced herself to think about the question, and more important to *feel* about it. It wasn't difficult. *Child Woman* had been her doomed attempt to exorcise her personal ghosts—the dreaded specters that slipped and slithered through the muck, dripping venom and devouring life as their foul smells wafted up to disturb her peace. Now her sister Jane had brought them back to life.

"Yes, I was twenty when I wrote *Child Woman*, but of course it's really about adolescence, and the conflicting demands of childhood and adulthood."

"You were very close to your father—Richard Bennett the

Shakespearean actor. Is Frederick, the father in the novel, modeled on him?"

Merv had mined this seam to good effect before, or so one of the researchers had reminded him. Girls and their feelings for Dad tended to play well with the housewives who watched his show, the ones who bought the Bennett books with a desperation bordering on the obsessional.

Julie bit determinedly into her bottom lip; her tear ducts filling to order as the psychological trigger words summoned the spirits from her heartland. "Yes, Frederick *was* Daddy. I think that the readers can identify with the pain, because they know it was real."

The tear squeezed itself out as Merv felt the ratings quiver, spike upward. Tears, naked feelings, public grief were food and drink to his audience. He watched her like a hawk. Julie watched him back. Would he go for the big one? He never had before. From time to time the braver souls did.

Merv tugged at his tie in the gesture that said he was going to take the plunge. Julie braced herself.

"In *Child Woman* there is a physical relationship between Frederick and his daughter, a relationship that is a contributing factor to his suicide. Where did you get the idea for that?"

Julie would be in close-up now, the camera zeroed in on her mouth, on her trembling upper lip. In her mind the data flashed. Only Phil sold more books than Merv. Only Donahue and Agronsky went out to more homes. Only *Hour* and *P.M.* and Oprah came close. She sucked the silence dry of its drama.

Incest. The big one. Was this the moment when TV America would hear it first? Sitting on fat asses, popping M&M's as they scooped the *Star*, the *Examiner*, and the *Enquirer* by doing nothing more than catching good old Merv.

"*Child Woman is* autobiographical . . ."

Merv and America leaned forward.

"All first novels are, to some extent. And I won't deny that I worshiped my father . . ."

Merv's hands were clasped in prayer, his face funeral serious. If Julie Bennett gave him this one, she'd get to come back next week. For an author—even a Julie Bennett—that was Holy Grail time.

"But of course the love scene between father and daughter is based on my imagination. Fantasy, if you like. I think a lot of daughters dream about that. The Freudains call it the Electra complex, which is the equivalent of the male Oedipal one."

"That's very interesting," lied Merv. Nearly. A good try.

"We'll take a break; then we'll be *right* back," he said, cradling his head in his hand, and turned back toward the camera to give his fans the encouraging elflike smile that would keep them going through the ads.

As the red lights on the cameras flicked off, he turned to Julie. "What are you working on right now? Going to be difficult to top *Sins of the Fathers*, sales-wise."

Electra complexes and incestuous fathers were already history. These two stars were pros. Julie was peddling books, and Merv was hawking advertising space, and their skill was to make America forget it.

"Listen, Merv, the book I'm doing now—I promise you— is going to be the first *genuine* mass-market hardback. Believe me."

"Save it, Julie. Save it for the next segue."

"No way. I don't want to go public with it just yet, but I don't mind you knowing."

"Give."

Julie let him wait for a fraction of a second.

"The sequel to *Gone With the Wind*."

He seemed genuinely surprised. "You can't do that. What about the Margaret Mitchell estate?"

"I did a deal with them and Macmillan. Bought the rights to the characters and continued story line of *Gone With the Wind*. I'm going to call it *Tomorrow Is Another Day*. Scarlett gets Rhett back. What do you think?"

"I think you should tell me about it in the next segue."

"I can't, Merv. Contracts and things. My lawyers tell me I have to keep quiet just now. Imagine what would happen if the studios get hold of it. They didn't do too badly with the original."

"Well, that's a wonderful idea, Julie. Did they make you pay?"

"Three and a half."

"Wow. That's a lot to make back on a book—even one of yours."

"Hardback royalties alone could pay that back, and then some. That's what Mort says anyway."

"Mort knows." Superagent Mort Janklow—Danielle Steele, Judith Krantz, Barbara Taylor Bradford—*knew*.

"How far are you with the book?"

"Pretty far. You fit me in for the tour?"

"You'd better believe it. Have Crown talk to my booker. Say I said 'definitely.' Okay. Back to work."

After Julie had filled in the world on *Sins of the Fathers* and sold another hundred thousand copies, Roger Moore came on to the James Bond theme, looking suitably ashamed, traditionally impish, and totally devoid of pretension. He talked about Bond, and Timothy Dalton, and disappointed Bonds, and whether or not *he* was Bond, what he thought of Bond, and of what it was like to be in Bondage. It transpired that being Bond was very nice because it meant that he was extremely rich and could do the things he really liked to do, which were to grow the grapes for his own wine in St. Paul de Vence, drink superb Calvados in Gstaad, and spend lots and lots of time with the family he loved.

Michael Caine joined him on the half-moon sofa and talked amusingly about the differences between the English and the Americans, how he could never make enough money to overcome his terminal financial insecurity, and how it was that a nice cockney boy had achieved the life-style to which he had become accustomed.

Merv asked them both if Mike had ever wanted to be Bond, and there had been a bit of confusion about that. Then Mike had mentioned that Julie's father had been a very fine actor, which was when things started to get nasty.

"Of course, Daddy was a *real* actor."

The audience made that wonderful moaning sound, as they anticipated a tangle.

Roger Moore took it on the chin. "Yes, he was."

Mike Caine—with far more artistic pretension than his best mate—didn't. "You say that, Julie, but you know Shakespeare's a very limited world and a lot of great Shakespearean actors found it necessary to spread their horizons just a little bit wider—lived dangerously, came over here, shot a few movies." It was sweet reason, but it was not sweet charity.

"And look what happened to them," Julie retorted. "Do you remember Burton in *The Klansman* and *Exorcist II*, and Laurence Olivier in the Harold Robbins movie about the automobile tycoon?" The scorn sprayed off the words. "No. Daddy was never a carpetbagger."

"Now hang on, Julie. You're English. You're over here selling a book or two." Roger Moore couldn't let that one go.

Julie had baited the trap. "But I'm not English. I'm an American citizen, and I have been for fourteen years." Not many people knew that.

The fierce determination bristled in Julie's words. God, if only she could have persuaded her father to do what Mike Caine had suggested. If only she had been able to snatch him from her mother's arms, and from the fetid jaws of the mean old world, to allow him to be reborn in the brave possibility of the new one. What a joy it would have been to have watched him emerge shiny and new beneath the Beverly Hills sun.

"I didn't know you were a naturalized citizen, Julie. What made you take that step?" Merv moved to defuse the ticking bomb. This wasn't *Donahue* or *Crossfire*.

Julie felt the warm glow of the spotlight as metaphorically she moved center stage. Not bad for the one on the end of the sofa when the other two were heavy-duty movie stars.

She leaned forward and spoke straight from the heart to the camera. "I love America because things *move* here. Because people aren't afraid to hope and to be optimistic and to dream. Here there are no points for pessimism, no applause for cynicism, no brickbats for rocking the boat. America is a place where to care is not naïve, to cry is not regarded as a weakness, to wish to change the status quo is not looked on as subversive. And I love it when I wake up, and I love it when I go to sleep, and I love it in between."

They clapped for her for a full twenty seconds, because

they knew it was true. Julie could never remember an audience doing that on Merv before. It almost made it all right. Almost, but not quite. Because there was still the problem of Jane.

THE TWO HUGE TEARS ROLLED UNEVENLY DOWN JANE'S PALE cheeks, and sitting on the floor she braced herself against the whitewashed wall, head in hands, as she fought to clear her mind. She felt like Kafka's K—an innocent thrown into the deep end of a nightmare for shadowy reasons she didn't begin to understand. It was quiet in the cell, but there was a background noise of terror in her brain that drowned thought and obliterated reason.

What was this awful man saying to her? She was so hot and tired and so very frightened, but she forced herself to concentrate on his questions as she looked up at him, her eyes bleary with the exhaustion and the crying.

"Tell me, Jane, just how long have you had the feeling that you are Julie Bennett's sister?" Dr. Carney perched calmly on the edge of the bed. He was quite unprepared for the violence of Jane's reaction.

She sprang forward like a jungle cat. In one sinuous movement she was across the cell and hovering over him, threatening, screaming at the top of her voice. "*Can't* you understand what I'm saying? I *am* Julie Bennett's sister! I've *always* been her sister, and I don't *know* what crazy game she's playing by lying about it!" She towered over the doctor, her fists clenched, the tears squeezing out of her eyes.

Dr. Carney bobbed back like a puppet and his dismayed face registered his miscalculation. Then his eyes narrowed. "Whoa, Jane. Don't get upset. I'm listening to you. I'm hearing what you're saying. I put my question badly. What I really wanted to hear about was your childhood—what it was like when Julie and you were growing up."

He'd made a beginner's mistake. Never deny a delusional system, even by implication. In psychosis, patients believed totally in their warped view of reality. To question it only made things worse. The interesting diagnostic question was whether this was a schizophrenic illness or the manic phase of a manic-depressive one. The quality of the delusion was definitely grandiose in his opinion—sister of a famous person, and the girl certainly looked exhausted, perhaps from the hyperactivity that accompanied manic mood swings. A careful history, and some information from somebody who knew the patient well, would be vital. In the meantime the treatment for both illnesses would be the same. Major tranquillizers to calm down the delusional thoughts and allow the tired body to rest at the same time. Later on, it might be different, with lithium for repeated episodes of manic-depression, and long-acting phenothiazines to prevent a recurrence of schizophrenic symptoms. His gut instinct told him this was paranoid schizophrenia.

Jane saw right through him. God, he was trying to humor her. The shrink thought she was crazy. She put her head in her hands as the panic bucked and reared within her. There must be a way out of this, something she could say that would persuade him that she was sane. But what? She must stay calm. They thought she was mad because her sister had done something mad. They were holding the wrong person, and there was no way to make them understand.

"My sister lied." She spoke slowly, distinctly, patiently, as if to a small, willful child. "I don't know why. I can't understand that. Perhaps it was something to do with things that happened before I was born. But she did lie, and that's why I'm here. It's the only reason I'm here."

Dr. Carney placed both forefingers at the corners of his mouth in a gesture that seemed to say he was thinking deeply. "Well, let's explore that possibility, Jane. Let's imagine your 'sister' did have a grudge against you. Wouldn't she just be very displeased to see you? Throw you out of the house, or something like that? I mean, to allow you to be arrested by the police seems something of an overreaction, wouldn't you agree?"

Jane took another step toward him, her feet motivated by a force far stronger than her will to stay calm. "God, oh God, can't you *understand*? I don't know. I don't *know*!!"

He hoped that his voice sounded firm as he spoke. "Jane, I

want you to trust me and have an injection that will help to calm you down. And I think we need to get you into a hospital for a few days' rest. Really, you must believe me. It would be for the best."

"No!" Jane shouted the word.

Dr. Carney stood up. Sometimes the riot act worked. "Jane, I'm afraid I'm going to insist that you have some medication. It's for your own good."

"I don't want an injection...I don't *need* any medicine... I'm just tired and all alone, and..." Jane's hands splayed out in the gesture of supplication. "Please, will you believe me...Please..."

He stood up and walked briskly to the door. "Officer!" In seconds he was gone.

In the station office outside the holding-cell area he was businesslike. He spoke to the sergeant. "Listen, Fred. We have a paranoid schizophrenic in there, and she's very excited. We'll have to move her out to the Patton in San Bernadino or the Metropolitan in L.A., but in the meantime I want her to have some Thorazine I.M. Do you have a couple of good strong officers—preferably female, to give me a hand?"

"I'd be pleased to. So'd Fritzie. I'll go get her." The voice came from behind him.

Carney turned around to confront the female officer. Apart from her spiky hair, the image that sprang irrepressibly to mind was that of a sumo wrestler. Whoever "Fritzie" was, she would hardly be needed. The she-mountain, however, was determined to find her, and as Dr. Carney filled the syringe with two hundred milligrams of Thorazine, she went off to look for her.

Fritzie wasn't at all like her friend. She was trim, and tight, and almost good looking, her hair cut short in a no-nonsense bob.

Carney hoped for her sake that his patient didn't put up too much of a struggle. It was equally clear that the gleaming eyes of the two women that they didn't share his ambition. The gorgeous young girl in the holding cell had not gone unnoticed.

"Where you goin' to put the needle, Doc?" Fritzie's voice, despite her appearance, was soft.

"Buttock, upper outer quadrant."

"She got those blue jeans painted on," the other woman said. "Be a real struggle getting them off." The prospect of the struggle didn't sound at all discouraging.

Jane backed away as the terrifying trio approached. This was it.

"Jane, I just want you to slip down your jeans and panties. Won't take a second . . . just a pinprick."

The second she saw the needle, she sprang at them, the awful vision of the future giving strength to her tired body. But of course it was absolutely no use at all.

Fritzie took her low, ducking under her outstretched arms and crashing her shoulder into Jane's legs just below the hip. The forward momentum of Jane's body sent her torso and upper body in a graceful arc—straight into the bear hug of the enormous policewoman.

Jane screamed as her pants were dragged down, and the needle found its mark.

It was the scream of the condemned. Hopeless, helpless, hapless, as she was forced to embark on the journey to oblivion.

SEVEN

JULIE BENNETT WALKED OVER TO THE PICTURE WIN-
dow and peered out at Palm Springs, stretched out like her
own private doormat below. She could see clear across the
Coachella Valley, across the fault line to the Santa Rosa
Mountains. Usually the magnificent grandeur of the view had
the power to lift the lowest of spirits. Today its sparkling
brightness, its spaciousness, its spiritual beauty were as moving and as meaningful as an Academy Awards acceptance
speech.

She turned around and her desperate eyes scanned the writing room. Nothingness stared back. Usually she liked it that
way, with its empty walls, the simple table, the out-of-date
IBM, the backless Balans chair that you knelt on to prevent
the spine caving in under the pressure of the sedentary life.
Yes, a monastic room, locked against the outside world, was
the best place to turn out the words at roughly twenty bucks
apiece. But not today. Today she was blocked up tighter than a
nun on codeine, and the frustration was driving her mad.

She flopped down onto the big sofa—the one she usually
avoided until the fifteen-hundred-word daily quota was finished—and reached for the cat.

"Orlando, darling," she murmured as she ran her fingers
through the thick orange fur. "I can't do it today. I can't do it,
darling. Perhaps I'll never be able to do it again."

Orlando ticked like an irritated time bomb. It was his way

of purring. He liked the back rub, but he could do without the chat. Being the Bennett cat wasn't all fish and mice.

"What do I do about writer's block, Orlando, darling? Tell me what I should do." Julie's fingers roamed absentmindedly through the soft fur. Orlando was like her, was a *part* of her. All alone, isolated in his cat world, oblivious to the universe and the noisy, nasty people who inhabited it.

Damn it. The maddening thing was that she thought she had gotten over this problem. On the talk shows she'd actually started to talk about it. Her theory had been deceptively simple, and now, confronted by the reality, she could see that it had been wrong. Writer's block, she had taken to saying pompously, was a disease suffered by inexperienced authors who expected things to come too easily. People who overvalued themselves as "artists" and believed that writing was a creative activity that sprang directly from the soul rather than from the sweat of the brow and the determination of the will. That was rubbish. It was not a question of vibrating in tune to some mystical melody, hitching a ride on some starlight express of the imagination. Instead it was blood, toil, sweat, and tears, and if the words didn't come you just had to sit there until they did.

So much for the theory. But why the hell did she feel that her prospects as a writer were quite suddenly as promising as the outlook for a lizard in a roadrunner's beak? There seemed no doubt about it. The reserves of talent had run out. The gushing well of creativity that had rocketed her into the upper echelons of the plutocracy was dry as the desert's dust. The world would never know what happened to Scarlett or what became of Rhett because she, Julie Bennett, was history. Limp, spent, as useful and as appetizing as a fly-blown condom on the roadside of life.

"You know who did this to me, don't you, darling?"

Orlando ticked away furiously.

"It was Jane, my love. My little sister, Jane." The Bennett fingers stiffened. Suddenly the rub was a bit more bracing. Therapeutic rather than pleasant. Orlando shifted nervously. He knew the signs.

"She had no right to come here. To my desert. This is my

place. My country. It always was. It took me in and made me someone. And it would have made Daddy someone, too."

A big tear formed in one big eye. She remembered it so well. The poolside room at the Sunset. For so many it had been the end of the line, the last stop on the descent of tinsel town downward drift. The Sunset had never been the real Hollywood—gritty and dirty and alive—like the Tropicana on Santa Monica where the rock bands' roadies stayed, or even one of the traditional "fresh-off-the-bus" stops like the Highlands off Hollywood Boulevard, to which a certain romance was attached. The Sunset was copper-bottom, end-of-the-line time for people who had been hanging on by their fingernails, unwilling or unable to read the writing on the wall, fearful of facing failure's music in the knowing looks of family and friends as they disembarked from the slow boat home.

But it hadn't been like that for Julie Bennett. It had been her new beginning, and the first step to riches beyond the wild dreams of even Sunset Motel dreamers. Each morning, surfing on a foaming sea of Brazilian coffee, she would beat the ancient Silver Reed to death in the gloomy, grubby, artistic palace of a room. *Child Woman* had written itself as the essays had always done at school, and as the pile of typescript had climbed higher, Julie had known that it was a masterpiece. She knew that out there they were all waiting for her guerrilla manual of family warfare, ready to cry with her, to dream with her, to die with her as they wallowed in their incestuous longings, their libidinous urges, and their James Dean rebellions.

All around her had been the music of failure as she had laid the foundations of her phenomenal success. The cigarette burns on the bedside table, the stains of a mercifully indeterminate type on the fluffy once-beige carpet, the drapes that had cleaned shoes. Through the grubby window she had looked out across an Astroturfed balcony to the thirty-foot kidney-shaped pool, and in her mind's eye she could still see the thin scum collected in the shallow end by the ancient, underpowered, and misplaced filter system. Where the bottom was visible through the detritus of dead leaves, spiders, and the occasional collapsed page of newsprint, the plaster had been flaked and cracked in a pathetic mosaic of decay. As her fingers had hammered at the keys and the ultimate blockbuster had been born, she had been but dimly aware of the human flotsam and jetsam that populated the failure-scape—the plump hooker, sweating in the low-seventies pseudoheat, her spare tire exploding over the edge of the mean synthetic leopardskin G-string; the bodybuilding gay, oiled and shiny, his cute little pecs all neat and round and plump as he flicked halfheartedly through *People* magazine; the greasy Arab, fatter by far than the hooker, eying her speculatively as he picked his nose.

For those people the Sunset had been the flames of Dante's Inferno, but for Julie, the Sunset had been the sunrise of a glorious dawn in the wonderful country that had given her a new home.

But now the long hand of her past was reaching for her. A girl whose looks would make the angels weep with jealousy had sprung from the damp, dank, distant homeland to plague and threaten her and turn her world upside down.

"We won't let her touch us, will we, Orlando? We'll know what to do with her, won't we? Because you know who she is, Orlando, my darling? She's Mummy. She's Mummy. She's *Mummy.*"

Julie Bennett sprang to her feet, wild eyed, as Orlando the marmalade cat took flight. Like a rocketship erupting from the Cape, the orange fireball blasted into orbit.

Julie Bennett stalked the room in ever-decreasing circles. Her target was the typewriter. The three-quarters-filled page contained about two hundred words. Four thousand bucks' worth of current market rates. She plucked the offending paper from the jaws of the machine, and crumpling it quickly, she threw it at the wall.

Damn. Damn. DAMN!

She needed somebody to *irritate*. Where the hell was Billy? Almost certainly in the studio at this time of the day. "Working," if that was what no-talent "artists" did. But there was just a chance he would be poolside. Just a chance.

She walked to the back window and looked out over the

pool. Good. There he was. His hormone-shifting body stretched out in the full-frontal sun, at peace with the desert world.

Julie Bennett felt her spirits rise as she hurried from the room and trotted down the marble stairway on her way to the pool.

"So the *artist* rests."

The world *artist* was a phonetic prizewinner conveying hilarity, patronization, infinite sarcasm, and a generous portion of plain old disgust. Both the intonation of the first syllable and the hissing sibilance of the *s* managed to imply that the word she had really been looking for was *arsehole*.

Billy Bingham looked out from the sun bed on which he lay and eyed his potential tormentor calmly.

"I can't think why you lie about in the direct sun like that. I suppose with your education you think melanoma is something sweet and sticky to buy the Valley girls at the drugstore." Julie plonked herself down beneath the big beige sun umbrella with the mahogany spokes, as she remorselessly turned up the rheostat of malice. Billy looked like a wild dream as usual, his hard, spare body burnished like a brand-new penny—the muscles shiny with Johnson's baby oil. She fought back desire and tried to cool it in the bowl of venom.

"Have you forgotten how to speak during the night, Billy? I know you've always found words difficult, but you might try to string a few together to give me the *illusion* of talking to someone."

"What do you want me to say, Julie? That yes, I'm stupid? That yes, I'm lazy? That yes, I'm inarticulate?" His voice was weary. He knew there was a ways to go.

Julie Bennett let out a war whoop of delight. "'Inarticulate'? 'Inarticulate'? Oh my God, you've been at the dictionary again. Or was it that book I gave you—*It Pays to Increase Your Word Power*? Lord Almighty, you even got the pronunciation right."

"Words aren't the only way to communicate, Julie. Sometimes you forget that. It's all that scribbling you do."

"Oh, really! Thus speaks the little hippie. I suppose you 'communicate' with cosmic vibrations, or magic auras or some other sixties method. God, you young people are so *unoriginal*. Just because short skirts are back you have to get all flower-power metaphysical. I suppose you'll be mincing around here in a paisley shirt listening to *Sergeant Pepper's Lonely Hearts Club Band* any minute now—dropping acid and going psychedelic. Christ, that'll be a stomach turner. And anyway, don't you forget that it's my 'scribbling,' as you so rudely call it, that's keeping you in paint to daub on those ridiculous canvases of yours."

There was triumph as she said the last words. What came before had been pinpricks. Anything rude about Billy's art would draw real blood. She sat back on the chair and waited.

Billy tried to stay calm. There was nothing tougher than this. His art was everything. It was his past, his present, and his future, and for it he was even prepared to endure Julie Bennett. He hated her, of course. As far as he was concerned she specialized in Evil.

Her agile mind was always searching for weakness to exploit, and her poisonous tongue missed no opportunity to flay his nerve endings. She lived to control, and to destroy, whatever and whoever was at the mercy of her power. And the worst part of it all was that so many gave themselves up to her. Billy himself had agonized over that, but the trap had been so cunningly baited. The sticky sweet aroma of money, the influence in the Industry, the open sesame to all the closed caves of a fertile imagination. There was something for everyone in the Bennett Aladdin's cave—and that was the trouble. Billy wanted so much, so very much.

He didn't want just the materialistic success, although that was a method of keeping the score. He wanted *recognition*. The wonderful, glorious recognition as the cognoscenti bowed and scraped and worshiped at the fountain of genius he knew he possessed. It was a strange kind of knowledge. He had enough faith in himself to move mountains, but he suffered dark nights of the soul when others could not see what he alone could see. When the paint flowed over the canvas he could feel the shining strength within him. Like sexuality, the force would dance and prance and fill him up with a wondrous joy as the colors wrestled with each other and the shapes flew into life.

Later he would stare in wonder at what he had made, and it had the power to move him. His eyes would fill with tears as the sunlight kissed the canvas, promising him that he had found a way to touch the hearts of others, with beauty, with hope. Then and only then could he banish the ghosts of insecurity—the ones that so insidiously mocked his pretension, joked at his pride, and ridiculed his most fervent belief in his ability.

Those were the demons that endlessly found voice in Julie Bennett's merciless mouth. From dawn to dusk she searched for ways to wound him, and she used every weapon in her armory: faint praise, black humor, violent abuse. And yet, perversely, she was in some fundamental way an important source of his art. In the shadow of her scorn he could never be lazy. The desire to prove her wrong fueled him, and the peace of the magnificent studio at the foot of the mountain was a balm only she could provide.

"Well?" said Julie, the disappointment in her voice scarcely disguised. She'd zapped the art. Sparks were supposed to fly.

"'Well' what?" said Billy Bingham, wondering if he could get away with slapping the headphones on and catching some U2 on the yellow waterproof Sony. Least of all could Julie Bennett stand being ignored. As a compromise he turned around on the Tropitone recliner and showed her his back. The intense heat of the low desert sun knifed down into his skin. Who cared that it was supposed to be bad for you? He was twenty-two and all the diseases of middle age lay a million miles away in the foreign country of the future. Right now he loved the heat on his body and the brilliance of the light—perfect antidotes to the bites of the Bennett serpent.

"Well, what do you think of your new Suzuki?"

That was clever. Julie effortlessly switched her attack. Motorcycles were the only things apart from the painting that seemed to excite him. The brand-new Suzuki Intruder had turned him on for sure. All chrome and slim-line slick, reeking of the late-sixties "choppers" that had been its design inspiration.

Julie had managed to make her question almost coquettish, a potent signal that love, not war, was on her mind—or rather sex, not love.

"I like it real fine, Julie. You know that."

"And what do all those biker weirdos and teen-marines down at Twentynine Bunch Palms think of it? If they're capable of thought, that is."

"Everyone likes it, Julie. It's a neat bike." Billy's voice was patient, wary.

"Maybe you could get around to thanking me sometime."

"I thanked you, Julie."

"I mean thanking me *properly.*"

Billy winced. He hated it when Julie made herself sound like a spoiled little girl. He didn't answer.

Julie felt her anger begin to boil. Why did she care about this boy? Why did she find him so incredibly attractive? A shrink would have some sort of an answer. Did it all stem from the loss of her child? After all, Billy was young enough to be her son. Maybe because she couldn't have a baby one way, she was having it another. Perhaps that was too obvious. But young boys were getting to be her habit.

From the outside Billy appeared to be just like all the others—young, tight flesh, the piquante sauce of youth's insane arrogance, the vacant-lot mind, the upwardly mobile heart—but there was something else, too. Billy had a destination; Billy had a purpose; Billy had a dream that wasn't just a college of Fred Segal, Maxfield, and Parachute.

Of course it was the art that made him special. It was easy enough to joke about—Art with a capital *F*—but much, much more difficult to ignore. Art had always been an enigma for Julie. She couldn't be sure about it, or artists. Just when she thought she knew they were rubbish they would turn around and make the world laugh at her and her rotten taste. There didn't seem to be any rules. Certainly she couldn't judge art from the sales figures or the movie gross, and that was disturbing—especially in southern California, where everyone needed overt signs of success to determine whether he need speak to you or not.

In England artists had always made the upper classes uneasy. They stood outside the social structure, and for that they were regarded as both weird and strangely admirable all at the same time—outcasts who had made the extraordinary decision not to play the only game worth playing, the class game. It was nice, of course, to have the odd Van Dyck or Reynolds on the wall to show that yours was old money, and it was acceptable to give wall space to the lastest Marlborough or Kasmin protégé to show that you were self-confident enough to "move with the times." But to be enthusiastic about artists and art was naïve, nouveau riche, and unacceptably effeminate in a culture in which buggery was what you did at Eton and then spent the rest of your life bad-mouthing.

Julie sensed she was on a dead-end street. Once again she changed tack. "I thought we might go and have a drink with Lord and Lady Hanson this evening. Geraldine called up and specifically invited you."

Billy sat up. Anything was better than Julie in a flirtatious mode. The change of subject was a welcome one. And he rather liked the tall, laconic multimillionaire James Hanson and his sparky, bright-eyed wife. "Okay. Fine. I'd like that." He paused. There was something on his mind. Was this the moment to raise it? "Carlos was saying there was some excitement around here the other night. Some freak pretending to be your sister or something."

Julie Bennett stopped breathing. For a moment or two she had buried the memory of Jane. Now Billy had scooped up the corpse from the rotten undergrowth. "What else did you hear?" Her voice was sharp.

"That the cops came and hauled her away. What else *was* there to hear?"

When next she spoke, Julie's voice was faraway, almost dreamy. "It *was* my sister."

"What?" Billy laughed. "You're not serious, are you?"

"Yes, I am." Julie wasn't quite sure why she was being so honest. A numbness seemed to have descended on her like a thick fog.

"You have a sister . . . and she came here . . . and you said you didn't know her . . . and you had the cops take her away."

Billy was deeply astounded. Surely even Julie Bennett couldn't have done a thing like that.

"She had no right to come and disturb me here." Julie's voice was childlike now, whining, almost plaintive, a little girl hurt.

"Have the cops let her go? Where is she now?"

"She pretended to be a policewoman to get through the gate. Apparently that's a felony. They charged her with it."

Billy Bingham exploded. "But you can't do that . . . to your own sister. Nobody could do that . . . You'd better call them up and tell them it was a mistake. I'll call. Right now." He leaped off the sun bed.

"Don't you *dare*!"

Billy dared. He walked toward her. There were things in this life that had to be said, just had to be done.

He stood there vibrating with indignation. "Listen, Julie. You mess me around, and you can mess the others around. It's part of the sick deal we've made. But you can't do that to your own sister. It's weird. It's just . . ." He paused as he tried to find the words to express his disgust. ". . . It's just . . . evil."

Julie Bennett smiled up at him nastily. Life was so full of surprises. She'd found the spot quite by accident, and now Billy Bingham was thoroughly upset. How *very* satisfactory.

Her accent was at its most English as she spoke. "And what, dear boy, do *you* intend to do about it? If *I* say I haven't got a sister, then I have no sister. Who the hell around here is going to listen to some two-bit hustler on the make? Christ, look at you! You look like one of the bum boys on Santa Monica trying to turn a cheap trick. You start trying to make waves for me in this town and you'll end up splattered all over the sidewalk where you belong."

The Queen's English and the L.A. street talk made uneasy bedfellows, giving a surreal quality to her monologue.

At first Billy didn't answer. His mind was whirling. Of course she was right. His only chance had been to persuade Julie to do the right thing, to phone the cops and straighten everything out. To attempt to intervene himself wouldn't achieve anything, except to land him on the street or in jail. As usual Julie Bennett had the big guns on her side. Damn it to *hell*. Why did she always win? Why did she always get her own way? What pact had she made with the devil to allow her to spread so much pain and remain immune from its consequences?

His lips tight with anger, he spat out the words, "You know what, Julie. I think you've done that sister of yours one big favor letting her stay in that jail. Because while she's in there all locked up, she's safe from you. You can't harm her now. God knows what you'd do to her if you had her here."

Julie Bennett eyed his retreating back. Mmmm. He was right, wasn't he? Jane in jail would always be a threat to her. The specter of her past would be forever lurking in the bushes, potentially ready to spring out and devour her. And Julie's revenge would be spent, finished, a cold meal consumed rather than an endless banquet. The only real exorcism of the ghosts would be in the slow and cunning destruction of the symbol of her pain. The enemy should be near her, where it could be watched, manipulated, tortured, and destroyed. It should not languish safely for a few days in the relative paradise of prison.

Julie Bennett sat for a moment, planning. Then she stood up and walked slowly toward the house. There was a telephone call she had to make.

"Captain Andrews? Oh, *hello*, Captain Andrews. This is Julie Bennett. No, that's right. Not since the police ball last year. Yes, it *was* fun, wasn't it? But wait till this year's one. I think I can guarantee it will be even more enjoyable. Frank and Barbara are definite, and I think Bob's going to be in town too. So a full house of the desert celebs, and I've got Willie Nelson for the cabaret. Yes, quite a coup. I'm quite pleased with myself."

The honey dripped from the Bennett lips. This was the Julie Bennett that was strictly for public consumption, the charming authoress who hadn't let money bend her mind, who still cared, and who pushed some of the winnings back into the game. Captain Andrews of the Palm Springs P.D. was a big, big fan—and with the very best of reasons. The security-conscious writer had seen to it that her relationship with the local police was a special one. Whenever a new VCR was needed for the station, whenever illness caused hardship for one of his officers, whenever there was a problem with the town council, then Julie Bennett would bend over backward to help. And the police ball—one of the major sources of funds for the luxuries of the police business, including the new canteen, the forty-eight-inch Mitsubishi wide-screen TV, the personalized food baskets at Christmas stuffed with whole Virginia hams, crystallized fruits, bottles of Johnny Walker Black and Taittinger champagne—was Julie Bennett's jealously guarded preserve. The other heavy hitters of the desert social circuit—Barbara Sinatra, Lee Annenberg, and Betty Ford—left the cop ball exclusively to Julie Bennett. Nobody had been disappointed yet.

"Captain Andrews, you're probably going to find this a little difficult to believe, but you know the girl you're holding at the moment—the one who came up here pretending to be a police officer..."

"Yes, Julie." He was proud that he was in a position to call her by her first name. "We never formally charged her as it's quite clear she's a nut case. Schizophrenic, probably. Dr. Carney, a psychiatrist from the Eisenhower, is dealing with it. In fact, I think he saw her yesterday, because I vaguely heard there was a plan to transfer her immediately to the Patton, a place for the criminally insane in San Bernadino. She might have gone already. I could check."

"Well, the tricky thing is . . . she *is* my sister."

"She's *what*?"

"She is my sister. You see, I hadn't seen her for fifteen years, and we haven't been in touch—for family reasons—and it was late, and the truth be told I'd had a couple of cocktails, and I just didn't recognize her."

"You didn't recognize your own sister?"

"That's the bottom line, I'm afraid. I genuinely didn't recognize her. I know it sounds unbelievable, but it was dark and I had no idea she was coming. Hadn't thought about her for years. . . . I just made an honest mistake."

"This report says you denied you ever *had* a sister."

Julie's voice was Teflon firm. "Oh no. The officer must have made a mistake."

"But Julie, we arrested the girl. We had her here in a holding cell. Right now Carney's probably got her in a back ward at the nut house filled up to the eyeballs with God knows what medication. We're all in the shit—Carney for malpractice, my department for wrongful arrest. If the girl was speaking the truth and if she's sane, then any lawyer who can stand up and stay sober is going to take us all to the cleaners, and it's all down to us believing what you said. Frankly, it stinks."

He was beginning to get angry, but he hadn't forgotten who he was talking to. Neither had Julie Bennett.

"Oh, come on, Seth. Don't do the drama bit. It's not *that* big a deal. It's no crime to make a mistake, and anyway when I sort it out with Jane she isn't going to be suing anybody. I can guarantee that. These things happen. It's just lucky we're all friends, and we know about sticking together and making things come out right. Outsiders don't have to get in on this one. It's all in the family."

Julie had made the tactical switch from "Captain Andrews" to "Seth" to offset the steely determination that had crept into her voice. IOUs were being called in. The reference to "outsiders" had been a shrewd one. This wasn't New York City, with wall-to-wall bleeding-heart liberals and closet-queen ACLU lawyers jamming up the smooth workings of life. This was Palm Springs. The desert. Where fine sensibilities and emotional indulgences were not allowed to disturb the peace, harmony, and tranquillity.

"Just let me get this quite straight, Julie, because we can't afford to screw up again. The girl is your sister, and she pretended to be a police officer to surprise you, right? That means we've got to spring her right now. Presumably she won't want anything to do with you after you got her pitched into the nut house. So what the hell do we do with her? It says here she's got no money."

"No, that's no problem. I'll deal with all that. I want her up here at the house. I can explain everything and get it all straightened out. She'll understand. You just get her to me, okay?"

"I guess that's what I'll have to do. God alone knows what I'll say to Carney. He'll go ape."

"Tell him the truth, Seth. Tell him anything. I'm sure you'll think of something. You're quite brilliant. I know that. That's why Palm Springs P.D. is the best in California. Why else would I be its most energetic cheerleader? You wait till you see what my ball pulls in this year. Oh, by the way, you and Betty will be my table guests, won't you?

"Well, okay, Julie. It sure is a mess, but I guess we can straighten it out somehow. I'll find out what's cooking and get right back to you to let you know when to expect her."

Julie Bennett put down the telephone. While she had been speaking, her face had provided an animated visual accompaniment to the roles that her voice had played. She had been arrogant, "silly-me" sorry, the down-to-earth realist, and the little woman in awe of powerful man. Now it was over, and as always she had gotten her own way. At first her face reflected that, too, a sort of grim satisfaction—but slowly, swirling form the murky depths, another expression began to build. The thick, dark mist creeped in from the corners of her face, millimeter by centimeter, centimeter by inch, until it lay dense across her features, suffusing them, impregnating them with the glow of hatred.

She reached down for the cat.

"Well, Orlando. What do you think of that?"

The dark green eyes gazed back at her.

"Believe Mummy, darling. The fun has only just begun. It's only just begun."

EIGHT

"DON'T LIE TO ME, JULIE. YOU KNEW EXACTLY WHO I was. You know now and you knew then. I only came back here because the doctors wouldn't send me anywhere else. So don't worry. I'm not going to wreck your cozy little world. The moment I've told you just what a bitch you are I'm going to go for good."

Like an Amazon, Jane stood foursquare on the priceless Shirvan carpet, beneath the approving eye of the old Velázquez soldier. Pale and wan and still gripped by the cotton-wool fingers of Thorazine, she nonetheless shook with rage.

On the edge of the slubbed-silk sofa Julie Bennett, her hands clasped tight together, was making it up as she went along. She hadn't expected Jane to believe her lie, and she had been right. Now she fell back on the truth. Jane had to stay with her. Jane had to trust her. So that Jane could be destroyed.

"You're right, Jane," said her still, small voice. "It's point-less to deny it. I did recognize you. Of course I did. But I wanted terribly to hurt you." She paused to let the drama of the unexpected honesty sink in. "Please, please—try to un-derstand what I did."

"For God's sake, Julie. What is there to understand? You had me thrown into jail. You convinced them I was a lunatic and they committed me to an asylum. Can you imagine that? They as good as raped me. They injected me with drugs and they locked me up with *mad* people and just because I came to see my sister who I hadn't seen for fifteen years. What's the *matter* with you, Julie? You ought to see a doctor. You just can't *do* things like that. *They* can't do things like that. What kind of a crazy country is this?"

Jane vibrated with righteous indignation, but she was curious too. What on earth had happened to make Julie behave like this?

Julie's voice acquired theatrical overtones—the soliloquy after the emotional storm. Quiet, the words slow, hesitant, her voice throbbed with sincerity. "God, how I loved him. You can never know that. How much I loved him."

The drama was heightened by the absence of the loved one's name, but Jane knew at the deepest level of her being that Julie was talking about their father—the shadowy figure she herself had hardly known.

"He was my whole life. Everything. I dreamed about him. I lived for him. And I only wanted him to be happy."

The little-girl-lost had moved to the center of the stage. Not much to ask—for a beloved father's happiness. What cruel, insensitive person would deny a request like that? At the tail end of anger, Jane braced herself for the entrance of the villain, who somehow she knew would be a villainess.

"But Mother didn't want him to be happy. She just wanted to own him. To have him as some performing poodle to parade before her smart friends. He would have had a chance here . . . with me. A chance for everything he'd ever dreamed of. And they were dying to give it to him. Pleading with him to let them make him a star. But he stayed behind. With her!" Julie's face twisted with fury as she shouted the dreaded word and she jumped up, transformed from wronged child to avenging angel.

Jane inhaled sharply, almost afraid. No wonder *Child Woman* had been such a success. Julie had just made the change from girl to woman in front of her eyes. But she didn't believe her sister for a second.

"Oh, don't talk such *nonsense*, Julie." Jane allowed her voice to blast a bit, too. "You talk about Dad as if he was a kid of ten. He had a wonderful career in England. Just because he didn't want to come and live in Disneyland doesn't make Mother his jailer. Mum wasn't perfect, but she was a terrific person in her own way. And she deserved some sort of gesture at her funeral. I thought it was *intolerable* that you didn't come, no flowers, nothing. What sort a daughter behaves like that? What sort of a *person* behaves like that? It sounds as if you had some sort of a crush on Dad, and it sounds pretty unhealthy to me."

Julie was white as the snows of winter. Her fists pumped, her pupils dilated, as she throbbed her indignation. "How dare you *talk* about Dad! You never knew him. You were five years old when he died. When that *bitch* killed her."

"What the hell do you mean, killed him? Mother didn't kill anyone, especially Dad. She loved him. She was always talking about him, and what a wonderful actor he was and how he loved us."

Julie Bennett's face flicked through the rage of emotions like an animated cartoon. She had reached incredulity, followed by the beginnings of understanding and disgust when she spoke next. "No, of course she wouldn't have told you, would she? Not Mother. What did she say it was? A car accident? A sudden illness? Something a bit more inventive probably. Like struck by lightning or zapped by a laser from outer *space*!"

"Stop talking in riddles, Julie. What is all this nonsense?" Jane couldn't help feeling that the role of the righteous wronged was slipping away from her.

"Do you want to know what really happened? Can you stand a bit of the truth about our happy family?"

"*Your* version of it."

"Yes, my version of it, Jane. Because Mum and Dad are both dead, and you were only a child. I'm the one who has to *live* with the tragedy. Every second of every minute of every day of my life." Julie was feeling it, being it, lost in the drama.

"What 'tragedy,' Julie?" The impatience poked out of the words.

"Daddy's suicide, Jane."

"What?" Jane stepped back as the force of the statement hit

her. There was a half smile on her sister's face as she watched
the impact, growing cruel as she toppled the playing cards of
all the most cherished beliefs.

"Yes, Daddy killed himself. He hanged himself from one
of those dark oak beams in the drawing room of the cottage in
Gloucestershire. Do you remember those beams, Jane? When
I was a child I used to think that they were so high that they
were like the scaffolding of heaven. I used to think God lived
up there in the beams. Did you have thoughts like that, Jane?"

Jane could see the demons now. Her sister's ghosts were
wailing and moaning before her, but she said not hing because
inside her a voice was telling her that there was more.

"Why did he do it? Why did he take a rope and put it
around his neck and hang himself from the old oak beams
until his legs stopped twitching, and his eyes popped from his
head, and his hands stopped clawing at the noose?"

The dreadful vision filled the silence as it was meant to do.

"Because Mother walked out on him. Because she deserted
him. Left him for another man. And he killed himself because
he couldn't stand it."

The words rolled around the room like thunder. They were
intoned rather than shouted, like some potent litany in a ceremony of exorcism.

"It's not true." Jane murmured the prayer that was no statement. It was true all right, and it explained so much. Her
mother had married Johnny Anstruther quite soon after her
father's "accidental" death. The excuse had been nothing more
inventive than brain cancer. Julie had been wrong about that.
But there was no doubt at all in Jane's mind that about everything else she had been frighteningly right.

There had been the bittersweet look in her mother's face
when she had talked about Richard, her eyes often averted as
she told the tales of his dramatic successes and his wonderful
skills. Somehow she had never seemed totally at ease with the
subject, and at the first opportunity she would dart gratefully
away from it on the pretext that "life must go on" and there
was no point "indulging oneself in sad memories."

About her father it was difficult for Jane to be sorry except
in a vacuum of feeling. She had hardly known him. And even

her mother was difficult to blame. Who knew the realities of the lives of others? Those were always a mystery. Divorces happened. People fell in love with people they weren't married to. It might not be the most admirable thing in the world, but it was far from the most uncommon. And she had always loved Johnny Anstruther as a surrogate father until the car crash that had killed both him and her mother. Judge not that ye be not judged: It was a comfortable verdict.

Julie sank down on the vast sofa and her head collapsed into her hands. The sobs mutilated the silence as they shook her ample frame. "She murdered him," she whispered. "She killed the mockingbird. And he was so beautiful, and so trusting and so kind and so true. If only you had known him, Jane, you would understand how I feel."

She peered up through her fingers. In the depth of her genuine grief the plan had not been forgotten. Jane was leaning toward her. She could see the turmoil behind the exquisite face as it forgot its own pain and began to concentrate on Julie's.

"And you *were* Sophie, Jane. You look so like her, too. When I saw you I could only think of her and of what she had done to Dad. You were the symbol of the love that killed him. I know its crazy and illogical and it doesn't make sense, but that's why I did what I did. And I'm sorry and ashamed, and I just hope and pray that one day you can forgive me." She sniffed back a sob and wiped a tear from the eyes that sparkled for Johnny and flashed for Merv.

"Can you understand this? When Mummy was pregnant with you I was so jealous I went right out and screwed some pop star when I was just *fifteen*. And while you were being born do you know what they were doing to me? They were cutting out my womb. They told me my baby was dead and they had to do a hysterectomy to stop the bleeding. You know what that *means*? I'm barren, Jane. I can never have a child, and there's a part of me that blames you for that. I'm not like other people. I'm like the desert."

Jane took a deep breath, overwhelmed. Nothing in her life so far had measured up to the intensity of this. The tour de force of Julie's emotion absolutely demanded not only attention but sympathy.

The sobs were coming again now. Stronger than before as self-pity gripped at Julie. Through tearstained fingers she said, "I'm half a woman, whose daddy died of a broken heart."

It was enough. More than enough for Jane. She sprang toward her, drawn by some magnet to the hurting figure who had harmed her, but who had been so deeply harmed herself. This was her sister Julie—heroine of the press cuttings and the scrapbooks and the full fantasies of her adolescence. Here, weeping in front of her, crying out for warmth and understanding, was her own flesh and blood, the only close family she had.

She bent down and wrapped her arms around her sister, holding her close. "Oh, Julie, how dreadful. How awful for you. I'm so sorry. I had no idea."

From the depths of her arms the little voice said, "Oh, Jane, can you forgive me? Can we start again?"

"Yes, yes. Of course I forgive you. Of course I do. It's all over now. It's all over."

NINE

ROBERT FOLEY SAW THE FLIES EVERYWHERE. NONE of them could be bothered to use their wings. Here in India it wasn't necessary. There was more than enough dirt and filth to go around. All flies had to do was crawl. They crawled on the wall, on the dirt floor, even on the arms of the ancient ceiling fan as it struggled to circulate the steaming air. But mostly they crawled in the eyes of the children.

"This isn't a clinic—it's an oven, a sewer, a Turkish bath —but it isn't a clinic." Robert Foley's voice had despair in it, but there was anger, too, anger at the poverty and the squalor and the unfairness of it all.

"But I am thinking that with a little money it could be fixed up, old chap. We could make it a jolly sight better than this or I'm a Dutchman's uncle." There were few more certain things in the world than that Dr. Chandresawa had no Dutch nephew. He was small and bespectacled and very Indian, and his sing-song voice rushed and darted as it wrapped itself around the curiously English idiom that was the legacy of the Raj.

The Foley laugh told him he was a liar. "No way. *No way.* The whole area is open drains. I can almost *see* the bacteria. Throwing money at this place would be like pissing it up against the wall." He reached out to touch a child, fondling the scrawny shoulder, smoothing his fingers through the matted hair.

Dr. Chandresawa looked at him uncertainly. Weren't

Americans supposed to like throwing money at things? "But, Dr. Foley, this is Bombay. The whole city is an open drain. We have to start somewhere." His hands fluttered the unspoken "or not at all."

Robert Foley sighed deeply. It was true. He'd only been in the city for four days, and it had been a revelation. The serried ranks of people sleeping on the sidewalks of the broad avenues—gigantic skid-row solutions to the housing "problem"; the cripples dancing, tumbling, displaying cheerfully their hideous deformities for the iced-chocolate-drinking tourists on the balcony of the Taj Hotel; the pubescent prostitutes—not jail bait here—tempting the passersby from the infamous "cages" of Falkland Road. And over it all, like a thin, threadbare blanket, the sickly sweet smell of decay—urine, ganja, curry, and excrement merging in the steam-pressed air.

Again he looked around the dark little room. Would this be a good place for Live Aid money? Or should it go elsewhere? To some more worthy project, if such a thing existed. Until the contaminated drinking water was eliminated, dysentery would survive. Until these people got proper food the TB would continue to feed on their lungs. And until their living conditions improved, infections would continue to invade their malnourished bodies. Treating the symptoms of disease in a place like this was like blowing in the wind.

Robert Foley put his hand to his high forehead and his steel-blue eyes flashed their fury. It would be his decision. Bob Geldof had asked him personally to spend five million dollars in this part of India. As a result of what he decided, some would live and others die. Possibly some of the little children in this very room. He was playing God again, and the reason he had to do so was that God had passed on the responsibility. On what black moment at what dark time had the Great Inventor dreamed up dead babies? What obscure divine purpose did these suffering children serve? Was it that the Live Aid donors should be given a chance to express their charity? That he, Robert Foley, should be allowed to feel good because he was able to give of himself so freely? Well, he had news for God. He didn't feel good at all. He felt rotten, and betrayed and tricked by the Dice Man who had created the sickness, the ugliness, and the poverty that lived in this room.

"It's not a very good show is it?" said the Peter Sellers voice of Dr. Chandresawa.

Robert Foley smiled grimly as he twined his fingers into the hand of a sleepy child whose big round eyes told the story of his malnutrition. On either side of him two cheerful children showed the distended bellies of protein-deficiency disease, the muscles of their stomach walls just not strong enough to do the job that nature had intended.

"No, Dr. Chandresawa, it's not a good show. Not a good show at all."

The river would be flowing now, home in the San Fernando Valley. A sizzling, speedy river of greased sugar coursing remorselessly into the fat cells of the "fortunate." Burp-burgers, and Fast-farters and Sloppy Meals for the kids, Whizzers and triple-decker Whammos and Bop-dogs floating on the surging sea of chemical carbohydrate—melon-cola, Phew!, and Nice-Ice drinks. And Mom and Dad and little Willie, already planning his homeward puke, wouldn't know or care about this place, where parents occasionally mutilated their children to provide fodder for the lucrative curb-side freak shows, and where age fifty was age eighty-five.

Dr. Chandresawa looked at him quizzically, as his restless, despairing hands plucked impotently at the children. "One feels so sorry for the little blighters," he offered, aware that somehow his words didn't do justice to the sentiment. True moral outrage of the kind that fired from the Foley eyes was a rare and beautiful thing. The Indian doctor had lived here all his life, and familiarity with the Third World poverty had bred a detached indifference, if not contempt. But this American, born in the latter-day Canaan, his land awash with milk, honey, opportunity, and glorious possibility, had clearly taken it personally, as an affront to human dignity, as an abomination for which someone should be held responsible, someone would have to pay. Dr. Foley did not look like a violent man, but Dr. Chandresawa could never remember seeing anybody as angry. A terrible controlled rage, all bottled up inside, one that he hoped and prayed he would not see unleashed.

"Have you any children of your own, Dr. Foley?" Talking about his children might calm him down a bit. Certainly he must have them—a fine man like him. A physician from California, where doctors were millionaires and the people had nothing to do all day except worry about their health. Married, probably divorced. His standards would be high. Not a particularly easy man to live with, unless for a dreamer who shared his lofty ideals.

Robert Foley turned to face him—this throwback to a bygone age of cucumber sandwiches and the gentle click of leather on willow on the cricket pitches of the country clubs. Why did this silly little man pose and strut and ape the accents and pretensions of the hypocrites and opportunists who had plundered a whole continent, leaving only terminal poverty and ignorance behind?

"No, I have no children. Never married." His voice had gone cold. In it there was more than mere disapproval of Dr. Chandresawa and of what he stood for. There was a deeper, more fundamental dissatisfaction. An unmistakable displeasure with himself.

Dr. Chandresawa heard the message between the lines. This line of questioning was the deadest of dead ends. Foley had never married, had never reproduced himself, and it would remain a mystery why. He looked at the sensitive, intelligent face, at the expressive deep blue eyes, the aquiline nose, and the firm, positive, no-nonsense chin. Broad shoulders, a tapered waist, the body of one who took a lot of exercise but with no hint of the bodybuilding narcissism that would have raised the specter of effeminacy as a cause of bachelorhood. No, Foley was not homosexual, or "gay" as the Americans liked to call it. His lean, spare frame was that of an ascetic, his long thin fingers totally at ease as they roamed professionally over the pathology of the children, his restless eyes speaking eloquently of deeper, more meaningful preoccupations than the mere gratification of the senses. One thing was absolutely certain. If Robert Foley had remained unattached in California, then the choice would have been *his* alone, a choice defended from dawn until dusk, and from dusk until dawn as the blond beauties of the beachland—a species not known in India for their reticence—aimed themselves at him.

"How much do you need to get this clinic going, Doctor?"

The eyes of the Asian sparkled. "How long is a piece of string?—as we say over here. Do you have that expression, Dr. Foley? It must all depend on what kind of end result you want."

Foley talked fast. "Mornings only. Two doctors. A couple of nurses. An X-ray machine and some basic blood-testing facilities. An O.R. for minor surgical procedures. Redecoration, plumbing, wiring, furniture—and a self-financing operating budget."

"For a million dollars we should be able to put together something jolly fine. Jolly fine."

Foley narrowed his eyes. He could deal too. "I'll give you seven hundred and fifty thousand and we start work yesterday. Okay. We can iron out the fine print back at the hotel if you agree."

Seven hundred and fifty thousand, Foley thought. That was the Mick Jagger/Tina Turner duet that had lifted the stadium temperature ten degrees? The marvelous Madonna set—all guts and gaiety as the spirit of a generation had confronted her public for the first time since *Penthouse* and *Playboy* and emerged triumphant? The extraordinary power and presence of Bono and U2 as the supergroup had uncaged joy and excitement in the hearts and minds of the global audience? To all those right-minded citizens who scoffed and sneered at the tawdry pretensions and materialistic values of the "pop" world, Dr. Robert Foley had a message. Today, here, and tomorrow children would live and love because of Live Aid and the wonderful men and women who had sweated and strutted their stuff upon a stage for sweet charity.

Dr. Chandresawa could think of nothing to say. It was not bad news, but it was hardly good news. It was not a triumph, but it was hardly tragedy. His hand expressed his dilemma.

"Well?" Robert Foley snapped the word as if breaking a twig. His jaw shot out pugnaciously as he prepared to do battle for the children. The gentle cut and thrust of haggling had no place here, among the bugs and the pain and the shit and the steam. Here, if Robert Foley had anything to do with it, there would be no murder of hope.

Dr. Chandresawa managed a watery smile. "I'm sure that for that sort of money we can end up with a jolly fine clinic."

"I'm counting on it, Dr. Chandresawa. Counting on you. 'A jolly fine clinic' is exactly what it must be."

As always, Robert Foley meant what he had said.

"C'MON, BABY. MAKE WITH THE PINK. HIT ME WITH THE PINK. Right on, babe. That's it. You're lookin' dirty, sweetheart. Boy, are you lookin' dirty. Makin' me weak at the knees. For sure. Fer *sure*!"

Lucy Masterson was hardly bothering to look through the lens. The technical side of things was on automatic pilot now. The trick was to keep the energy level up, the inhibitions way down low, and inject the magic onto the celluloid. That was what sorted out the real photographers from the also-rans. The whir of the motor drive, the upbeat tempo of the Bangels, and the insistent flashes of the strobe light were the background to her moaning, pleading, breathless commentary.

Out to the side of the teenage Valley girl, Joshua Sheahan contorted himself into impossible shapes as he strained and stretched to keep the silver reflector board on target, and yet out of shot at the same time. To the unpracticed eye the assistant's efforts were totally unnecessary, but to the expert they made all the difference between the ordinary and the extraordinary—amplifying the light at the precise spot that the reader's eyes were meant to focus. Not that the readers of *Anything* magazine really needed the direction.

"Hey, Jishy boy, ain't we seein' sweet things today? Little Karen's got me turned on like a Christmas tree. Keep it comin', honey. How's she doin', Jish? Give me some feedback. She turnin' you straight, baby? She goin' to make you kiss the boys good-bye?"

Joshua Sheahan laughed good-naturedly. This was the famous Lucy style. Her teasing, sexy banter got the models going—relaxing them and flattering them into giving just that little bit extra, the tiny bit more that gave the soft porn a cutting edge. Compared to the souped-up Lucy Masterson *Anything* girls, the *Penthouse* Pets looked like the sterile models in *Gray's Anatomy* update.

"Yeah, you got it, Lucy. I think I just seen the light. Road to Damascus time. No question. No question." Joshua laughed as he lied.

"That ain't the light, honey. That for sure ain't the light. *That* is the prettiest pink you ever did see." Lucy crouched over the Nikon and flipped the zoom to the 105mm close-up slot. "Mmmm," she murmured appreciatively as the frames clicked on.

Joshua Sheahan watched her, the admiration shining in his eyes. It had been a lucky break to get to work for Lucy. In West Hollywood, homosexual capital of the world, where even the mayor had been a lesbian, the gays seldom hired the opposite sex. But Lucy Masterson had crossed gender lines to take on her assistant, and he would always be grateful to her for that.

"Okay, Jishy. That does it for this shot. Let's hold the lighting the way it is and go wide—like twenty-eight millimeter. And let's try it in Kodachrome. Gotta make the colors sing, baby. Gotta get Karen playing gorgeous *tunes*." She stepped back from the camera—hands on hips—as she surveyed her domain, and Joshua, juggling film and equipment on the matte-black studio trolley, watched her. Big, butch, ballsy Lucy Masterson. She was still beautiful—just—but the looks were brittle now. The blond hair color was bottled, and the cut was geometrical—Vidal Sassoon Rodeo Drive haute punk—with severe bangs and long sloping sides that ran backward to a sharp point at the nape of her neck. There were freckles around the upturned nose, an Aryan hardness in the deep blue eyes, and her melon-ripe lips—hungry, mocking— were coated in pink Fred Segal gloss, a dramatic contrast to the even, standard-issue California suntan. The body was a Matrix One production, serious L.A. coachwork honed and sculpted in the daily workout sessions, which were the latter-day Hollywood equivalent of organized religion. Her legs exploded proudly from the microscopic miniskirt, and her breasts, iron hard, bored angrily through the oversize white shoulder-padded T-shirt. She was about forty, maybe more, and behind the wheel of the Volkswagen Bug she was the standard stuff of the California dream, the cannon fodder for a thousand traffic-light fantasies. Male fantasies that would never, ever, be actualized.

"How ya doin', Karen? Warm enough? You sure look hot. Like, there's steam risin' in here." Lucy took a step toward the model, still stretched out languorously across the severe contours of the black Eames chair.

Karen smiled vacuously and tried to switch herself into thinking mode. Getting the neurons all fired up for that was often a problem, and most of her waking life she was on stuff that made it more difficult still. "Feels good," she managed at last. In Karen's world, feelings were the old thing that mattered. She ran her tongue provocatively over her lower lip to emphasize her point.

"And it *looks* good, honey." Lucy's eyes ran hungrily over her, like a fine art connoisseur considering the purchase of a high-ticket item. "But maybe we should have a little oil for the next shot. Make the colors throb." She called over her shoulder. "Hey, Joshua. Throw over the baby oil. We're goin' to slick young Karen up some. Have the colors *communicate*."

"Comin' up. You wanna put it on yourself? Like, you know how much you're gonna need."

"Oh, if I *must*. Can't get the hired help to do anything these days." Lucy laughed as she took the transparent bottle. "Oh, and Jish, beef up the strobes to the high slot, and focus in the heads a bit tighter. I want to light the laser in for this shot. We'll close down a stop or two and pick up a bit more depth of field. Not that anyone's goin' to want to see the stinking chair, but we'll have a real sharp ass line to go with the main attraction."

She squirted a generous slug of baby oil onto the flat of her hand and reached out for Karen.

The young girl was ready for it. Lucy could see it in her Los Angeles eyes. People knew about Lucy. And if they wanted to work with her, then they did what it took. Karen sat up, legs still unselfconsciously splayed open, and let her full, firm, adolescent tits push out at the photographer.

Lucy swallowed. "Oh, yes, baby," she murmured. "Pre-pregnancy pink. Pregravity. Precocious."

The professionals were always saying that it was never like this. Lucy assumed that Helmut Newton "never" got turned on by his models. For David Bailey they were, she imagined, just things, to be insulted and abused if he didn't like the way they flirted with his camera. To Scavullo they were, perhaps, just money-making machines. To Penn and Avedon they were geometrical shapes, clothes horses whose sole purpose was to participate in the creation of beautiful "Art." To Lucy they were sex—warm, hot, quivering contraptions made of sweet-smelling secret places, and smooth doe-skinned loveliness, to be desired, wanted, and, most important of all, had. She couldn't take a good photograph unless the model turned her on, and once turned on, she couldn't rest until she had experienced the girl. It was almost a ritual, a way of life. Their soft lips, soft bodies, soft minds melting into hers, merged themselves into her hungry flesh, fuel for the feminine love machine.

Lucy's eyes held Karen's in hers as she reached forward shamelessly for the young girl's beckoning breasts. "All for art," she half joked, half lied, as her hands closed over their targets.

Karen's lazy smile of acknowledgment said most of it. Her Teflon-hard nipples said the rest. She pushed them at the exploring fingers. No mistake now about the gift that would be given. No question but that later there would be more, much more.

Lucy didn't hurry. Her hands had all the time in the world. She loved the yielding flesh, the humble surrender, the promise of ecstasy in the so young eyes of the sexual voyager. When would it happen? Later that night? In the tiny hours of the morning after the all-night rampage through the after-hours clubs. Then, minds melted by substances, brains bent by the decibels of the Chili Peppers and Theolonius Monster, their bodies tired by the frenetic dancing, they would be one-time lovers . . . before the endless game began once more.

Down, down went the hands to the smooth flat stomach and still the eye contact held, as Lucy saw the feeling build in the wide-open teenager. Lower still, with both hands, reaching together, seeking, feeling, for the place where the contract would be signed, the ultimate deal done. There. The pleasure source. Hot and wet and grateful for the fingers' touch. Pushing shyly at the oil-covered hands, welcoming, nervous, a soft and frightened bird feeding at the hand of the powerful alien.

For a second or two it lasted. Karen held firm by the elder girl's hands, her soul mesmerized by the twin beams of longing in Lucy Masterson's eyes. And then she gave voice to the awesome feeling that raged through her. The sigh was dragged from her by the tide of longing, pulled roughly from her throat by the fist of passion. "Ooooh," she moaned, as the shudder of desire racked her throbbing, oil-slicked body.

Lucy smiled her triumph. One hand stayed where it was. The other flew gently to the teenage lips, dry and parched with the sudden desire. She rested a finger on Karen's cheek.

"Tonight we'll make love," she promised.

TEN

THE HOT WIND FLEW IN LOW FROM THE FOOTHILLS, caressing, insistent, bathing the world in a lapping sea of heat. There was no escape. Everything had surrendered to it, and the desert was still and silent. Even the ravens, their wings set, were content to ride the currents of warm air, passengers on the thick breeze, a passive audience for the inert, sun-bleached world below.

Billy Bingham lay against the white terrycloth of the sun bed, his slick mahogany body taking the full force of the burning rays. In the 107-degree heat of the low desert afternoon even he had bothered to cover himself in oil. Nothing too heavy, just Bain de Soleil, number 2. The scent was terrific.

"You don't look like an artist." Jane lay close to him but was shielded from the burning rays by the umbrella. She lay on her side, watching him, the material of the dramatic Christie Brinkley one-piece clinging to her magnificent body. Already her English skin was a delicate shade of honey brown, and most of it was visible, thanks to the design of the swimsuit: round panels of flesh beneath muscular upper arms, the crotch cut away high to reveal most of the firm buttocks and all of the sculpted thighs.

Billy laughed his reply. "What do you want? A black beret, a funny mustache, and an expression of semipermanent pain on my long-suffering face?"

"Well, I suppose so. I mean, you look too peaceful. You ought to be more haunted. And you shouldn't look so fit. Artists are underfed, and they never take any exercise, and they're always pale. You certainly have no right to be that color."

Billy smiled his lazy smile. He liked her. Very much. It had been three short days since he had rescued her from the horrors of her cell and already there was a part of him that was lost to the beautiful girl with the forgiving heart.

"Maybe in Europe artists are like that, but in southern California they have suntans. Everyone has suntans. Even behind the ears."

"Behind the ears?" Jane giggled.

"It's pretty easy. All you do is drop the convertible top and ride away from the sun."

He propped himself up on one elbow and stared at her, aware of the powerful contours of his upper body, the strong shoulders, the sexy, oil-slicked smoothness of his steam-ironed stomach.

Jane saw the sudden intensity in the brown eyes, despite the jokiness of the conversation, and recognized the self-conscious physicality of a young man who knows his body is beautiful and is not ashamed to use it to get what he wants.

For three days she had watched him watch her, and now she wanted to know more about him. "You really care about your work, don't you, Billy?"

Billy's look was thoughtful. There was so much to reveal, but nobody yet had understood him. Perhaps it wasn't possible to describe his desires, his ambition, and his art. Could mere words paint the emotions, the desperate needs that racked him?

Certainly his parents had never known about such things. They had stood back, hurt and uncomprehending, as he had struggled to tell them that their world was not his. So he had thrown off the security blanket of the family electrical business and left the comforting, stifling anonymity of small-town Ohio for California, cauldron of dreams, crucible of hope, murderer of innocence.

And when he'd gotten there he had painted it—the deep

rich blues of the sky, the purple haze of the dreamscape, the Big Orange Heaven that doubled as Hell—and the raw energy of his vision, undiluted by art-school pretension, had screamed from the canvas and yelled its promise from the dripping brushstrokes, until he could hardly bear the genius he alone could see. The days and nights had merged as creation had coursed through him. He had fed on life and tried to hold on to the exploding joy in his head. But he had no money. No friends. No lovers. And worse, worst of all by far, no recognition, no artistic respect. Then, at last, he had begun to consider the scarcely to be believed possibility that his single-mindedness was nothing but madness.

One night, lightheaded from hunger and deeply worried, he had found a bar, and a biker who had suggested a weekend ride in the desert to do some dope, drink some beer, and sleep in the quiet beneath the stars.

Julie Bennett had caught him on Palm Canyon Drive like a rabbit in a steel trap. And he had caught her. It was seven short months ago, but the conversation remained as clear in his mind as today's Palm Springs sky.

She had stopped the snow-white Maserati right up close to the beat-up old Harley, and she had looked at him directly as she spoke.

"What's your name?" she said. As she spoke her eyes had undressed him. They had undone the buttons of the filthy 501s and ripped off the dirty Jockey shorts. They had stripped away the grime-covered T-shirt, and they had yanked off the Dexter ankle boots and had roamed freely over his naked body. Then her eyes had dived aggressively toward his secret places, picking and plucking at him as they sized him up like steak on a butcher's slab.

"Billy Bingham," he had replied as he had taken in the almost good-looking, heavy features, the mane of lionlike hair, the bicycle-pumped breasts, the fleshy upper arms. As he answered he had sniffed the heady scent of diamond-hard cash as it hovered about her in easy alliance with the force field of Giorgio and the red leather upholstery of the Italian dream machine that enveloped her like a second skin. And he had heard the refrain of lust playing in the Maserati air, with its high-stepping descant of decadent despair.

"Billy Bingham," she had repeated, her voice heavy with the surrogate humor of sarcasm, as her eyes had continued to trespass over his body.

Billy had been quite unable to get the idea out of his mind that this extraordinary vision was in fact a cat, a huge, hungry leopard preparing to pounce. He had the unmistakable feeling that she would flow all over him, engulf him, take him into herself, and then digest him with a giggle and a burp.

Which, in a way, was exactly how it had happened.

She had reached over to the passenger door with a knowing smile. "Get in, Billy Bingham," she had ordered.

Like a sleepwalker had had obeyed her, and an extraordinary feeling had zipped through him as he had moved to do her bidding. In that moment there had been a flight from freedom, a headlong retreat from responsibility as he had obeyed this iron-willed stranger, and into the vacuum created by the surrender of control had flowed the alien liquid of masochistic desire.

She had hardly spoken on the drive to her home, but she had looked at him speculatively from time to time. At the vast gates of her compound, she had spoken at last. "My name's Julie Bennett. I write books. You've almost certainly heard of me."

And of course he had.

With the noise of the huge brass doors still resounding in his ears she had turned around to look at him, this thing that the cat had brought in. She had seen the awe in his eyes—at the money that the name "Julie Bennett" implied, at the astounding artwork that dripped from the walls of the mighty anteroom well-recognized from the pages of *Art* and *Graphics* magazine, at the brazen effrontery of the outsize feline that had captured him. And she had seen the physical sign through the dirty Levi's, the symptom of passive lust, the signal that he was aware of what must be, and that his body at least willed it. So she had laughed at him then, at his insignificance, and his poverty, at his dirt and his inconsequentiality, and she had bared her teeth to show her hunger for his lean body and his youth. She had taken two paces toward him and hitched up the immaculate white linen skirt to reveal the formidable upper thighs and the angry bristling place that waited to devour him. She wore no panties.

"Fuck me now. Here. Standing up. You dirty little asshole," she had said simply.

On the sun bed Billy Bingham swallowed hard as he forced the disturbing vision from his mind. Julie Bennett was no hypocrite. She had started out as she had continued, and he had been a participant in the weird conspiracy. But here and now was the sister, soft and beautiful, gentle and kind, precious as a cactus flower framed in the early light of a desert dawn, haunting in her loveliness, asking him if he really cared about his art.

"Yes. I care. It's all I care about really. All this"—he waved his hand to take in the ten-million-dollar estate, the sparkling sixty-foot pool, the Henry Moore sculptures dotted like pebbles across the emerald-green lawns—"is dog shit." He looked at her carefully. Did she believe him? Why did he mind?

Jane said nothing, but her eyes said that she understood.

"I mean . . . I had to live . . . to paint, and to do the sculptures. It takes money for that. Quite a lot. Julie does all that side of things for me . . . and in return . . . Well, I . . . kinda . . . you know what I'm trying to say . . . I . . ."

"You're 'nice' to her." Jane laughed as she supplied the euphemism. The English used words like that a lot. They believed that some things—most things, perhaps even all things—were better left unsaid.

Billy laughed, too. "Yes, I guess you can say I'm 'nice' to her. And while I'm being 'nice' to her she's being nasty to me. That's her little game. I know she's your sister, but sometimes I think she needs a shrink."

"No, I think she's just lonely, and very unhappy. I mean, that trick she played on me—she was so sorry for that, and we talked for hours, and she told me all sorts of things that I had never known—about Mummy and Daddy and the things that went on when she was small and I wasn't even around. She made me feel so sad for her. I began to understand all the hurt and the pain that had built up inside her. Does she ever discuss things like that with you?"

"No way. She doesn't 'talk' to me, she *insults* me. There have been others you know. I mean, a lot of others."

"Yes, I know. The scandal magazines call you 'toy boys,' don't they?"

Billy's face darkened. "That's right, they do. And perhaps they're right. About the others. But not about me. I'm going to be someone, the *biggest* someone in the world. Bigger than Julie frigging Bennett . . . than . . . anyone. When you see my work you'll know that. It says it all. The future is right there on the canvas. Now. I swear it."

It was as if Billy spoke a catechism, a litany, a solemn promise to the gods in their heaven. By his belief alone Billy Bingham would make his dreams come true. Jane felt a shudder run down her spine. Feelings like this were foreign to her. They didn't talk like this in the drawing rooms of Gloucestershire, or the dining rooms of Eaton Square. It was strangely stirring out here in the real world. A future where exciting things could happen, where things could actually change, where feelings and desires and ambitions would mean something—something fine, and noble and worthwhile—in complete contrast to the unbroken circle of life in England, where things were "good" only insofar as they remained the same.

There was so much more to this young boy than the world would think. He was interesting all right, fascinating, and very, very attractive. Jane fought against the idea. It was quite impossible; whatever their relationship was, he *belonged* to Julie.

"Can I see your work?"

For a moment he didn't speak. "I'd want to know you better first."

"Oh." She didn't know what he meant. There were several possibilities—and one at least was far too hot to handle.

"I mean, I'd want to know what you felt about painting, and its purpose and its meaning, and who you admired and who you hated. All those kinds of things. I couldn't bear it if you couldn't 'see' and just said things about it being 'pretty' or 'strange' or asking what it *meant*. I'm not saying you would, but I'd just like to be sure first. I'm sorry if that all sounds pompous, or precious, or whatever."

"No, it doesn't sound like that. I hear what you are saying." Jane smiled encouragingly at him. She sat up on the Tropitone sun bed and clasped her hands around her long legs as she watched him.

"Great, well, let's have something to drink. I'm drying up like a prune out here. What about some peach juice and champagne? It's wonderful."

"God, how decadent. Sounds great, though. Will they have to open a whole bottle specially?"

"Listen, Jane. Do you realize how much Julie got for the hardback and paperback rights of her last novel? Just the U.S. rights, I'm talking about."

"No idea."

"Five million dollars guaranteed. So don't worry about the Taittinger. *Money* is not her problem."

"Okay, okay. She can afford the champagne." Jane lifted both hands in mock surrender.

Billy picked up the poolside phone and ordered the drinks. "Oh, and bring some nuts—cashews, macadamias, pistachios. Yeah, that's right—a selection," he added.

"Billy."

"Yup?"

"If I can't see your work, will you take me for a ride on your motorbike?"

Billy smiled at her. "For sure, I will. Later on, when the sun gets lower. As long as you promise to hold on tight."

"Oh, I promise. I promise," said Jane, trying to suppress the frisson of guilt that shot through her as she spoke.

"DO YOU SEE THAT, ORLANDO? DO YOU *SEE* THAT?"

Julie Bennett plucked feverishly at the bristling fur as she hissed her question. Forty feet above the pool and to one side of it, she had watched it all unfold. Usually she would be chained to the typewriter at this stage of the afternoon, lost in the world that authors sought on the other side of reality's looking glass. But today, once again, when she'd attempted to climb through the mirror all she'd gotten was a metaphorical bloody nose. The escape route to fantasy was blocked and she had exhausted every trick in her substantial repertoire to get around it. So she had wandered over to the window—the one whose smoked glass kept out prying eyes as well as the ubiquitous rays of the desert sun—and stared down morosely at the pool.

Beneath her, ridiculously beautiful, obscenely attractive in the figure-hugging swimsuit, was the sister she hated. Staring into her eyes as if he expected to find the secret of life itself hidden in their depths was her toy boy, the thing she *owned*.

Even in the riptide of her rage Julie couldn't help thinking about the comparison between herself and her younger sister. The similarity couldn't be denied, but it was the differences that caught the attention. When the genetic cards had been dealt she had been left holding the nines and tens while the royal cards had gone to Jane. Julie's proportions were fine, but she was so damn *big,* and Jane, in contrast, so effortlessly "right." A sidelong glance at the mirror told the whole story. The ample white caftan hid most of it—the big round curves that were muscled and tight from the tennis and golf but lay like a continent a million miles from the graceful lines of her sister's body; the wrinkly, button-type, cherry-on-the-ice-cream nipples that lost the contest with the splendid bottom-of-the-cone variety that crowned Jane's *Vogue*-worthy breasts; the ample hammer-and-anvil buttocks a miserable also-ran in the race with her sister's bottom, whose lines would have required Matisse on a good day to capture. And the face? Again no match. Julie was quite fine looking in a way, and the mouse-colored hair swept back before being allowed to cascade forward over her plump neck was definitely a fine feature, but her forehead was too broad, her cheeks too ruddy and too round, the voluptuous mouth with its pearly white tombstone teeth just a fraction too full. And her feet, crammed unhappily into golden open-toe sandals, were slain by the opposition—Jane's pink-toed beauties, fine and delicate, the wild fantasy of some perfectionistic podiatrist high on Ecstasy. Even the vast diamond-encrusted leopard bracelets and the matching feline earrings—Cartier at its best—fell short of making Julie elegant; instead she looked bold and brassy.

"He's flirting with her, darling. Do you know that? He's flirting with her, and she's *lapping* it up." The marmalade cat struggled impotently in the iron embrace.

The Bennett mouth was a surgical slash across her unmade-up skin, cold, determined, and deadly. From her eyes the hate bored out through the thick smoked glass and into Jane, as inside her mind the dreadful silent movie played. The one that starred Jane and Billy.

"He's mine," she murmured.

"He's *mine*," she screamed, as she cast Orlando into space and dived toward the phone.

"Carlos," she barked into the receiver. "Go to the pool and get Mr. Bingham. Tell him to come to my bedroom immediately. This moment. *Me entiende? Pronto!*"

She waited just long enough to see the scurrying figure of the butler as he rushed onto the patio, before she herself hurried to the door.

BILLY BINGHAM WAS STANDING IN THE DOORWAY.

For what seemed like forever Julie Bennett just looked at him. The sort of look you gave the pony-tailed, whacked-out dope fiend your sixteen-year-old daughter brought back from the Roxy.

But of course Billy Bingham didn't look like that at all. For a start he was clean as a newly minted penny, and about the same color. The tan was a masterpiece, and the thin film of oil that covered it was varnish on the painting. He stood there like an athlete, his arms dangling by his sides, one muscled leg cocked forward, its downy hairs glistening in the sunlight that filtered into the vast room through the forty-foot retractable ceiling. Even in the full spate of her anger, Julie Bennett was still able to see his beauty. He was twenty-two tender years, but if anything the face was younger. Dark brooding eyes, the type that got called sensitive, a strong Roman nose, just a little too big but great nonetheless because it excluded the face from the dreaded "male model" category. Perfectly proportioned mouth and jaw. Standard-issue surfer's teeth. It was clear that he sensed he was in some kind of trouble. Clear, too, that he didn't give a damn.

Julie felt the well-known sensation coursing through her. Anger and jealousy were already making the trip to the back burner, and in the front of the stove the cauldron of lust was beginning to bubble. Billy could do this to her, more than any of the others. It was the insolence, perhaps, the "screw you" vibes that beamed out of him even when he was asleep in the sun. She couldn't touch him where it mattered, because his heart didn't want the things she could provide. He would accept the presents—the custom-painted Suzuki Intruder, the Maserati Bi-Turbo convertible—but he didn't really *care* about them. Even during the lovemaking, or rather the sex, he wasn't really *there*, and he turned in his faultless performance with absolutely no effort at all. But she had seen the light in his eyes as he worked on his canvases in the vast solarium that had been converted into his studio. That was where the real Billy Bingham lived and had his being. Everything else, including Julie Bennett—especially Julie Bennett—was totally unimportant to him.

Billy Bingham felt the wave of passivity pass through him. There was a way of doing this, a method of surviving it. He *had* signed his contract with the devil to buy time for his art. The space, the materials, the peace of the desert had all been bought with the hard currency of his body. His body wasn't his anymore. He had sold it, and Julie Bennett was its owner.

"Come here." Julie's tone was not remotely coquettish. It was an order, pure and simple.

Billy felt the first stirrings in the Dolfin shorts as he did as he was told.

It was weird, almost impossible, but there was excitement in this, excitement and horror, the excitement *of* horror. God, what vast animal did she resemble, lying there, as she waited for him?

"What do you want me to do?"

"Eat me!"

Quite suddenly Billy had ceased to be a person. He was now a pleasure instrument, no longer a human being, and with the evaporation of responsibility came a wonderful sense of release that merged with gratitude toward the one who had engineered it. This was what the led felt about leaders. The burdensome decisions were no longer his to make. A whole area of his being—the most onerous part—had been lifted away from him.

Julie Bennett lay back on her two-thousand-dollar ivory-and-beige striped Pratesi silk sheets, and the smile of delicious anticipation played over her full, parted lips and her wide eyes widened as she looked at her present. Now he would pay for his mental lapse from grace with Jane—and those other lapses, physical ones, that were unknown and unseen but as certain as Christmas and wrong numbers. At moments like this Billy Bingham was different no more. He was just like all the others, and all those who would follow after him. He was not a mind, he was a body. She didn't want to know what he thought or felt, whether he was enjoying himself or not, what philosophy motivated him. Words were a waste of time, a perversion, even. His tongue had other, infinitely more useful purposes.

She splayed herself open for him—big muscled thighs streaming out to the generous buttocks and rolling down to quite passable knees and pleasant, if rather stringy, lower legs. The sheet-sized caftan raced upward.

Suddenly Billy had the idea he had been searching for. A whale on the beach. That was it. A sperm whale blown in by some storm at sea. Immobile now, but this awesome thing so very far from helpless.

But he bent in toward her, to do her bidding, and the dark dampness swallowed him up.

THE WILD HOT WIND PLUCKED AT THEM AS BILLY BINGHAM opened up the throttle of the 750cc Suzuki Intruder. The heat shimmered from the sticky tarmac of the road and the tacky mess of Cathedral City was already a rapidly fading memory.

Jane squeezed in tight against Billy's shoulders as the bike picked up speed and headed into the long curve of Highway 111. It felt good, his cut-off khaki tank top plastered up against her breasts, her arms locked firm around the whiplash waist, her head nuzzled down at the nape of his neck sheltered from the insistent blast of the moaning wind.

She shouted above the roar of the enigne. "What was that place we just went through?"

"Forget it. Bars and gays. We're just coming up to where the real bucks are. Rancho Mirage."

He twisted his head as he spoke, the words tumbling out of the corner of his mouth as Jane pressed her head near his lips to pick up his voice. In the small of his back he could feel her breasts, firm and pointed, warm and disturbing, as the scent of her raced into his mind, merging with the dusty wind and the kaleidoscope colors of the desert evening. This girl was getting to him, not that she was trying. She was not the poaching type at all. But there was a gentle, easy feeling about her, a powerful aura that lit up her phenomenal beauty and bathed her in an out-of-this-world loveliness he had never met before. She was kind but she wasn't weak; straightforward but not naïve; forgiving but not gullible. She was funny and she was bright, direct and perceptive, unselfconscious and unselfish, and of course, he was beginning to fall in love with her.

"Who lives in Rancho Mirage?"

"The way you tell is to look at the road names. There—see Frank Sinatra Drive. A mile or two up it merges with Bob Hope Drive, and the intersection is where the third heavy hitter lives— Walter Annenberg, Nixon's pal and the publisher of the most profitable magazine in the world—*TV Guide*! Actually, Bob Hope doesn't live in the desert at all, but he keeps a sort of a museum here and flies in and out from L.A. for the golf. Everybody likes to pretend he's a resident because in this country he's almost as important as God!"

"Where does Gerry Ford live?"

"You just seen him or something? He lives right in there at the Thunderbird with Ginger Rogers and Lucille Ball." Billy flipped out a thumb to indicate the formidably guarded entrance to the country club. No rubbernecking tourists would be hit by the ex-president's hooks and slices. "Not the sort of place for a redneck biker like me."

"You neck isn't red. It's the color of chocolate cake." And

I'd like to lick it. Jane felt the little thrill as the lascivious and unexpected thought zipped through her mind.

Billy's laugh was lost in the wind and in the rush of feeling that surged through him. Her voice could touch him like that —the exuberant British accent, so deliciously strange as her voluptuous lips wrapped themselves around the rich syllables. The powerful vibrations of the Suzuki cruiser shuddered between his legs and amplified the sounds of the little awakenings that played throughout his body.

The road creamed past his alert eyes and he made the sharp right-hand turn that sent them speeding through Palm Desert, the latest "in" place with its Rodeo Drive/Worth Avenue shops. Then they were off 111 and heading up toward the twilit sky on State Route 74, the highway to the *real* stars, the manmade masterpiece that was literally carved from the mountains.

There on the twisting canyon road the Intruder weaved and wound its way around the hairpin turns, forcing closer the bodies whose minds were already close. Jane clung to him— limpet tight—and Billy shamelessly threw the bike into the chicanes, the toes of his Reebok sneakers sandpapering the hot surface of the road, as he milked the moment for every ounce of its physical promise.

Beneath her feet Jane could sense the scalding pipes of the Suzuki's exhaust, and her whole mind was filled with the deep-throated roar of the engine that was the descant to the unmistakable music of desire. His bottom was plastered against her crotch. Her groin was thrust against his rock-hard buttocks as a warm wetness of their bodies fought to merge. She leaned her head against his back and breathed in deeply to smell the scent of his body, through the damp khaki of the tank top, pushing her nose into the sweat-soaked material, and spraying her mind with the hard honest aroma, gasoline for the flickering flames of lust that danced within her.

But it was still the phony war of would-be lovers, the childlike games of rough and tumble, the hot bodies near but not yet committed, the charade of counterfeit closeness. She clung to him for safety as the bike made crazy patterns on the mountain road. He pushed back at her to provide a firm anchor, to protect her from danger. On the surface they were friends. But millimeters below surface they were already so much more than that.

The Suzuki climbed remorselessly upward, past desert bighorn sheep clinging precariously to their rocky promontories; past meager herds of cattle scratching unhappily at the sparse grass of roadside ranches as they browsed among carpets of barrel, fishhook, and beavertail cactus. The colors were changing now, and it was not only the altitude—over four thousand feet above the desert floor—that was cooling the still balmy air. The sun was tired. Balanced like an orange football on the steel-blue peaks of Mount Jacinto, it was almost ready to surrender to the night. Its warm glow was soft now, bathing the valley in gentle light, daubing the Painted Hills to the east in pastel pinks, mauves, and vivid purples and the mighty mountains to the west in battleship grays and rich chocolate browns.

"It'll soon be dark. Let's stop and watch the sun go down." Billy's voice wafted back on the wailing wind.

In answer she squeezed his waist and ground her hardening nipples into his back. Nightfall on the mountain, alone with this boy who had sold his body to buy his dreams. Alone with the body that belonged to her sister. Jane shuddered at the illicit thought, and at the memory of the sun-bronzed flesh, and at the wondrous smell of it that filled her nostrils, here and now, on the dusky road.

The bumpy scrub replaced the smooth tarmac as the bike slowed and stopped and the eingine died. The sudden quiet imploded in on them, concentrating thought and underlining intention. For a second neither moved. They were a sculpture of still, twin bodies in the embrace of safety when safety was superfluous. In a little longer, the admission would be made, and the real reason for their closeness exposed.

Billy looked back over his shoulder at Jane, and she unwound from him and watched his eyes as he struggled to find the words that would make possible what he wanted. She smiled back at him in encouragement and understanding.

"Speak to me, artist," her smile said. "Tell me that you want me as much as you want your recognition, your success, and your glorious future. Let me hear you speak. Communicate with your tongue, not with your paint, your clay, and your talking hands."

The shadows were dancing behind his head as Billy wrestled with his moment. The sun was mobilizing its forces for a last desperate stand against the all but victorious night. Behind him the angry orb of violent color—orange red in the deep navy blue of the evening sky—was poised on top of the mountain range, radiating its last messages, caressing the sparkling chrome of the Intruder and silhouetting his handsome profile against the darkening desert. Then, suddenly the sun was gone, lost behind Mount Jacinto, and the world was plunged into a blackness relieved only by the brave brightness of the twinkling stars.

In the inspiration of the darkness Billy found his words. "I want you, Jane," he said simply.

Jane felt the breath rush through her parted lips, as her lungs and her heart quickened. But even as she stepped into the no-man's-land of the love battle, her mind was at war with her feelings. This was her sister's lover. Julie, who had suffered so much, was about to be betrayed by her own flesh and blood. Once again.

But youth's hot fire was burning in her body, devouring doubt and scalding caution. There was a personal score to be settled with Julie. This would wipe the slate clean. Anyway, what right had her sister to take advantage of Billy? To use his poverty, his ambitions, and his youth was obscene, a peverted, cruel misuse of somebody who deserved better. Of somebody who was about to *get* what he deserved.

So she reached around his body and her hands found the hot hard place, and she moved her face close to his so that she could smell his breath as she whispered. "If you want me you can have me."

Relief and desire crashed into each other on Billy's face. He swung around to confront her, swiveling on his buttocks as his athletic legs arced easily over the pear-shaped gas tank, until he sat before her in the wonderfully small bucket seat of the bike.

For sweet seconds they stared into each other's eyes—two hungry children lost in awe, not knowing where to start.

Billy's hands reached out across the inches that separated them, and he took her breasts in his hands as he gazed with longing into her eyes. Through the T-shirt they moved against his exploring fingers, alive, tight as the skin of a snare drum, as they throbbed with need. He reached down, but Jane had anticipated him. The Mexican conch belt that gripped the waist of her faded jeans was loose. The material of the sweatshirt was already free. He lifted the cotton, slowly, with reverence, as still he held her eyes and swallowed hard at the thought of the beauty that would soon be his. Then, his body trembling, he allowed his eyes to be sucked down. With the arrogance of the terminally beautiful she thrust her chest at him, her breasts, two perfect sculptures, smooth and proud, and confident of their supremacy. Billy stared hungrily at the honey-brown skin and the pale pink of the delicate, hard nipples, at the sure geometry of the sharp rose-petal-colored cones. They stood there, all on their own, laughing at his need and mocking the gravity to which they were immune, secure in the knowledge that they defined themselves, that they were the standard against which all others should be judged. Shaking with desire, Billy Bingham bathed her glorious breasts in his warm breath, as he dared to disturb the picture in his mind with the added sensation of touch.

Wonderingly, his fingers traced their contours. The creamy skin was firm and resilient—hot and slippery with the thinnest film of sweat squeezed out by the body heat in the early dawn of arousal. He laid his hands upon them and the hard, tense points surged against his moist palms. Then he bent in toward her, his tongue pushing shly through dry lips.

Jane moaned quietly, like the wind, as tongue and nipple met and her whole body quivered with the exquisite delicacy of the sensation. The fullness in her breasts was almost unbearable as the blood raced to them, crowding into the cramped space as it heated and energized the parts of her body that her lover touched. Her breast gloriously imprisoned in Billy's mouth, she squirmed and struggled to open herself up to the certainty of bliss, and her fumbling fingers found the waist of her jeans.

Jane arched her back and thrust down toward the hot, wet leather of the Intruder's seat as the blue denim surrendered. Down, down it went, below her bottom, halfway down her sculpted thighs, carrying with it the already soaked panties. Exhausted by the effort, anxious for the escalation of the pleasure dance, she stretched back, tearing herself away from the mouth that held her. Her arms were above her head, and the upright of the Suzuki's passenger seat was in the small of her back, as her long legs opened wide. On her face was the half smile of lust as she watched the helplessness in Billy's. She knew what she wanted, knew, too, that she was irresistible. Now her breasts and the knife slash of her belly button were aimed at the black velvet sky. Down below—its peach-pink lips pouting in the starlight—the glistening, musky silkiness of her core was framed by the crude, crumpled cloth of the bleached-out jeans that had clothed it.

On some astral plane of joy Billy heard her unspoken command. Willingly he hurried to obey her, and her hands accepted his head.

The anthems of triumph sang in Jane as he nuzzled into her, and her legs reached out for him as her hands had done. She twined them around him, binding him to her, his face buried in her beauty. She crushed her thighs against his cheeks, and both hands clasped against the back of his head, she pushed him in toward her, grinding his lips against hers, as she fought to drown him in her molten depths. Against his back her feet beat their tattoo, now perched against his shoulder blades, then reaching down to drum insistently against his spine. His tongue was a butterfly inside her, and as the explosions of pleasure racked her brain, Jane increased the tempo of the dance. Harder, more cruel, she crushed him, daring him to inhale the essence of her, to become her.

Sliding on the slippery slope at the edge of oblivion, Jane fought to save the moment. Her muscles strained and stretched as she dominated the mouth that pleased her, forcing it to stop when it wanted to continue, to start when it struggled to rest. Then, quite suddenly she was at the point from which there could be no return. Like a ski jumper, she crouched down low, tensing every muscle before the flight into the wildness of space. Down, down she swooped toward the takeoff point, her body shuddering, shaking with the effort—and the scenery rushed past as she roared toward her destination. The cry was conceived at the back of her throat, a gurgling, groaning, growing thing to be thrown at the uncaring hills and discarded by the unseen canyons—winging back to her on the complaining wind in the echo that guarded the precious moment.

"Yes, yeeeeeeeeeeeeees," she screamed as thought and mind took flight and she poured herself gloriously into the mouth of the man who loved her.

"Looks like Turner vomited up MGM. Bit off more than he could chew."

Julie Bennett addressed the clam as if it were something she would like to take to bed. Her big red lips sort of sneaked up on it, gave it a quick lick, and then went for it like an Italian tart in a fellatio contest. As it slithered into her, she reached for the ice-cold Corton Charlemagne '82 and peered suspiciously at Daniel Galvin III.

Beneath the patent leather Bryl-creamed hair the exuberant Galvin suntan broke into a pleased smile. "Yeah, those boys think they can handle anything. Now Turner's cut and run, and look at the trouble Boesky's got himself into. Personally I'd have Congress chop 'em all off at the knees."

Daniel Galvin spoke as if Congress were an institution that existed entirely for his own purposes. That they hadn't outlawed corporate raiders was merely because he hadn't so far —for reasons of his own—issued the relevant instructions.

Julie smiled at the pomposity, but she knew it was not entirely without foundation. As chairman, chief executive officer, and largest stockholder of the vast ABS network, Daniel Galvin stood at the right hand of God. He would have liked her crack against Turner, the ebulient, brash chairman of CNN, because it was only recently that he'd tried and failed to take over CBS, one of ABS's main competitors. In the musical chairs of the communications industry—Columbia swallowed by Coca-Cola, the proud NBC peacock zapped by RCA, and ABC forced into a shotgun wedding with Capital Cities—a lot of people were looking nervously over their shoulders, and scrambling to be in the right place when the music stopped.

"Anybody sniffing around at you?" Julie eyed him carefully out of the corner of her eye as she seduced another clam.

"Good God, no!" Daniel Galvin shot out the denial in irritation. Clearly there were a few things Julie Bennett didn't know about business. It was unlike him to accept a luncheon invitation from somebody he hardly knew, but Gerry Ford had insisted he come along, and now he was beginning to wonder why he'd bothered. Limeys were all the same. They thought the sun shone out of their asses and that if you weren't royal you didn't count. She must know he *owned* ABS—well, with the trusts a good twenty-five percent anyway. And any two-bit, smarmy hustler who tried to move in on his action was going to end up the pepperoni on the pizza. Even if the profits weren't billiant right now, the institutions, who held the balance of the shares, would stick with him. He was their kind—Phi Beta Kappa, Harvard Law, Bohemian Club—and he could count on their support against any outsider. Still, sometimes at night, at 3 A.M. when the martinis wore off, there was the odd nervous moment, which accounted for his reaction to Julie Bennett's remark and the bad mood that it had so effortlessly summoned up.

Gerry Ford moved into the unpromising conversation. He made something of a specialty of healing wounds. "Daniel was telling me their entertainment division's cooked up a series called *Beverly Hills Nights* that's going to blast Cosby right off the top of the ratings. Sort of up-market *Dynasty*—that right, Dan?"

"Yeah." Daniel Galvin brightened as he thought about the new program. "The whole company is high as a kite on the idea. Real gung ho." Technically it wasn't his particular responsibility and so he couldn't take all the credit, but at ABS nobody broke wind without either asking him first or hitting him with a memo about it afterward.

"We've got Pete Rivkin producing it. His show *All To-*

gether was the best thing I've ever seen, and his last mini-series just raped the Nielsens."

Carlos bent over him to pour some more wine, and he reaced for it immediately, drinking greedily. He was feeling better. Much better. This was *good* burgundy. In his opinion only a Le Montrachet beat a Corton Charlemagne of the same year. It was a bit too cold though. That was a common mistake in the desert. Everything got left in the Sub-Zero too long. He looked up and down the long table as the wine mellowed him. Most of the people here he knew a bit. Gerry and Betty of course. Elliott Roosevelt and Neil Simon, scribbling friends of the hostess, presumably. Old pals John and Bonnie Swearingen of Standard Oil. Allen Paulson of Gulfstream Aerospace, who'd just sold ABS a couple of corporate jets. Halfway down and across the table from him was an absolutely gorgeous girl. She was very young, but quite amazing and unfortunately locked in deep conversation with some guy who was too good looking by half.

Julie Bennett followed his eyes . . . and his thoughts.

Her mind flashed back to last night. It had been dinner for three in the formal dining room, except that she had been the only diner. Time and time again she had checked her 1920s Cartier diamond-and-emerald-encrusted bracelet watch, and the minutes had ticked by as the fury had grown within her. She had looked right, and then left, and the empty places had stared back at her. Jane's place. Billy's place.

Julie Bennett was the most successful novelist the world had ever known. She knew about plots and motivation, and characters, and about what in life was likely, and what was not. Superimposed on what she had seen by the pool that afternoon, her conclusion had been inescapable. The two absent dinner companions were either lovers or, if one was feeling charitable, would-be lovers. And it was a long time since Julie had experienced the feeling of charity.

She had remained calm in the eye of her hurricane of hatred. She'd practiced that. From the day they had lowered her father into the damp earth of the cemetery—her mother's lies about "cause of death" still staining her lips—she had lived in suspended animation—a gigantic moneymaking machine, her fingers attached to the keys of the typewriter as the words had flown out of her otherwise unmotivated mind. She didn't think about it, she did it, and the work had been an anesthetic of sorts. The pain had not gone away but its edge had been dulled. Into that bit of her brain where the memory and the emotions lived she had squirted some kind of preservative fluid, and they endured as fossilized monuments to her past. Until Jane had changed everything, and wakened her to confront her demons.

The music that had played over the housewide sound system last night had matched her mood. Melancholy Mendelssohn, Violin Concerto, E Minor. The plaintive, heart-wrenching beauty of the violin solo had been a suitable background to what she knew she must do. As she sat there she had constructed the plan like one of the plots of her novels. It hadn't been written down on the yellow legal pads that she liked to use for outlines in the early stages of a book. Instead it had been written in the wiry pathways of her brain, where now it grew and grew, thanks to the behavior of the two people who had indirectly brought it into being.

Billy and Jane were unaware of the electricity that sparkled between them. Everyone at the long luncheon table could see it but them, and several of the more daring guests at the less grand end of the table had tittered when somebody had stage-whispered, "Looks like the pet fuck hasn't been properly house trained."

"If you split to L.A., then I'm coming with you," whispered Billy urgently.

"No!" Jane shook her head to emphasize her determination. "Billy, you can't. I mean . . . I can't. She's my *sister*. And anyway, what about your work? Your work is here. In L.A. you'd have nothing. Here you've got everything."

"I wouldn't have you." Billy's big brown eyes were in soulful model. In his mind he could still see the moonlit vision. Taste it.

"Billy. It was a *mistake*. We shouldn't have . . . It was crazy. You know that."

"No, Jane. Don't say that. It wasn't that. I really like you. I mean I really do. You know that. It was so beautiful. So goddamn *beautiful* . . ." He hissed the words at her, as the ears round about strained to hear.

"It was mad, Billy." Jane was definite. "I like you. Of course I do. But don't make it too heavy. Please. Don't spoil it."

"I'm not fucking spoiling it. Christ, Jane, I love you!" His voice had crept louder, as the desperation began to seep into the words.

"Billy, Jane, are we all allowed to know what you're talking about? It looks so *interesting*. We all feel *quite* left out."

Jane felt the adrenaline rush as Julie lobbed the verbal grenade. "I was just telling Billy that I'd be leaving for L.A. pretty soon." She blurted it out. In situations like this, when she had to talk fast, it was best to stick close as possible to the truth.

"Oh dear, dear, how sad. Poor Billy will miss you dreadfully. Won't you, darling? We all will, but especially Billy. He does so like to have someone his own age to talk to. He finds it such a *strain* always being with the grown-ups."

"Being with *you*." Billy's eyes flashed down the table, as the lunch guests sat back to enjoy the drama that was erupting in their midst.

"Billy's from L.A.," Julie continued. "But then you must know that, Jane. I'm sure he's told you everything about himself. What I always say is that L.A.'s exactly like Granola—all nuts, flakes, and fruits. Come to think of it, Billy's a bit like Granola. Good roughage. Keeps me regular." She laughed wickedly.

Several people joined in. L.A. bashing was par for the course in the desert, where the money tended to be older by a year or two, the people older by a few more years than *that*, and where Industry wasn't just another word for the movie business.

"Good gracious, Julie. In that case Billy deserves a medal. It doesn't look as if *anything* could keep you regular." Jane struck back without thinking.

Julie eyed her coolly. "How very sweet of you to say so, darling. How kind. Tell me, darling, has Billy shown you his 'paintings' yet? One usually gets to see almost *everything* else Billy has to show before one gets a look at those. But you must persist. It's worth it. They're absolutely *hilarious*. Funnier than Whoopi Goldberg on a good day. No really, I promise. It's belly laughs. Take my advice. Go to the loo first."

The arrival of the main course confused the moment. It was a work of art, delicate strips of pink English lamb in a port wine sauce arranged like the petals of a flower around a central green mound of broccoli soufflé. The white burgundy had become, to Daniel Galvin's enormous satisfaction, an extraordinarily generous Lafite Rothschild '61. He was impressed; a first growth of that year traded at over four hundred bucks a bottle in New York.

Billy Bingham stood up—daggers in his eyes—threw his linen napkin onto the table, and walked directly from the room.

"Dear me. Have I said the wrong thing? The young are so sensitive, aren't they? Jane, do you think you'd better rush after him and say I'm sorry? We don't want tears or tantrums, do we, or I'll have to go and raid the toy cupboard to quiet things down."

Julie was purring like a Cheshire cat. Cream, milk, fish eyes, succulent mice—she looked like she'd had them all.

"Why are you so unhappy, Julie?" Jane's voice was quiet, direct, slap bang on target.

The table watched and waited as claret poured into crystal, Limoges china plates landed on sporting print placemats, and Malvern water gurgled into Irish Waterford tumblers.

The smile faded from Julie's face. The answer had asked the question. The cause had queried the result.

Betty Ford, sipping gloomily on a glass of Perrier, interjedcted. "Oh, really, I don't think Julie's *remotely* unhappy."

It was more than just routine politeness to a generous hostess under fire. In the desert Julie Bennett had a reputation for a fine, if marginally black, sense of humor. Anyway, desert ranks could naturally be expected to close against an outsider, especially one who looked as if she might well be an actress, or worse, a *young* actress. The movie crowd may have invented Palm Springs in the far-off days when Charlie Farrell had started the Racquet Club and everyone from Gable to the Lone Ranger (excluding Tonto, of course) had rushed lemminglike to the cancer zone, but things had changed. They were still welcome, but no longer on most-favored-citizen basis. What the desert wanted and got was sleek, gray-haired business people from the real California growth industries like building, aerospace, microchips, and "financial services." It was they who bought the Steve Chase–designed houses, cavorted in the seven thousand swimming pools, and did deals on the seventy-odd golf courses.

But Jane didn't see or hear the ranks closing. Neither did Julie. This was a private war, not remotely a part of the old Beverly Hills/Palm Springs tension.

Julie's eyes narrowed to pillbox slits and her mouth to a line drawn by the hardest pencil across her face. It was clear to everyone that she was about to become an act of God, a tempest, a tornado, a flash flood. If she had been happy before Jane had spoken, she was not happy now.

But not for the first time or the last, the amateur weather forecasters were wrong. Julie's storm didn't break. Instead it disappeared inside her, to be compressed down to its fundamentals and stored as the raw energy that fueled her—the high-octane liquid of hatred. Julie was back. She had held on to herself. Her cards were still secret.

She stared dreamily down the long table. It was one of her better al fresco lunches. The six ceiling fans of the bougainvillaea-bedecked, Mexican-tiled terrace cooled the midday heat, while hanging baskets of impatiens lurked in the shade and pots of blood-red geraniums and birds of paradise bloomed in the direct, vertical sunlight. As a back-drop the mountain, always different, constantly the same, reached for the sky across the rippling waters of the black-tiled pool.

She beamed around at her guests, and her suddenly cheerful eyes came to rest on Jane. "Darling, when you get to L.A.," she said with the innocence of an asp, "you must look up my good friend Lucy Masterson. I just know she'd only be too happy to fix you up with a job. She's one of the very best photographers in town, and I know she'd just *love* you to model for her. You're so pretty. Isn't she, everyone? Lucy will just love you to *death*."

Nobody could quite understand why her voice went so very shrill on the last word of all.

PART THREE

THE
MELROSE
WALK

"West Hollywood's full of young people," said Lauren pertly
as she lowered the dripping asparagus tip into her mouth.
  "Good gracious, is it?" said Betty, rapping her blood-
red talons on the polished Honduran mahogany.
  "Thank God they never come to Beverly Hills."

Julie Bennett, *The Melrose Walk*

ELEVEN

JANE NEEDN'T HAVE WORRIED ABOUT RECOGNIZING Lucy Masterson. Big, blond, brassy, and beautiful, a larger-than-life figure buzzing with energy and infectious jollity, she rushed up like a desert dawn, spraying rays of good-humored light all over the anxious travelers who milled about the arrival gate at LAX.

"Ohmigod! Ohmigod! It's not true! Julie Bennett promised me an angel and she *delivered*. Gee, honey, you're so goddamn pretty it *hurts*. Do you hear? I'm in *pain!*"

Jane laughed to cover her embarrassment, but it was a great beginning. She liked people who thought she was beautiful, although she'd have preferred it if half the airport hadn't been in on the compliment.

Lucy grabbed at the Vuitton carryall and spirited Jane toward the baggage carousels, words bubbling from her as she wafted Jane along.

"How do you know Julie Bennett? She just said you were a good friend. Well, let me tell you something, she's a good friend of mine. *Now*. To be brutally frank I'd only ever met her a few times before she telephoned me the other day about you. Said you would photograph like a dream. And was she *right*! The Nikon's goin' to have an orgasm the moment I take off the lens cap an' let it see you, babe."

Again Jane laughed at the zaniness of the compliment, but already her mind was at work—as far as thought was possible in the presence of someone like Lucy. The conversation with Julie was still fresh in her mind. She could see her sister now, cat in hand, sugar and spice dripping from her tongue.

"Darling, you know I mentioned the other day about my friend in L.A., Lucy Masterson. If you're really set on going there and getting a job, she'd be the very best person to oversee your Hollywood launch. She's a really close friend of mine, a brilliant photographer, and she knows that hellhole like the back of her hand. She'd fill you in on all the angles, find you somewhere to stay, and get your started in the business. The first thing you need in seedy city is some really good snaps. What do you think?"

"Great," Jane had said, surprised. And she still felt great. But the "close friend" bit was clearly a bending of the truth. What else was?

LAX rushed by like Disneyland from the monorail, neurotic noisy, the whiff of panic just below the surface as the inhabitants of earthquake land scurried back to their wrecked marriages, their meaty mortgages, and their sex wet dreams.

In the canary-yellow Baja Bug with its mountainous rubber wheels, Jane tried to stem the flow of Lucy's rapid-fire chat. "It's really kind of you to help out like this. Do you think you can do something with me? I don't know a catwalk from a boardwalk." Actually Jane was hardly sure what either was.

Lucy didn't allow the murderous San Diego Freeway to stand in the way of a little flesh pressing. She lunged out and grabbed Jane's bare thigh where it thrust out from the very short, plain, white cotton dress and turned away from the traffic to face her.

"You listen to me, Jane Cummin. You may be the best-lookin' chick I ever *seen,* and, baby, you better believe I seen some in twenty-three years takin' photographs."

Jane laughed, but a discordant note rang in her mind. She was Jane *Cummin,* now. That had been another of Julie's ideas. She had been quite definite about it.

"Believe it or not, darling, Hollywood doesn't like nepotism. Contrary to popular opinion, in tinsel town the son-in-law does *not* also rise. The funny thing is they all like to believe that what they do is based on something called 'talent,' and that they are all 'artists.' Extraordinary idea, isn't it? Of course *we* know that all those 'artists' can't tell Chopin from a chainsaw, and that the only reason that the cigar-chomping incompetents went into the Industry in the first place was to get their filthy fingers on some chicks who were so desperate to make it they would cheerfully ignore hairlessness, hernias, and halitosis. Still, the charade must go on. So I think you really ought to change your surname. For your own good. They won't want anyone thinking that they hired you because of me. Another advantage is that you get the satisfaction of knowing that when you *do* make it—and I promise you will—you'll have done it all yourself."

It had seemed like a good idea, and she had agreed instantly. She had a fresh future in the brave new world. The mystery girl from nowhere was about to corner the market in the fame and fortune that was the lifeblood of celluloid city. So now she had a new name—culled from the pages of *Architectural Digest,* where the various houses of her attractive superrich new namesake were on semipermanent display. And she had a new secret—one that she was determined to keep from everybody until the day of her arrival on the pinnacle of success, when her arms would be wrapped around Johnny, when she would be insulted by Joan and mocked by Dave, and when Robin Leach's camp camera would be stuffed as far as it would go into the creamy heart of her famous life-style.

Lucy flicked on KROQ and they listened to the Talking Heads while they drove, the sun roaring into the convertible Volkswagen and lighting them up like actresses center stage. On every side, the freeway veterans zoomed in for a closer look—truck drivers, Ferrari Arabs, Mazda manqués, Mercedes mercenaries. They were two blondes high on life, and God knows what else, riding the freeway in a yellow Bug, powerful ikons indeed in the southern-California dream.

The wind plucked at them and Lucy roared above it. "Hey, I'm glad I picked you up personally. Let's go get some lunch. I could use a drink or two. We'll celebrate you gettin' into town. You heard of the Hard Rock Café? We could go there."

"I know the one in London. They have queues outside even when it's snowing."

"Yeah, Peter Morton started it there. Then when they were coming over here he and his partner fell out, so they carved up America along the middle and Peter got the West and his partner got the East. It's a great place, fantastic ribs, and I like music while I eat."

They parked the Bug in the Beverly Center and swept past the line of kids outside the Hard Rock. At the reception desk Lucy waved the platinum-colored plastic, modeled on the American Express card, that Peter Morton distributed to the haute café-society movers and shakers.

"That card lets you jump the queue?" Jane wasn't used to that sort of thing. In England queues were sacred. You queued even when you didn't need to queue and to queue-jump was a crime so heinous as to rank with insulting the royal family, kicking a Corgi, or striking up a conversation that wasn't about the weather with a stranger on a train.

"Sure does, honey. Straight through, any time of day or night. Wouldn't be able to use the place without it."

"But don't the other people object?"

"Why should they? They just go out and work a bit harder and plan to have one of their own someday. This is L.A., sweetheart. Nobody *belongs* here. They all come here because they *want* to be here, and they know the rules. When you make it you get perks—why the hell else would anybody bother?"

Jane tried to take it in. It was like a caste system, but with free mobility between the classes. In England there would have been mutiny among the waiting customers, because however hard they worked they could never have made it to the plastic-card-equivalent stage. That was the basis of class envy, and was also why the "haves" conspicuously avoided parading their "have" status in front of the "have-nots." She could see that she had a lot to learn about America.

The Hard Rock was overwhelming, with its sixties-going-on-late-fifties, all-American-dinette-style of decoration, college banners merging happily with rock 'n' roll memorabilia, checkered tablecloths, almost pretty waitresses in tight nurse-like uniforms, at once strict yet reassuring, and the whole seasoned with the endless sauce of not-quite-too-loud rock music.

Lucy sat down heavily at the banquette on the raised dais and took the menu from the perky waitress. "Christ," she said irreverently, "you chicks make me think of hospitals. Don't know whether to ask for ribs or a high colonic. Better settle for a couple of bloody marys. That should be suitably surgical."

The framed telegram on the wall was a groveling apology from John Lennon to some Liverpudlian middleman of long ago for some unidentified peccadillo. Next to it, shielded in plastic, was a pair of beaten-up black velvet slippers, the heels worn away, a once-proud leopard emblem now decidedly moth-eaten. The plaque announced that "Sir" Bob Geldof had worn them every day on a tour of famine-torn Ethiopia.

Lucy eyed them suspiciously. "I hope that plastic case is airtight."

Jane looked around her. There were lots of kids, wearing just about everything. A female punk-rock group at a table near the back were decked out in plastic miniskirts, peace signs, and black plastic raincoats. Sitting beside Jane and Lucy was a bevy of *Less than Zero* kids, all in stone-washed 501s, Wayfarers, white shirts, string ties, and expensive soft leather jackets—the modified John Belushi look that said they were fueled on coke rocks or crack, or just a little Ecstasy. Peter Morton himself was catching a quick burger with what looked like a business associate, hot from the tennis court and still in Coldwater Canyon, standard-issue Fred Perry. There were Beverly Hillbillies—the older girls, blond and beautiful, silk I. Magnin shirts with shoulder pads, and waisted Yves St. Laurent blazers over the eternal razor-creased Levi's and Maud Frizon slip-ons; there were Ralph Lauren pseudo-preppies; medallion men, mostly record-business types on the lookout for passing jail-bait trade; the odd Cerruti suitor and Armani man; and a gaggle of Industry teenage daughters, with beehive hair, pinked-out lips, Muzak minds, mostly in unreconstructed sixties gear, short "sack" dresses that might even have Biba, Bazaar, Topgear, or Countdown labels if Dad was really riding high.

One thing was certain. Everybody had tried. Everyone was saying something. And nobody seemed to care or even to notice that it had all been said before.

Lucy grabbed at the drink. "Gotta have some mary in my blood-stream," she muttered as she drank deep. "Here's to you, sweetheart. Welcome to my town."

The eyes came in now, over the rim of the glass. Hungry, unavoidable, passionately interested. "Now, Jane Cummin, what are we goin' to do with you?" She made Jane sound like some exotic present, enormously expensive, and extremely beautiful, but with no immediately apparent use. "Well, first you gotta have somewhere to stay, and that's easy because I got a spare room that's real neat, an' it's empty and so it's yours. It's just off Melrose, next to my studio."

Jane tried to protest, but she was only going through the motions. Lucy Masterson looked like a lot of fun. Loneliness would *not* be a problem.

"I'll take you back there after lunch, and you can check it out, but it's great, and it's free—with my love." Lucy made a sort of sweeping motion with her right hand as if she were distributing largess in some Renaissance costume drama.

"That sounds just great. You are kind. Really, I . . ." Americans believed in instant friendship, but this was ridiculous, but wonderfully ridiculous. Already the desert seemed light-years away.

"An' tonight we'll hit the 'after hours' scene. You like to dance?"

"You mean, nightclubs?"

"Almost. But these aren't really like clubs. They're illegal places, unlicensed, and the cops are always trying to close them down, 'cept that the cops can't find them because they happen all over, at different places each week. It's where the kids go, and all the fun is. The traditional places—like Tramp and Helena's—are horseshit, you know, full of middle-aged trendies with nose problems from too much pharmaceutical. Christ, if you want to pee in places like those you have to do it in the sink—the toilets are permanently occupied by the coke-heads."

"Sounds like fun."

"An' we'll take Jishy along. He's my assistant. He knows the scene. An' he's gay, so he won't grope you, honey—but he dances up a storm."

So they ate ribs, listened to Sergeant Pepper, put away a bottle of Valpolicella Bolla and watched the kids hang out.

Over the coffee, Jane popped the question that had been on her mind. "Lucy, this is all just great. But what on earth am I going to *do*? I mean, I've got to earn some money. I'm just about broke."

The lights danced in Lucy Masterson's eyes as she answered. "My God, didn't I tell you? Honey, you're goin' to be a model. The best model in town. The best model in the whole wide world. Sweetheart, you heard of *Anything* magazine?"

EVAN KOESTLER WAS SMALL BUT PERFECTLY FORMED. He knew that because he was feeling his perfect proportions beneath the bubbles in the tub at the Bel-Air Hotel. Sixty years was old for a born-and-raised New Yorker, but Evan had never followed the East Coast fashion of bodily neglect. In fact, Evan Koestler had never followed fashion at all. Instead he had made his fortune by inventing it.

Up and down the small hard body his manicured fingers roamed, over the flat little stomach, the tight little ass, the powerful little legs—saved from scrawniness by a careful attention to diet and the daily workout on the stationary bicycle in the bedroom of the Fifth Avenue triplex apartment. His body was something of which he was certainly not ashamed if not exactly proud.

The telephone by the side of the bath was a nice touch and typically L.A., where you needed the telephone to prove to yourself that the outside world still existed, and more important, that it still *wanted* you. But to get the ego message of the incomings you had to put out with the outgoings. Evan reached for the phone and punched the numbers with his neat little fingers. He held the telephone in his left hand. With his right, he stroked absentmindedly at his dick.

Seven o'clock. So 10 P.M. in New York. He hadn't thought twice about calling his secretary at home. She was used to that. "Lisa? Evan. Yup. Did the Texas asshole close on the Titian?"

A pause. Then a mini-explosion. "He doesn't know what 'provenance' is. Didn't he see the letter from the wop professor from Florence? And the limey from the National Gallery? Christ. Doesn't he realize that our boy is *history,* boxed, dead, not quick? Yeah, yeah. No, smooth him over. Keep him on ice till I get back. Yeah, let him have it in the Pierre for as long as he likes, the asshole. Just make sure the insurance boys know when he farts. Okay? You did the Dun and Bradstreet on his company, and the Moody's and the bank inquiries through Morgan's? Good. Yeah. Those oily boys are hurting for sure right now. Can't give away real estate in Houston. Okay, sweetheart. Anything else? Yeah, L.A.'s fine. You know the crap. Sun shines, etcetera. Thought I'd go slumming tonight. Couple of off-the-wall galleries. Never know what you might find among the junk, and it keeps me young. Okay, sweetheart. Back on Thursdsay. Keep on top of it. Right."

Evan Koestler reached for the dark Johnnie Walker Black and club soda. No ice. He had learned that perversion from the Sotheby's and Christie's boys during dank, dark weekends in Wiltshire. He never really liked the taste, but he felt it was good for him. Purged the soul, and it was certainly not as fattening as the negronis that he so much preferred.

He sighed in contentment. Through the open door of the marble bathroom he could just about see the edge of the Picasso he had just sold. It had been an incredible deal. The hotshot producer had sat on the edge of the sofa, panting to be persuaded to buy, as Evan had pitched him the indifferent painting. Funny how they didn't recognize trash in this town; after all, they more or less had the copyright on the stuff. But no, they were the biggest suckers of all. And boy did they love a *story*! So did every loser in the art world for that matter. They needed a story to make the paint come alive, a story that would make their own particular picture brilliantly individual, a story that would be told and retold until their long-suffering friends cried for mercy.

The introduction had come right from the top, as it nearly always did with Evan. The megamoney wasn't in the film industry in this town. That was where the egos, the heartache, the glory, and the sexual power lived. But people like Edward William Carter rose effortlessly above all that. He had started the County Museum of Art with a donation of two hundred million. Spielberg and Lucas hardly had a net worth of that, and compared to *them*, the rest of the Industry crowd were financial minnows. So when Carter had sent along the producer-of-the-moment to buy some instant status from Evan Koestler, the deal had been as good as done before the fat philistine had walked into the room.

"Now, I don't have to tell you anything about cubism, I can see that. I sense you're a man who knows his art, and also knows what he likes."

Every man believes he knows what he likes. Few do.

"But what you may not know about this marvelous, enormously important painting is what Paloma told me about it."

Wide-eyed, the producer had swallowed it all: the lunch at Mortimer's with the Erteguns and Brooke Astor, Paloma Picasso's anecdote about the painting that dear old Evan had persuaded her to sell. That far-off day beneath the Provençal sun, bouncing on Daddy's knee. "Of all your cubist work, Daddy, which is your favorite?"

"And do you know . . . can you believe . . . well, that's your painting, Mr. Estevito." The producer had nearly had an orgasm trying to write the check. "No, dear no, Mr. Estevito. All that can be done later. I'll send it around to you tomorrow. No problem. It's marvelous to know that it has found a home where it will be appreciated as much as the artist appreciated it. I'll tell Paloma next week. She'll be as relieved as I am."

Evan laughed out loud. Was it a con? Not really. The painting was genuine. It had come from Paloma's private collection. He had teased it out of her at Mortimer's. But the truth of course was that she had sold it because it was run-of-the-mill, no better, no worse than scores of others. The "story" had made all the difference. The producer would never retrieve his four hundred thousand when he tried to push the painting through the auction rooms the moment his film career went cold, and his wife left him, and his mistress decided she could do without his dandruff, his fallen arches, and his cocaine habit. Did all that make Evan a thief? No. It was a case of caveat emptor. Besides, Mr. Estevito would have years and years of pleasure from the painting, or rather the story about the painting, and if he was sufficiently good at storytelling he might be able to move it on himself at an even fancier price.

So Evan felt good and, even more important, he felt richer. It was beautiful to be at the top. Few people were: the president. Spielberg. Volcker. Johnny. Baryshnikov. Donahue. But everyone else was little more than a first among equals—Michener looking over his shoulder at Clavell, Streisand at Madonna, Rather at Brokaw. But Evan Koestler, in the incestuous world of fine art, was out there on his own. He was an opinion maker, a guru, whose magic eye could not only see talent when it existed, but divine its presence even before it existed. Evan Koestler could make people and he could break people and he gained an almost orgasmic pleasure from doing both.

Reluctantly he abandoned the delicious contemplation. He heaved himself out of the bath and admired his trim frame in the mirror. Weekends in the Palm Beach, South Ocean Boulevard Mizner a door or two away from the Trumps and the Whitmores took care of the even suntan that the Californians were congenitally drawn to. He had beautifully manicured feet, a clipped gray mustache, a full head of rich gray hair, so reassuring, so safe. Yes, all things considered he looked pretty good. But it was time to get going, to see what fruits the L.A. evening could provide. Would he get lucky? Would the right little boy come along?

It was a myth that in the art world they understood about such things. The world of beauty was a cruel world, and anything and everything would be used against Evan in the ugly scramble up the ladder to the place in the sun. So he had learned to curb the impulses that steamed within him. In New York he was a walker—Nan, Brooke, Pat, and even, on one hallowed and auspicious occasion, Nancy herself, and he had a reputation to protect as a "safe" man, endlessly charming, unfailingly urbane, the life and soul of the party. But the yearnings did not go away, and somehow in L.A., boystown of America, they bubbled nearer to the surface. Like tonight. He would have dinner with a the group of sexually indeterminate at Spago, followed by a free-for-all opening at the trendy Affront Gallery on Melrose, and then . . . and then . . . the Los Angeles night, infinitely unpredictable, nerve-rackingly uncertain, hopelessly alluring.

The telephone cut into his reverie and Evan hurried to the drawing room to answer it, grabbing at the hotel's white terrycloth dressing gown and the large bottle of Calvin Klein Obsession eau de toilette as he did so. "Oh, yeah. Tell him to wait. I'll be down in about half an hour."

He slammed down the receiver and walked over to the closet. New York was so easy. The Saville Row tailored suits from Huntsman or Anderson and Sheppard were right for any potential occasion. But L.A.'s P.R. held that it was mellow, laid back, casually relaxed. Bullshit, but it was wise to humor them. So he chose navy slacks, matching polo, and a rustbrown tweed hacking jacket, pinched in just a little at the waist. The outfit was just racy enough for the racy things that he half hoped, half feared, might happen to him on a play-it-by-ear Hollywood night such as this.

In Bungalow 3 at the Chateau Marmont, the room where Belushi got his, Billy Bingham was coexisting with the MTV. You didn't really watch the music program, rather it sort of watched you, and you sat there in a state of suspended animation that was neither pleasant nor unpleasant, but was more like some Oriental religion's goal of nonbeing, a kind of disembodied state of unreality where nothing much happened but where time passed. Occasionally there was the sensation of *listening* to it, when some particularly insistent song tweaked at the neurons, but mostly it was a question of simple endurance. Billy recognized that with the MTV life was happening to him, rather than he happening to life, but somehow in L.A., in the Chateau, a few feet from the Strip, there was absolutely nothing wrong with that.

The Zenith Chromocolor II had been around a bit, and possibly had tales to tell. Had it survived the redecoration that had followed the tragic night in March 1982 when the ex-groupie drug dealer Cathy Smith had "wired" Belushi for the last time? Billy shuddered at the morbid thought. He hadn't asked for this particular cottage on purpose. Just for somewhere near the pool and a place to park his car. Bungalow 3 with its steep steps to the pool area and private garage had fitted the bill, and the $250 hadn't been an issue. Already whatever redecoration had been done had melted into the indefinable uniqueness of the Chateau's ambience—nineteenth-century Transylvania merging with fifties motel style haute tack. There was dung-colored stucco, candlewick bedspreads, and safes that looked like they might be needed, and throughout it all wafted the mystery of Hollywood myth. Garbo, Harlow, and Flynn had all cavorted here in the hotel where the talented stayed before they were discovered, and after they had failed.

Why the Chateau? The gold American Express card that Julie allowed him, and that existed mainly for the ease with which it could be canceled, had permitted him the choice of any hotel in L.A. for his evening's stay. When he was with her they stayed at the Bel-Air, among the old money and the classy people, safe beyond the little bridge, in privacy among the swans. The Bel-Air was the aristocrat of L.A. hotels and suitably distant from the perils and delights of the wild and woolly city. Or he could have gone for the pink lushness of the Beverly Hills Hotel. It was more nouveau, naughtier, but still right up there in the top three despite the ongoing irritation of its seemingly permanent facelift, and its recent tendency to change hands. The other option had been the Beverly Wilshire—hard by Rodeo and its credit-card-melting shops, but a little impersonal now, a little too businesslike. Which left the Chateau. Proud and old, with no restaurant and no bar, but with Hollywood "history" on its side. Billy could ignore the nasties he sometimes found in the pool, or the noises that the plumbing made, or the things, and the people, that went bump in the night. After all, in the Chateau, he might want to do a little bumping of his own.

But more important than the question, Why the Chateau? was the question, Why L.A. at all? There were two sorts of answers to *that* question, the surface ones, and the real ones. For instance, it was great to be free of Julie—of her clamorous, voracious, all-enveloping presence. And an artist couldn't live forever tucked away out of sight and out of mind. Sooner or later it was necessary to get out into the marketplace and try to persuade the world that what you did mattered. Those were two of the reasons that when Julie had been invited to an after-dinner show at the Affront Gallery on Melrose and shown no inclination to accept, he had decided to go in her place. But the real reason he was there, alone in L.A. watching smooth Dweezil Zappa on MTV and waiting for ten o'clock, was not called art, or ambition or even escape. It was called Jane.

God, how much he wanted to see her again. The hours apart already seemed like weeks of harrowing despair. He needed to see the face, to feel the body, to smell the smell of her and cool the fires of his longing by holding her in his arms once again, as he had held her in the foothills of the mountains as the orange sun had died and black night had swallowed them up.

Whitney Houston was whispering her creamy nothings at him, brown, sugary sweetness from the Marmont box. Already the Myers rum, warm in his stomach, was changing his schemes. He had planned to see her tomorrow, and to endure tonight without her. But now he wasn't so sure.

His hand reached for the phone. The number was in his head.

It was an answering machine. "This is Lucy Masterson. Boy, am I *not here* at the moment. Leave your message and all that jazz but if you *really* want to find me, good luck! I'm gone dancin'. Try the Pink, or the Crack, or the ones that are newer than that. If you can find them. Biyeeeee!"

Billy slammed down the phone. His life would have to wait for a few more hours.

JOSHUA SHEAHAN FANNED OUT THE FIVE INVITATIONS AS IF they were playing cards, which, in a way, they were: invitations to "after-hours" play. Like a magician about to perform a trick he shuffled them, giving chance a chance to lift the responsibility from him. He was the master of ceremonies tonight. The success or failure of the evening might rest with him. It could well depend on the order of events, the clubs visited in prime time, when booze and drugs were still working for you rather than against you, and before the spiders of the late, late night and early morning started marching spikily over your spines, killing the pleasure and ushering in the pain.

The Crack. Photograph. Delilah. Speedy Gonzales. The Pink. At which one would fun become something else?

The cards themselves only hinted at what they represented. A geometric design. A casually drawn girl. A scratchy map. Nothing much really, but to the cognoscenti they conjured up the camaraderie of the insiders, who alone knew the site of each movable feast of experience. These illegal clubs were never still; their illicit bars, their mobile sound systems, their warehouse venues never more than a week away from the hovering presence of the vice squad. That was part of the thrill, of course—the sense of persecution, of impending disaster, of unity in the face of a common enemy. There would be no "door policy" at any of these places—the dreadful New York attempt to manufacture a spurious exclusivity by giving to goons the right to decide who was and who was not allowed in to dance to the music. In L.A. they had no need of such things. If you were there at all you were all right. You went out with the "in" crowd, because you had learned the secret of the constantly changing address—a secret that was not easy to learn.

The chemistry was in the total mix. The group who had been there last week might come again. Certainly the D.J.s were vital, their track record laid down in after-hours folklore, the time-honored veterans of the now dead clubs of yesteryear —Plastic Passion, Station, The Bitter End, Dirt Box, Ariel, and Z. The bars and the light shows and the go-go dancers and the location would all have to be assessed in their contribution to the overall equation.

So Joshua Sheahan turned up the volume and let Trouble Funk into his wide-open mind as he pondered on his awesome responsibility. Lucy had, as always, left the details up to him. Tonight, with the English beauty in tow, and the lovelight in her eyes, she would want the very best.

* * *

POP! THE FLASH CUBE ON THE POLAROID DID ITS STUFF, AND Jane yelped in mock outrage. "Hey, watch it, Lucy, I think you caught my tit that time."

"You'd better *believe* it, beautiful girl."

Lucy ran her tongue over suddenly dry lips. Before her the vision squirmed and twisted as she tried to squeeze into the skin-tight black leather miniskirt. Jane, bare legged, her extraordinary ass jutting and thrusting as it sought to lose itself in the clinging strip of material, was getting all the juices flowing. Every now and again the black leather bomber jacket would twist off center and one or another of the ice cream cone tits and fantasy isle nipples would flash into view. Lucy had bided her time, and now she had the wonderful thing on celluloid.

"Here, let me see." Jane held out her hand for the film.

Lucy waved it once or twice in the air to speed the developing process and took a quick peep before passing it over. From her kneeling position on the floor she watched and waited. The reaction to this one was important.

"There. I told you. One monster breast. That one undoubtedly goes in the rubbish bin." She handed the picture back with a laugh.

"No way. That one's for the wall over my bed." On purpose Lucy didn't laugh when she said that. She looked straight at Jane. It was time to raise the stakes. She had been watching this girl for a couple of hours now and it wasn't just a question of liking what she saw.

"Oh, so you want my body, do you?" Jane giggled nervously and toyed with the zipper on the leather skirt.

"Well, I certainly want to photograph your body."

"What do you mean? With no clothes on?" She stopped struggling with the skirt and stood there watching Lucy. The base of the triangle of white pants peeped through the slit in the still undone leather apron. Above it there was a tiny line of soft blond hair, and a large, absolutely eye-capturing beauty spot. The line of her young breasts barely curved back into the outsize, unzipped Claude Montana jacket.

"Yes. For *Anything* mag. That's the deal, isn't it?"

"What is this *Anything* magazine? And no, it's not the deal. How could it be the deal? What's this all about, Lucy?"

Lucy stood up. She had expected some resistance. There was always resistance. Her girls thought they owed it to themselves not to cave in too precipitously. After all, there were parents back in Wisconsin, and promises in church, and all the baggage of traditional middle-American morality. Obviously, the same situation applied in England. There were two ways of doing this. Lucy could come straight to the point or lead in gently. She opted for the former. Walking quickly to the bookshelf, she pulled down a big leather-bound portfolio.

"Perhaps you'd better see some of the pix I take. Remember, the money's good. Real good. I'm talkin' thousands of dollars, Jane."

Jane took the book, her heart thumping now, suddenly aware of her seminudity. She zipped up her jacket but still felt exposed. She took a deep breath, and then another, and then another. "Oh dear," she said at last. "There's been a terrible mistake."

"What's with the 'mistake,' honey? Julie Bennett said you were real anxious to get into the photography business. I mean, real anxious."

"But my si—I mean, Julie—she didn't know that you took . . . I mean . . . these sorts of photographs."

"For sure she knew. She interviewed me a couple of times when she was researching a character for a book she was writing. One of the earlier ones."

"Oh, no, she can't have known. I mean, I would never have done photos even remotely like this . . . she must have got it wrong, not understood or forgotten, maybe. Maybe she got you confused with some other photographer who took things for *Vogue* and *Harper's* and magazines like that."

Lucy tried hard to make sense of it. She could remember the conversation with Julie clearly: "Lucy, you still turning out those shots for the porno mags? Well, have I got the model for you! Friend of mine from England, really wild, open for anything, and just dying to get to L.A. to experience it *all,* and do I mean *all.* She's a friend of a friend and wanted me to get her an introduction, and I thought of you. Can you look her over and do your best for her? I don't think you'd be sorry. In fact I can guarantee you wouldn't be. She's just made for you. Just the sort of girl who could do a bit part in one of my novels. In fact, after you've shown her around I must just pick her brains and use her for that. Anyway, see what you can do. Big favor. Thanks, Lucy. I owe you one. If you ever get out to the desert, look me up." Clearly games were being played.

Lucy cocked her head to one side. "How well do you know Julie Bennett?" She wanted it to be Jane who was lying. Perhaps it was a ploy to raise a price a bit, but Jane seemed honestly innocent.

Jane tensed. Careful. "Not very well at all, really. My family in England knew her a bit. And they gave me an introduction."

"Any reason for her to be jealous of you, or anything?"

Billy Bingham. The tortured eyes. The hot lips. The tight waist beneath her fingers.

"No, I don't think so." What on earth had Julie been up to? She wouldn't have anywhere to stay now. Tonight she could be on the street. No money. No friends. The fun scene had turned into a nightmare. She didn't flinch. Proud, defiant, the blood of Rumania in her veins, she stared straight at Lucy.

"Listen, Lucy. I'm not disgusted by these photographs. Actually I think they're rather beautiful—some of them. But they are not for me. Absolutely not. I don't know how you got the idea that I might be game for them. But I'm not, and that's the end of it. I suppose that means you want me out of here. Of course, I'll go." She paused. "Though it would be really great if you could let me stay tonight."

Lucy Masterson felt the big-band music strike up in her soul. The missing ingredient so far had now been plenteously provided. The girl who had everything that a woman could possibly wish for had yet another attribute. Balls. Wham, bam, and thank you ma'am. It had happened at last. Lucy Masterson had fallen in love.

TWELVE

"THIS INVITATION SAYS JULIE BENNETT AND GUEST. Presumably *you're* not Julie Bennett."

The receptionist/guardian of the door "list" at the Affront Gallery on Melrose was the unhappiest of people, plain as a pikestaff, middle aged, and living in L.A. The dreadful vibes of her appalling position as a perennial wallflower in lotusland had destroyed any good humor that she might have possessed, and so now she could only irritate folk like Billy Bingham from her punny pinnacle of temporary power.

"Julie Bennett's coming right along. She's losing the wheels." His weary, don't-give-me-too-much-hassle tone of voice combined nicely with the overt politeness of the lie.

The surrogate policewoman chose to ignore the fact that the gallery had valet parkers. After all, Julie Bennett was a "face," and there weren't too many of them on the guest list. This asshole could be her brother, her agent, even her husband. In this town people could surprise you. She waved him through.

Billy Bingham slid gloomily into the glass-and-chrome techno-trip gallery and tried to avoid looking at the stainless steel that was trying to be sculpture and the turgid, vomit-colored triptychs that were pretending desperately to be "art." He grabbed at a glass of passing champagne and winced as the waiter blew him a kiss and whispered, "Go for it, Bruce."

It was true. He'd gone as Bruce Springsteen to the Affront

Gallery opening. He hadn't done it consciously of course, but the deeply faded 501s with the worn-through knee, the brand new K-Swiss sneakers, and the simple white Jockey T-shirt over the brown, muscular body reeked of the ragged, sweaty earthiness of the singer. He knew he looked good, and he was there to do himself some good, but it was a drag that the hired help had insinuated that he was some cheap lookalike.

Evan Koestler saw Billy Bingham across the crowded room—saw the Sean Penn bad-boy pout, the latter-day Jimmy Dean rebellion, the brat-pack insolence, and the De Niro aloofness, and somehow he knew, even then, that good things, supremely good things, were going to happen. He saw too, the hard, smart torso, the proud chin, the lickable lips, and the waspish waist. He also saw the longing and the want, the desperation and the need for the things that he, Evan Koestler, could almost certainly provide, and the vision was more than enough to propel his little legs through the Red Sea of parting party people toward Billy.

As Evan Koestler knifed through the packed humanity toward his destination he couldn't help noticing it wasn't all flotsam and jetsam. He caught sight of Marcia Weisman, the legendary Beverly Hills collector; Rosamund Felsen, aristocratic Pasadena-born dealer-guru to the "new" L.A. artists; and a smattering of the older, established art crowd, like the indestructible biker/painter Billy Al Bengston, jovial abstractionist Richard Diebenkorn, and mustachioed Bob Graham, whose sculpted nude had graced the gate of the 1984 Olympic stadium.

But most of the people were art-scene groupies: a few nearly rich embryonic "collectors" who were on the verge of graduating from photography to the real thing; a bustle of party addicts who'd cheerfully attend the opening of an envelope; a clutch of sallowfaced art matrons with slack tits, useless degrees, and sandpaper minds; and of course the usual L.A. gaggle of sword-tongued gays, their Sports Connection bodies Bijaned and Fred Segaled and Maxfielded, their Dorothy Parker minds sharpened and ready for bloodshed. Evan winced at the whispered mutterings of awed recognition that surged around him as he fended off would-be friends and lovers, half-remembered acquaintances, the near celebrities and almost has-beens who were the eternal extras in the movie of his life.

Billy watched him come. He saw the cutting of the swathe through the ranks of what were clearly lesser men. He saw, too, the sparkling eyes of welcome, deep set in the expensive face, the amused contortions of the mouth around the well-kept teeth—and he both loved and loathed what he saw. Because although Evan Koestler liked to think he lived in the closet, the Billy Binghams of this world knew his secret.

Evan's assault was full frontal. "Hello," he said, as he put out his hand. "Evan Koestler. What do you think of the art?"

Billy blinked. *The* Evan Koestler. The *gallery* Koestler? He looked the dapper figure up and down, as his pulse quickened. It looked more than possible. "What art?" he said.

Evan laughed, too loud, and his hands darted to Billy's naked forearm. "You're right. It stinks. How clever of you to know. Are you in the business?"

Monosyllables at first. "Yes." And then. "I'm an artist. . . . No, the desert. . . . I live with Julie Bennett. . . . Yes, she sure does write books. . . . Oh, only a few months."

Then Evan had his turn, and things loosened up a bit as the California champagne formed an alliance in Billy's mind with the earlier MTV/Marmont Cuba libres.

"I love America, but I have vowed never to drink its wines." How very sophisticated, urbane, *expensive*. "You may have heard of my little galleries in New York and here in L.A." How understated, modest, *exciting*.

And then the magical, other-worldly, "I'd very much like to see your work. I have a funny feeling in my gut that it's going to be well worth seeing."

Some more champagne. Another scotch and soda. Do you have Bell's? If not, Teacher's will be fine. No ice. Yes, that's right, I said no ice.

"Do you know the little prick who runs this place? Inherited his money. Milk cartons, I think. Got all the taste of a lottery winner from an Alaskan oil rig. Come on, I'll introduce you to him. Give you a good laugh."

Billy accepted the invitation to join the conspiracy, dazed, flattered against his will by the "us" against "them."

Through it all the bottom line kept repeating itself. Evan Koestler wanted to see his work.

"By the way, I don't know your name."

"Billy Bingham."

"Billy Bingham. Billy Bingham. Well, I would hope the art world is going to hear a great deal more of that name." He smiled easily, his hand at Billy's elbow as he propelled him through the impressed crowd toward their host.

"Willie, I'd like you to meet Billy Bingham. He's a painter. Lives out in the desert. Staying at Julie Bennett's house. I have one of my funny feelings about him. Last time I had it was with Jackson Pollock. What do you say to that?"

Willie Garrigues only wanted to say what Evan Koestler wanted to hear. He peered at Billy carefully. He didn't know postmodernism from monkeyshit but he could recognize a nice piece of trade when he saw it.

"Hi, Billy boy. Love to see your work sometime. Make a date with my girl. I mean it. No bullshit."

"First refusal's mine." Evan Koestler's voice was quite sharp. The point of this conversation was to show the moody boy-god that Koestler could use Garrigues like a piece of Kleenex. *Not* to have him making moves on the merchandise.

"Of course, Evan. Of course. Didn't mean to step out of line." He licked nervous lips and his eyes darted around the room. "What do you think of the work?"

Evan laughed nastily, and his playful eyes made contact with Billy's. "He's not going to make it, is he, Willie?"

Willie's heart fell as he thought of the good money he had just lost on his artist.

The boy was already steaming around Venice in a matte-black Laredo, running up bills at the West Beach Café and 72 Market Street. Now he was over against the wall in head-to-toe Parachute supremely oblivious to the fact that artistically he was no longer alive.

"You don't like the work, Evan? Too direct? Too brash? He's a young boy, Evan. Plenty of time to mature."

Evan laughed again. "No, Willie my dear. I wasn't expressing an *opinion*. I was stating a *fact*." He smiled to himself, and for Billy. The message was not subtle. In the art world most people made subjective judgments; one could take them or leave them. But Evan's judgments were self-fulfilling prophesies. In his column in the *New York Times* his "likes" became the likes of others, while his dislikes were the kiss of death. The functions of a dealer and a critic had never been combined before. But Evan Koestler was above "conflict of interest" carping. He *was* the New York art market, as J. P. Morgan had once been Wall Street. And there was nothing that anyone could do about it.

"I'm very disappointed that you think that, Evan."

Was that a tear in the Garrigues's eye? A fortune in milk cartons could take Willie only so far. It *mattered* how his gallery did. If he went down the tubes so would the Richard Neutra contemporary at the top of Laurel Canyon, the Ferrari Testarossa, the house in Marrakech, and the poolside pretty boys with the AIDS-free, herpes-clean medical certificates.

Evan Koestler waved a forgiving arm. "Don't worry, my dear. We all make mistakes. I made one once." His sunburned brow puckered in concentration as he sought an example of the rare phenomenon. "Ah, yes, that was it. Let Lichtenstein go to the Pace in the late sixties. Mind you, with the benefit of hindsight one could argue that he was over the top."

The boy who pirouetted up to the group was Cyndi Lauper cute—pixie pretty and long on "personality." "Willie. When this thing wraps do you want to come dancing with us? We're all going to try to find the Crack." He giggled encouragingly at the double entendre.

Willie looked uncertain.

Evan prepared to spirit Billy away from the planned communal activities. Billy, however, was not to be spirited. "Did you say the Crack?"

"That's right."

"I'd really like to come with you."

"Great. Fantastic. Who are your friends, Willie? Aren't you going to introduce me?"

"What's the Crack? Some nightclub?" Evan asked his question quickly. He had turned toward the group again. He wasn't going to lose this one. If it took a nightclub, then so be it. "Have any of you been to Helena's . . . ?" he tried hopefully. Helena Kallianiotes, raven-haired tango-queen proprietress of rich Hollywood's trendiest private club, could be relied upon for the warmth of her greeting. More still for the likely faces at neighboring tables—Jack 'n' Anjelica, bratpacker guru Harry Dean Stanton, and a snarl of his acolytes, Mickey, Emilio, and Rob escorting a pout of their dates— Ally, Demi, and Melanie.

Cyndi Lauper didn't want to have *that* sort of fun at all. "Oh *no*! No way. Not all those *movie* people. That was *last* year."

"Well, I've never heard of this place . . . the Crack." Evan didn't like to be talked down to. He was on the verge of irritation.

"But that's the whole *point*. Nobody's heard of it, because it only exists for a night, and it's hardly ever in the same place twice. It drives the glossy magazines crazy 'cause they can never get a bead on what's goin' down. *Vanity Fair* sent Bret Easton Ellis and Judd Nelson on assignment to find the Mud Club, and it didn't exist at all. We just invented it to send them off on a wild-goose chase. *Details* and *Interview* didn't do much better."

"Well, I'm definitely going," said Billy Bingham definitely. "You know how to get there?"

"You'd better believe I know," said Cyndi Lauper.

"I'm game," agreed Evan gamely.

"Suits me," said Willie suitably.

Billy smiled. He had captured Evan Koestler, who could make his future come true. And he was on his way into the L.A. night to find Jane.

"HEY CATCH THE GO-GOS. PENIS PINK!" Lucy whooped with excitement as she grabbed Jane's arm.

On top of two outsize loudspeakers two boys whirled and twisted dervishlike to the sixties-vintage T Rex. They wore nothing at all except for skimpy G-strings full of the jiggling cargoes that were the only hard evidence they were boys.

Head to toe they glittered in lustrous Day-Glow pink body paint, and the strobe and black lights played over their writhing skin.

"Now I know what that English boy meant about the 'entertainment.'" Jane laughed back at her new friend, totally in love with L.A. It was their third stop in as many hours and the best yet. From the outside, the illegal clubs looked much the same. The difficult thing was to find them, and that was all part of the night games. The maps on the advertisement flyers were purposely vague. To get there you really had to want to *be* there, and the collective desire gave the places their indefinable atmosphere. At the door—guarded by a make-believe cop—badge, uniform, nightstick, big flashlight—the English guy with the lank hair had pushed out the words as if they were an incantation to ward off evil spirits. "Welcome. You realize that this is a private party, but we are pleased to accept your contribution of five dollars each as a donation toward the cost of the entertainment."

"Okay brand-new beautiful assistant," said Lucy, "let's dance. I'm your boss now. You can't refuse. You have to humor me if you care about climbing the corporate ladder."

Lucy—in midthigh denim miniskirt, long-sleeved, knuckle-length faded-out Georges Marciano denim jacket, strapless gold lurex blouse, gold braid draped from coat and skirt, hair zapped back with gel in a Tony Curtis duck's ass—laughed her challenge at Jane. Big and butch, she shone out like fireworks, hand on belted hip, toe tapping to the Tyrannosaurus, a bright beacon of sexual come-on on the edge of the jumping crowd.

Jane, her smile wide-open, took the gauntlet. She was letting go, and it felt like heaven. It had all turned out fine. One moment she was nearly a bag lady on the streets of sin city; in the next, she was assistant to the assistant at Lucy Masterson Photography, Inc. America was like a roller coaster. England, preciously predictable, monotonously motionless, was another planet. If Lucy had been disappointed when she had refused to show everything for *Anything* magazine, she had a funny way of showing it. Now Jane had a new friend and a new job, an amazing, strange job in what was already to her the most curious town on earth.

"First time I've danced with a girl since dancing classes at school."

"Honey, you've been wastin' your life."

They laughed, delighting in their night anarchy, as the downtown warehouse throbbed to the rough, raucous music that tumbled out of the huge, antiquated speakers.

Lucy took Jane's hand and led her toward the roaring dance floor. Knotted around her long, proud neck, Jane wore a leather handkerchief sporting the badges of the wild night bands—Flesh for Lulu, Gene Loves Jezebel, Fine Young Cannibals, Pet Shop Boys. The neat geometry of the jet-black Vidal Sassoon wig perfectly complemented the heavy leather, modified-Twisted-Sister outfit. She was gloriously, deliriously unrecognizable from the simple, straightforward beauty of the morning at LAX, and Lucy's hormones surged as she eyeballed her Cinderella.

Across the cavernous room with its cathedral wood-beamed ceilings, its big, industrial-size windows, and its hard cement floor already awash with spilled beer and abandoned cigarettes, Evan Koestler was having a nervously good time.

"Well, well, well, it's certainly all happening here, isn't it?" He turned to look at Billy, but Billy wasn't listening. Instead he was scanning the tight-packed mobile human sea: two thousand leaping, rearing teenagers—paisley parrots, psychedelic sirens, pseudopreppies, modern "mods," leather ladies, and motorcycle maniacs.

"Do you know any of these people?" Evan tried again. He wasn't used to being ignored; part of him liked it, part of him didn't. Who was he, this beautiful, sulky, complicated boy with the body of Mercury and the depth of the ocean floor? But as the delicious thrill of excitement ran through little Evan and his eyes devoured his prey, it collided with another emotion. Jealousy. Billy was clearly looking for someone in the crowd. And an ego the size of his had problems adjusting to the idea that there might have been life for Billy before Evan.

"What did you say, Evan? Sorry, I was looking for someone." Billy half turned toward him. Preoccupied, the anxiety penciled in around his mouth, his eyes still scanned the crowd.

"Not important. Not important." Evan waved his hand to emphasize his words. But he had wanted to ask "who?" He peered uncomfortably around the room. Without Billy it would be a hellhole. He didn't like nightclubs, but at one time or another he'd suffered most of the ones in New York, from the overdesigned Palladium with its *Vogue* artists, to the laid-back night chat of Nell's, the smart-assed artiness of Area and the backlash classiness of the Surf Club. He rather liked their door policy. There was a gauntlet to be run at the entrance, as supercool legislators of trend-chic decided on a whim who would be allowed through the gates of the temporary paradise, and who condemned to the cold, damp pavements to lick the wounds of their rejection. On the few occasions *he* ventured out, however, it was always on most-favored-guest basis. He would sweep past the sidewalk losers, through the groveling welcome, on a surging sea of superiority as he headed toward the inner sanctum that most of the clubs set aside for those celebrities who communed most closely with God. Here, in contrast, everyone was welcome, if you knew where the party was. Did that mean New York was more elitist than L.A. or just less subtle? Whatever. How did he score this boy?

It would be a help if he could get to *communicate*. "Billy, you're the artist. What's the verdict on the decoration here?" He laughed easily, the art guru humbly seeking the opinion of the lowly student. He peered grandly around the room. Some sort of "statement" had been made. There were flickering black-and-white TV sets tuned to impossibly unwatchable stations; painted mesh curtains hanging from the walls everywhere but over the windows; and hundreds of feet of industrial plastic tubing of obscure decorative purpose. At the far end of the ten-thousand-square-foot space, behind the D.J.'s station and to the right of the bar, a pornographic movie, watched by no one, was projected onto a filthy, once-pink sheet. The overall result was a cross between bad performance art and bad art, period. The interesting question was whether all the badness was intentional. Evan was inclined to think it was. Which made it quite good.

He had Billy's attention now. He had mentioned the magic word. *Art*.

His head jerked back toward Evan. At that precise moment he saw her.

A dark-haired girl in a microscopic skirt. A girl who was so very like Jane, but black haired, butch in leather, dancing with a big buxom blond. It couldn't be. But those legs.

A sleepwalker, he moved toward her, oblivious to the small talk of the art hero, lost in the urgent necessity of the present. He was close behind her now and still he wasn't sure, but his heart was racing as he tapped her shoulder.

She turned. Friendly. Open. A free spirit among her colleagues of the night.

"Billy! Billy Bingham!"

"Jane?"

"You mean you didn't recognize me? Just picking up some stranger, Billy? I'd never have believed it."

Her eyes laughed at him, and her obvious pleasure at seeing him lit up Billy's heart. "God, Jane. I'm so glad I found you. I got the message on the machine that you might be here. I've been searching Los Angeles. Wow!" He reached out for her hands and held them as he stared at her, reassuring himself that she was real. Then, on the edge of vision, something called his eyes away. The big girl with the sassy breasts and the outsize grin was not the sort of person you could ignore.

"Oh, Billy, this is Lucy Masterson. You know ... we talked about her. Anyway, meet my new boss. I'm the assistant to the assistant—that state-of-the-art trend setter dancing over there." Jane jerked a thumb at Jishy, lost in the intricacies of an interpretive dance a few feet away. "And Lucy, this is Billy Bingham. He's a close friend of Julie Bennett."

Jane was getting the hang of L.A. introductions. Everyone came with a descriptive sentence: "My cousin, the brain surgeon," or rather, "My cousin the *well-known* brain surgeon," or "This is Tracey. Did you see her last week on *Miami Vice*?"

Lucy held out her hand as she bopped to the Bowie. "My, another friend of Ms. Bennett's. Gee, does she have *pretty* friends."

Billy smiled wanly at the compliment and wondered why

he disliked Lucy Masterson on sight. Because she was dancing with Jane? Hardly.

"Are you one of Julie Bennett's *very* close friends?"

"Lucy!" said Jane, mock-shocked.

Billy ignored her, and smile tenderly at Jane. "I've missed
you."

Jane deflected his intensity. "God, how on earth did you
find me down here? It's supposed to be impossible."

"Where there's a will..." He left the mystery in the air
where it worked best, mingled in with the techno-funk and the
excitement.

He tugged at her outstretched hands. "Come on, let's go
and get a drink."

"Great, let's *all* go and get a drink. I'm burning up."

But Lucy had gotten the message. So the boy liked her girl.
Well, he had good taste, but time was on her side. A gigolo
would never leave the book queen—not with her royalties—
however slick the chick. She stepped forward quickly, and
leaning right over Billy's arms, she kissed Jane directly on the
mouth, hard and long. "So long, you two. Have fun. Catch
you later." She giggled into the oasis of startled silence that
suddenly existed in the middle of the night noise. Then, grabbing an off-balance Jish and sliding a cheeky hand up the
thigh of the girl he was dancing with, she spirited them both
away into the frantic crowd. As she did so she turned toward
the duo she was deserting and a mammoth wink screwed up
one side of her flushed, amused face.

"Christ, what was *that* all about?"

Jane laughed to cover her embarrassment. "Oh, that's just
Lucy."

"Whaddya mean, 'just Lucy.' She's a dyke, Jane, and she's
got the hots for you. You ought not to be working for someone
like that."

"Oh, balls, Billy. She's just affectionate. It's no big deal.
Come on, let's get that drink." Jane took control. Billy looked
doubtful, and she chose not to explain the porno pictures on
top of the kiss. "Are you here by yourself?" She squeezed his
hand encouragingly, willing him to lighten up and have the
fun that she was having.

"Sort of. I came with a crowd of people."

"He came with me."

Evan Koestler's voice was sharp. He wasn't a crowd. Crowds *followed* people. And he, Evan Koestler, followed absolutely no one. The frown on his face said it all, said that he had caught the body language as the dance-floor scene had unfolded; said he had seen Billy flirting with the beautiful girl. Well, Billy should know that in any competition—for bodies, for souls—he, Evan Koestler, would be a formidable opponent.

Billy did the introductions with conspicious lack of enthusiasm.

"The art Evan Koestler?" Jane asked.

"Ah, you know the art world?" Evan was surprised. Up close, the girl was more than beautiful.

"I've heard of *you*. Are you and Billy old friends?"

"Actually, we met this evening at a gallery opening. Had a long talk about art, and you know L.A. evenings. No telling where you'll end up."

"Strangers in the night," said Jane enigmatically, looking at Billy as she spoke. The line "lovers at first sight" hung like an accusation in the fetid air.

Billy moved fast to break the unpromising impasse. Taking Jane firmly by the hand, he steered her back toward the dance floor.

Safe in the anonymity of the massed humanity, he spoke urgently, holding her close to him as the music and the bodies swirled around them. "Jane. Listen. I'm finished with Julie. I'm moving out. Gonna get a place in Venice. Will you come with me? Will you come and live with me?"

The words tumbled over themselves. They were speaking themselves, inventing his future. To see her like this made decisions superfluous. Nothing mattered now but her, not even the art, not even his ambitions, not Koestler. He was vaguely aware that there would be problems, like money, and extricating himself from the stickiness of the Julie Bennett web. But first and above all he had to persuade this perfect creature to do what he so suddenly and so desperately wanted.

Jane fought to take it all in. It seemed like someone had

thrown the tape of her life into "fast forward." "Billy, that's really sweet. But I mean . . . I've just moved in with Lucy. I've got this job. And Julie and you . . ." Her voice trailed off uncertainly.

"But you could *keep* the job. I mean, you'd have wheels. Venice isn't that far. What sort of a job is it, anyway?"

Jane took a deep breath. "You'll think I'm crazy probably, but Lucy Masterson takes soft porno pictures. Not so 'soft' actually, but she's all right. She's a great person and I like her a lot." She held her head back—defiant, the big girl who could look after herself in the wicked old world.

Billy stared at her, incredulous.

Jane plowed on. "At first she wanted me to pose. Can you believe it? Obviously Julie got things completely mixed up. She didn't know anything about the sort of pictures Lucy took. Anyway, I straightened it all out and now she's given me a job. It'll be a fantastic opportunity to learn about photography."

Billy's face had clouded over. He stood stock-still in the middle of the bouncing dancers as the anger built within him. "For Chrissakes, Jane, don't you know what's going down here? Can't you understand what's happening?"

"What do you mean?"

"I *mean*, your loving sister is trying to destroy you. That's what I mean."

"Oh, don't be ridiculous, Billy. She didn't do it on purpose. I mean she's probably a bit out of touch, sitting in the desert year in year out. One thinks she's got her finger on the pulse because of all her P.R., but most likely she just hangs out in her ivory tower and doesn't know anything. Maybe she got confused."

Billy breathed in deeply and his eyes rolled up to the ceiling. His voice tried to be patient. "Jane, you've got to believe me. This whole thing has been a setup. First she gets you slung into prison. Now she has you living with some psychopathic lesbian who's in the skin business and God knows what else. Drugs, prostitution—you name it. I mean, *look* at her. She kissed you. On the *mouth*. She's crazy and she's stuck on you."

"Billy—don't be so dramatic. This is the twentieth century. You sound like some Puritan throwback. It's no crime to be gay, and she's hardly going to rape me."

Jane laughed. Americans liked to live as if life were the movies and they were the lead role. It was important to express *emotion*, and if you didn't have any particularly strong ones then you could always make them up. After all, "actorliness," with cleanliness, was next to godliness.

Billy shook his head in disbelief. "Jane, try to understand. This is L.A. It may look fun and wild and safe to you, but beneath the surface it's an open sewer. Girls like you drift into town every day, Hollywood and Vine dreamers with no gutter savvy, no street smarts, and thousands of miles from home. You know what happens to them? They meet some fun person who promises to be their 'friend' and to put their feet on the ladder to the stars and in no time at all they're in the meat trade. And you know what happens next? They're ashamed and they've got no bread, and they're lonely and they hurt and all those wonderful friends float crack at them and black-tar horse and Ecstasy, and they take them for the pain because they don't know what they are, and pretty soon they don't care. And it's booze and Happy Valleys and uppers and downers and sideways pills and tricks to pay for it all. Then there's nothing left but the worms and the slime and the crawling maggots of the Hollywood underbelly until it's all over at last. Mortuary time. Please believe me, Jane. It happens. It's happening right now while we speak. Your sister wanted it to happen to you, and I won't let it." His knuckles were white, his fists tight.

"Billy. Billy. Stop! You're talking to me like I'm a child. I don't take drugs. I never would. And I'm not going to make it with Lucy. She's the one who's gay. Not me. Remember?" Her voice went soft and slinky and flirtatious, and her hand reached for Billy's.

"Jane, please. Say you'll come with me. Promise me. This minute. Let me look after you. I love you. Say you'll come and live with me."

"Billy, I don't know what to say. I don't even know what I

feel . . . I mean about you . . . about us. I *really* like you. A lot. But I don't think it's love."

"I'll *make* it love. Just give me a chance." There were tears in Billy's eyes. She held out her hands, uncertain, and inside she fought to make sense of her feelings. Whatever else it was, this wasn't the love of her life. But there was more than enough lust and he was wonderfully attractive, and his fierce ambition would give him a shot at the greatness that he so firmly believed was his birthright. Life in a Venice studio with Billy Bingham would surely be exciting, a marvelous world of creativity and togetherness; of strange, wonderful people and burning intense conversations into the night. Did it matter in L.A.—in the late eighties—that she was not yet deeply in love? All he was asking for was for her to share his bed, his body, and his dreams. Surely eternity could wait.

Jane stepped forward and her arms reached out around his waist as she stared up into his anxious eyes. He loved her. As much as his art would let him love. It was enough.

"Yes, I'll come with you, Billy Bingham. If you want me, I'll come."

Relief shone from Billy's eyes, but the haunted look remained. He shook with emotion. "Jane, that's wonderful. Wonderful. Now listen, Jane, very carefully. You've got to do exactly what I say. I'm going to leave. Right now. I'm going straight back to the desert to get my things, and then to Venice to find us somewhere to live. You have to move out of Lucy's. Do you hear? It's important. Don't stay there. Not even tonight. Go to the Chateau Marmont Hotel on Sunset. I'll leave an Express card imprint at the desk on my way to Palm Springs. Here, and you'd better take this." He fumbled in the pocket of his jeans for some cash and thrust it at Jane.

"Okay. You'll do what I say? I'll contact you at the Marmont in a couple of days."

"Billy, what on *earth* do you mean? I don't need money. Lucy has given me some. Do you have to go now? This minute? Why do I need a hotel?"

"Just *do* it, Jane. Okay? I can't explain here in this zoo. Just do what I say."

Jane smiled helplessly. It was pointless to argue with him.

He sounded as if he had inside knowledge of the imminent ending of the world.

He leaned in toward her and his lips brushed the edge of hers. "Be safe, my love. Be careful and be safe. I'll be back for you. Trust me."

Then he was gone, and Jane tried to shout above the music as he pushed through the crowd toward the exit. "Why 'be safe'? I'm not in any danger. I'm fine. It's great. Everything's wonderful." But the words were lost in the frantic hard rock, the heartbeat of the L.A. night.

THIRTEEN

THE DESERT DAWN WAS A PERFECT BACKGROUND for Billy Bingham's mood as he drove into Palm Springs. The blood-red sun, sly and cunning, was peering over the tips of the Santa Rosa Mountains as it crept up on the now-conquered armies of the night. Already its advance troops were making inroads into the outskirts of the town, painting the buildings pastel pink. The yellow moon had surrendered only minutes before, sinking down gracefully below the peaks of Mount Jacinto, and now it was the sun's turn to rule the desert skies.

Billy pushed the button that sent the Maserati's electric windows down, and he breathed in deeply. He would miss the clarity of the early desert morning, the smell of the already warming air, soft and sexual. He was tired from the sleepless night, from the two-hour drive, from the booze and cigarette smoke of the roaring evening. But the adrenaline was keeping him awake.

Today he would leave Julie Bennett. Julie Bennett, who had never been left before—who liked, demanded, to do the leaving herself. She would go ape: the cat flying through the air like a trapeze artist, the air-conditioned atmosphere turned blue with her insults. He could cope with that, but there was a problem.

Julie Bennett had a hostage, a roomful of hostages. Locked away in the studio of her all but impregnable house were the paintings that were all he had to show for his life so far, the paintings without which he would have no future. Somehow, in some way he would have to get them from her, and that meant he would have to cap his anger and inject diplomacy into his act.

There was so much to lose, so much to gain—the soft girl plucked from the clutches of the hard enemy, his glittering future rising phoenixlike from the desert, freedom from the shackles of sexual slavery.

He drove fast through Las Palmas, and at the gate there was no difficulty for the boy who belonged to Ms. Bennett. It was six forty as he hurried up the stairs of the house. She would be awake, but not yet up, and her fertile mind would be planning the day's work as she lay back on the pillows of the big bed. He knocked briefly but entered the room before she had time to ask who it was.

She lay there—voluptuous, far larger than life—radiating equal mixtures of power, charm, charisma, and jaundiced bile. Her fingers irritated the hair of the inevitable Orlando who sat, pashalike, on her ample breast.

Was that pleasure on Julie's face as she saw him? "My, my! Mr. Billy Bingham. Back from Hell-A. Couldn't stay away from me. Not even for twenty-four hours. What happened? Art world not interested? Did they turn off the American Express card tap? Not on *my* instructions, if that's the problem."

The banter was cheerful, standard Julie stuff.

"Why did you do it, Julie? What have you got against Jane? A pornographic photographer. A crazy lesbian. In L.A.? You must have known what that could mean for someone like Jane, who doesn't understand the game, with no money..."

Billy, exhausted, spoke more in sorrow than in anger. His life had been too tough, his desires too strong, for moral indignation to come easily to him.

Julie's big round eyes narrowed dangerously. "Ooh. I *see*. The lovebirds have been reunited. It wasn't a gallery show after all. It was a lover's tryst—a dirty, stinking betrayal. *That's* what it was." She spat out the last words.

Billy fought to stay cool. He couldn't blow it all away, not when she held all the paintings.

"You know it wasn't like that, Julie. Jane wouldn't do that to you even if I would. We met by accident." The half lie slipped out easily, and he moved back to the offensive. "Why did you try to destroy her? What have you got against her, Julie?"

A darkening blush of anger spread rapidly across Julie's broad face. "Don't you dare question me! How *dare* you stand there in my house and question me! Who the hell do you think you are, you little punk? You're nothing around here. You remember that. A great-big round zero. Do you hear? You exist because I want you to exist and for absolutely no other reason at all. The second I stop wanting that, you're *history*. Do you know what you are, Billy Bingham? You're my perversion. You're my dirty, squalid little sexual perversion, and don't you forget it." She sat up in the bed, her bosom heaving with the force of her delivery as she threw the words at Billy like hatchets.

"I'm leaving, Julie. It's over," said Billy simply.

The alarm bells rang in Julie's mind. Leaving? Billy Bingham? He wasn't *allowed* to do that. It was against the rules. In a second or two he was supposed to crawl across the floor and breakfast off her.

"Hah! Where would you go? You've got nothing."

Billy could see that she was worried. "I've got less than nothing here, so I'm going, Julie."

"You're going to Jane."

There was pain in her voice now. A terrible hurt he had never heard before.

"I'm just going, Julie."

"You'll be back. They always try to come back, you know. But I don't have them back. The moment you walk through those gates it's over. Forever."

Was that glistening thing a tear?

"I can live with that."

"And what, Billy Bingham, if I should decide to keep you after all? What, for instance, if I wrote you a check for one hundred thousand dollars? Would you come over here and do what you do so well?"

Coquettish. Flirtatious. Why wasn't she an actress? Billy thought. The range. The depth. The *bitch*.

"No, I wouldn't, Julie. Not even if you gave me one hundred thousand dollars." He had to laugh, and he did so as he spoke. She was amazing. She took his breath away, this outrageous she-mountain with the alley cat's morals and the brazenness of brass.

Julie laughed then, too. Their conspiracy of mutual need was not dead. He would leave now, to search for the green grass on the other side of the hill, but he would never find it. When his dreams died and his ambitions were atomized, he would crawl back.

In his mind Billy felt for the moment. Was this it? She was laughing at him, but with him as well. She believed he would return. It was time. He held his breath and then fought to sound casual. "I'll send for the paintings in a day or two—if you don't mind holding on to them until then." His life was in her hands.

"Oh *God*! Can't they go with you? The thought of those monstrosities polluting my house fills me with utter horror. But I suppose they'd hardly fit into the Maserati. Yes, they can stay for a day or two. After that they get junked."

Billy felt relief surge through him. For once she had missed an opportunity for destruction. Or, more likely, she had saved her trump card for some later time. Oddly enough, it was her belief in the ugliness of his art that had saved it. To her it was a passport to the failure that would bring him groveling back to her. To him it was his brilliant future. Only one of them would be proved right.

"Good-bye, Julie."

"Get the hell out, loser. You'll be back."

But as the door closed behind him Julie wasn't so sure, and she couldn't bear to think of the possibility. But already her hurt was swamped by fury. She had been deserted before, once, by the only man she had ever loved. Her father had turned his back on her and chosen her mother . . . and Jane. Now Billy was leaving—the toy boy, the recreational drug that both deadened her pain and gave her temporary pleasure

—and once again the reason was the sister who wouldn't go away. Jane. Always Jane.

Julie pressed her hand to her brow and bent her head as the well-known feeling throbbed and burned within her. "I hate her so much, Orlando," she whispered. "Can you understand so much hate?"

Orlando stiffened.

"But we haven't finished with her yet, have we, darling? Haven't started, really. Or with Billy. What a silly billy, isn't he, sweetheart? We'll cut them up small, both of them, won't we, and stick them in your dinner."

Revenge became a raging furnace in her belly. But she couldn't keep the emotion inside. "Aaaaagh," she screamed at the world that had mistreated her, and the orange cat rocket took flight as the Pratesi sheets twisted and turned beneath her squirming body.

"THERE ARE THREE KINDS OF 'NOT GETTING ENOUGH TO EAT' in Third World places like the ones you see on the screen. Not enough calories. Not enough protein. And not enough vitamins, which leads to diseases like scurvy, pellagra, and beri-beri."

It had been bold of Pete Rivkin to hit the party with Robert Foley's after-dinner screening of life among the Indian have-nots. Usually the banquet would be followed by some hot-from-the-press movie, a conversation churner that would allow the lucky viewer star billing at the town-of-the-talk fund-raisers for at least three weeks. But this was hardball, especially after the food. The mild flavor of the Pacific tray oysters, nestling seductively in their thin, fluted shells, had been offset to perfection by the flinty charm of the delicate Pouilly Fumé, 1982, from the Loire. The witty grilled turkey breast in pomegranate and juniper-berry sauce—nuevo Mexicano cuisine for those nervous Beverly Hills waistlines—washed down by the more than respectable claret, a Chateau Beychevelle, 1966, had been tasty, "safe" protein. Nor had there been anything health- or diet-threatening about the dessert. Three little individual bowls per person. Blue for the blueberries. Raspberry for the raspberries. A delicate lime green for the iced Muscat grapes. The guests had drunk a bottle or two of vintage Taittinger Rosé champagne with that, and they were still drinking it—with rather less pleasure—as they stared bravely at the sores of the children, at the flies and the filth and the squalor and the awful, accusing hunger. If Pete Rivkin hadn't been hotter than the atmosphere for an Apollo reentry—a small-screen guru hot on the heels of Aaron Spelling—they would have made their excuses and walked. As it was, they were glued to the aggressively comfortable seats of the private Rivkin screening room, and the women, and at least one—possibly two—of the men, were passing the time by wondering what Robert Foley would be like in bed.

Cybill Shepherd leaned toward David Puttnam, studio boss of Columbia Pictures. "All this talk of hunger is making me hungry. I think I want to eat *him*." She winked as she jerked a thumb toward Robert Foley as he stood, pointer in hand, beside the flickering screen.

Cybill's *Tonight* appearance had elevated the *Moonlighting* maneater to legendary Mae West status. Johnny had upset his drink. Quick as a flash Cybill had said, "If you'd spilled that in your lap I'd have mopped it up."

Robert Foley weighed his audience carefully. Mixing dinner with hunger was always a risk, especially among the guilty rich who wore their liberalism on their sleeves to disguise the fact that the thing beating in their chests was nothing more than a meter for counting the money. The way his Bombay home movie was working on their digestive systems they'd rather be on Tums than Taittinger.

"Now, I know that Packwood and Rostenkowski haven't made it any cheaper for you folks to pass on some of your earnings, but I want you to know that these children need your help desperately. You can see what they are suffering, but you can't smell it, hear it, feel it. I did, and believe me, that experience will stay with me always. I want to try to share it with you, which is why Pete Rivkin asked me here tonight."

His piercing blue eyes scanned the room, locking onto those of the Industry heavy hitters, scorching through to elusive conscience, targeting in on squirming guilt. He sought them out, summed them up, and found them wanting; all around the room hard exteriors were melting as the guests mentally reached for their checkbooks.

"Who *is* he, Elizabeth? How come I never *heard* of this one? Does he do drug rehab? Could I get him for my animal thing? Boy, has he *got* it. I feel a hundred thou coming on. I mean it."

"No way. I tried to get him for AIDS, and I know he turned down Barbara Sinatra's abused children. He's strictly a Bob Geldof production. He does this part time. Mostly he works at a clinic down in the Watts area. At-cost, nonprofit medicine. Isn't he wild?"

Elizabeth Taylor didn't bestow compliments lightly. The compassion commissar who had questioned her was duly impressed. The hundred grand was firming up.

"What's Pete in for? Big ones?" Like everything else in Beverly Hills, charity was follow-my-leader. The good-worker didn't want to be in the "wrong" good work.

"I bet. That ABS show he's doing—*Beverly Hills Nights* —is going to be huge. They're spending a fortune on it. Unto them that hath . . ." Liz Taylor laughed, aware that she was as good an example of the biblical saying as anyone.

Robert Foley saw that they were with him. They liked his style. He could afford to squeeze a bit. He tugged at an ear, apologetic, grinning to himself, eyes momentarily downcast, as he prepared to sock it to them. "Of course, here in southern California we think we have problems with food. Too many calories. So we book a week at the Golden Door or the Cal-a-Vie, phone our personal trainers and order a little low-impact aerobics, wander down to Hunter's and pick up a copy of the latest diet book." His eyes found Liz Taylor's. She had one out any minute. "Or we worry that we're taking in too much protein. Cholesterol. Animal fat. All that might take a couple of years off our three score and ten. And of course we're all vitamin freaks and trace-element fiends. Is calcium still hot around here? I'm betting magnesium's gonna be the next craze. But, you see, in India to be forty is to be ancient, and they're *thrilled* if they get old enough to have Alzheimer's."

He talked fast, the whip-stroke words lashing them merci-lessly, the pain hardly lessened by the transparency of his use of the pronoun "we." The whispers had crackled like wildfire around the room. This M.D. was no millionaire. He lived in the humble Valley, worked with the poor in Watts, and thought Spago was a children's game, which, perhaps, in a way, it was. He wouldn't have known the inside of a fat farm from the inside of a starlet, and he would be about as interested in his own health as a hotshot agent in the health of a has-been's wife.

"Now, you've seen the clinic that we started in Bombay. That clinic will be called the Rivkin Clinic because of the extraordinary generosity and kindness of our host this eve-ning. I have in my pocket a check drawn on the Bank of America . . . hope they've still got the money . . . for . . . a quarter of a million dollars." He pulled it out and waved it above his head as the collective gasp was replaced by the odd bravo and the round of polite, marginally anxious applause.

Robert Foley's voice went shrewd. This was a low one, but the hell with it. The end more than justified the means. He knew little of war and next to nothing of love, but in charity, for the children, all was fair.

"I know that not all of you can afford a large amount like that. Pete is a lovely, wonderful man who also happens to be very, very rich. But I would so appreciate it if I could accept from each and every one of you some little contribution for the children. They are so small, so vulnerable, so in need. You've seen that tonight. Let them touch your hearts as they captured mine. Let the children live, so that the future of all of us on this planet can be assured. Whatever you can afford—from each according to his means—as the precious gift of life to those in the valley of the shadow of death. I thank you all."

The room was vibrating now. Enthusiasm gripped the high rollers. But there was something else there, too, as Robert Foley had intended there to be: the spirit that kept America great—free competition, keeping up with the Joneses, or in this case the Rivkins. In California, and especially in Beverly Hills, to be rich and successful was a moral duty. To be *seen* to be so was even more important. Robert Foley had put them all on the spot. To give small meant you *were* small. To give big meant you were big. To give biggest meant you were best.

The Cartier diamonds flicked nervously on the sunburned fingers. Augmented breasts heaved and swelled in Lagerfeld; reduced ones prickled and pouted in Claude Montana. Toes squiggled excitedly in Maude Frizon; lifted faces did what they could to register appropriate expression.

Pete Rivkin was on his feet. The most successful TV producer in Hollywood, he was thin, fit, and forty-five, casually good looking. He beamed around the room at the business associates who doubled as his "friends." He was going to speak, but success was speaking for him. He didn't have to talk at all.

He smiled across the room at Robert Foley. Dear, funny, haunted Robert—as different from the Beverly Hills crowd as Kraft from Camembert. It was a bizarre place for him to be—in his off-the-rack tuxedo, hanging unhappily from the strong shoulders, with his pale, sensitive face that could have used an hour or two in the sun, and his abrupt, no-nonsense manner so different from that of the greasy, money-grabbing bandits who passed for physicians in southern California.

"Robert, thank you. In you the poor of the world have a mighty champion. A mighty champion indeed." He paused, as the room filled with the applause.

"Right on, Pete," said a Tanqueray-deep throat.

"Hear, hear," agreed a J&B Rare one.

"This could be a long night." Cybill Shepherd's irreverent stage whisper was dangerously audible.

"Thank you. Thank you all." He'd heard her. And already the crack was in the memory Filofax. *Moonlighting* had better run and *run*.

"Sometimes, here in Hollywood . . ." He used the generic term as did all Industry people, ". . . we lose ourselves in our own dreams and schemes. We worry about our points and our grosses, our break-evens and our awards, and it's good that we should. It makes the world go round, and our wonderful business vibrant and healthy, and of course it makes us rich. And that's good too, because sometimes, like tonight, we find ourselves in a position to do great and wonderful things. Some of you here this evening know what it's like to be poor. Not as poor and as deprived as these unfortunate children, but poor enough." He paused for the collective reverential memory.

Around the room the calculator minds worked out how much they could afford, wondered if anyone would cap the Rivkin contribution, worried whether it would be wise or foolish to do so.

". . . So please, in Robert Foley's words, 'for the sake of the children,' give with your hearts."

Elizabeth Taylor was on her feet, and her electric presence crackled around the room. "Thank you, Pete. And thank you, Dr. Foley. You have touched me. Touched me very deeply this evening and made me want to do something that I'll probably regret. But that doesn't matter. What matters is the children. I want to give them this."

The room went quiet. Liz Taylor had the respect of the entire world, for her courage, her dignity, and the warmth of her heart. She had put every ounce of her formidable energy and charisma into the desperate battle against AIDS.

She walked forward and as she did so she pulled from her finger an egg-size diamond ring.

Slowly, the room began to hum.

Wendy Stark couldn't help herself. "Liz, not the Winston diamond."

"No," said Elizabeth Taylor. "The Richard Burton one. He would have wanted the children to have it."

POOLSIDE AT THE BEL-AIR HOTEL, EVAN KOESTLER STARED gloomily at the names on the Cartier pad in front of him. He should call all of them at some stage of his trip: the big collectors—Armand Hammer, Eli Broad, the Annenbergs, Aaron Spelling; the politicos like Bradley and Waxman and the high-visibility Industry people like Griffin, Weintraub, and Wasserman. But right now he didn't have the stomach for any of it. He was hung over, tired, and hovering on the brink of a dangerous obsession. The boy with the haunting eyes had walked out on him without so much as a single word of farewell. It hadn't been some cheap street hustler's ploy to turn him on.

Billy Bingham was an artist, and he had been introduced to Evan Koestler and he didn't *care*. It was an abomination against the natural order of things, and it had turned Evan's usually well-ordered life upside down.

It was more than just physical attraction. For some reason that Evan couldn't understand, he had an insuperable desire to hitch himself to Billy's comet—a magnetic determination to submerge himself in Billy's ambition, to acquire some of the *meaning* that he seemed so comprehensively to have acquired. Evan knew that he himself was a success. His clients were the people who had run out of toys to buy, who had more houses than they had time to visit, a longer stock list than they had time to read, who had more mistresses than they had time to satisfy. It was his vocation in life to minister to them in their hour of need, and as his smooth tongue rolled around the syllables, he would relieve them of the burden of their wealth, lightening their load as he exchanged their money for strange-colored paintings and weird-shaped sculptures that would put them one up on the rivals who pretended to be their friends.

But compared to the ambition he had seen shining in Billy Bingham's eyes, his whole career had about as much purpose as the male nipple.

Petulantly he bit the end of the torpedo-shaped Montecristo No. 2 Havana cigar and caught the eye of the great-looking, long-haired guy who was in charge of the Bel-Air poolside. "Robert, can you bring me a bullshot. Lots of lemon juice and a couple of shots of Tabasco. Don't hold back on the pepper."

"Coming up right away, Mr. Koestler." At the Bel-Air all the staff knew your name.

The midday sun was coming on strong, but that was fine. Aristotle Onassis had been right. When asked what was the most important thing to know if you wanted to make money, he had replied, "Always have a suntan." Well, Evan had a suntan—and he hadn't even made the traditional Hollywood mistake of doing the front only. His back was brown, too, and his buttocks. Evan let out a sigh of satisfaction. This was one of the few deeply relaxing places in L.A. Nothing happened fast, but when the food and drink finally came, it was the best. He looked up at the walls of the canyon, the tall palm trees reaching toward the blue sky, and then back across the oval pool to the table laden with fruit, towels, and baskets of various suntan oils, which the hotel made available for its guests. Yes, it was an enormously civilized place. The sort of place that Billy Bingham might like . . .

The thought was running around in his mind as the waiter approached with his drink—the stylishly shaped plastic glass upside down on his tray, its mouth covered with Saran-wrap, an idiosyncratic way to prevent spillage.

"Can you bring me a telephone," he said.

She wouldn't be in the directory, but with his contacts it should only take a minute or two to find her. What time did they eat lunch in the desert? Almost certainly not quite yet, although they behaved in a peculiar way out there. Whatever. Julie Bennett would talk to Evan Koestler. He couldn't think why he'd never sold her a painting. Perhaps he'd buy something from her. But it wasn't art that was on his mind.

JULIE BENNETT WANDERED MOODILY THROUGH THE SCULPture garden. Usually she loved this place, a seventy-foot green postage stamp at the bottom of the towering mountain, dramatic in its fertile contrast to the sun-washed slopes of the foothills that towered over her. But it was really the mountain that was her soul mate, desolate, vast, unyielding in the face of the adversity of the elements. It seemed to mock the lush oasis nestled at its feet, the thousands of gallons of precious water squandered for a rich woman's whim. It sneered and snarled its monumental superiority—"I may be a peasant, but I am lean and hard and enduring, and one day, effete aristocrat of the valley, I will come in the night to make you mine once more."

There was a strange hope in the desert's endless struggle, in its difficulty, in its awe-inspiring, alien charm, in its effortless survival of the torment that endlessly plagued it. She could lose herself in the low desert and bury her individuality in its fearsome vastness, and although civilization had come to the valley it was there under sufferance, and nature was still in control. Here she was living on the edge of a place that did not easily give birth and that understood about life, about stark death, and about leaving behind no trace of what had gone before. Which was why Julie Bennett's essence communed with it. It was the place, perhaps the only one, for a woman with no womb.

In the Coachella Valley she could forget about the green fertility of her homeland and the exuberant life of lawn-sprinklered Beverly Hills, from where the movie riffraff rushed each week to court her. Julie Bennett, the bankable writer, the one whose books could sell the flicks on which the mortgages, the mistresses, and the Maseratis depended.

The midday sun was heavy on her shoulders now. Mad dogs and Englishwomen. But whoever had written that didn't know about Palm Springs. Here, where the temperature liked to climb into the 120s at this time of day, the mind-bleaching effect was a cure for madness, not its cause. What pain could survive to irritate the neurons when the sun turned the frail tissue into a bubbling cauldron? What pain indeed?

Julie reached out with her finger to touch the smooth, round contour of a Henry Moore sculpture. She did so with maximum caution. To rest her hand on it for any length of time would sear her skin. The burning metal stroked her mind, the feeling pleasant in its sharpness yet divorced from meaning, and she thought again of Billy Bingham.

Billy had gone, just four or five short hours ago. Already she missed him. The others she had never missed, but Billy was different. Although she had tried to make him believe he was just a thing to scratch her itch, a living joke, a moving target for her whiplash tongue, he had not believed it, and, at heart, neither had she. Time and again she had tried to tell herself that he was a nothing, a piece of prick like all the ones she had had before, but she had fallen victim to his inner strength, his faith in himself, his sense of purpose. Julie Bennett wanted him back. And she would have her wish. It was part of the vow she had made to herself those long years ago. Life would always be hard, but at least she would have her own way.

The butler's voice slithered through the heat. "A telephone call, Meez Bennett. A Mr. Evan Koestler." In his hand was the cordless telephone. He looked quite pleased with his "Koestler." "Shall I say you are not in?"

Julie Bennett did not want to talk to Evan Koestler, or to anyone for that matter. But she was curious. Over the years most famous people got to meet each other. It was that, more than anything else, that destroyed the illusion of fame. But she had never met Koestler, though she knew all about him. Anyone who spent as much money as she did on art had heard of little Evan.

She held her hand out for the telephone. "This is Julie Bennett speaking."

"Ah, Julie Bennett. Evan Koestler. I do hope you don't mind my calling you like this. I got your telephone number from Allan Carr who insisted that you would not be offended, and who, incidentally, sent all his love."

"No, that's fine, Mr. Koestler. I'm surprised our paths haven't crossed before—we must have hundreds of mutual friends. What can I do for you?"

"Well, actually I'm trying to locate somebody called Billy Bingham. I met him yesterday evening in L.A., at a gallery opening, and stupidly didn't take his telephone number. He told me that he was staying with you."

Julie felt her heart begin to race. Evan Koestler, the most important art dealer in the world. And Billy, the artist. The dreadful paintings stacked in the studio. Billy who had walked out on her, that very morning. She had thought it was because of Jane. He had intimated that, too. But did he have bigger fish to fry? Fish of the outlandish proportions of tiny Evan Koestler.

She moved slowly now. Wary, her Renaissance mind was on maximum alert. "He's not around right now."

"You see, I'm very anxious to reach him. We had such a good discussion, and I found him so interesting, and I'd just love to see his paintings. He made them sound so wonderful."

In between the lines Julie Bennett, the novelist who understood character, translated the words. Evan Koestler wanted Billy; effortlessly, the boy had made another conquest. It was all clear now.

If Koestler was going to be a sexual rival, he would be a

powerful one, given Billy's longing for artistic recognition. But Evan didn't know where Billy was, and neither did she. Did that mean that Billy had gone to Jane? The bile rose in Julie's throat. She made her decision quickly. Evan would be an ally against Jane, and that was the only thing that really mattered.

Her mind made up, she moved fast. "Listen, Mr. Koestler, I'm a little tied up right now, but I am going to be in Los Angeles sometime later this afternoon. Would there be any chance of our meeting for a drink? I'd love to meet you, having heard so much about you, and perhaps pick your brains on what I should be buying. We could discuss Billy then."

"That would be marvelous. Perhaps you would do me the honor of letting me take you out to dinner. Can you bear Spago? I'm rather fond of it."

"That sounds wonderful. I'll look forward to it. I'll be staying at the Bel-Air."

"Well, that's just perfect. So am I. Why don't I give you a call in your suite around eight o'clock?"

"Eight it is."

Evan Koestler was a dealer. But Julie Bennett knew how to deal, too. Between them they would work out what to do about Billy Bingham. And Billy would have no say in it at all.

FOURTEEN

IN THE BAR, AND CLUSTERED AROUND THE RESERVAtion desk at Spago, the atmosphere was one of scarcely controlled panic. It had been bad enough in the parking lot where the Rollers, Mercs, Beamers, and Pinninfarina-bodied Italian beauties cruised dangerously, occasionally vomiting up beautiful people to run the gauntlet of the free-lance photographers who clustered like vultures around the door of the most desirable restaurant in the world.

The panic was only partially about getting tables. It was also about *what* tables, and even more important *when* tables. In the bar stood the nameless, faceless, no-hopers—the ones who, despite the fact that they had a reservation, had been bullied into waiting for tables for an hour or two, maybe even more. They were there all right, and it was *almost* enough, but when they tried to speed the snaillike table allocation process they ran slap bang into the immovable object of the maître d' and his long-haired female sidekick of the mysterious eyes and haughty expression. To cover their humiliation they were getting drunk, and sometimes, in between drinks, they would surge out individually and collectively to make their pitch to the power broker whose ears were closed to their pleas and whose job it was to humor them until they were too zoned or too socially browbeaten to care.

There was a second group, trying desperately to remain distinct from the losers in the bar. These were the B group.

People to be reckoned with who had rated a table, even a "good" table, but whose table wasn't quite ready "just yet." They tended to hang in close by the wooden lectern, not risking the descent into anonymity threatened by the seething mass in the bar. Mostly they knew each other, or at least knew *of* each other, and they talked among themselves as they pretended to have a good time, their nervous eyes roaming the restaurant in search of the table that might possibly become "theirs." The B group were careful to remain totally friendly to the powers that be; that ploy had been lost on the dead enders at the bar, whose belligerence rose with their blood alcohol levels. To fall out with the table people at Spago was not only a short-term disaster, but a long-term one, too, in a town built on the shifting sands of fashion from the bricks and mortar of superficiality.

The nervous tension of the tight-knit group around the lectern was heightened by the fact that their invidious position could be seen by just about everyone seated in the packed restaurant. They were in effect center stage with their pants down, the spotlight playing revealingly over them. Usually in L.A., center stage was the place to be, but this situation was an exception. *Le tout monde* could also see that you were being kept waiting, and for how long. They could also see which table would be your eventual destination. From that evidence it was not impossible to calculate how your movie was doing at the box office, what your net worth was, whether or not you had a chance at an Oscar nomination.

The third group wouldn't have liked to have thought of themselves as a group at all. They were the card-carrying bona-fide stars, the ones who rode effortlessly above it all. They did not have to wait for their tables. If they had been told to wait, they would have turned tail and walked right out again and never, ever come back. And if by some organizational mischance "their" table had gone, then another table would have been made—literally created out of thin air, the table and chairs hustled into place. These people sat against the window, overlooking the billboard on the other side of Sunset Strip. They sat nowhere else at all, unless they were in a party of more than four, when they sat one table in from the window. It was as simple as that.

Swifty Lazar—a fully paid-up member of the A team, whose incredibly "in" Oscars-night party was now held at Spago—would run lizard-like right through the B groupers on his way to his vacant table, the would-be friends bouncing right off his armor-plated scales, as he set his eyes straight ahead.

Allan Carr, chubby and cheerful, a ship in full sail, would cruise majestically through the flotsam and jetsam on his happy way to a bellyful of duck-sausage pizza.

Evan Koestler, a remote-controlled guided missile, scattered the lectern loiterers like pigeons as, Julie Bennett on his arm, he turned right at Sean Penn, left at Sylvester Stallone, and made for the table by the window that he knew was "his."

As he sat down he nodded to the long-legged, full-breasted beauty at the next table. Christina Ferrare—A.M. show hostess, former Mrs. John DeLorean and now married to the thickset man of Greek origin who sat by her side and just *happened* to be chairman of a little company called United Artists—waved back cheerfully.

"Oh, my word. How very grand. The billboard outside is showing your latest book. Don't say you organized it specially to impress me—though I *am* impressed."

Julie laughed. "I'd no idea." But she was pleased. It was a nice coincidence, and around the room she could see that several people had noticed it and were whispering to their friends. The Sunset billboards didn't sell any books, but they were a present to the author from the publisher. They said, "We want you. We need you. We think you're wonderful." Which were the only words anyone wanted to hear in Los Angeles.

"So, Julie Bennett, how is it that you have managed to amass one of the finest and certainly the most interesting collections of art in America and managed to avoid me in the process? It can hardly have been by chance."

Again the puff camouflaged in mocking banter. Evan was good, very good. He knew exactly how to flatter, and there were few things in this life more vital, especially when dealing with the rich and famous, who had long since ceased to care about the "truth," whatever that was, and who now dealt only in the quality and quantity of the compliments.

"I can't afford your prices, Evan."

"Ah 'afford.' Such an ambiguous word. So many of the things I think I can't afford are the things I can't afford to do without."

Again Julie found herself laughing. Could she "like" this man? Could she "like" anyone? Indeed, could she *afford* to?

"Will you join me in a glass of champagne, while we order?"

Julie nodded. He was taking control, or trying to. Men often made that mistake with her. Usually they regretted it.

"So you want to find Billy Bingham do you, Evan?"

He didn't answer at first, burying his head in the wine list as if lost in the decision-making process. But the twin red spots high up on his cheeks said he *had* heard her.

"Yes, a bottle of Pol Roger rosé. Nice and cold." There were no half bottles for the Julie Bennetts and Evan Koestlers of this world. They would have a glass each of the champagne, possibly a glass and a half, before moving on to the claret.

"Sorry, Julie, you were saying . . . ?"

"I was saying 'Billy Bingham.'"

"Billy Bingham. Ah yes, Billy Bingham."

Evan Koestler said the name as if he were practicing it, a name that needed tongue time to increase familiarity. He had rather hoped the subject of Billy could be broached at a time of his own choosing. Clearly Julie Bennett was not a bush beater.

"Is he your lover?"

Julie allowed the surprise to register. That was very direct for a smoothie like Koestler. But she could play hardball too.

"Would you like him to be yours?"

Evan took the direct hit right between the eyes. He wouldn't like to sell a painting to this one. She'd probably get it for cost . . . or worse.

"Touché, Julie Bennett."

Julie's eyes sparkled. This was rather fun. Evan was a

match for her, and it wasn't every day that she got to joust with someone who was that.

The champagne arrived and the pretty boy waiter poured it deferentially, sensitive enough to realize that his out-of-work-actor riff wasn't required at *this* table. Crushed pink rose petals. Churchill's favorite champagne, and a weakness of all English men and women who understood such things. Had Koestler known that?

It was her turn again. "Leaving aside what Billy is, was, or might yet be to either of us, the fact of the matter is that he has disappeared."

Evan cocked his head to one side in an expression that said he was not quite convinced.

"He walked out this morning and said he wasn't coming back. I wondered if your meeting with him had anything to do with it."

Cards were often better on the table next to the lark-tongue-and-camel-eyelash pizza or whatever was the latest exotica that Wolfgang Puck was serving up nowadays.

Evan recognized straight talk when he heard it. When you dealt in soft soap you knew how to recognize the smell of carbolic. "I don't think it was anything to do with me, although it might well be something to do with a blue-eyed beauty called Jane. A gaggle of us went to a rather amusing club, and he met up with her there—by chance, I think."

The icy fingers were at Julie's throat. "Did they leave together?"

"No, he left alone." He peered at Julie carefully, noting the flush on her cheeks. There were things here that he knew nothing about, but he knew what he wanted. He wanted to see the sad-eyed boy again.

Billy was not with Evan, not with Jane, and not with Julie. The streets of Los Angeles had swallowed him up. A frisson of panic swept through her. He must be found, and maybe Evan could help. She was thinking out loud when she said, "The paintings are still in my house. All the paintings. He said he would come back for them. He *will* do that."

Evan's eyes sparkled and shone. He tried to sound casual. "What are they like . . . the paintings?"

"Oh, you know. . ." Julie flung out a dismissive arm. "Big, bright, rather clumsy . . . sort of fierce, I suppose."

"Fierce . . . like Billy." Evan Koestler was suddenly talking to himself. When next he spoke there was a terrible urgency in his voice. "I'd like very much to see them, Julie. Could I do that?"

Yes. That was it. This dreamer, this lover of young men, had a fantasy about Billy. That he was a great artist—undiscovered, unknown, waiting for the seeing eye to reveal his genius. When confronted by the harsh reality of the canvases the dream would explode. Evan Koestler would be bitterly disappointed and his obsession would be blown away into thin air. He would withdraw in embarrassed confusion. He would be a threat no more. Then, when Billy slunk back to pick up his paintings she would be able to crow in triumph. The great Koestler had seen the paintings and pronounced them worse than worthless—labeled as trash by the man who knew. Billy's faith would not withstand that blow, and she would buy him back, castrated, his pride in ruins, his magnificent purpose nothing more than a hollow memory.

She rushed to give Evan what he wanted. What in a few short hours he would not want at all.

"Of course, Evan. Drive out with me to the desert tomorrow morning. Have lunch. See Billy's paintings. You can even see mine and tell me which are the fakes! I'll send the chauffeur back with you in the afternoon. I'd thoroughly enjoy it." Julie smiled.

THEY WERE THE VERY BEST DAYS JANE HAD EVER HAD. Mostly it had been Melrose. Funky, chic, elegant, flashy-trashy, gaudy, sexy-shiny, glitzed-out Melrose, the street that symbolized the new L.A. They had shopped on it. Winkle-picker brothel-creepers and leather motorcycle jackets at birth-of-the-sixties Let It Rock, sneering now at retropunk and Pepper psychedelia. Wipe-off polyester and lurex party frocks at Neo 80 and Bruce Halperin. Postnuclear-survival stuff at Warbabies and fake pearls, multiple belts, rhinestone obsessions, and Wild West kitsch from most everywhere. There had been metal throb-rubber and vinyl-net-Spandex, chic-a-boom trinkets and shades, of course, from the L.A. Eyeworks. Among the zapped-out, up-to-the-millisecond counter detritus there had even been the odd pretty thing from Olivia Newton John's Koala Blue and Fred Segal's Fred Segal. Then there had been the long leisurely white-wined lunches, parmigiani at the Cucina, sex-Mex at the state-of-the-trend Border Grill, and sushi at the place that started it all way back in the woolly times of September '82—Tommy Tang's. In the late afternoon they had hung out at the brat-pack haunt I Love Juicy, rented videos at Aron, browsed for magazines at Centerfold News on Fairfax. And all the time they had been watched, been the people high on "now" and down on "then."

In the evenings they had caught the movies in Westwood —and their happy feet had devoured the hot, student-crushed sidewalks as they had cruised for ice cream and cookies, not minding the traffic, not minding the lines, not minding the all-but-impossible parking. And later, roof down, Blaupunkt cranked up high, they would point the yellow Bug down Sunset to the sea to walk and laugh on the sand, drink California Coolers on the sidewalk in Venice, loiter grandly beneath the Bob Graham industrial-strength art in cuddly Dudley Moore's chic 72 Market Street restaurant. Then it had been after hours, and the early morning chiliburgers at Tommy's on West Beverly, a browse through Tower Records on the Strip before the mellow, sleeped-out journey home to crash exhausted in the tiny apartment.

In the mornings they had worked. The languid long-legged girls had wandered in at the crack of dawn, and the studio hummed with activity, as the models hustled to fill time and to fill coffers until the movie roles came and one more little piece of the dream slotted into place. They exposed their bodies to the celluloid with a cheerful resignation and a black good humor as the hairdressers fussed about and the sharp-tongued makeup artists gave them lip against the fantasy-rousing background of chick pop, Madonna, Janet Jackson, and the Bangles. To Jane it was an amazing world of bare skin and brightly colored background paper, flashing strobes and peeping pink, whirring pretty youngsters contorted and cavorted to give America the thrills it demanded. Lucy would stand there among the cheerful chaos, orchestrating the packaging of the lust, her big breasts falling out of the T-shirt that read SEX WAX, her finger playing with the shutter release as her professional eye roamed hungrily over the visuals.

It had certainly been a bit of a shock to experience the reality of what Lucy Masterson did for a living, but Jane had been able to live with it. Lucy's own attitude had helped. She was not remotely ashamed of what she did, and her attitude was contagious. "Listen, honey, the girls want money. The mags want the pix. The johns have got to jerk off on something. Don't you believe in *freedom*?"

And Jane had been just too busy to consider the wider implications of what was going on. There was so much to learn, so much to do: meter readings, adjusting the reflectors, getting the glasses of cold, sour Gallo for the hungover hairdressers, providing instant psychotherapy for the inventively neurotic models. Later they would all sit around in various stages of undress and talk and talk of their dreams and their schemes, and tell the horror stories of how they had been used and abused, of how they had been caught up in the lies and the exaggerations, the processed fantasies and near psychotic delusions, of how they had wallowed in the murky waters of the sea of pretension and promises, of petty politics and possible, passable passion, of balance sheets and bullshit.

Now, Lucy's sigh of contentment came right up from the depths. It was Sunday night, and life was good. But if it was ace Sunday, it had also been awesome Saturday, truly outrageous Friday, and totally fab Thursday. So near, yet so far, the cause of all the liquid joy sat next to her on the sofa. Jane Cummin.

This was what it was like to be in "passion," in "lust," in "desire." Somehow the feeling was a new one. She'd *wanted* it before—with this one and with that one—but this was more like hunger. It gnawed at her guts. Jane made everything exciting, each happening squirted full of life and fun and promise.

She turned toward Jane, stretching like a sleepy cat. "And

you look disgustingly beautiful this evening. There ought to be a law against people like you."

"Why thank you, ma'am. You sure know how to compliment a lady." Jane mimicked the southern accent and smiled easily.

Lucy was coming on strong and had been these last few wild days. It was nothing Jane couldn't handle. But it was one thing Billy Bingham had been right about. Where on earth was he? He had sunk without a trace, despite his earnest promises to return for her and his scary predictions of murder and mayhem and tinsel-town creepy-crawlies. Thank God she hadn't taken him at his word and blown her job and her bedroom for the uncertainty of the Marmont, waiting for a Godot who wouldn't show. She had been too busy, having too much fun to worry about him. Maybe he'd called the Marmont and lost interest when she hadn't checked in. Perhaps he wanted only to control her; maybe he was a bit of a flake beneath the soulful eyes, and the Teflon body, and the steely purpose. Still, Billy knew where he could find her. Right now Jane was young and beautiful and in L.A., and the merry-go-round was spinning as the music played. Nothing else mattered.

Lucy twisted on the sofa to look Jane over once more, feeling the delicious wonderful *pain* of it all. In California you got used to beauty—especially in her business. But around Jane it was difficult for her to breathe. The packaging was picture perfect, from the tight, hard, tender torso to the lickable lips and lovable legs, from the life-loving eyes to the spine-liquidizing skin. She had tried every trick in her telephone-directory-size book to seduce her, but to no avail. Jane had deflected the advances as if she had a star-wars defense system all around her heart.

Lucy laughed out loud, at her predicament, at the zipping excitement of the chase. She jumped up. "Come on, sweetheart, let's grab the Bug an' cruise around some. Maybe score some pizza, pick up some Valpolicella, rent a tape or two, and spend an evenin' in. I'm zapped from all these late nights, an' I gotta do sweet beaver for *Hustler* in the morning. Sound good?"

"Sounds good, boss woman."

Jane stood up. Her shoulders were bare. A faded denim bodice from Guess? cupped her breasts, and from it a snow-white bra peeped out, its shoulder straps contrasting seductively with the sun-washed skin. Her pencil denim skirt ended at the knees, and her thick white ankle socks were turned down over the soft brown leather of short cowboy boots.

"How do I look?"

"State of the tart."

Jane aimed the dropkick at Lucy's backside, the toe of her boot disappearing up the black leather miniskirt.

"Hey, baby, we made contact at last! Come again."

"Okay, Lucy. Pepperoni and Häagen-Dazs?"

"Yeah, and Bolla and booze. I feel like gettin' blitzed and zoned and fuckin' out of it tonight, honey. An' we'll get some real rotten movies. Real bad ones. An' some skins maybe— *Super Vixens* and *I Spit on Your Grave*. You never tried my rum punch, did you? Baby, we gonna *party* tonight."

Jane laughed her excitement. Another crazy evening in Xanadu.

And it would be a crazy evening.

A crazed evening.

A mad, sad evening in L.A.

EVAN KOESTLER SAT DOWN HEAVILY ON THE PAINT-SPATTERED director's chair and tried to take control of his chaotic senses. The paintings were everywhere. Stacked against the white walls, lying on the white-tiled floor, in untidy heaps in the corners of the huge room. Everywhere the light played upon them, caressing them, making the colors sing, rolling luxuriantly from the thick texture of the paint. Canvas to eye, eye to brain, brain to essence. The communication was direct, elemental in its marvelous simplicity, haunting in its fervent honesty. There was no way to categorize it. For once the concepts failed Evan Koestler. Usually he would have been able to slot it in somewhere—as his tongue would fly over the rich syllables, dripping erudition and long words that only the cognoscenti could understand. Postconceptualist, neo-this, retro-that, the influence of what's-his-name, the style of you-know-who—all that was irrelevant now. These paintings had never been painted before. Here was a singular vision of breathtaking originality. Never in his entire life had Evan Koestler stood so close to so much wonder. The tears of pleasure poured down his sunburned face.

"Surely not *that* bad, Evan."

Julie Bennett looked at him with an amused interest. Tears! God, that was a bit of an overreaction. He'd been smitten by Billy Bingham, but could it matter *this* much that the "artist" would have screwed up a five-year-old's paint-by-numbers kit?

"Silly of me. Silly of me," muttered Evan as he tried to regain his composure.

He couldn't believe his eyes. Billy's studio was brim full of genius. He walked to a pile of canvases, but still he couldn't bring himself to touch them.

"Bit of a contrast to my collection eh, Evan?" Julie was positively preening.

"Dear yes. Oh, dear me, yes," said Evan, the smile breaking through the tears of happiness. "What a contrast. What an extraordinary, fascinating contrast." It was true. The Bennett collection was good. Some might say it was very good. But it had been put together by a businessman working in tandem with a businesswoman. Together they had done the clever things, the fashionable things, the safe things, but there was no spark to ignite the whole, no concept to give meaning to the collection, and as such it was pedestrian, despite its occasionally flashy brilliance and its considerable pretension. Here, however, was the real thing. This was what the wild, deep eyes had seen. Utterly grand. Absolutely genuine. Born from sacrifice, built on pain.

"Now you begin to understand the problem with Billy Bingham, don't you, Evan?"

He knew she was mocking him. She was baiting him and it was deeply, meaningfully wonderful. Because she didn't begin to understand; she was standing in the middle of the incarnation of beauty, and she saw it not. He wanted to laugh, and to cry. But even at the most triumphant moment of his life, his wily brain did not drown in the floodtide of emotion.

"Yes. I see his problem. What a terrible burden it must be to have a problem like that." These paintings which were worth the world were locked up in her house. How could he get them from her without alerting her to their value?

"What will become of them?" said Evan with the innocence of the viper.

"I wish you would cart them away for me, but I suppose poor Billy might object," said Julie, letting out a sigh of contentment that masqueraded as resignation.

Evan again suppressed the mad desire to laugh.

"So, I imagine I'll just leave them here until the great artist comes to reclaim. He'll be back in a day or two," she continued.

Julie was playing with him now. Probably he still wanted Billy, despite the revelation that he was incapable even of painting the town. The Evans of this world would forget about the lack of talent when confronted by the lean, boyish body. Not that poor Evan was going to get a crack at that; the beauty of the situation was that he had dealt *himself* out of the equation. By his reaction to Billy's paintings—by actually crying at their ghastliness—he had provided the most potent ammunition for her. When Billy turned up in a day or so she would take the greatest pleasure in telling him that his dreadful "art" had actually reduced the great Evan Koestler to *tears*. Then, over the months, she would drip the poison on him every time he irritated her, and even when he didn't. It would be wonderful.

"Perhaps you will tell Billy that I was trying to get hold of him, and maybe give him my telephone number. I'd very much appreciate that. Tell him I . . . adore his paintings."

"Why of course, Evan. Of course I'll do just that."

Her smile of triumph said it all. The name of Evan Koestler would never pass her lips in anything like the context that Evan had just suggested. Instead there would be the stories of what he had said—the scorn he had heaped on the paintings, lies springing from the mind of the most successful novelist in America.

"Well, it's been the most wonderfully interesting day and I ought to think about getting back to Los Angeles. I think a plane would suit me better than the car if you don't mind. Perhaps I could call about the flights, and if your man could drop me off at the airport I'd be most grateful . . ."

"Well, Evan, I've thoroughly enjoyed it. And you must let me know when next you have something you think might interest me. You've seen the collection—so you know the kind of things I like."

At the airport Evan hadn't caught the plane. Instead he had taken a cab to the Racquet Club, making sure that the Bennett driver was long gone before he had ventured out to the taxi line.

Once there he had checked into one of the quieter suites, in the colony area away from the main clubhouse, and he had dialed room service and ordered a bottle of Louis Roederer's Cristal champagne, a plate of black olives, some smoked-salmon sandwiches thinly cut, brown bread with some sliced lemons—not limes. Then he had reached for the telephone directory and flicked through the pages until he had come to the listing for Checkmate Security systems. He had dialed the number, and soon had been talking to Steve Kaufer, the president of the firm. Then, at last, he had kicked off his shoes, turned up the air-conditioning, and lain down on the bed to stare at the grandeur of Mount Jacinto as he contemplated the almost impossible brilliance of his future.

FIFTEEN

FOR BILLY BINGHAM IT HAD BEEN A TERRIBLE FEW days. To be unable to work was bad enough. To be separated from the work was much worse. In his nightmares Julie Bennett stalked the house, a carving knife in one hand, a lighter in the other—and he would wake drenched in sweat as she slashed at his pictures and muttered her curses, and the flames licked at his past and his future.

He had driven the Maserati to Santa Monica and sold it eventually for cash. But it had taken time, precious time, as the dealers had insisted on checking that the car was not hot, was indeed his. All the time, at the back of his mind, fighting for pride of place with his artistic ambitions, had been the thoughts of Jane. Jane in danger, beautiful Jane waiting for him in the teeth of the dragon and yet unaware of her predicament. As soon as he could he would go to her, and he prayed that it was not already too late. First he had had to find a place to work and a safe place for the paintings, but until the car was sold he had no money for the advance rent. Eventually he had found a place, a ramshackle former shop on Market Street with a door that was thick and unobtrusive at the same time— solid and unpretentious enough to keep out the vandals and freaks.

So now there was only one thing left to do before he could keep the promise he had made to Jane. Once more to the scene of his humiliation. Once more to the insults and the bribes.

To get the paintings back he would have to see Julie Bennett once again.

JULIE BENNETT WAS READY FOR HIM, BUT SHE WAS STRANGELY nervous as she looked for the umpteenth time at her watch.

He had sounded cold on the telephone, cold and calm, not sorry. Unrepentant. He would be there this evening, for the paintings. He had found a place to live—never mind where —and if Julie would just let him pick up the canvases then he would be out of her life forever.

On the slubbed-silk sofa Julie Bennett flicked impatiently at the remote control and turned up the Vivaldi until it drowned out her thoughts. She drank deep on the dark beaker of Glenlivet. It was funny how her taste for malt whiskey had survived the early disaster that had seared her. Funny how this legacy from the cold and the damp could survive in the dancing heat and the shimmering colors of the low desert.

How best to deal with Billy? She would have to have him back of course. There was no question about that. And there was always the awful possibility that his insane pride would sabotage her desires, and the unthinkable possibility that his feelings for Jane would tip the balance against her.

Julie stood up as the intercom buzzed. "Yes, let him in. I'm expecting him," she said curtly.

He stood for a moment in the doorway, angry, distant, and seemingly reluctant to fight.

Julie got up, and as she did so the plans vanished. There had been a way to do this, but there wasn't anymore. The dirty jeans, the dirty T-shirt, the dirty sneakers clamped tight around the body that could bend her mind were responsible for that. There was only instinct left, and anger and frustration and all the accumulated hurt and pain of the years.

"Well, Billy Bingham—the prodigal returns," she had managed at last. "Welcome back," she added halfheartedly, immediately regretting it as too conciliatory.

"I'm here for the paintings, Julie. I've got a truck outside."

"Oh, of course, it's the *paintings*, isn't it, that you've come to see. How silly of me to forget. For one second there I thought you might just have come to see me. But obviously I have outlived my usefulness, which presumably means that somebody else is paying you to fuck."

"I don't want to fight, Julie. I just want to get the paintings and go."

Damn him to hell, he was really going to go through with it. She moved quickly to the big guns. "You know, for just one crazy minute I thought that it might be Evan Koestler who was getting your body."

She watched him carefully. The flush sprang up on his cheeks.

"How did you know about Evan Koestler?" The witch had had him followed. Could she ever be beaten? Would he ever be rid of her? He felt his resolution seep from him.

"Oh, little Evan called me up. He was very taken with you, you know. And when you walked out on him in some godforsaken club his pride was hurt. Do you know what he wanted to do? How's this for a perversion? He wanted to see your paintings."

Again she paused. It was going rather well. His face was white now, and so were his knuckles. All the things he cared about were juicy targets in the middle of her sights, and the guns were loaded.

Billy's voice was small. "You didn't let him see my paintings."

"Ah, but I did, Billy. I knew how *proud* you were of them. It was a marvelous opportunity to let a real expert express an opinion on them. I must admit I could never see the point of them, but as you were always saying, 'Who am I?' Well, we *all* know exactly who Even Koestler is, don't we, Billy darling?"

Billy felt faint. Evan Koestler, who walked with the Art Gods, who talked to them, had his being with them. Evan with the all-seeing eye, that even his enemies recognized as being the ultimate judge of beauty and importance. Evan had told him that he wanted to see his paintings, but Billy had recoiled from the enormity of what that could mean. In the face of Koestler's disapproval could he keep the faith alive, the faith in his genius that had survived the worst that Julie

Bennett could throw at him, that had outlived the world's lack of recognition? What would his life be without that faith? It was his belief in his art that had sustained him through the dark nights of the soul in the valley of the shadow, during all the long hours, days, and weeks of despair. Without his art he was an empty vessel, devoid of meaning in a cruel and capricious world. Without his art Julie Bennett would win and he would lose, and there would be no escape anymore from the awful truth of that. He would *be* the no-good, no-hope sponging bum that she always maintained he was, and there would be nothing left but to embrace her. There and then he would have to crawl across the floor and beg her forgiveness as she readied her mighty body for pleasure. It was all too awful to contemplate, but in seconds that could be what he'd have to do.

"Don't you want to know what Evan thought about your paintings, Billy?"

Billy opened his mouth to speak, but there was no point in words.

This could not be good news. Julie Bennett was enjoying herself and she didn't do that when the messages she brought were good messages. The writing was on the wall of her face, smirking on the corners of her feline features, so round and self-satisfied, so vicious in their cruelty. If Evan had liked the paintings, then Billy as an artist would be vindicated and Billy as a lowlife lover would vanish as if he had never been. So he said nothing as he waited for the sharp blade to descend and wipe away the only life he had ever wanted.

"Well, you know, at first Evan didn't say anything at all. He had to sit down, poor man. And do you know what he did then? I wouldn't have believed it unless I had seen it myself." She drew herself up, and her gargantuan breast filled like the chest of an opera singer.

Billy braced himself.

"He cried. He wept, Billy. So much ugliness. All that ugliness actually made him cry." She was triumphant, her voice rising in a glorying descant above the meaning of the words she uttered. They were a life sentence to hell and eternal damnation and they were filling her heart with a terrible joy.

There were tears in Billy's eyes now.

She saw them, and they encouraged her to continue. He was at bay. Later there would be time for a little rebuilding, but now it must be total destruction, the liquidation of his will to resist her.

"We talked about it, Evan and I. Frankly, he was shaken. It was the arrogance of the ugliness that had upset him so. The self-confidence that had allowed the 'dreadful repetitions'— those were his words. I'd never known he was so sensitive. You know, you always think of those big dealers as having checkbooks where their hearts should be. But no, your work really got to him. I thought I was going to have to give him a brandy to bring him round." And she laughed at that and looked at his stricken face, and then she had the awful nerve to try to dilute the pain.

"Of course, I told him he was overreacting, and that really it wasn't all that bad. You know what drama queens those closet gays can be. I said that maybe...after a few lessons..."

Billy looked at her. Was this his future? Was there any alternative now? She was prattling a sort of victory speech, he supposed.

"Come back to me, Billy. Who cares about little creeps like Koestler? You're safe here with me. We're so good together. We need each other. And you could even have some money of your own. How about that? A trust fund maybe, that you got the income on—with the capital in say five years...or perhaps ten. What about that? We could start it off at say a quarter of a million and then add to it if things worked out..."

Billy was hovering on the brink. He didn't know what he was going to say. Then the thought came to him, the thought that allowed him to live. It was called "Jane."

Jane, who this fiend had tried to destroy, who even at this moment might be in dreadful danger. Jane, to whom he had promised to return. Whom he had promised to protect. Into his mind swam the steamy memories of the touch of her body, the taste of her lips. Like a mantra he murmured her name to himself, and it strengthened him for his decision.

"Go straight to hell, where you belong, Julie Bennett."

DESPITE THE AIR-CONDITIONING, IT WAS STILL HOT IN THE BACK of the Checkmate Security van. Evan Koestler shifted uncomfortably in the back seat and looked at his watch once more. "That's three hours he's been in there, isn't it?"

"Yup. Must be close on three now." The burly security man, bent almost double in the space in which Evan sat upright, could hardly keep the boredom out of his voice.

Evan's mind was playing tricks on him. Floating on a sea of the champagne in the Racquet Club, he had thought his plan foolproof. When the telephone had rung in the palatial suite with the message the somebody answering the description of Billy Bingham had just driven through the gates of the Bennett compound in a U-Haul truck, his heart had leaped. The Hertz Cadillac had been waiting outside and—desert tourist that he was—he had burned his fingers on the sun-baked door handle, again on the metal ignition key, and his bottom on the leather of the driver's seat. In the womblike furnace, the heat amplified by the fiery blast from the air-conditioner he had just turned on, he had raced up the Racquet Club road, made the left on Palm Canyon, and the right on Las Palmas.

One thing at least he had got right. He had known that at some stage in the next day or two Billy would return for the paintings, for the art that he loved. So Evan had set up a twenty-four-hour watch. An unmarked van had loitered outside the gate of the Bennett estate in constant radio contact with the head office of Checkmate Security, who in turn were to telephone Evan the second they had anything to report. Part one of the plan had worked. On part two the jury was still out.

There had been two possibilities. The first was to intercept Billy before he entered the house to confront his former lover. The second was to wait until afterward. The problem with the first plan was that at that stage he wouldn't have the paintings.

The problem with the second was that he might never get the chance. It was possible that Billy would succumb to the lures that Evan knew Julie would float at him to persuade him to stay and that he would never reemerge in time.

Evan chewed on a manicured nail as he wondered if he had done the right thing by waiting, and he tried to imagine the course of the conversation a quarter of a mile up the hill. One thing was certain. Julie would not have told Billy Evan's real feelings about the paintings. She hadn't sensed them, and even if she had she would have kept quiet. It was no part of Julie Bennett's game to tell her lover that he was on the verge of becoming an art star. That was not at all what you wanted your gigolo to hear. Almost certainly she had used his name as a stick to beat Billy, telling him that the art guru was indifferent to his work at best, loathed it at worst. Billy would hardly be overjoyed to see him when and if he finally emerged from the lioness's lair.

"At two ten they went in, right?"

The security man didn't even bother to reply. He'd answered the question ten times already. It was nearly quarter past five.

In his mind Evan rehearsed the phrases he prayed he would have a chance to deliver. It would be a formal speech. The appreciator of great beauty humble at the feet of the Creator. There would be talk of privilege, and honor, and pride and of hope, of certainty of the brilliant future. The misconceptions would be rectified, and wrong would be made right.

Then he saw the truck—brightly painted, and with its infinitely precious cargo—waiting for the automatic gates of the Bennett estate to swing open and let it pass.

"HERE, SWEETHEART, YOU GRAB THE FOOD. I'LL DO THE drink."

There was a funny feeling at the back of Lucy's head. It was tickling in between her shoulder blades and roaming around the other places, too. She had been here before, but this was different; she still didn't know whether she'd do it, and even her indecision was deliciously exciting.

The raw materials were all there—the big pepperoni-and-mushroom from the pizzeria opposite the Fairfax High, a couple of bottles of Italian liquid headache, and a pint or two of chocolate-chip Häagen-Dazs ice cream from the 7 c. Market opposite Body Express. It was trash, crash food for a wipe-out evening.

"Christ, we're going to need intensive care if we do this lot. La Costa, at least." Jane laughed happily.

"Before we do *anything*, you gotta get to know my rum punch, darlin'. You just sit there an' in two seconds you're gonna be a cloud-nine tour guide. That pretty hair of yours goin' stand on *end*, babe. Believe me."

In the kitchen Lucy worked fast. Dark Mount Gay Barbados rum, white Myers Jamaican—equal measures—fresh orange juice, pineapple juice—half frozen from the ice box—a splash or two of Angostura, a slug of pink Grenadine. She paused. It was time. To do it, or not to do it. The little vial with its clear liquid was where it always was, tucked down deep in the bottle of all-but-indigestible yeast tablets that *nobody* used anymore. Lucy plucked it out and rolled it around in the palm of her hand, and still she hadn't a clue whether she would use it or not.

She took a swig of the browny pink drink and the rum raced for the lining of her empty stomach. It was like mainlining booze. The 10cc of concentrated barbiturate stared at her. So many of the others had unknowingly swallowed her knockout drops and loved the feeling as the body let go and the alcohol bonded with the sleeper to melt inhibitions and burn away responsibility. But Jane was real, not some burned-out Val from Van Nuys who did an upper when they played a song she didn't like on MTV, and a 'lude because the upper strung her out.

The silent debate roared on. The hell with it. There was only one way to find out, and the rum alone wasn't going to make the difference.

She thumbed the rust-colored rubber stopper from the glass vial, took a deep breath, and upended it into one of the drinks. Then she splashed in some extra Grenadine and a few more lumps of ice to disguise the bitter taste of the barb.

"Lucy's punch comin' right up, honey. You gotta drink it *fast*. While it's laughin' at you." She sashayed into the room.

Jane reached out for the drink. "Knock out drop, is it, Lucy?"

"Babe, you'll never know." She sank down on the sofa inches from her target, while Tom Brokaw rolled his locked jaw around the latest from South America.

Jane took a sip. "Wow, Lucy, that's *powerful*."

"Good for you, sweetheart. We gotta *sleep* tonight, ya know. This morning I damn near dropped off in the middle of a shoot."

Jane could almost feel the drink talking to her brain. The rabbit-food, Rob-Lowe-watching lunch at I Love Juicy hadn't really been enough to fill her stomach, and now the alcohol was racing into her bloodstream. What the hell, she thought. It's a quiet evening. I'll be in bed by nine. And it wouldn't matter if she got pissed with Lucy. Lucy was really sweet, in such a very short time such a very good friend. She felt safe with her.

She took another sip, a deeper one. It was good, but with rather a bitter aftertaste, too much of that stuff that her mother's really heavy-drinking friends liked to splash into their gin. She stretched out her long bejeaned legs and pushed back into the pillows. This was great. Really relaxing. Nothing to do. Mind in neutral. Everything on hold.

Lucy put it into words. "Well, here's to hardships. I guess it ain't all sushi and sunglasses in silly city—despite what they say."

She held up her glass to Jane and laughed at her with her eyes. Then she drank deep on the powerful drink—the one whose power came from the alcohol alone—and watched Jane start to go under.

The rum and the liquid barbiturate were melting her. They were undoing her, dismantling her defenses, opening up her secret gates.

Lucy could feel the beating of her heart. "What's the drink like, darling? Pretty neat? You have to use the best rum. Myers or Mount Gay. That's the secret." She was testing, probing to check what was going on in the mind of her delicious prey.

"S'wonderful, Lucy. Best in the world." Jane heard herself slur the words. Felt herself not mind. She took another sip. A big one. The world looked good now, a cozy, soft, furry place with blurred edges and a mellow, gentle "feel."

Lucy's hand snaked out and found the nape of Jane's neck. "It's so good to have you here with me. So very good."

Jane let the fingers rub gently at the base of her head. Somehow it was right that they should be there, both for the pleasure it gave her and for the pleasure it would be giving her friend. Poor Lucy. She had been rather cruel to her. And Lucy had been so very kind, having her to live here, giving her a job, personally supervising her crash course in L.A. living. Yes, she hadn't been good enough to Lucy. Dear, sweet Lucy. As big as all of southern California, and she *was* beautiful. Jane laughed out loud and turned on the sofa to watch her friend as she massaged the back of her neck. She sipped again at the drink. My, it had almost all gone. One needed a rum punch every evening of one's life.

"What's the joke, sweetheart?"

"I was thinking that you had a Venus flytrap mouth."

Now Lucy laughed. "Oh, I *do*, do I?" She moved playfully toward Jane, her hand firm on the young girl's neck. "And do you know that mouths like that go out and devour whatever they want to. Did you know that, beautiful Jane?"

Jane saw it coming, and somehow there was nothing in her that minded at all. She's going to kiss you. She's going to put those big lips on your lips and she's going to open her mouth, and you'll know what she tastes like, and she'll know what you taste like and it'll be strange but not at all nasty. In fact it'll be rather nice.

Her mind slowed down another fraction and she closed her eyes as Lucy moved toward her. In acquiescence. In surrender, in the very beginnings of lust.

For a second she could feel the heat of her, before the lips touched. There was warm, sweet-smelling breath and the sensation of darkness—of being enveloped by a powder-puff cloud that hovered over and around her. The arm was strong behind her head, stroking her no more but holding her, positioning her for the alien kiss.

But it wasn't the lips that touched her first. It was a tongue; wet and warm and soft as velvet it slid along her dry, closed lips, teasing them, moistening them, daring them to part, to open up and to take it in. At the corners of her mouth it paused, exploring, tantalizing. Then its confidence grew. Now it ruled her, patronized her, mocked her, and laughed at her, and she kept her eyes shut tight to avoid encroaching on the delicious illusion. Up it went on its self-confident tour of conquest to the base of her nose, darting daringly into first one nostril, then the other. Down then it went, to trace the contours of the chin, leaving the wet trail of passion, before slipping back to the lips that would surrender to it. Any moment now.

A wave seemed to break across Jane's mind, the foam-flecked surf crashing headlong into the breakwater of sleepiness. She felt so good, so secure, so wonderful, and the tongue must have its way and do whatever it must do. She wanted that, was quite clear about that one thing as the drowsy numbness stroked, not pained, her senses.

So she opened her eyes as she opened her mouth, and the lovelight bore into her as the love tongue dove into its rightful home. The two tongues were hungry, slipping and sliding in their desperate, liquid embrace, as their lips tried to bruise themselves on each other, struggling for a closer closeness. Her lover was drinking from her, searching for her moisture, to take it in and make it her own.

Jane felt the star burst down below. She could feel the glorious wetness between her legs as they splayed apart, and she loved the feeling, demanding it go on and on and on until whatever sweet conclusion nature, and this wild woman, would give to her.

The moan of passion was hard and guttural in the back of Lucy Masterson's throat. Like the cry of some wild animal it spoke to other senses besides hearing. It spoke with the heart and communed with the eyes, and all the time the bits and pieces of the jigsaw of love were fitting into place. Nostrils, wet skin, the lushness of lips, the ripeness of tongues.

And now there was the hand on her stomach, hot, determined, so very welcome. Up, with its ally, to take her breasts in their glorious grasp. Jane felt the fire raging in her, its flames licking at the sleepiness, pushing it back as it fought to keep the enemy at bay. Lucy's fingers had their victory now, and they marveled at the incredible ripeness of the tense nipples, the arrogant fullness, the throbbing helplessness, which cried out to be used for pleasure and submerged completely in the wild equation of lust.

"Lick them, Lucy. Put my tits in your mouth. Please. Do it now," Jane heard herself say.

Lucy knelt across her and beheld the half-open mouth, the restive tongue that licked at its own dryness, and the sleepy eyes with their dilated pupils, which called for her to do what she would do.

She lifted up the white T-shirt. Erect, unbelievably hard beneath her fingers, the panic-stricken nipples, murderous in their loveliness, called out to her. She bent her head and her mouth closed over the thing that it had longed for. The salt of the young girl's sweat was sharp and wonderful on her tongue, and inside her mouth at last, Jane's nipple bucked and reared, riding her teeth, luxuriating in the wetness, thrusting itself greedily into the moisture.

It was only the beginning.

Already Jane was ahead of her. The young girl was hooked on the helter-skelter ride of passion. Now she wanted it all, more than she had ever known that she could want. It would be a headlong descent into ecstasy, where nothing mattered but the final explosion, when the intellect was purged in the celebration of the senses and reason was prostrate before the mighty strength of desire.

Jane reached down and as she did so she lifted her bottom off the sofa, taking hold of the blue jeans on either side and thrusting them away from her as if they were on fire. She pushed down as Lucy made free with her breast, groaning her pleasure, until the part she wanted was free—the soft blond hairs glistening, the soaked pure white panties framing the pleasure center, the soft Levi's crumpled deliciously around the muscular thighs. Jane's right hand went to the place it had to be. She had to hold on to herself. Her finger slipped deep into her own heat, marveling at the thing that had happened to her as her mind fought on to ride the tiger of wild physical joy that ran between her legs.

Lucy could smell the scent of her now, the angry, greedy, demanding perfume. It beckoned her, overriding even the insistent demands of the sharp nipple that so loved her mouth.

Slipping down onto the floor Lucy knelt in reverence between the thrusting, grinding legs.

Jane watched her.

"Lick me, Lucy. Put your tongue inside me."

Lucy bent forward, her chin resting gently on the soaked cotton of Jane's panties, her chest on the crumpled bridge of the Levi's. For long seconds she waited at the gate, trying to hold it in her mind. Then, slowly, she lowered her head farther, her sigh rushing through parted teeth.

Jane watched her, and her hands reached out in gratitude to guide her home. One hand on either side of her lover's head, she held on tightly, as if to the rail of a roller coaster. Never before. This thing. But there was an innate knowledge of the ecstatic dream she would now dream as fantasy prepared for its meeting with the reality that would not destroy it.

She thrust herself upward to meet the mouth, and like a hibiscus flower at the first kiss of the early morning sun she felt herself open up to her lover.

But once again her mind was fading. She was going somewhere and she wasn't sure where it was, and there seemed to be no resisting this insistent feeling. Her body was suddenly heavy, not hers anymore, and the wonderful feelings that called to her from below were at once muffled and faint. She knew what was happening and that she wanted it, but she had forgotten why. The meaning seemed to be flying away. She felt her head fall away to the side, and she caught it before it fell and with a superhuman effort made it right itself, but her eyelids were leaden and kept wanting to close, and she was so tired. Yes, it was tiredness, an unnatural tiredness. The rum. It was rum, wasn't it? Or something else. Something else to make her sleep, but why? God! The tongue was in her now. Secure at last in her secret place, and she was going to sleep while the head of her lover buried itself in her wetness and enslaved her. She was going to go to sleep. Lucy had made her go to sleep.

"No, Lucy, please don't . . ."

Lucy felt her go.

On the tip of her delirious tongue she felt the muscles relax, the shudder of surrender as Jane lost the battle against the powerful barbiturate.

Lucy knelt over the sleeping beauty. She ran her hands over the hot, subservient flesh she owned and the forbidden delight coursed through her. Now Jane was hers. Nothing stood in her way. The girl she wanted was hers to enjoy at last.

Lucy stood up, her legs shaky. This was the moment of which she had dreamed and she knew exactly what she must do. It couldn't die in the momentless present. This deed must live on, into the future. It must be immortalized in the best and most efficient way possible. Then, if it were never to be repeated, at least it would have some reality, some existence . . . forever.

She walked quickly to the closet and opened the door. There it was, the strobe unit with the model's light. On the shelf were two or three Nikons—all loaded with Kodachrome, and one with a motor drive attached. She hauled the equipment into the room as her body sang and her mind burned with excitement. Luckily she didn't even have to think about the procedure as she plugged in the lighting, screwed the camera to the tripod, and attached the remote-control lead to the trigger of the motorized unit. She crouched briefly behind the lens and adjusted the screws, before focusing in on the target—the sweet place that already she had loved, that she would love again. She flicked the 85mm–135mm zoom to midrange and checked the exposure in the through-the-lens meter. The shutter speed was automatic with the strobe— 1/125 of a second, way fast enough to capture sudden movement without blurring, and the f/11 aperture would give good depth of field to make sure that the focus was sharp.

It was ready. Jane, arms flung out above her head, lay prostrate, half on, half off the sofa. Her magnificent breasts rose and fell with the even breathing of her deep, dead sleep. The jeans, the crumpled panties, the glistening heart of her sexuality said it all. She was in flagrante, caught abandoned in the middle of mad, wild lust, her eyes closed not in sleep but in ecstasy.

Or so it seemed. So it would seem.

The ice cream was in the refrigerator, where she had left it. The virgin carton of Häagen-Dazs chocolate chip ice cream, cold and delicious, thick and sticky. Lucy reached in for it. She took the big wooden spoon from the kitchen drawer and hurried back.

Then, slowly and deliberately, with reverence almost, she knelt down beside Jane.

The spoon swam down into the yielding Häagen-Dazs, and emerged full. Her eyes sparkling in the harsh light. Lucy Masterson moved toward her destination. She daubed on the food, blond on blond, sweet on sweet, smooth on smooth. Cold on hot. Firm on soft. Cream on dream.

And then it was time.

With her right hand Lucy Masterson squeezed the shutter release cord, and as the music of the motor drive began to play and the insistent flashing of the strobe light lit up the little room, Lucy bent down to consume the banquet of love.

SIXTEEN

THE DRILLS WERE DIGGING UP THE ROAD INSIDE
Jane's head. It was a crippling headache—the sort that made
all movement agony—but it was absolutely insignificant
compared to the anger and frustration coursing through her.
As she lay on the bed, bits and pieces of the jigsaw were
already fitting into place. There had been something in the
drink. Lucy Masterson had drugged her. She had been slipped
—what was the ridiculous old-fashioned term for it?—a
Mickey Finn.

Jane lay still, both to minimize the agony and to collect her
senses. She had been allowing Lucy to make love to her, and
she had even been enjoying it, loving it actually—but then the
river of desire had speeded up and the frightening, wonderful
ride had become something else as the bubbling stream had
approached the rapids. She had suddenly wanted it to stop, but
the tiredness, the paralysis, the creeping numbness of sleep
had taken away her control and captured her mind. And it was
only then, when it was way too late, that she had realized
what was happening to her.

Jane tried to sit up and the room swam in and out of focus
as the hammers pounded. She was lying half naked on the
bed, her jeans and panties wrecked and torn. There was a
soreness deep inside her at the bottom of her stomach and
everything seemed to be unaccountably wet and sticky. The
woman hadn't stopped when Jane had crashed out. She'd gone

on making love to her while she was unconscious, and from the awful feelings and the state of her clothes and upper legs, she knew she had been horribly abused. The sudden rush of fury collided with the pain.

Billy Bingham had been right. There had been danger all around her, and she, poor naïve fool, had refused to see it. Lucy Masterson, dear, funny, mad Lucy had been a devil in disguise—Lucy, whom Julie had said would be the best person to look after her. . . . Julie! Julie had been behind it all! First getting her thrown into prison, and now this! Damn them all!

She must get up and get out of this place. It wouldn't matter where. Anywhere would do.

With a superhuman effort Jane sat up once more and swung her legs over the side of the bed. Which was when she saw the photographs.

They were everywhere. A pile of them lay in an untidy heap on the foot of the bed. Some were pinned to the cork-board on the wall that Lucy used to write herself messages. Another pile nestled on the bedside table. A large lavender sheet of writing paper was propped against the lamp a couple of feet from Jane's sleep-filled eyes. The writing was in large capitals, the ink red.

WOW, THAT WAS FUN, SWEETHEART! LET'S GO FOR THE ACTION REPLAY. BACK LATER. LOVE, LUCY.

With shaking hands Jane reached for the photographs. There were so many of them, eight-by-twelve prints and the focus perfect, the lighting a dream. Their subject matter lit the fires of a disgusted rage in Jane's still half-awake mind.

She was invaded. She was used. She was open. The unspeakable things she appeared to be enjoying were recorded for posterity.

Jane's legs could hardly hold her as she struggled to get up from the bed. She felt weak, drained of energy, but already she was running on the fuel of her anger, which burned away the cobwebs in her brain. Her initial thought had been that this was the end, the end of her life, that nothing could withstand the dreadful shame; but those thoughts were now history. It was a watershed all right.

It was the end of the old Jane, but it would be the beginning of a new one. She had allowed all these things to happen to her. She had been manipulated and misused—she had been tricked and shamed but she herself was ultimately responsible. She had been trusting where she should have been suspicious and she had forgiven where she should have learned to hate. She had been the optimist in spite of the wise warnings, and she had suffered bitterly as a result. Well, experience was the name women gave to their mistakes. But she would learn from it and no one, nobody on this earth, would ever, *ever* be in a position to treat her like this again.

Later, much later there would be time for revenge. But now there was only one thought in her mind: escape.

She looked at her watch. Christ! Five P.M. She'd slept all night and most of the next day.

Where the hell could she go? She had hardly any money, and no friends. God, if she had just listened to Billy.

The thought pushed its way through the cotton candy in her head. Billy would help her—if she only knew where he was.

She stumbled across to the telephone, and her fingers worked the buttons. The Marmont hadn't a clue. No, there were no messages left for a Jane Cummin. There had been a reservation for a Jane Cummin a few days earlier but she had been a no-show. That left the desert. Had he gone back? It was worth a try, and if not there might be a forwarding address. The trick would be to bypass Julie. With an effort Jane plucked the phone number from the mess of memory.

The butler was on the line. What the hell was his name? Gonzales. Pedro. Something Mexican. Pete? She tried to sound full of authority. The growing fury helped.

"It's Jane, Julie's sister. No, I don't want to speak to Julie ...I..." Her mouth was numb. The words wouldn't come. She knew what she wanted to say but translation to speech was hard, and then the thought would slip away again.

"Is Mr. Bingham there?" That was it. "Where to?...What I mean...is where did he go to?...Yes, the address.... Thirty-three Market Street. You sure?"

Jane banged the receiver down. Thank God! At least now she had somewhere to go. In half an hour she would be safe. Her life could start all over again.

As she staggered across the room she managed to pull up the polluted jeans and panties. No time to change her clothes. She just had to get *out* of here. She sleepwalked through the wrecked living room, its accusing photographic gear still in place, the stained carpet, the pillows scattered about as if by some crazed burglar. She half fell, half walked through the front door and down the little staircase to the parking lot. In her mind there was nothing but the all-consuming redness, the fury, and the self-hatred at the failings that allowed her life to come to this. She had never thought of herself as either stupid or naïve, but now she saw clearly through the swirling mists that that was precisely what she had been—the innocent among the wickedness, the lamb ripe for the slaughter. Well, she would be a lamb no more. They would all have to take account of Jane Cummin from now on. The name change had started out merely as a bright idea—a tinsel-town ploy. Now it was something entirely different. It was a potent symbol of the new Jane—the one whom people would mess with only at their mortal peril.

She lurched drunkenly across the lot, her determination holding her together. There was the Bug. And Lucy left the keys in it, her little affectation. Lucy Masterson doesn't lock her car in L.A.; that was a big joke. Well, Lucy had better keep laughing while she could, because one fine day Jane was going to bury her for what she had done, in the same grave as her sister, side by side to rot forever.

She all but collapsed behind the steering wheel, turned the key, and to the accompaniment of the wails of a hundred horns and the screams of infuriated abuse, she headed out into the early evening traffic.

ON THE STRETCH OF SUNSET BOULEVARD FROM WEST HOLLY-wood to the sea, the cars of L.A. exercised the people they owned.

The character of the road was always changing. There were

bowel-churning chicanes in Holmby Hills, bladder-relaxing bends around UCLA, and tight turns around the edges of Topanga and the Santa Inez Lake. But Jane was blissfully unaware of it all. The Bug buzzed like an angry insect as it churned the miles, and all around the cars, those highly polished statements of their owner's financial position, recoiled from her in horror. On every side the horns howled and the stricken faces of the automobile worshipers twisted in rage as they hurled their unheard insults at the inept conductress of the Bug. Jane didn't bother to wonder why she didn't hit anything. The reason was simply that the others didn't want to be hit. They were doing her driving for her.

It wasn't easy to find Venice. It was less easy to find Market Street. But 33 was where it should be, between 31 and 35. The Volkswagen came to rest, like a drunk thrown out of a bar, half on, half off the pavement. The door of the building was open. Someone had pissed on the floor. The stairs were straight ahead. Jane forced her leaden feet to climb them.

Weakly, she called out, "Billy!"

And then, there he was, standing at the top of the stairs, looking down at her, with that extraordinary expression on his face.

"Jane!"

"Oh, Billy." She smiled—her face lopsided. "Oh, boy!" She sat down heavily on the stone of the stairs. She'd arrived at her oasis.

"Jane. What are you doing here? How did you find me here?" Billy sounded less than ecstatic to see her. He remained at the top of the stairs. "You never went to the Marmont." It sounded as if he wanted to put her in the wrong.

"No, I didn't go. I stayed with Lucy. I should have listened to you, Billy . . . but I didn't." She was tired. Why couldn't he walk down to her, pick her up in his strong arms, and put her to bed?

"Are you all right, Jane? You look awful." He walked down toward her. "What the hell's been happening to you?"

"Bad things, Billy. Like you said. Bad things." Again the wan smile, but talking was impossible. She didn't want to explain. She wanted only to be understood.

He knelt down beside her, and she could see the concern in his face now. But where had the longing gone? There had been so much of that in the intense eyes when he had promised her his life and his future and his home.

"You don't want me here, do you, Billy?"

"Of course I want you here. It's wonderful to see you." He tried, but he didn't succeed. There was a part of him that wanted it, but it was no longer the biggest part. The biggest part wanted something else—the future Evan had promised.

He saw that she knew.

"But I'm going away. To New York. I was just getting some things together. I'm catching a flight from LAX in a couple of hours. Hey, Jane, are you *on* something?"

He picked up her chin with his forefinger and her head lolled upward, her unfocused eyes wandering over his face. "Christ, Jane, I warned you about that. Damn it to hell, I warned you."

"Are you going to New York with Koestler, Billy?"

He nodded, and his eyes flicked down away from hers. "Listen, Jane. You can stay here. I won't be here, but you can stay and I can send you some money. . . ."

"For the drugs you think I'm on?"

He looked away. Dear God, this was all he needed. How could the world change so completely? The other night had been another galaxy, another time. Then, love and lust and this beautiful girl had mattered more than anything. That night he had wanted only a human life, an ordinary life of simple, straightforward things and of honest, predictable people—and Jane. But Fate had intervened and played one of its oldest and most popular party tricks. At the very moment when he had been on the verge of giving up his ambition, the devilish dealer had dealt him the perfect hand. Evan Koestler had sworn to make Billy the art star he had always longed to be. He had been on the verge of giving up, but then all the wild wishes had rushed back into the forefront of his mind, and Evan had massaged them, titillated them, stroked and played with them until there was only being and becoming, and being *seen* to be, *seen* to become. There was nothing Jane could ever give him that could compare with that.

And yet, she needed him. She didn't want to tell him about the disaster that had so clearly befallen her until he had shown her that he cared enough to hear it. And he didn't want to hear it, because he knew that he could no longer afford to care.

They spoke these difficult things in the long silence on the dirty stairs.

Jane dropped her head. She thought she had hit the low point, but it seemed there was further to go. Billy didn't want her. Lucy wanted to abuse her. Julie wanted to kill her.

She stood up and grabbed the iron banister to stop herself from falling. "Don't worry, Billy. I won't get in your way. I'm fed up to the teeth with getting in people's way, and I've had it with people getting in mine." She turned around.

"Jane, stay here. For God's sake. You can't go out like this. Use the apartment."

"Fuck the apartment. Fuck you," said Jane quietly as she stumbled down the stairs.

SHE WAS OUT IN THE NEON NIGHT NOW, CARVING HER WAY through the nervous city. It was funny how the colors merged. The headlights seemed to trail like vapor clouds and the red taillights made magic patterns on eyes that Jane could scarcely keep open. There was a purple haze around her brain and the angry red and merging magenta of the recently departed sun lit up the sky in sympathy with her mad anger.

All around her the cars darted and danced at her, their horns blaring as the inhabitants of the City of the Angels recorded their irritation at the ultimate crime—Jane's winding, weaving threat to the cars they loved as much as the sound of applause.

Jane was on the freeway—Santa Monica? San Diego? Ventura? It didn't matter. It was just good to be alone, to be away from where she had been, and to be going to wherever it was she seemed to be going.

The messages were coming in too slowly, or she was processing them too slowly. Whatever, it was a standard sort of an accident. The car stopping, the foot slow to respond, wheel wrenched over to the right as the brakes screamed. And then?

Nothing much really. No pain, just unbearable light and deafening noise and odd smells and people pricking at her and saying funny things like "Look at me" and "Can you move your legs?" Followed by absolutely nothing at all as the darkness swallowed her.

SEVENTEEN

THE PAN AMERICAN JET HAD ONLY JUST TAKEN OFF from LAX on the five-hour flight for Kennedy, but Billy Bingham knew that he had already arrived.

It helped that he was traveling first class. Julie had never taken him on author tours and this was his first experience of how the other fifteenth traveled: champagne on the tarmac, the envious eyes of the coach-class passengers, self-consciously avoiding his as they filed through the spacious first-class cabin with its piles of newly minted glossy magazines and its noticeably more attractive flight attendants, on their way to the packed oblivion of the coach-class cattle truck.

But it was much more than that. It was Evan Koestler, sitting beside him and radiating self-confidence, bonhomie, and lust in an extraordinarily exhilarating mixture. Oddly it was Evan's lust that was the most potent ingredient of all, and it wasn't just lust for Billy's body. Rather it was lust for his future—lust for the incredible wealth that he knew his discovery would bring him, lust above all for the accolades that would be heaped on the man who had seen the greatness that nobody else had seen. Billy knew all about Evan's lusts, because Evan had told him, in the greatest possible detail. And Billy had had no problem at all believing him. Evan Koestler *was* the art world, and quintessentially the New York art world, the place Billy knew he had to *be* to succeed.

Billy sipped at the champagne. He didn't really like it, but it was a sign of something, a potent symbol that he was on his way at last. He could even tell that it wasn't very good, which somehow made it even better. It lacked the crisp dryness of the stuff he was used to drinking. It was too acid to compare favorably with the vintage Krug he would drink before lunch at Julie's. Maybe he should send it back. Billy Bingham, the art titan, was now a man of taste, no more the redneck biker in the paint-spattered jeans, no more the gigolo bending down to service a cat woman in a shower of abuse and humiliation. Eat your heart out, Julie Bennett; it's your turn now.

He laughed out loud at the thought. Julie Bennett. How near he had been to believing her incredible lies. He had been milliseconds away from wrecking his life, and his mind still boggled at the inventiveness of her evil. Koestler had deliberately misled her about his opinions on the paintings, but she had elaborated, twisting his words, until truth had lain bleeding on the floor. She wanted him destroyed, if not by her then by the poverty and anonymity that would have corroded his life. But now he stood poised on the brink of a glorious future. This little man whose reputation was so great had promised him the world, and Billy believed him because he had always believed in himself. There were many facets to the glittering diamond of his suddenly brilliant future and one of them was the sweet revenge he would now be able to take on the woman who had tormented him. On every rung of the ladder to the stars, he would bad-mouth her. In the art magazines, in the newspaper profiles, on television, and in every dusty corner of the lowliest of the media, he would mock her lack of taste.

Evan looked over at him. "May I share the joke?"

"I was just thinking of Julie."

Evan laughed too. "We outmaneuvered her. I don't think she'll forget that in a hurry."

"She'll never be allowed to. Not while I'm alive."

Evan watched him. This young man's iron determination was the essential element in the chemistry, more important even than the talent. Others were sidetracked. They wanted, but they wanted other things as well—to be loved, to be rich, to be happy. The true genius wanted nothing so mundane. What was money or contentedness, or the distracting presence of friends and loved ones compared to art? It was a question of focus and of priorities, of fundamental disregard for the moments of doubt and fear that derailed lesser mortals. Billy Bingham would achieve greatness because he had thrust it upon himself. Evan Koestler knew he was just a fixer, an expediter who had speeded the inevitable process of the rise of Billy Bingham.

He saw the cloud pass across Billy's sunburned face.

"It really is important to be in New York, isn't it?" Billy asked.

"Yes, it's vital. New York is where it's at. In art L.A.'s really just a backwater. They think actors are artists, and singers, too. There's no reality there, and art can't exist on fantasy alone. It starves. Or it gets all bleached out by the sun and becomes anemic and insipid. God knows how you've managed to avoid all that, but you have."

"Oh, I don't know that I go for all that crap," Billy said, shifting uncomfortably in his seat. "You don't have to suffer to paint. You don't have to be cold and uncomfortable and poor. It's an affectation. All that Neo-Expressionistic rubbish in New York is just fashion. It's a self-perpetuating thing. It works the other way around. Art just *is*, and nobody knows why. I couldn't have made all those paintings hanging around Venice. I couldn't afford food, or paint, or anything."

Evan smiled, but it was an interested smile. Anything a genius like Billy said was interesting. But he did know more than Billy about the selling of art and the invention of artists, and that meant New York and not L.A. New York was where the press was—the vitally important *Artforum*, *Art in America*, and *Arts* magazines. It was where the collectors were, and the place to which they came from the South, from Europe, from Latin America. It was the home of the auction houses and the densely packed Madison Avenue galleries such as his own. New York knew about art, and more important it *cared* about art. In L.A. art was nothing much more than a complicated method of keeping the score.

"You may be right, Billy. But we have to plan what to do. That's what's really important now. We know what you have made, but we have to show other people what you've done, and in a way that creates maximum impact. We'll have a huge show, of course, but before it we have to build the excitement, and I think I know how to do that. First I place two or three of your paintings with the opinion makers, with Brooke Astor, with C.Z. Whitmore—maybe the Saatchis, and with one of the hot museums, like the Whitney. Then we let them talk. The world can't wait for the show and it sells out. But we have a whole lot of paintings in reserve. In the back room, and we hold them tightly as the price roars up and demand outstrips supply..."

There was a beatific expression on Evan Koestler's face. It would happen, because the paintings were spectacular. The public could not be fooled, but if you had the product it could be milked.

Billy's spirits soared. Then, like a bird caught dead in the shotgun blast, his soaring fantasy crashed to the ground.

Jane.

He had had to choose, and art had won while she had lost.

In those proud eyes he had seen that there was no possibility of having it all.

Jane would not share him. Neither would Evan Koestler. It had not been spelled out, but Billy knew. With lesser people, it might have been possible but not with the A team; and both Jane and Evan, in their different ways, were quite definitely that. And so was he. So he had made the impossible choice on the stairs while she had watched him. To gain his world he was abandoning her to hers, the slippery slope of L.A. lowlife on the brink of which she already hovered. He wasn't proud of what he'd done, but he'd done it because there was no alternative. He had to leave. He'd had to cut out the love and the lust and the respect and the wanting. In the flight to success there was no place for extra weight.

Billy Bingham scowled at his champagne. It wasn't easy to be a star.

JULIE BENNETT HAD ENJOYED THE DRIVE TO LOS ANGELES. Usually she flipped into LAX in the Lear and had a limo meet her there, but today she'd had the chauffeur take her in the

Rolls. There had been so much to think about, and during the two-hour trip her mind had picked over the facts as if they were the skeleton of a fish.

In her lap Orlando made all the right noises as her fingers explored his fur. She could hear the ticking of the famed Roller clock, the purring of the marmalade cat, and the whirring of her own brain.

It had seemed like a good idea to check in with Lucy Masterson the evening before, and it had turned out to be a brilliant one. "Lucy Masterson? Julie Bennett. Hello, luv. How are things going? Did you manage to meet up with my friend Jane Cummin?"

"Wow! Julie Bennett, you sure are a fairy godmother. Did we meet up? Hey, baby, we met, okay. Collided. My head's still spinnin', honey."

"Did you get her to model for you? I know how persuasive you are, you wicked woman." Julie laughed like a partner in crime.

"Yeah. In the end, but maybe it wasn't such a hot idea, 'cause she blew the scene. She took my car and she split. You know where she is? I got no bead, an' I'd really like to see her again. I mean *really*."

"What do you mean? She did some pictures for you? Have they been published? Are they going to be?" Julie had hardly been able to control her excitement. How the *hell* had she gotten Jane to pose? What else had she gotten her to do? Drugs? Tricks? Johns? Chicks?

"Yeah, I was a bit naughty, honey. She was like, movin' slow, so I laid some downer on her and then got clever with the motor drive. Guess she flipped out. No note. Nothing. There was some kid called Billy something sniffing around, a friend of yours. You know about that? Maybe she split with him. Whatever. I for sure'd like to dance with that one again. I mean she really hit the spot with me."

"Goodness me, Lucy. Sounds pretty heavy. Pretty wild." Julie enjoyed mimicking Lucy's style. "Bit like one of my books. You got the photographs?"

"Sure. You wanna see them? You hot for her or somethin'? Didn't know it was your bag, sweetheart. Thought you liked those skinny boys." She had giggled helplessly down the telephone.

Julie had joined in. "So she's disappeared completely."

"Yeah, and she took my wheels. But it was worth it."

"Lucy, listen, it would be wonderful to meet up with you again. It's ages since we met. Which book was it? The Melrose one? *Hard Rock, L.A.*? You know, I've been meaning to give you a little something for all your help. I know it's ages ago, but it's been tucked away at the back of my mind. Any chance of your lunching with me tomorrow? I'm going to be in town, and we could dish the dirt at the Ivy or Le Dôme. Somewhere like that."

"Sounds like fun. Yeah. I'm free tomorrow."

"Where shall I pick you up?"

"You mobile? You could find my studio."

It had been a good conversation. The L.A. outskirts flashed by. Now it was Melrose.

"Oh, dear, Orlando. I think we've struck gold, you know. Aren't we lucky people? How much do you think she'll take for the feelthy pictures, sweetheart? A nice, big butch photographer with bills to pay and girls to buy? Twenty thousand? More? Do you really think so, darling? I'm not sure you're right. But it doesn't matter because Mummy is a wise virgin. She's brought a hundred big ones. Just in case. Yes, darling, you can never be sure, can you? You're quite right."

But would Lucy sell? Morals were a funny thing; they were always turning up when and where you least expected them.

They had arrived. The bottom door said STUDIO. The apartment was obviously at the top of the stairs.

The chauffeur was dispatched inside the studio. He came out immediately with what looked to Julie like a punk, with bits of unnatural green in its hair. She pushed the button to lower the window.

"Miss Bennett, Lucy is expecting you. She said could you wait upstairs. She had to go and look at some prints across town. She won't be long. You can go straight up. The door's not locked," said the Lucy Masterson assistant.

Julie paced around the tiny apartment. God, how people lived. You couldn't swing a cat in this place. Her eyes wandered over the couch. Was that where it had happened? The thing she had so brilliantly planned? Her heart began a little war dance as the idea occurred to her.

This was Lucy's apartment. The pictures would be here. They were "personal." They wouldn't be filed away in the studio downstairs. Why should Julie buy what she could steal? She'd save the money, and no way could Lucy complain that somebody had stolen her porno pictures. That was not at all the sort of thing that West Hollywood cops would get upset about. With the pictures of Jane in flagrante in her pocket, Julie would possess her ultimate weapon. They could be used anywhere, anytime, to produce the maximum in pain and humiliation.

She worked fast. The bedroom was most likely.

It was so unbelievably simple. The bedside table. The top drawer. Underneath a copy of last year's *L.A. Style*.

For a second or two Julie feasted on them, but the adrenaline hurried her along. Christ, they were heavy! Was that ice cream? What a way to blow a diet. They were very clever. If Jane had been unconscious she sure didn't look it, which was all that mattered.

Thank God she had brought her Banana Republic tote bag. She shoveled the photographs inside.

It was only a minute or two before the steps on the stairs said Lucy had arrived. She blew in like the wind on a Chicago street—fresh and invigorating, a rush of life. "Hi, sweetheart. Long time. Wanna drink or shall we get one at the restaurant?"

"Let's get one there. You know how they just love to give your table away if you're a second late in this town."

"*Your* table? Forget it!"

Of course, nobody was in the business of giving away Julie Bennett's table.

The patio at the Ivy was pretty as usual. It was funny how the restaurant fashion changed over the years. The Ivy was almost as old as Los Angeles; it had been there at *least* a year or two. Now, suddenly, it was "hot" again. For Julie, who hated the town and everything it stood for, it was important nonetheless to keep her novelist's finger on the fickle pulse of fashion, so she played with her mind-numbing Jack Daniels mint julep and leaned back to enjoy the show.

Hot/cool Bruce Willis with cool/hot Kim Basinger and some studio people. Belinda Carlisle, divine-looking, speedy-living ex-Go Go, lunching with Jimmy Iovine. Cooking a record deal? Tina Turner and Norma Moriceau, brilliant costume designer for the *Mad Max* and *Crocodile Dundee* movies. Another postatomic epic for the sexiest woman in the world?

The Ivy possessed the enormous advantage of being open for lunch and in the evening it was much less frenetic than Spago, with less of the supercharged high-energy social intercourse of Morton's or the smug "we-found-it-first" elitism of membership-tight Helena's. The Ivy was quiet, very pretty, serving excellent Cajun-oriented food. It was for those trendies who were not prepared to forsake their appetites in the cause of being seen in the "right" place. There were big portions of macho mesquite-grilled things like ribs and Louisiana shrimp and redfish, mouth-watering fodder for the Marlboro man, and saliva-shifting puddings, or what Americans preferred to call desserts. The chocolate truffle tort, that mighty enemy of thinness, singlehandedly kept the diet-book department at the Beverly Wilshire Brentano's in hustling, hassling business.

Beneath the table, resting snugly against her ankle, was the bag, with its strange bedfellows nestling anxiously together, one hundred thousand crisp dollars, which would not be needed, beside a few dozen glossy celluloids, which would be.

Lucy Masterson smiled across the table. The Cajun martini—made with potato vodka and spiced with red and green hot peppers—had done nothing to take the shine off her. She had dressed "up," whether for the Ivy or for Julie it was difficult to say. She wore a figure-hugging Azzedine Alaïa pencil skirt in black gabardine, slit up to the thigh, with a green leather wide-shouldered jacket by the same designer, and Manolo Blahnik high-heeled shoes.

Julie smiled back. "So you liked my Jane."

"Yeah, she was a lot of fun. *Is* a lotta fun. Where do you think she split to?"

"Well, Billy Bingham moved out of my place. Maybe they're shacked up together somewhere. One thing's certain: Bingham hasn't got a pot to piss in, or the window to throw it out of. And he'd have to find a blind man to buy one of his paintings."

Julie couldn't keep the bitterness out of her voice.

"Looks like we've both been loved and left." Lucy made it sound like that was a fun thing to be.

They ordered: tomato, Maui onion, and basil salad in the house vinaigrette; baked red peppers stuffed with risotto and chili; New York strip steaks—seared on the outside; rare within—basted in the Ivy's special marinade; and Jordan, the superb Napa Valley red at thirty-five bucks a bottle.

What Julie wanted was information, not commiseration. The really important objective had already been achieved. "You still doing a lot of work for *Playboy*?" That was the best sort of L.A. question—the kind you already knew the answer to. In this town, exaggeration was just about the only art form there was, and it was such fun to watch people telling lies.

"No, I really got tired of *Playboy*."

Lucy looked down. Fell out with Hef. Blew it with Marilyn. Screwed up with Carrie Leigh. Broke the hallowed look-but-don't-touch-unless-I-tell-you rule at the Holmby Hills fun palace. Since then it had been down, down, down for sleazy Lucy, which was why she had been selected for the task that she had so perfectly performed.

"Well, good for you. New frontiers. New anything, for that matter. The trouble with this town is that it thinks it is open to new ideas, but it's all fantasy. People are terrified of losing everything, so nobody dares to take a risk. This place has the most conservative liberals in the world."

Lucy laughed deferentially. What was the scribbler gabbling on about? Christ, did she have some sort of leopard complex—imagining herself reincarnated from one in a former life, perhaps? Leopard-skin armlets, a sort of leopard-skin jerkin out of which the earth-shattering tits poked like a reasonably-difficult-to-climb mountain range, and that great

mane of lionlike hair. She looked like a rug in a Dallas designer's *Out of Africa* creation, or possibly a shop-worn Thun-
dercat in a Toys 'R Us sale. Ugh, thought Lucy. I'd rather go
down on a broken bottle.

Julie sipped reflectively on her wine. There was something
she needed to know. "Lucy. Those pictures you took of Jane.
What are you going to do with them?"

"What d'ya mean, 'do with them'?"

"Well, would you publish them?"

"Heck no. They're personal."

"Or sell them?"

"No way. You offerin' or something?" Lucy's eyes were
twinkling, intrigued. Was Julie Bennett a closet dyke?

"No, but what would you do if somebody offered you several thousand dollars, or even more. I'm fascinated by motivation. It's a perversion of mine. What would you really do?"

Lucy thought for a second or two. "Well, I can always use
more bread, but I wouldn't do a thing like that. Not to Jane.
She was kinda special. Is kinda special. Don't know why I
talk of her as if she's dead." She laughed nervously.

Julie laughed too. She was inclined to think Lucy was telling the truth. Stealing them would have been the only way to
get the photographs. It was her lucky day, Jane's unlucky one.
Oh, yes, and Lucy was right: Jane might not be dead yet, but
when Julie had finished with her she would wish that she
were.

"Now, Lucy, what are we going to have for pudding? How
about some ice cream? You look like the sort of person who'd
be fond of that."

"WELL, HOW ARE YOU FEELING, BEAUTIFUL MYSTERY LADY?"

Jane's eyes weren't open but the voice was warm, safe,
deep, reassuring, if anything could be reassuring in this miserable city. She tried to focus and his face swam in toward her.

"I'm not sure. Pretty rotten, I suppose."

He was about forty, and his eyes were sort of sad, but he
was beautiful. Yes, that was really the right word. He had a
kind of saintlike beauty, like a stained-glass window, radiating

goodness, just the way a doctor should look. And because this was L.A. and because she knew what she now knew about people and the things they wanted, that probably meant that he was a child-molesting necrophiliac, or worse.

"I'm just going to peer into the back of your eyes if you don't mind. Try to look straight up and focus on some part of the ceiling."

Now there was the smell of him as his face approached, right up against her, his chest brushing hers as he leaned over the bed.

"That's fine. That's just fine."

His warm breath was sweet as it fanned her cheek, and there was the vaguest scent of something pleasantly antiseptic to go with his white coat, open-necked blue shirt, and casual stethoscope.

"You know, you've just survived an accident that would have killed or maimed ninety-nine percent of the people who went through it, and you're hardly touched? No damage anywhere except for an egg-size bump on the head and maybe just a bit of concussion. If you believe in God, it's a miracle. That's what I'm calling it."

"Was anyone else hurt?"

"No. Just your car. It was totaled."

He reached for her pulse. His fingers were firm and confident. Jane checked herself. Don't trust anyone. The second he found she hadn't got Blue Cross she'd be on the street, *after* he'd done the gynecological exam—"just in case."

"I can't remember much about what happened."

"That's not unusual. A bang on the head like that can wipe out the short-term memory. You'd taken some sleepers, and perhaps a whole load of booze. Were you running from something?"

His hand was still on her wrist. It was not so much a tingling sensation, but a heightened awareness that he was touching her, which was somehow more important than the things he was saying.

Silence was Jane's answer. People could use the things they knew.

"Don't feel like talking?"

"I like to know whom I'm talking to."

Robert Foley laughed. "God, you're right. I'm sorry. You don't know who the hell I am, or where you are, do you? Well, my name's Robert Foley and I'm an M.D. This is my clinic. It's in the Watts area of L.A., if you know where that is. Central, I guess. It's not the Cedars but we get the job done. You were cruising down the Harbor Freeway when you came unstuck."

"I've heard of Watts."

"But never visited until now?" He laughed again, a little raspy, as if he weren't very used to laughing, but had tried because he wanted her to feel good.

With what seemed like an effort he drew his hand away from Jane's. "Don't worry. It's not important. You're safe and you're in one piece. One great big beautiful piece. That's all that matters. Can I know who you are?"

Jane managed a weak laugh. That was the second time he had called her beautiful. But it didn't sound smarmy and smooth like so many L.A. compliments.

"Yes, of course. I'm Jane Cummin. Can't remember my rank and serial number."

"Oh, don't worry. Vee haf vays of making you talk. Truth serum. The rack. Red-hot pokers. Seriously, though—anyone we should contact who might be worried about you?"

"Seriously, though. No." Jane had picked up on the fact that his cool question wasn't *quite* as cool as it ought to have sounded in a world where doctors didn't call their patients "beautiful," so her tone mocked him, but she was far from being cross.

"Well, I guess after you've had a few hours sleep you'll be well enough to leave, though I promised the L.A.P.D. that I'd let them know where you're going to be. I'm afraid you're going to need a good lawyer. I don't think traffic school's going to cut this one."

"Actually, I don't live anywhere at the moment. Sort of in between, you might say. 'No fixed address' is the expression in England."

"But you have somewhere to go, haven't you?"

"Not really."

And of course there was nothing remotely funny about that, but somehow both Robert Foley and Jane Cummin agreed that there was. The tentative mutual laughter said so.

So the mystery lady had nowhere to go. In Watts, homelessness was a perennial worry—poverty, hunger, helplessness. But why on earth did Robert Foley feel that it was the best piece of news he'd heard in months?

PART FOUR

LIFE AND DEATH IN BEVERLY HILLS

"Is there life after success?" asked Mandy cunningly, across the prestigious table in front of the palm fronds at Morton's.

"I've got a feeling you're never going to find out," said Petra.

Julie Bennett, *Life and Death in Beverly Hills*

EIGHTEEN

THE ORANGE CLOUD CLUNG TO THE VALLEY LIKE A hungry pup at a bitch's teat. It sucked at the burning earth and swallowed up the air so that there was none left to breathe. The one-hundred-degree temperature sapped the will, emptying out all purpose and meaning and leaving nothing but the determination to endure. It was summer in the San Fernando, on the wrong side of the freeway, in one of the little boxes where the Valley people lived.

Robert Foley loved it here, in the faceless motorscape of America. It was Los Angeles, too, but it was where Los Angeles merged with the rest of the nation. Here Moon Unit Zappa clones roamed the shopping malls in a gas-pump paradise of fast food and do-it-yourself car washes, of pet paradises and neon liquor marts, of faded jeans and jaded dreams. Only the heat made the Valley different—it was mother and father of the smog, grandparent of the stonewashed minds and the browned-down bodies. Far from the street depression of Watts and mercifully remote from the facile fertility of Beverly Hills, it was an unrepentantly suburban place where plumbers and manicurists ruled and where a man could strive for the anonymity that he craved in the forlorn effort to escape his spiritual demons.

Dr. Robert Foley sometimes wondered if, in making him, God had been joking. Life was a paradox—everyone knew that—but his was mystery of such extraordinary complexity that he had all but given up trying to solve it. The driving force was guilt, of course. Guilt made him get up in the morning, drove him remorselessly through the day, and plucked at him cruelly when he tried to sleep. He had chosen to spend his waking hours among the vomit and bacteria of Watts, the drug addicts and the drunks, the TB and the cancer, the venereal disease and the vitamin deficiencies. All he ever wanted to do was to serve humanity. To put things right and to be God's servant on an imperfect earth. Intellectually he knew it was a worthy ambition and that, in attempting to make it real, he should reap the rewards of his selflessness. But here was the paradox. Doing good didn't make him feel good, and not doing good made him feel worse. Somehow all this was God's fault, and with God Robert Foley had a love/hate relationship.

When he looked at himself in the mirror, which was not often, Robert Foley, M.D., saw no signs of the psychological struggle. At forty-five he looked good, like a football player who had kept in shape in retirement—lean, rangy, the flecks of gray hair looking as if they had been put there by a highlight artist rather than by time. And, of course, he felt guilty about looking so good, so his clothes in compensation were always a bit of a mess, and he tended to block out women, especially the ones—and there were very many—who came on to him. His house was monastic, his tastes ascetic, and his pleasures all but nonexistent. All of which made him, in this particular town, a very unusual person indeed.

But now a dream had wafted into his clinic. A depth charge had exploded without warning in the stagnant pool where his emotions lived and Robert Foley had been rearranged.

In the kitchen the ceiling fan twisted listlessly and the ancient refrigerator groaned with effort. Usually things like that didn't faze Robert Foley. Half-melted ice, milk going sour, prickly heat—what were they in the scheme of things, when dark forces roamed the earth and the horsemen dealt out their death and disease, their famine and their wars?

He peered out through the tattered screen to the yard. She was there, standing by the pool, topless. Robert Foley's guilt collided with desire.

He called out to her. "I'm afraid the beer isn't very cold."

"Couldn't matter less as long as it's wet." She turned toward him, dripping with sweat. Across the shimmering air the breasts danced into his brain, warping his mind and churning up his body. This desire was so different. So real. So threateningly tangible. The bleeding crowd was always there, reassuring in its remoteness. You could care for it, love it even, at arm's length—hidden behind the cloak of professionalism, wearing the doctor's mask. But here, now there was the want that was called lust. The extraordinary, unavoidable emotion that had lived in the woodshed of Robert Foley's psyche for so very long. His life was supposed to be about God—about all the skirmishes and mini-wars as he sought to find the meaning that had always remained just out of reach. But now the idle luxury of philosophical doubt and abstract love had made it to the back burner. In front of his eyes was Jane Cummin. Jane Cummin. Jane Cummin. Robert Foley repeated the words silently like a response in church. He had touched this body. His hands had played over it as he had checked for the injuries that mercifully had not been there: the rib cage; the soft, yielding abdomen; the pelvic bones all in one beautiful piece around the perfect blond triangle of love; long limbs, thankfully intact; the pupils—big, round, and closing symmetrically as his flashlight shone on them; the neat, infinitely alluring toes turning down gratifyingly as he had run his nail along the sole of her foot. And it was called Jane Cummin, this beauty of the night who had arrived in his world like a message from the God who wouldn't leave him alone.

"Robert, aren't you going to come out here and take some sun? It *is* your day off. You ought to go through the motions of *trying* to relax." There was laughter in Jane's voice mixed with the truth and the concern.

Who the *hell* was she? She had started out a mystery and she had remained one. Robert Foley was not an inquisitive man, but even the remotest hints that it would be nice to know a bit about her had been met with a stone wall of silence. Some things seemed obvious. That she had been let down, badly hurt by somebody, and that to protect herself she had acquired a jaundiced view of the world. Well, he had been able to sympathize with that. "You can stay with me," he had

said. "Hide with me from the cruel world," had been the implication. In the valley beyond the Ventura Freeway where
"nobody" lived except maybe the gardeners, the pool men,
and the people who made broken things work. Which was, of
course, what he did—make broken people work.

"I'm coming right out, Jane—what's the air like out there?
It doesn't *look* too good."

"It's okay—marginally 'healthful.'" *Healthful* was a word
the English didn't have in their dictionaries. In L.A. it had
almost religious connotations.

The sun lanced into his shoulders as he left the relative cool
of the kitchen and walked outside, but he was hardly aware of
the arrogant heat. He didn't know exactly what he was feeling. Certainly he felt desire, and confusion—but why irritation? That was the most puzzling of all. It was true he had a
reputation for running on a short fuse. His patients didn't see
it, but fools did, and poseurs and hypocrites, and selfish people and those who didn't care about the people who *needed*
them to care. People who stood in his way would be hit by Dr.
Foley's anger right between the eyes as they tried to deflect
him from his single-minded purpose, the helping of those who
were unable to help themselves. But Jane wasn't in any of
those categories. She was a wonderful, caring dream girl with
a mystical charm, and he wondered if he was beginning to
love her. Was that the thing that irritated him?

In the business of love Robert Foley was a novice. Wise in
the ways of the world, he had allowed no time at all for TV
love, paperback love, celluloid love, or for the genuine article. And perhaps that was the thing that was frustrating and
irritating him—that he felt like a child in the California game
of hearts in which so many of the players were experts.

Robert Foley thrust the beer at her impatiently as he tried to
control his eyes.

Jane watched him. She could see the confusion, but she
didn't understand it, and there was a part of her that didn't
want to. This man was making her feel all the things she had
promised herself not to feel. In the few days since she had
moved into his house, she had become intrigued by his
haunted reticence, his prickly exterior, and by the mysteries

that lurked and lingered in the fascinating undergrowth of his mind. For some reason she knew she threatened him. But she could only discover him by opening up herself. And that she was far from ready to do. The hurt was still too real.

"You don't really belong here, do you, Robert Foley? I mean here, in L.A."

He flopped down on the sun bed and smiled warily at her question. Did anyone *belong* here, on the edge of the world, on the fault line—in the plastic paradise of wheels and pills and desperate dreams? "A doctor belongs where the pathology is, I guess." He knew that wasn't what she meant, but he wanted to confuse her, as she had confused him.

"But L.A.—even here in the Valley—it's . . ." She struggled to find words that wouldn't sound odd, then gave up. A honey-brown arm swept out to encompass the impossibility of it all—the jogging, the eating, the tanning, the sex, and the est.

He put the beer to his mouth and smiled at her, his eyes thanking her for the attempt at the compliment he could never accept. "Will *you* stay here?"

It was a funny mixture of a question and a request.

Jane knelt down beside him—her breasts inches from him —oiled, shining orbs, the tense pink of the nipples glistening with her sweat. Robert Foley swallowed hard. He had always believed until now that nothing surpassed the beauty of holiness.

"I'd like to, Robert. For a bit anyway." She looked at him carefully. "But I've got to get some work."

"Well, it's Hollywood. You could always act."

They both laughed at the joke. Then they stopped. There was something in the air of the place that stifled the humor of jokes about the essence of L.A.

Jane was half serious when she spoke next. "You need training, I suppose, and a good casting-couch technique."

"And an agent. In this town even ministers have agents . . . and then you'd need steely ambition and armor-plated skin and . . ."

"Stop. Stop!" Jane threw up her hands in mock horror, raising her breasts toward the yellow haze of the sky.

Robert Foley looked at her, glistening and beautiful. Like it or not, she did belong here in California. A woman like Jane Cummin could have whatever it had to give.

"I suppose I could introduce you to Pete Rivkin," he said.

To say that Pete Rivkin was on a roll was a serious understatement in a town that didn't forgive such things. Pete Rivkin was a green-light man, a Nielsen gnostic, a mighty moneymaking machine, and as such he possessed ultimate power in a city that worshiped little else. But this man who swam up and down the drinkable pool of his Coldwater Canyon contemporary, had a vision. It would be a vision strange to anyone who didn't understand Hollywood and the sorts of things it cared about—a stomach churner, even, to anyone who fancied himself a paid-up member of the intelligentsia. Pete Rivkin wanted to produce the most successful prime-time soap that TV, or the world, which were basically the same thing, had ever known.

And he was well on the way to doing just that. The pilot had already been successfully pitched to the network, and now the dailies had the ABS network execs drooling like teeny boppers at a brat-pack communal shower. *Beverly Hills Nights* was off to the races and the word on the street and, more important, in the vital "trades," *Variety* and *Hollywood Reporter*, was that it was going to be bigger than huge, far larger than vast.

Pete Rivkin carried off the racing turn like an otter changing its mind. All the energy fell in place as he cut through the water, and he savored the feelings of stretch and strain in his extended muscles; everything was right with his world. *Beverly Hills Nights* was going to be magnificent; there was absolutely no question at all in the mind that knew.

Rivkin was an unusual figure in Hollywood, an original in a town of cardboard-cutout men—A-sexual, A-scetic, A-ttractive for those who liked their men dark and dangerous looking with sandpaper eyes and stiletto tongues. He was tight and lean, uncoked, unsmoked, undrugged. But he read balance sheets with the avidity of a housewife devouring a Julie

Bennett novel. At the same time he just loved to make good TV—and this rare combination scored the highest marks in the boardrooms of the conglomerates that liked to spend their petty cash buying up slices of entertainment America. It was the newest game in town as fantasy tempted the industrial mainstream to "Go Hollywood." Why churn out Coca-Cola when you could be making celluloid dreams? Why waste your time turning trees into fish wrappers when you could be rubbing bits of yourself against Kelly McGillis? Why be a Denver oil boy when you could be a Hollywood oily one?

But after the party came the surly light of dawn. The would-be movie boys, faced with the wasteful, free-spending ways of the "artistic" filmmaking fraternity, would rush for their slide rules, do the math, then call their shrinks as they popped the Valium. As the cutbacks came, the "creative elements" would call "foul." What did the faceless MBAs in their Brooks Brothers suits know about the magic of the movies? You didn't learn how to melt box offices in Ivy League law schools. Of course it would be conveniently forgotten that you didn't learn how to do that in Hollywood either—that hits were thrust upon you by the kindness of Fate, to be found no more nor less frequently in the seat of a dreamer's pants than in the market surveys in which the Big Apple big businessmen put their trust.

In Pete Rivkin, David Stockman met the ghost of Cecil B. De Mille, which was why everybody loved him. His last two sitcoms had creamed the ratings, and in him money and creative talent merged into that most eighties phenomenon—business art. The only problem for Pete Rivkin was to find a bank in America safe enough to stash the loot.

It helped that he was vertically integrated. Usually an executive producer with his own production company would buy an idea, sell the development deal to ABC or CBS, and then use the network money to hire a writer to get a script on the property. If the network liked the script, it would green light the two-hour pilot and finance that, too. At that stage the executive producer would hire an on-the-line producer to take care of the nuts and bolts of production, and *that* producer would then hire an assistant producer—freeing the Pete Rivkins of this world for the development of other deals. Rivkin, however, didn't work that way. He had dreamed up the idea for *Beverly Hills Nights*, written the teleplay for the pilot, and produced the whole thing himself. He was everywhere—the casting, scouting the locations with the production manager, overseeing the props, staffing the crew, attending the wardrobe meetings. The director, never particularly important in TV anyway as opposed to his vital importance on the big screen, was pretty much of a rubber stamp on a Pete Rivkin production. All this meant that Rivkin Enterprizes, Inc. never had many deals on the front burner at the same time. It also meant that the ones it had cooking were the hottest in town, and a by-product of that was that Rivkin could afford both to charge and to pay top dollar.

So ABS had paid out half a million for the preproduction and three and a half for the two-hour pilot, and Rivkin, who could have made it for two and pocketed the difference, had backed the project to the hilt and blown four million. The investment showed. For Rivkin, the nights in Beverly Hills would be Giorgio-scented dreams as beauties cavorted on Pratesi sheets in houses that belonged to real people like Cher (her retractable ceiling gave a new dimension to the term *starfucker*), the George Hamilton/Nabila Kashoggi house (all those *mirrors*), and the Barbra Streisand Malibu pad (the world's only art deco ranch). The network had already committed itself to forty-eight episodes at two million dollars each. It was mouth-watering money, and to someone who cared as much as Pete Rivkin, it was nail-biting time, too. Now he had to deliver.

So far there had been one major falling out, and as he sliced through the eighty-degree water, his body humming and his mind singing, he thought back on the Russian Tea Room lunch with the programming chief of ABS.

"Listen, Pete. If we're putting up all this money, you gotta come up with some name stars. I know I can't tell you who to cast, but you gotta see my point, and run with someone bankable. I mean, this isn't chickenshit we're laying out here. This is big-budget TV. You persuade someone like Sally Field to do it, an' however much it costs, you got a hit and the Nielsens take care of themselves. Nobody ever got hurt taking insurance, and Galvin's on my case like you can't believe. The asshole's crawling all over us, ranting and raving and screaming for hits. My guts'll be garters if we blow this one. You've heard the rumors on the street. If ABS doesn't jack its profits up, it could be on the block."

Pete Rivkin had groaned. The popular wisdom always made him do that. "That's crap, Dave, and it's old crap. We pay out everything on the stars and we can't afford a decent set to stick them in. There'll be nothing in the kitty for really great scripts, terrific clothes, wild props, and knockout P.R. My way, we get the *show* right. We do that and the public will *make* my unknowns into stars. That's the smart-money way to go. These actors are going into millions of homes, night after night. The public gets to know the characters better than their husbands, their wives, and their kids—and they like 'em a *whole* lot better."

"But, Pete—look at *Dallas*. Larry Hagman was and is the show, and then they bring in Mrs. Elvis Presley, and Howard Keel. You gotta have the names. *Dynasty*'s the same."

"Balls. Anyway, *Dallas* is last year. All those 'super-rich' Ewings have no one to serve them breakfast in the morning, live in a rabbit hutch with a thirty-foot dip pool, and travel first class on airplanes. Not a private jet in sight. They look like they're on welfare. The girls have to save up for their facelifts. At least in *Dynasty* they have chauffeurs, and somebody's made an effort with the clothes. But the point is that the *idea* of these shows caught on. You've got it the wrong way around. Okay, so they pull in some biggies like Heston, but Joan Collins and Linda Evans are biggest of them all, and before the public latched on to *Dynasty* they were about as visible as the small print on an insurance policy. My series is going to show how the heavy hitters *really* part with it. None of this *Lifestyles of the Rich and Famous* bull—a whole lot of poseurs showing off their overmortgaged houses and boats— but the real McCoy. The public is going to love it, because I'm giving them reality, and they're going to recognize it. They always do. They're always right. Trust me."

He had carried the point, just. But the money men were

really only giving him the benefit of the doubt. If the mix didn't turn out the perfect cake then the chef would be the ingredients in the next one.

It meant that the casting was vital—a mining operation that just *had* to turn up some spectacular rough diamonds— and of course Pete Rivkin was overseeing it personally. In the last three weeks it seemed to him as if he had seen every girl in Hollywood, the long, the short, and the tall. He tended to see most of them in the evenings, and at home. Somehow, catching them in the palatial surroundings of his Richard Martin–designed, award-winning modern home made it easier to sort out the gold from the dross. Technically, it was the business of the casting director—an ugly bitch whose face had the form of an exuberant Jackson Pollock—but the job was far too important to leave to her. He had her sit in on the cattle calls anyway. She could tell a sheep from a goat in the clinches.

Seventy-five lengths of the forty-foot pool. About half a mile. Around twenty minutes. Pete Rivkin hauled himself from the water and peered at his matte-black Tiffany watch. Six o'clock. The cattle would be rounded up in the dining room, the Juilliard graduates trying to remain superior to hookers, waitresses, and hat-check girls. Starlets with credits peering down pert noses at models with portfolios but no parts, the odd "once-was" genuine article hiding her pride behind blacker-than-night L.A. Eyeworks shades. The word had gone out—"Cast the net wide"—and even though the hopefuls had been screened by minions, and the card-carrying dogs weeded out, what was left would run all the way from the sublime to the ridiculous and back.

The girl they were really looking for at the moment would be called Camellia. An unusual name for what he hoped would be an unusual actress, one who could combine the facets of a right California raver with a certain European sophistication and charm. Sort of a sexy Catherine Oxenberg, a younger Jane Seymour.

So he had already endured and would have to endure further an endless succession of Camellias. Vamp Camellias, cold-on-the-outside-but-warm-within Camellias, decadent

Camellias, less-than-zero Camellias. A few, very few actually, would call him up at home and suggest lunch, more than prepared over the Soave for a tactless "confession" that they had this thing about "father figures." But mostly they would just look helpless, desperate, and determined—and resigned, of course, to the ongoing process of rejection. Pete Rivkin could never get used to it. How did these people have the stamina to carry on? There would be big names, too, on his carpet, reading as if their lives depended on it—people America knew and cared about, stars whose *Lifestyles* profiles suggested that they would never have to work again. And yet there they'd be, competing with the "models," the masseuses, and the aerobics instructors who'd wormed their way into the cattle call because some key player in the psychodrama of production wanted to impress them, or screw them, or both.

The Filipino butler had stood there for twenty minutes and watched his employer swim. Now he moved forward with the big white terrycloth robe, the Rivkin initials scripted in deep red over the left breast. "Most of the girls arrive, sir. And Miss Hirsch waiting in drawing room."

Pete Rivkin disappeared into the dressing gown and stole a last look at the dusk settling like dust over Century City, watched the sparkling, strange colors of magic hour painting patterns on the rippling pool, and breathed in deeply to smell the jasmine already floating on the heavy evening air.

Then he turned around and plunged into the house. "Tell Ida Hirsch I'll be right there," he said over his shoulder.

A couple of minutes later he reappeared barefoot in white Levi's and a light gray T-shirt. "Hi, Ida. Sorry I'm late. What have we got?"

She half stood and then half sat.

"Don't move." He held up a God-like hand to stop the charade of slavelike indecision.

"Well, we have fifteen in all. The last three are short-listed. I've seen those myself and they're possible. I wanted your opinion. The first one—Jane Cummin—I don't know at all. Your secretary said you would know about her."

There was the faintest accusation in her voice. Some chick you met at a party? Coming on to the big producer? Not that she really believed it. Pete Rivkin had a bigger reputation than that, and he wouldn't debase it by playing cheap Hollywood games. Still people did get "discovered." Dino de Laurentiis had "found" the most popular actress in China, Joan Chen, in an L.A. parking lot for his movie *Tai-Pan*.

"Oh, yeah. Friend of mine said we should see her."

Ida Hirsch looked quizzical. It was not really a good enough answer, but you didn't question Pete Rivkin.

"Okay, let's see Ms. Cummin."

Pete Rivkin sat back on the deep cushions of the sofa. He would get the worst over with first. The last person on God's earth he had ever expected to ask him for a "see-my-actress" favor had been Robert Foley. But he hadn't even considered refusing. Robert Foley was one of the very few people he had ever met who was wholly and totally admirable. It seemed to Pete Rivkin that God had created him as a sort of prototype of selfless goodness, and although they were both roughly the same age, he respected him in a way that bordered on hero worship. They had known each other for several years now, and they were friends, although the single-minded zeal with which each man pursued his personal goals left little time, and not too much inclination, for intimacy. Robert Foley was not an easy man to know, but he was one hundred percent bull-shit-free in a town that had invented the stuff, and to Pete Rivkin, who cared almost as much about giving his money away as he did about making it, Foley's devotion to the cause of those the world had forgotten put him on a lonely pedestal indeed.

Never before had Foley asked him for a favor that was not obviously a worthy one, which made the unknown Jane Cummin very interesting. What sort of person had turned on the man with his saintlike fingers in the gutters of the world?

One minute later he knew. He could see.

Head-to-toe Azzedine Alaïa, black as the devil's heart, her blond hair shining, Jane Cummin bounded into the room. It seemed to Pete Rivkin that there were trumpets playing, bands rejoicing, choirs singing their joy as the vision drifted toward him. Her face—alight, alive. Her smile, welcoming as the gates of paradise. The whole of her was a treasure trove of star quality that Pete Rivkin had dreamed of all his life but never expected to find.

He had to clear his throat before he could even try to speak. "Good evening, Ms. Cummin. Thanks for taking time to be here."

"Thanks for letting me come."

It was not the greatest line in the world. Not Shakespeare. Not Goldman. But it brought Pete Rivkin to the very edge of the Kindel sofa and the Hirsch woman to the outer limits of the formidably uncomfortable sixties Eames chair.

It was the voice. The English had softened into mid-Atlantic-silky, sexy, like the fur on a peach.

"Have you any acting experience, Ms. Cummin?"

Third banana in some repertory fruit scene, probably, Rivkin thought, and all the fairy castles would fall. "I was twenty-fifth from the right in the front row of the 'I'd like to teach the world to sing' Coke commercial." Worse? He'd heard worse before.

"No, none."

The voice again. How did you make, "No, none" sound wonderful?

"It's not important. So no card?"

"No, I'm afraid not."

"Oh, that's okay. We can fix that."

"And your agent?"

"I don't have an agent."

Agents had agents. Needed them anyway. On paper this sounded worse than the "character" slot in the Miss America pageant. But that was paper and what did paper know? Paper could not explain this girl, communicate the gorgeous lilt of her voice, translate the forthright blue eyes or the phenomenal, absolutely stupendous breasts he could almost, so very nearly see. . . . Pete Rivkin made a conscious effort to stop staring at them. He actually wanted to take this girl out to *dinner*—him, Pete Rivkin, the man with the iced cock.

"No agent." Somehow that needed repeating.

"No agent."

Pete Rivkin searched his mind for something to say. Did this girl *want* the show? Of course she *had* it. And a reshoot part in the pilot, too. Pete Rivkin wiped his brow and turned to Ms. Hirsch, who sat beside him as ugly as apartheid, and with all the charm of a cockroach in a jar of face cream. She would need to be persuaded.

But Pete was wrong about that. Ms. Hirsch, still on the edge of her chair, was glowing like a Chernobyl chicken, and her appalling foot was reaching across the carpet toward his bare one. Apparently the Cummin sex appeal was a gender bender.

"Wonderful," the latex lips mouthed soundlessly at him.

Pete Rivkin felt relief and excitement collide. *Nights* was a wrap. It would go all the way to the top of the Nielsens on the back of this mysterious fantasy girl.

He took a deep breath.

"Congratulations, Ms. Cummin. We would like you very much to work with us. I might say that usually at this point we ask you to read for us, and if that goes okay, to test for us. Then we need time to consider. Then we call your agent. In this case we are going to dispense with all that, and not just because you have no agent . . ." He laughed nervously. "I just know that you are going to be a very big credit to *Beverly Hills Nights*."

Sometimes—much later—Pete Rivkin would remember that line, and he'd laugh and he'd laugh.

All the way to the bank.

JANE RIPPED AT THE ALAÏA DRESS AS IF IT WERE ON FIRE. BUT despite her hurry she was careful not to tear it. It had been Robert Foley's present to her for the audition, and for him to pay a price like that for a *dress* made it a very significant dress indeed.

"Damn! *Damn!*" she shouted at the night air as she twisted and turned in the front seat of the old Chevy. But she was laughing, too, laughing at the glorious wonder of it all, and the blissful future that lay stretched out before her like the lights of the San Fernando Valley below. Christ, these dresses were like body paint. Maybe Alaïa wasn't into rapid undressing, but sometimes a girl needed that option. Jane was seconds away from giving the best news in the world to the person she cared most about, and she wanted to do it in the T-shirt and jeans in which she felt comfortable.

At last the dress was history, thrust down among the bubble gum, empty Coke cans, and other car detritus that gunked up the floor of a non-L.A. wreck like Robert's. She wiggled into the jeans, her long legs slipping into them like a pianist's fingers into buckskin gloves, and then pulled the T-shirt over her chest. As a final touch she tore at her hair, messing it up irretrievably into a wanton Kelly McGillis jungle. She surveyed the result in the cracked mirror. Watch out, Robert Foley! Prepare to meet your match, bromide man!

For a second she sighed deeply as she tried to hold the dream still. A few minutes ago she had been nothing more than a no-hope Hollywood and Vine fantasist, winging it on a prayer and a phone call, lost in the desert of maybe. But now—right now—she was riding the shooting star she knew would carve her initials on the firmament of America. Her life had begun.

She flicked the ignition key, jammed the car noisily into gear, and peeled into the Mulholland traffic.

Jane zipped down Beverly Glen, through Sherman Oaks, past the newsstand where she liked to browse, and soon she was racing down Van Nuys under the freeway, to the place where she and Robert lived. In the back of the car, wrapped tight in brown paper to keep it cold, was the bottle of vintage Krug from the liquor store on Sunset and Doheny. Seventy-five bucks had seemed expensive, even on the eve of her triumph. It was just about the last of the money she had left from England, but now it couldn't matter less.

What would Robert *say*? She prayed he'd be home by now. She wrenched the wheel over to the right and roared into the small driveway, narrowly avoiding the mailbox.

Banging the ancient door so hard that it nearly shattered, she rushed into the hallway, champagne in hand, the crazy joy spilling out from every pore of her body.

"Robert? Robert! I'm home. Where the hell are you?"

He jumped up from his chair, the alarm all over his face as Jane exploded into the room like a hurricane surge tide.

"I got the part, Robert. *I got the part!* Can you believe it?" They gave it to *me*. Your friend Rivkin gave it to *me*!"

The smile broke across Robert Foley's face. "What? Just like that? There and then? I thought there was some sort of a procedure to go through. I mean reading, screen tests, don't call us . . ." His head was cocked to one side. Was this some sort of joke?

"Yes. Yes. He shook my hand and said I definitely had it. And there were *stars* in that room. Do you know that English actress Jenny Agutter? I can't *believe* it. Rivkin said they could fix up the contract later, but he wants to pay me ten thousand for each episode and there would be a minimum of forty-eight. Can he have meant that? Surely he must have got it wrong."

"Jane, that's wonderful. I mean it's just *fantastic*." The Foley smile was more than that now. It was a celebration. He tried to move toward her. She *saw* him try. He wanted to touch her and she wanted to be touched by him, to be swept up in his arms and kissed and hugged and loved at this best moment of her life. But an unseen hand was at his shoulder, some invisible glass barrier was in front of him. Like so many times before, Robert Foley was holding back, was held back.

He sat back into his chair as the moment vanished.

"Listen, Jane, if Pete says you've got it, then you do. His bullshit reading's unrecordable. He's hot enough right now to get a forty-eight-episode commitment. In this town nobody knows how to guarantee a hit series—so they just throw money and power at the guy who made the last one, and that's Pete."

Jane struck a pose, hand on jutting hip, letting geometry talk to him. She smiled as she watched him watch her, desire flashing into his eyes, his tongue moving to moisten dry lips.

"So, Robert Foley. How does it feel to be shacked up with a TV star?"

The deliberate suggestion of her question mocked at him. He stretched his hands above his head and smiled at her. "I'll be Mr. Cummin in *People* magazine."

"Let's hear it for Dr. Jane!" She twirled around and threw the joke over her shoulder as she headed for the kitchen.

"Robert, we are going to drink some *champagne*. I just paid seventy-five bucks for this stuff. Guess we'll have to drink it out of tumblers, as your kitchen doesn't seem to run to champagne glasses. Yet!"

"God, Jane, you can't spend that kind of money on wine."

He hadn't seen Jane like this before. She had a devil-may-care vitality about her and a deliciously dangerous spontaneity that threatened to upset his precarious status quo.

"Listen, sweetheart, watch out or I just might spend money on *you*. No, I've got a better idea. I might just pour it all over your clinic—like sticky treacle. And then what would you do, Robert Foley? What would you do then? Would *that* be the way to your heart?"

She was back, two tall glasses of cold champagne in her hands.

"Well, you sure will have enough. Ten times forty-eight is around half a million bucks. Not bad for an evening's work. I guess you could get me a new stethoscope with that."

She bent down to put the glass in front of him. "How about a new life?"

For a moment neither spoke as the mood grew serious.

It was true. Things would not remain the same after this. Jane's tide had turned. Now, taken at the ebb, it could lead to mighty fortune. And in Hollywood fame and money changed life. That was the only point of them.

"When do they want you to start?"

"Tomorrow. I report to the studio, and then they put me through the mincer. Drama coaches, people to dress me, people to change the way I look, lawyers, contracts, instant green card, bank accounts, script briefings, meeting the cast, photo sessions, the P.R. people . . ." She made a winding motion of the hand as she recited the litany and her voice petered out as she realized what Robert's question had really meant.

There would be no time. No time for them. No time for them to become what they both wanted to be, what both had such difficulty in becoming.

Success would have no time for rivals.

"I'd like to stay here with you." Jane sipped at the champagne, as the bubbles began to evaporate from her mood.

"I'd like that too. I wonder if Rivkin would."

"Forget Rivkin."

In the face of the threat from the outside world they grew closer now—closer than they had ever been. They were fighting to be with each other, admitting it.

"He's a very forceful man, you know. He'll want all of you. Lock, stock, and barrel sold to the company store."

"I haven't got all of me to give."

Robert Foley looked down. She had a part of him, too, a part that was growing by the week, by the day, by the second. Why couldn't he tell her? Of course there was an answer, the same timeless answer: the promise he had broken; the promise that he was cursed to keep.

Jane knelt down in front of him. She reached out and lifted his chin until her eyes met his.

"I think I love you, Robert," she said quietly.

"Jane . . . I . . ." He shook his head from side to side, and moisture glistened suddenly in his eyes as the doubt, pain, and guilt rushed through him.

"What is it, Robert? What is it?"

Jane knew there was an enemy inside him, her enemy, the foe that would let him want her but not allow him to love her. The adversary would permit him only to love humanity, the soulless, heartless, faceless monster that could only take, and knew not how to give.

She knew she would have to fight for him.

She leaned forward and took his head in her hands and moved her mouth close to the lips she must have.

"Kiss me, Robert."

Robert Foley had had enough, enough of the preaching and the cant, all the pomp and the soul-searching, of all the poverty and the pretense.

He pulled her toward him, roughly, and crushed her to him. Her body plastered against his, the way it had been in so very many dreams. Her smell was in his nostrils, her warmth beneath his hands.

He no longer wanted to speak. There had been too much time for talk. He wanted only to feel.

"Jane...," he said, as the love flowed from his eyes into hers and his lips melted against her hungry mouth.

NINETEEN

THE WORLD AND ITS MISTRESS WERE THERE. THE trust funds prowled like hungry dogs, foundations snapped and snarled at each other as they sought to claim their prizes, the museums pranced and postured as they dithered over the impossible selection. In the Evan Koestler Gallery success's heady smell was already battling with the Joy and the Chanel Number Five, and that suited Billy Bingham just fine.

The assistant scurrying around with the little red "sold" stickers looked like the man in charge of the lifeboats on the *Titanic*. He couldn't satisfy everyone, but who should he leave out? Ashton Hawkins from the Met, Donald Trump, or John Walsh from the Getty Museum? All would have cheerfully parted with female grandchildren to get their hands on a Bingham piece, and some of them were destined for disappointment. Already people had given up the idea of choice. Even if the blue really was a much better bet for the Southampton drawing room than the red, the rooms could always be redecorated. The trick was to nail down as many as possible. Already it was rumored that C.Z. Whitmore had acquired three.

Warhol looked traditionally bemused, Schnabel, Clemente, and Haring deeply pissed off, and Phelan, the art guy from the *Times*, as if he had found paradise in the proverbial parking lot.

Evan Koestler was smiling. He turned to Billy. "You're a

star, sweetheart. I've made you a star. Together we can go anywhere from here. Tomorrow we triple your prices, and everyone who's bought tonight feels like they've broken the bank at Monte Carlo. They'll love you forever for that. All these people will love us forever."

It was true. The really rich adored the idea of a quick profit in the way that a meritocrat could never understand. The nouveau riche thought that money was for spending. But the true plutocrat knew that money was not even for mentioning. Like religion and the biological activities, it was present but not seen, obscure and mystical. It was, after all, the thing that *made* these people—the stuff of which they were constructed. Not for them the security of achievement. Great grandpapa of the hungry eyes and fearsome countenance had been the one for that. But to make money—buckets of it—overnight from a judicious exercise of their *artistic* judgment, the judgment that the crude, breadwinning forebear had known nothing at all about—that was for the big-digit sociocrats the sweetest thing imaginable.

Billy Bingham's smile was a work of art, as layered, joyous, and complicated as the canvases on the white walls of the Madison Avenue gallery. He had heard Evan Koestler's "we's" and his "togethers" and a response to that lay in the smile, too.

For the moment he would even endure Evan's hand patting away at his hard rump, the beautifully manicured fingers plucking unctuously at the brown skin of his forearm. For now. Later he would dump him, without ceremony, sorrow, or a second thought. So he turned to his mentor and allowed the knowing smile to soften until gratitude just might have been its creator. He fought back against the thought that Evan was getting fifty percent of all this.

"We really did it, Evan, didn't we? Just like you said we would."

Evan laughed and grabbed at a glass of circulating Moët. "Just wait till you see Phelan's review. He nearly did it in his pants when I introduced you. I've never seen anything like it. By tomorrow you'll have started a school. They'll be copying you all over New York, but it won't matter. Because everyone knows now that you were first."

He actually rubbed his hands together in anticipation. "But you know what I'm thinking of, Billy, my sweetheart?" he paused theatrically. "The back room."

In the room in back of the gallery were forty virgin Billy Bingham canvases, and nobody knew they were there. The thirty or so paintings running off the walls before their eyes at thirty-five thousand a throw were in effect loss leaders. Over the next few weeks as the heavy hitters spread the word to the lesser mortals of their amazing acumen in getting a Bingham at the source, the hoi-polloi groupies would be drawn into the net—gladly paying three times what their superiors had paid for their chance to share in the art-fashion bonanza. Then the original buyers would be back, buying in force, secure in the knowledge that the average unit cost for the instant master-pieces was way down, thanks to the bargains they had picked up on that electrifying first night of the Billy Bingham feeding frenzy.

The back room was where the spare art was. Spare art at three times the price. Thirty times thirty-five thousand before his eyes. Forty times one hundred thousand when the price tripled tomorrow. As Billy stood there sipping at his Diet Pepsi, he was standing as close as it was possible to get to a half share of five million dollars. He was rich.

Suddenly, and at last, he had it all and he wondered what he felt about it. Was it as good as it should have been? Better? He raced through the inventory of emotions, and was almost surprised to find that behind pleasure, self-respect, ecstasy, lay a subtle little mixture of worry and love and longing. It went by the name of Jane Cummin.

JULIE BENNETT TOOK ONE IMMACULATE IRISH WATERFORD cut-glass tumbler and dropped it with great precision onto the Mexican tile of the patio. Then she dropped the wineglass, full of rather good Puligny Montrachet, 1979. Then the Li-moges china plate, with its cargo of cold shrimp, lobster, and crab. Next she stood up in the mess she had made, and as loud as she possibly could, which was quite loud, she said, or rather shouted, *"Fuck!"*

Only Orlando witnessed the charade of annoyance. His orange fur rigid with fright, he leaped several feet into the air and fled.

The *New York Times* Arts and Leisure section lay open on the table. Phelan's column and Billy Bingham's photograph sprang from the page.

A STAR IS BORN AT THE KOESTLER GALLERY

I hope that by now the readers of my reviews will know that I am not addicted to hyperbole. However, there is a time in all our lives when we can learn something from the motion-picture industry. Such a time is now.

Last night, I visited the Evan Koestler Gallery on Madison Avenue. I am still in a state of shock from the experience. I am numb. I am bewildered. I am suddenly aware of the inadequacy of the words from which I make my living.

On the walls of the gallery are thirty paintings of such staggering beauty and originality, of such brilliant shape and form, of such gorgeous, glorious color and texture that the brain can scarcely believe what the eye sees. The name of the man who painted these masterpieces is Billy Bingham. I shall repeat the name. Billy Bingham. Please remember it. He is one of the greatest artists the world has seen in a very long time.

Julie stalked furiously into the house through the big sliding smoked-glass windows into the cavernous drawing room. Phelan's words were branded into her brain. Smoke was rising. She slumped down on the sofa and put up her feet on the Thai silk cushions, showering them with bits of cold crustacean, crystal, and mayonnaise.

The pictures she had reviled, whose point had totally eluded her, were quite suddenly the hottest properties in the art world, bar none. And the toy boy who had dared to leave her—the peasant she had invented—was now the toast of *le tout* New York, and almost certainly a paper millionaire already.

She ground her teeth with fury. It was the cruelest, most bizarre joke imaginable. Her Billy, the art cretin, the dreadful dauber, whose extraordinary, ugly paintings had polluted her house, had been transformed overnight by the Koestler wand into some latter-day El Greco. It was unbelievable, unbearable, unbelievably unbearable.

But then an even more terrible idea occurred to her. Jane had disappeared, and both she and Lucy had agreed that it was likely that she had gone with loser Billy—poor man, soon to be beggar man, possibly even thief. It had been a thought that had comforted Julie after she had recovered from the initial anger at losing her lover to her hated sister. She had been sustained by the knowledge that somewhere out there Billy and Jane would be bumping along the bottom of life, scavengers feeding in the mud and the ooze where the lesser creatures lived.

But now Billy was a rich man, and if Jane was still with him she was rich too, rich and untouchable, the prestigious lover of the art hero.

Julie had to know. She reached for the telephone and in minutes she was talking to the Evan Koestler Gallery. Thank God for the time difference from the coast! It would be around five in New York. She might just catch Billy before he left for what would presumably now be a brilliant and hectic social life. The gallery said he was staying at the Carlyle.

He answered immediately.

"Congratulations, Billy. So those funny paintings weren't so bad after all. You should have left me a couple in exchange for the rent."

"What the hell do you want, Julie?"

"The gallery told me I'd find you at the Carlyle. What good taste to stay there, but then I suppose we must all defer to your taste from now on. That's what Phelan says in the *Times* anyway. He particularly liked the figurative paintings of all those nubile young girls. Weird, isn't it? I'd always rather believed in Phelan before."

"You're responsible for those in a way, Julie. After all

those months of your body I had to escape into the pretty ones."

"Oh, do you really think little Evan has a pretty body? Thank God I've never had to see it, but I expect you're an *expert* on it by now."

"What do you want to say to me, Julie? I don't have to take your rubbish anymore. You know that."

Careful. How to get him to tell the truth. "Actually, Billy, I was ringing for another reason. Not just a remembrance of times pissed. I really wanted a word with Jane."

Silence.

"She's not here."

"Where is she then?"

Again a silence.

"I don't know." His tone of voice said he didn't like admitting that.

"We thought she was with you."

"Who's we?" He was wary. He wanted information, but he didn't want to be seen asking.

"Lucy Masterson and I."

"She's not with Lucy?"

There was worry in there with the words now. It was quite unmistakable. Julie felt the relief flow through her. He was telling her the truth.

"No, she blew the Lucy Masterson nest. Lucy was quite upset. Disappeared into the Big Orange. Did you drop her in it, Billy? My poor little sister? Did you dump on her and fly away with Evan to fame and fortune? You're an ambitious little chap, aren't you, Billy Bingham?"

But the line had gone dead. He'd hung up on her.

Julie turned to stroke Orlando, who, at last, had dared to reappear on her lap. "Hello, darling. Hello, my sweetheart. Well, it's not quite as bad as it might have been, my darling. Billy's flying high, but it looks, my lovely, as if Jane is deep in shit's ditch."

PETE RIVKIN'S ALMIGHTY HIT WAS COMING TOGETHER LIKE A beautiful dream, and he knew the reason why. He didn't need market research or viewer sampling to tell him. The humblest grip knew the score. *Nights* was a winner and the reason was Jane. Whole sections of the pilot that had opened the series had been rewritten and reshot to include her, and in the first few vital episodes she had most of the lines and the majority of the footage. Anticipating the tremendous viewer reaction, Rivkin had starred Jane in all the commercials for the show, and across America, on cue, there had been a reversal of life patterns. Now people went out to get the beer five minutes *before* the commercials. The P.R. blitz had saturated the country—and the word-of-mouth buildup had caught like nuclear fission. On the evening that *Nights* aired, restaurant business in Beverly Hills had been off fifty percent and Peter Morton had actually telephoned Pete Rivkin, tongue in cheek, to complain. It had been the same everywhere, wipe-out business, as the show had lifted *Cosby* and *Family Ties* off the top of the Nielsens. In the same week Jane Cummin had appeared on the covers of *Newsweek* and *Rolling Stone, US, Interview,* and the *National Enquirer.* In short, she was that all but unheard of commodity—an overnight success.

Already Pete Rivkin had jacked up Jane's per-episode fee. From a more than generous starter of ten thousand dollars, to twenty-five thousand, to a Don Johnsonesque seventy-five thousand. She was within spitting distance from Larry Hagman, if a million miles from Bill Cosby, but she was worth every penny, and Pete Rivkin had never been a nickel-and-dime man. But Rivkin's money was already merely the tip of the iceberg. Jane was sliding like a knife through warm butter into the heart of America. In exchange for its ecstasy it did what it did best of all; it threw not roses but money at her. The big cosmetics companies bid for her endorsement of their products. So did the battling bottlers in the cola wars, the jeans men, and even, in a desperate attempt to shore up confidence, the failing, ailing banks. Pepsi had paid Michael Jackson fifteen million in their effort to identify with the young at heart, but Jackson couldn't sell everything. Jane could—up to and including partridges in pear trees, soul food in Palm Beach, and the Reagan foreign policy to Colonel Khadaffi. On the *Tonight* show Johnny was careful, and on the Murdoch "network" even Joan Rivers was deferential. No one messed with the dream, and that was what Jane had become.

Pete Rivkin felt the thrill course through him as he contemplated the brilliant fantasy that had become reality, and his heart went out to the bright-eyed beauty who had made it possible.

All around him the voices were droning on. He forced himself to concentrate. He slipped his feet, shod in battered Topsiders worn Florida style with no socks, onto a desk the size of a helicopter landing pad. He was "taking" a meeting, but he wasn't really thinking about it. He didn't have to anymore. In Hollywood, "meetings" were excuses for not taking phone calls that doubled as "work," but of course they weren't really work at all. They were mutual masturbation sessions, and in his office the scent of déjà vu was as overpowering as Giorgio.

For a second or two he allowed himself the luxury of memory. Most of the Hollywood power panjandrums had a version of his: the too hot/too cold apartment that the roaches allowed him to share, the endless tuna sandwiches to stretch out the precious bucks, the desperate check-in-the-mail excuses to keep the vital telephone in play. Keeping frail hope alive had been the art form in those early days as his knuckles had rapped the closed doors and his raw fingers had spun the dial on a million calls that never quite got through. Yes, they had all lined up to dump on his dreams. But he had survived the ordeal of poverty and anonymity in the vicious city and now he could get them to do anything. They would cheat on their wives, steal from their mothers, and murder his enemies—if in a casual aside he should wish to be rid of some turbulent antagonist in the tinsel-town sharkscape. They closed their mouths when he opened his, and they fell over themselves laughing at the jokes that even he realized weren't funny. They opened doors for him, leaped to their feet when he entered the room, and one or two of the more shameless had started to call him "sir."

But power over the Industry people wasn't really what turned him on, although he accepted it as the way things were, the natural law of the Hollywood Medes and Persians that altered not. What he really loved was the power that came from doing the TV that glued Americans to the tube, and had them about as willing to flick the dial to a rival station as they would be to turn the switch on their own electric chair.

The rest of it was scorekeeping. He no longer had to endure the dreadful humiliation of attempting to secure "drive-ons" to the studio lot—and appalling patronization of the security men at the gates, those power peddlers who made St. Peter look like a broken-down janitor in a fly-blown block of the East Village. Now there was the palatial office, with its view of the Hollywood Hills, and there was a double parking space for the Gemballa custom Porsche that had set him back the best part of two hundred grand. And outside there were wall-to-wall receptionists, all of them nearly beautiful, to dispense the Classic caffeine-free Diet Coke and Perrier to the lesser mortals as they were kept hanging around for the statutory few minutes before they were ushered into the hallowed presence of the hit maker. In the old days there had been one battered, overworked telephone, great on dialing, not so good at ringing. Now there were telephones everywhere—one on each end of the half-inch-thick glass coffee table that ran the length of the sofa that sat eight, another on the walnut desk— all with five lines and an intercom to the secretary. Apart from the flowers—three generous azalea bushes—there was little else in the cavernous room except the antique Sheraton dining table with its eight matching chairs and yet another telephone, three David Hockney "swimming-pool" oils, and an elegant Perspex-and-brushed-aluminum media console containing Beta and VHS format VCRs, a stereo-sound Sony Trinitron, Nagamichi tape deck, Carver amplifier and tuner, and Guss speakers. Scripts, papers, trade mags, pens, pencils, and the paraphernalia of office life were conspicuous by their absence. Media men would get the message; the really heavy hitters must have their lives cleared of the minutiae so that they could concentrate on the big picture—the decisions that would change the face of the earth, or of Hollywood, which were basically one and the same thing.

A scriptwriter, a species with the employment lifespan of a virgin in Hades, was droning on while he could. In his game he never knew when the grim reaper in the shape of the rewrite man would loom up to obliterate him.

His speech should really have been directed at Ida Hirsch of casting, but like everyone else in the room he looked at Pete Rivkin as he spoke. "I think we all agree on the name Melissa, right? Sort of southern-California vanity-plate-fantasy churner? So for the Melissa role we need a rather unsophisticated girl-next-door, all-American type, to offset Jane's Camellia—not too beautiful but who the kids can relate to—a bit like Ally Sheedy, Molly Ringwald... Maybe a younger ... an older... a taller... a shorter..."

Pete Rivkin groaned inside. How many times had he played the "a bit like" game? This was where the overgrown schoolboys who dreamed of making movies would get into the act. It was worse on the big screen, but it was bad enough on the small one. "Who was that girl in whatsisname's movie... you know, the one that ended up in the Sahara eating snakes?" The would-be moguls would name everyone who'd been in a Nielsen creamer over the last eighteen months, anyone who might score the speaker a few extra points for originality or the extent of his encyclopedic knowledge of TV trivia, his senseless savvy.

Right now as they sat there, hundreds of such name-the-star meetings were taking place all over town, among foreigners in rented bungalows on the grounds of the Beverly Hills Hotel with the promise of movie money from some bogus sheik; among golden oldies in the Marmont dreaming of the time they have been regulars in now-defunct Ma Maison; among con men and freeloaders, dreamers and psychotics, cowboys and psychopaths. They were all knee deep in big names like Streisand and Streep, Taylor and Turner, Goldberg and Gibson—stars, Pete Rivkin knew, who wouldn't have bothered to cross the street to piss on them if they'd been on fire.

"I don't know about the name Melissa. I think it's a bit Val."

Suddenly nobody knew about Melissa anymore.

Pete Rivkin smiled as the conversation went into reverse. It was no longer Who would be Melissa? It was Who would

Melissa be? Nobody seemed at all put out by the change of emphasis.

The young guy from the studio, whom Pete allowed to sit in as an observer, said that he had always rather liked "Jennifer." He looked about twenty-one—blue jeans, khaki shirt, black string tie, and lightweight bomber jacket. Most probably he was a lawyer or a Harvard MBA who thought that it was the thing to do to dress down because it was the Industry.

Pete Rivkin smiled. Sometimes power was fun. "How about 'Lisa'?" He peered around the room for dissent.

He was general secretary of the Politburo, Attila the Hun with a hangover. Good. That was one decision that tongues could relax over. Now, what was it that Lisa had to look like?

He reached out for the intercom and punched the button. The receptionist had been holding his calls. "What have you got?" he asked curtly.

It was another power play. His meeting, his office—etiquette said he could take calls, make them. The gesture said that he was bored, that he needed some personal contact—because in Hollywood everyone knew it was far more personal to talk on the telephone than face to face. He knew that there would be nobody *really* important. Rules, after all, were made to be broken, and "hold my calls" meant "hold the assholes" —a network boss like Galvin, top agents like Michael Ovitz (Redford, Hoffman, Newman) and Sam Cohn (Woody Allen, Streep, Minnelli), or an all-purpose mover and shaker like Ray Stark would have been through instantly.

"Tell Fred I'll catch him later," he barked as he banged down the receiver amid a barrage of significant looks exchanged. They all knew who Fred was. They'd all thought he was hot. Now they all knew he was off the boil.

"I think 'Lisa' is a brilliant idea, Mr. Rivkin. Natural, but stylish. Southern California but with a bit of class," said somebody greasily.

But Pete Rivkin wasn't listening again. He was thinking about his telephone calls and wondering why his antennae, those finely tuned, sixth-sense trouble detectors, were twitching like masts on a high sea.

That was the second time that Julie Bennett had called. What the hell did she want?

"HAVE YOU BEEN EATING WELL?"

The black man shook his head. "Don' seem to be hungry, Doc."

"Nausea? Have you been feeling sick?"

"More I've had no energy. Don' seem to be able to do nothin'."

He looked thin. Emaciated, really. He was still in his fifties. The general picture and the history tied in with the examination. Dullness to percussion at the left lung base and reduced air entry over the area of dullness. The man had been losing weight, had coughed some blood, and had been a heavy smoker all his life. There wasn't much room for doubt. The X ray would show a tumor.

Robert Foley felt the familiar anger. Why had God *made* cancer? Why the pain and the sickness, the horror and the despair? Why was it good for us to suffer? Couldn't an all-powerful God have made other, less unpleasant, things "good" for us? And what perverse desire to play at dice had made him bother to create the world in the first place? What fatal flaw in his makeup, what lack of self-confidence made him crave our freely given praise and worship, and if there was an insufficiency in his character then what of his much vaunted perfection? All the doubts and fears were so brilliantly answered by the simple act of faith. After all, how could mere minds explain a Divine purpose? But where to go when faith had gone?

"James, I'd like to have your chest X-rayed. And I'll have to do some blood tests to find out exactly what's going on here." He hoped the smile was reassuring.

He tried not to let his anger show. Bronchial cancer. Five-year survival rate, thirty percent. The husbandless wife. The fatherless children. Life sucks and then you're dead.

"Anything wrong, Doc?"

"I don't think so, but we ought to be sure. To be safe."

In Beverly Hills he'd have had to tell the truth, and it wouldn't have been in the best interests of the patient to hear it. The malpractice lawyers would be the ones he was *really* treating. Here, in this free clinic, he could save this man needless anxiety and ease his passage with reassurance, and later, when the pain came, with heroin and hope. This man would never sue him, because the greasy contingency lawyers would never come beating on the door of the shack he called home. So James would die in dignity and peace and with the mind-soothing possibility of a cure that would never come. Nobody wanted to be told he would die, and the ones who protested most loudly that they did were the ones least capable of hearing it.

"How are the boys, James . . . and Mary? I'll never forget those cookies she baked. When little Joey had the meningitis."

"Oh, they's fine, Doc Foley. They's fine. I'm just hopin' this chest thing ain' gonna stop me workin'. Mary's birthday nex' week."

"You work for the city, don't you? If you had to take a few days off you'd be insured. I could fix that, no problem."

James smiled.

"It's the evenin' work pays for things like presents."

"Well, don't you worry, James. This is almost certainly an infection. Anyway, one good thing is you won't have to worry about the medical bills. There'll be no charge here. Unless you want to go and see the 'real' doctors somewhere like Mount Sinai."

They both laughed.

"Them sawbones'd have slim pickins with me. They'd call the cops if I tried to get into a place like that."

Robert Foley smiled grimly. It was almost true.

He wrote out the forms quickly. Full blood profile. Hemoglobin—to detect the anemia of chronic disease. White-cell count and sed. rate—both often raised in advanced malignancy. AP and lateral chest X ray. That was the important one. There was no point going overboard with the other tests right now, another advantage of a lawyer-clean environment. God, what he'd give for a CAT scanner. He handed the test forms across the desk to his patient and stood up. "Okay, James, take these to the nurse outside and she'll take some blood and fix up an appointment for the X ray. Now, don't you worry, okay? Promise?"

"Not if you says so, Doc. And thanks."

Robert Foley sat down and stared with unseeing eyes at the closed door. A dying man, brimful of false hope.

Life was hell, but life was also heaven, and above all it was paradox. Above all else it was Jane.

He didn't know what to do about her. He loved her, but there wasn't time for love. And he had loved like this before. Just once, but it had been the wildest affair that a man could have, and the fires of his passion had consumed him completely. They had burned and raged through his teenage years, eating up his youth, and they had flickered and flamed around the edges of his early middle age. There was no part of him that the blaze had not scorched and even now the mad love was not quite dead. But it had begun to die, because he had begun to see that he had been betrayed. Slowly, painfully slowly, the wild passion had begun to listen to the still, small voice of reason, to allow the possibility of doubt, and as the doubts had grown so had the realization that his was an unrequited love. His lover had lied to him, whispering the sweet words that had fanned the furnace of the desire for oneness, but all the while allowing the dreadful things that ultimately made a mockery of trust, loyalty, commitment, faith.

It had been a bitter, sad awakening, but he had torn himself away and plunged himself into a new commitment that could never let him down. He had tried to forget his old life completely, gone to medical school and immersed himself in the service of humanity. He had triumphed in his profession and given himself to the poor, the needy, and the sick in the desperate attempt to lose his past in the foreign legion of forgetfulness. To an extent it had worked, but try as he might, he could not forget the lover who had owned him, the lover who had pleasured him, the lover whose guilty presence hovered over him, now, this moment, and at every other second of his existence.

Could Jane battle with such a power? Could he? Could they together?

In her arms he had thought that the answer was yes. He had

kissed her and his mind had stopped and his soul had exploded with joy, but even then he had shrunk back from the awesome brink. Now, and every second since, he regretted it.

His prediction had been painfully accurate. Rivkin's magic wand had transformed his Cinderella into the ultimate princess, and now he was not the only man who wanted her. At the last census there were just under one hundred twenty-five million male Americans and the vast majority of those over puberty shared his desire. He smiled at the thought. She had been plucked from his grasp like a jewel from a beggar's hand and spirited away ito a world of frantic materialism, in which he could hardly breathe. They still saw each other, but it was always a rushed meeting. A few minutes of togetherness torn from a schedule so full it threatened to explode, showering a surprised world with appointments and photo calls, makeup sessions and publicity appearances, talk shows and business conferences.

On Sundays she was free, but on Sundays, like today, *he* was busy, seeing the people who could not afford to take time from work to visit their doctor. So now, this very minute, she would be lying alone, on top of the world that loved her, and maybe, just maybe, thinking of him.

Robert Foley groaned his anxiety at the white walls. How much longer would she remember him?

Soon it would be the time-honored phone call from Warren, and then all the glory boys would be clustering around: the whiter-shade-of-pale pop stars with their sly looks and drugged-out cool; the Russian ballet stars with their mocking, sparkling eyes and their steel-strut bodies—all cock and congratulations; the Pulitzer Prize—winning writers with faces like old raincoats and egos the size of the Latin American debt; the Jerry Brown/John Tunney-type politicos with their razor-sharp charm and their aroma of behind-the-scenes power. There would be check-forging studio heads and knock-kneed geriatric money men, Kashoggi children and teen-dream idols—all sniffing around her like a bitch in heat.

Where did that leave the Valley M.D. with the clinic in Watts?

Robert Foley stood up. He flicked the switch of the intercom. "Nurse, how many are still waiting outside?"

"About fifteen."

"Do any look serious?"

"Not really."

"I'm afraid they're going to have to be rescheduled. I've got an emergency. You can reach me on the beeper. Okay?"

"Okay, Dr. Foley."

It was true. He had an emergency. Himself and Jane.

TWENTY

JANE STRETCHED HER ARMS TOWARD THE POWDER-blue sky and tried to remember when last she had been so happy. *Nights* and Robert's vital introduction to Pete Rivkin had turned her world around, and now it was spinning like a nursery top. Shooting the series was a nightmare to everyone except her. She loved every hair-raising, nail-biting, bone-wrecking moment of it. She knew that she was astoundingly, breathtakingly good. Knew, too, that the camera lens was besotted by her. It wasn't bigheaded of her to know those things. They were facts. The moment she was on camera the scenes came alive like Sleeping Beauty at the touch of the prince's lips, and when they all watched the tapes at the end of the day she was gloriously aware of the hushed reverence that spoke so eloquently of the birth of a star. She could see it in their eyes and hear it in their voices—awe and humility, the unspoken appreciation that now she walked on a rarefied plane, where demigods and goddesses cavorted. There were other, more tangible, signs of the wonderful things that had happened to her, like the Benedict Canyon house, two million dollars' worth of California dreaming that had left change from the Estée Lauder contract alone. In the garage there was a blood-red 560 SL Mercedes convertible roadster, that powerful ikon of the Hollywood dream down to its sheepskin-covered seats, its Nardi steering wheel, and its license plate stating simply MERCEDES BENZ. Next to it, for company, were the black custom Suzuki Samurai 4 × 4 jeep-style runaround, the show-ready 1965 white Mustang fastback, and, representing the high end, a sleek gray BWM 735i. At the back of the house was the fifty-foot pool surrounded by Mexican tile and a built-in mosaic hot tub for sipping champagne, staring at the stars, and coming to serious grips with the material world. Beneath the pool, jutting out over a lower level of the canyon, lay the floodlit North/South tennis court with its own separate pavilion, ice-water machine, and TV monitor plugged into the camera system that oversaw the entrance to the electrically operated cast-iron gates of the three-acre estate.

Inside the house the glory continued: the futuristic kitchen with its Carrara marble floor, the three Sub-Zero fridges, Poggenpohl fitted cupboards, the Jenn-Air range and the Kitchen-Aid dishwashers. She had a built-in Sony TV with its own VCR for playback of video recipes or soap watching while she cooked, a Krupps coffee maker, a myriad of sexy black Braun appliances from Bullock's in the Beverly Center, and a compactor that mashed the trash into manageable proportions.

There was a computerized Westec burglar-alarm system (code word Star 90) with strategically placed "panic buttons" and piped music throughout the house from the central console; not to mention the fully equipped exercise room with its sprung floor, mirrored walls, hydraulic-resistance exercise machines, and its cardiovascular-system-monitoring stationary bikes. The cavernous poolside cabana contained a Mr. Steam cabinet, a sauna, and a massage area with its own marble-pedestal massage slab, in addition to the multiple jet showers. The billiard room was off the screening room, while the media room merged into the oak-paneled library. The "mistress" bedroom would have solved the housing problems of a dozen middle-class families, and the closets were themselves big enough to be living rooms in more ordinary homes. Browns on beiges, oranges and yellows floated into one another in the relaxing color schemes, and everywhere picture windows opened up great canyon vistas to the wondering eye.

Jane smiled to herself as she lay back on the rough white terrycloth of the sun bed and let the happiness explode from the back of her throat. It was a sigh of the purest contentment

—the sort she could only experience in contrast to the deepest sadness, the most fundamental disappointments. For sure she had had enough of those, but she wasn't going to spoil the beauty of the moment by thinking about them now. She took inventory of her singing senses, determined to preserve them for memory. Days like this couldn't be allowed to go away.

In her nostrils was the sublime smell of the mahogany-brown Ambre Solaire—so well remembered from childhood holidays in Ibiza and the south of France, merging in glorious harmony with the hot dry scents of the midafternoon canyon. It was bliss, too divine for words, as the burning sun torched down on her all-but-naked body, making love to the uncovered breasts that America dreamed about, and fathering the little bubbles of moisture that exploded all over her stomach. The hawks, climbing lazily on the faint breeze, searched for food among the purple scrub of the canyon walls and above her head a squirrel inched suspiciously along the branch of a poolside acacia tree as an anxious bluebird harassed it. Protecting a nest? Well, Jane could understand that. At last *she* had a nest to protect.

Fifty feet away, the guy from Wilshire Maintenance was going through the motions of cleaning the immaculate pool. Should she bother to tell him about the plastic glass she had dropped in the Jacuzzi? No, it would be a test of thoroughness whether he found it or not. It was wonderful to do absolutely nothing while somebody else "worked"—if that was what you could call vacuuming a spotless pool in eighty degrees of sunshine. Later on the gardeners would arrive and spend an hour or two pushing leaves from one place to another and hosing water into the pots of azaleas and ficus that the twenty-four-station computerized Rainbird sprinkler system didn't reach. Probably she ought to go through the motions of covering herself up, but the hell with it. This was her kingdom. She was its queen.

Languorously Jane sat up, and again she sighed her satisfaction. The pool was cut into the hillside below the house and from it there was a panoramic view all the way to the distant sea. She walked lazily to the rail at the end of the seventy-foot sun terrace and peered out over the canyon. To the right and above her there was the dull thud of music coming from a copse of trees. Her neighbor, Don Henley, was jamming it up with a few friends. Down below lay the old Ann-Margret estate, eighty brilliant acres of canyon prime, and nestling below the far hill was Cher's "Egyptian" blockhouse, built on the cash from the Vegas cabaret, shared with young Josh Donen and presently on the auction block for around four million. Out there somewhere—Jane had never figured out exactly where—was the ill-fated house that had belonged to Doris Day's son. Cielo Drive. Roman Polanski had rented it for his pregnant wife Sharon Tate. And one dreadful evening the Manson "family" had come to call.

She shut her eyes against the wild beauty of the canyon. Jane felt she had been reborn, brand new beneath the Beverly Hills sun. God, she loved this place, loved it all, even the orange yellow haze that licked at the city like a child at a lollipop. Mostly it was above the smog here, a few hundred feet below Mulholland Drive, but there was the acrid hint of it in the ozone air, reminding you that this place was real and that its terrible beauty could harm as well as haunt you. Jane loved that, too, the hidden danger of the canyons. She could sense it in the fierce heat of the Santa Ana winds that mocked her tranquillity. Their legacy was the invigorating aroma of gentle menace that permeated the sage-green hills with the beguiling energy of fear. A careless match and the intense beauty of these tinder-dry canyons would ignite in a blazing inferno of death and destruction. At nights the coyotes would crawl down from the hills and feed on the kittens and worry the dogs, and the weirdos would spill over from the Valley and the nighttime prowlers would crawl from the city gutters and roam the rich roads in search of prey. Then, in the winter rains, the mountains would slip and slide, raining rocks down onto the winding highway, smashing cars and filling the pools with slime and the landscaped paradise with mud.

And one day—one day soon—the earth would open and the ultimate disaster would strike in the form that Californians refused to contemplate. Then the houses would tumble into the valleys, and the gas mains would burst, and the freeways would become the hell they so often resembled, as fire and brimstone swept the vision of the future into the murky depths of the San Andreas. The rest of America would click its teeth and pretend to sympathize as God's thunderbolt struck down the Gomorrah that had been given too much. But nobody would cry for Los Angeles. Envy would see to that.

Yes, there was pain here, and fear and loathing and lost innocence, but Jane loved it. There was pain because there was so much possibility; there was failure and fear of failure because there was success and the hope of success; there was hatred because there was so much love. Here in California there was movement and optimism, and being and becoming in a beautiful place where to care was not considered naïve, to cry not regarded as weakness, to wish to change the status quo not looked upon as subversive. Sometimes it was difficult to imagine that the homeland she had left behind was part of the same planet.

She wandered back to the sun bed, the tiles hot beneath her feet. It was good to do nothing when there was nothing to do. Sundays were the only day off and Pete Rivkin expected them to be used exclusively for the recharging of batteries. So she flopped down onto the welcoming softness and ground her face downward into the sweet-smelling toweling as the faint strains of Genesis from the house sound system merged with the muffled but throbbing base from the cross-canyon recording studio. Lunch had been good—swordfish blackened Cajun style, a crisp green salad with a *real* French dressing rather than the cloudy, counterfeit concoction that passed for the genuine article in this part of the world, and a couple of Corona beers. All of it had been prepared by the cook, and now it was tempting sleep from the depths of the stomach on which America wanted to lay its head.

There was a peaceful, easy feeling in her soul, the one Don Henley had written about in the Eagles song, and there was only one thing missing from her world. The man she loved.

Jane shifted deliciously at the thought of him. Robert Foley and his gaunt body. The silver streaks in his worried hair. His innocent lips. His mysterious past. She felt the pounding of her heart, its pace quickening in time to the baton of thought, and she ground her pelvis into the foam-rubber softness to touch the part of her that needed to be touched.

She had made a parachuteless jump from a million feet, and he had been her soft landing. He had rescued her from humiliation, from poverty, from the edges of destruction and been instrumental in her extraordinary success, but her feelings for him weren't really to do with all that. From the first moment when she had awakened in the strange clinic in the middle of nowhere, there had been an intangible excitement, an electric feeling when his supposedly professional fingers had touched her, the weird awareness that she was hovering on the borders of a new state of consciousness. She had fought against it in her determination to leave the old Jane behind, but although she had achieved *that*, the strange feelings didn't go away. They grew, and they were growing still. She had nowhere to go and he had taken her in. There had been tension in the handsome face and the touch of an indecision that she sensed was not usually there when he had offered her his home. In sin city the screenplay would have called for all sorts of suspect motives—all kinds of steamy, sizzling conclusions—and her newly suspicious mind had considered most of them. But her heart had accepted, and it hadn't been like that at all. The mystic, sweet conclusion had never occurred, and as the days had passed Jane had begun to wonder why the hell not, and then to want the thing she had at first feared.

Slowly it had begun to dawn on her. This was the man she needed, a deep man, a selfless man, a man with direction and a diamond-hard sense of purpose. Foley was no Billy Bingham—a boy with adolescent dreams of power and revenge. He was formed, complete, whole, and his life was dedicated to an ambition so noble that she had to stand in awe of it. And she had to *compete* with it. It was like another woman, his love for a beautiful thing that was beyond criticism and above reproach. It sowed the seeds for an exotic flower of jealousy whose sweet scent added a piquant element to the dilemma called love.

But events had moved too fast, and the two of them had moved too slowly. From the moment of the fateful meeting with Pete Rivkin Jane's life had all but ceased to be hers. He had enveloped her like a benevolent cloud, and all the un-known details of the life she now led had been taken care of by the mighty people machine he organized. Investments, in-surance, the Benedict Canyon house—cast-aside plaything of a German industrialist who had tired of his "Hollywood phase"—the cars, the acting coaches, green card, staff had all appeared almost overnight. Platinum Amex cards, golden Visas, manila envelopes stuffed with hundred-dollar bills had come with the army of hairdressers and makeup artists, mas-seuses and chauffeurs, maids and manicurists who descended on her at unearthly hours of the morning when the world was asleep. All day long it was the grueling, backbreaking busi-ness of canning *Nights*, and all night long it was the business of trying to sleep through the excitement and the fantasy of her runaway world.

Of course she had moved out of Robert's house in the Val-ley and into the Beverly Hills Xanadu. At odd times they would meet—for sandwiches in the studio canteen, for snatched dinners after the day's shooting and before the early-to-bed evenings that alone made possible the crack-of-dawn awakenings—but the daunting distance between them had wi-dened with the separation and her unbelievable success. It had driven her mad then, in the Valley, because she had known that he wanted her. A thousand times she had seen it in his gestures, the fires of desire burning deep in his longing eyes. And she had wanted him—God, how very much—through the clammy San Fernando nights, when the heat ladled itself over her, and turned her lonely bed into a battlefield of silent desire—the sheets damp, her T-shirt soaked with sweat as she endured the darkness and prayed for the quietly opening door, and the whispered words of the nighttime lover.

One earth-moving kiss, and then nothing more. He had torn himself away from her as if he had committed a crime— a criminal act that he recoiled from as he wanted it more than life itself. What force had blocked his passion? What power stayed his arm and prevented him from acting out the mes-sages of his heart? He had wanted her but he had not l??? her, and she was there, ready, crying out to be loved. Each day they had lived as man and wife—shopping at Ralph's on the weekend, eating pasta at Frank's, reading books, separate but wonderfully together in the living room of the stucco house, horseplay on the weekend afternoons in the tiny pool. There had been so many possibilities, so many tantalizing chances at intimacy, but the clouds had always blotted out the sun of passion, and at moments when things had been so very "right," the unknown thing had intervened that made them wrong.

Jane had never been able to work out what it was, but she supposed there was a reason and that it was rooted in the past that he wouldn't discuss. He hadn't always been a doctor. He had taken it up later in life. That much she knew. But what had he done before? Who, if anyone, had loved him? Whom, if any, had he loved? It was a mystery to her. By mutual consent neither of them had probed too deep.

Jane allowed her thoughts to drift. Robert Foley. Sweet dreams on a canyon afternoon.

Her breathing was steady now, the rhythms playing over the firm brown skin of her breasts. She moistened her lips with a lazy tongue and closed her eyes; then she was poised on the diving board seconds from the plunge into the welcoming pool of sleep.

NOBODY WAS ANSWERING THE BUZZER AT THE GATE.

Robert Foley wasn't in a waiting mood. He left the car where it was on the road, and vaulted over the heavy iron gate.

The front door was open, and the warm canyon breeze was rustling through the leaves of the succulent ficus plants in the Mexican tiled hallway, caressing the lilies on the heavy oak chest, fanning through the areca palms that guarded the entrance to the drawing room.

"Jane?"

She wasn't there.

He walked through several rooms, calling out quietly to The rooms stared back at him. They weren't hers yet. There had been no time for her to impose her personality on the formidable house.

He walked through the outside barbecue area, to the cabana, to the pool. Nothing.

Then he saw her, right at the edge of the terrace, stretched out on the brink of the hazy canyon.

Robert Foley quickened his step as he moved toward her, and his darting heart outran his feet.

He stood over her, his face awash with wonder at the sight of her, this girl who had dragged him from the dungeon that had been his past life. She was asleep, one long brown arm flung upward to shield her eyes from the relentless sun. Beneath it the sweat glistened on the downy hair, and the sweeping line of her pectoral muscles slid gracefully down to the naked breasts. They rose and fell, measuring her breathing, proud monuments pointing toward the clear blue sky, and they spoke to Robert Foley's very essence.

"Jane!" His voice was quiet, unwilling to disturb her sleep, but wanting to add sound to the visual symphony. Then he knelt down beside her, and his lips brushed against hers, his tongue licking gently at the moisture shining from her upper lip.

THE WIND FROM THE DESERT TOUCHED THE LOVERS.

Jane moved her hand slowly to greet it. Languorously she held it up, and turned it around, to feel the soft kiss of the Santa Ana. She smiled at him, the pain gone from his eyes now, his whole face bathed in a loving quietness she had never seen before. Soon there would be words. But not now, not yet.

Her leg was across his, the honey brown of its delicate contours a contrast to his paler skin. Robert, the man with little time to worship the sun, the man with the world's worries on his mind, had loved her at last.

She was full of him, gloriously, deliciously full of him, and the harrowing screams of his almighty sweet conclusion still reverberated through her. Never had she dreamed that such a hardened dam could break. There had been so much held and for so very long, but as the bricks had broken and the concrete cracked, the deluge of desire had flowed directly into the core of her being. And now it was inside her, as he was inside her, joined in the joy of the aftermath of first-time love.

She traced the outline of his half-parted lips with her fore-finger, lingering at the corner, exploring the body that now was hers. Her mouth moved soundlessly around the words *I love you*.

He nuzzled into her then, his tired head against her breast, loving the thin film of wetness and the radiating heat that was the legacy of passion. She was all around him. This girl that he adored. This creature of endless beauty who had unraveled his mind and untied the knots that bound him to the gray drabness of his pleasure-free life. Of course he had fallen from the hard unforgiving throne of perfection. Now he was merely mortal—a grasping, wanting, feeling person at last. He mut-tered against the damp, welcoming skin, "I love you, Jane. I love you so much."

She wrapped her long arms around him and pulled him in toward her. Closer, and more close, as she crushed him against the body America wanted, in a desperate attempt to hide him inside her where he could be her, and she him. That was the sum total of her desire, and all the grinding, twitch-ing, threshing of the love dance was merely grasping for that impossibility. Cocooned in her body he moved happily against her, and distrustful of the bonds of arms, Jane reached hun-grily for him with her legs, too. Urgently, they thrust out for him, wrapping themselves around his, lest he slip away. And deep within, in grateful thanks for the envelope of passion that she had fashioned for him, she felt him grow once more.

She bent down to kiss the wet hair of his head—bathed in the sweat of his longing—and, her hands clasped tightly around his firm back, she clamped the soft silk walls of her about him.

"Yes. Yes, Robert," her voice said, low and husky in the quiet before the hurricane's return.

His body replied to her. Hesitant at first, then, strengthen-ing its resolve and discarding diffidence, it rejoiced in its re-discovered power, its once again resolute purpose.

Beneath his mouth her tense nipples, tight with longing,

pushed eagerly against his face. Then his lips were on them, insistent, demanding, sucking angrily at the fevered skin.

Backward and forward the borderline flew as tenderness warred with want. They were two alien figures—merging and then springing apart once again, in a desperate equilibrium that neither could control. They fed from each other, to kill the hunger that would never die, and the warm wind lapped at them and teased them with its touch.

He reached for her now. Strong, anxious arms burrowing beneath her to find the hard muscles and creamy skin of her bottom and he drew her toward him, at the same time pushing out, plunging himself once more into the deep delight.

Jane moaned her acquiescence, and her legs splayed out wide to welcome him. He moved on top of her—his hands still on her breasts, his stomach flat against hers, his eyes shining.

She lay back and stretched out her arms above her head as she gloried in the vision of his mastery. Up above her, deep inside her, all around her this man she loved had accepted the precious gift of her flesh. He must use her as he wished, enjoy her selfishly.

He saw it in her eyes—the demand for assertion, and he moved to do her bidding. Long and hard, he stroked at her. He thrust deep and cruel, and his pace quickened as he darted at her, rocking her body, crashing into the heart of her. On and on, harder and harder, he hammered her, watching her face wince with the delirious pain as the vicious strokes shook her. On his bottom he could feel her fingers pulling at him, urging him on, and around his lips the words gathered as he took her, strange alien words of lust and aggression that mocked the love that was in his heart and mind. And she nodded to him in encouragement.

It's all right. To do this to me. Like this. I love it, as I love you. Bury yourself in bliss, as you lose yourself in me.

His fingers squeezed mercilessly at the rock-hard nipples, and he renewed the violent assault until there was nothing but the searing rhythms of the dance, and the crazy crashing of his heart as he rode her. Now his hands were behind her, his nails buried deep in the firm flesh of her buttocks as hers raked at his. Blood and bruises would be the badges for the rough riders of love.

Like stars doomed to collide, they headed toward each other, the other planets flashing by, irrelevant spectators to the consummation that was about to be. Before, he had paused at the magic moment as he had tried to calm his senses, the better to feel the ultimate feeling—but now the unholy alliance demanded a headlong flight into the chaos of mystery as they raced together for the raging moon.

He opened his mouth to shout for her, and lips parted in the snarl of joy, she called back to him as their wild voices joined to welcome the clash of worlds. Far out on the canyon breeze, borne effortlessly by the knowing Santa Ana wind, the cry of the two lovers was a single thing.

ROBERT FOLEY SLIPPED HIS HAND INTO JANE'S BENEATH THE dazzling white tablecloth. Usually the charity people, with their diseased social ambitions and their speed-limit IQs, gave him hives, and the tuxedo torture of a Century Plaza charity ball threatened a nervous breakdown. Tonight, however, he was with Jane, and she was with him.

"What does this remind you of?" he whispered to her. "Barracudas feeding? The *Invasion of the Body Snatchers*?"

Jane laughed. It was true. The L.A. caviar generals were out in force and it was not a pretty sight. Right now they were table hopping, showing off their estate jewels, their Dr. Frank Kramer and/or Dr. John Williams facelifts, and their husbands of the month. All the time their anxious eyes kept the score. Who was with them? Who against them? Who was overly pleased to bask in their shade, who positioning himself subtly to avoid it? There were perhaps a hundred tables—eight or twelve of the charitable guilty at each—and at two hundred and fifty bucks a ticket, this benefit for retinitis pigmentosa, known as the Eye Ball, would score upwards of two hundred thousand from the evening.

"You're just pissed off that all this loot is for eyes, and not for your clinic."

Jane squeezed his hand under the table, and her laughter

bubbled from the back of her throat as she loved him, loved her life, loved everything and everyone in the world.

They were joined now. Whatever had held Robert Foley back was holding him back no longer. Born again into the world by the midwife of passion, in the glorious new dawn he was making up for lost time. During the days she shot *Nights*, but during the nights she immersed herself in the wonder of his body, and in the wild ways of love. The intensity of the experience had left its marks all over her, and the vibrant, unleashed sexuality now formed a terrible alliance with her beauty to send the enslaved country crazy. *Nights* was a miracle. The advertising rates were already seven hundred thousand for each thirty-second slot (three hundred thousand more than *The Cosby Show*), giving a per-episode revenue to ABS of a mouth-watering eight and a half million dollars, and a profit of over four million. It was serious success, and all around the room the rubber-necking fame-and-fortune lovers were peering and craning to catch a glimpse of Pete Rivkin's star discovery.

"I can't think why all these rich people don't just sit down and write a quiet check without putting us through all this goddamn business." Robert Foley's "irritation" was a sham.

Pete Rivkin leaned across the table. "Typical of you, Robert. Absolutely typical. No finesse. No patience at all for the bullshit to which we are all addicted. Don't you understand? This isn't for charity. This is an excuse to give a *party*. You see, the great beauty of a *charity* party is the collective responsibility. Any one of these megabuck ladies could have thrown a bash like this for herself. But what if no one had showed? Or what if only the no-hopers, the has-beens, and the also-rans had come? And what if everyone had laughed at the food, or the flowers, or the entertainment?"

He drew his finger dramatically across his neck. "Social death," he intoned mischievously. "You see, this town isn't like the East Coast, where social structures are set in cement. If the Phippses give a party in Palm Beach or the Van Alens in Newport they could serve cold cat and cabbage and dance to a jukebox and everyone would say "How clever," or "How very sophisticated." But here, social self-confidence is an endangered species. You're only as good as your latest husband and he's only as good as his last movie or TV series. Okay, so you can minimize the risks of disaster by getting Punky Brewster's mom, Mother Moon, or Chasens, or Candy Spelling's company to do the catering and Bijan to do the favors, but if you want to play it really safe it's best to take insurance and throw the party for charity."

"Well, I think you're all far too cynical," Jane said. "I think it's a wonderful party. Look at all these beautiful white gardenias. At the London parties, it's dreadful faded carnations, half-cold food, and teenage old Etonians throwing rolls and throwing up."

Jane sighed her happiness. Even the Rose ball at the Grosvenor House with its glutinous chicken Kiev, dreaded Bombe Surprise, and its shiny faced, chinless-wonder public school wankers would seem like paradise if Robert were holding her hand.

Pete Rivkin turned toward her solicitously. He was under no illusions about who had made him the colossus he had become.

"Sweet of you to say so, darling, and this town's great at all sorts of things, but at the end of the day California's got no class. A few nice little old ladies in Pasadena, maybe, Mrs. Chandler and the Dohenys, but basically the place gets its rocks off on money, fame, and, above all, power."

"I didn't know you did a sideline in social anthropology, Pete." Robert studied his wineglass. "My theory is that it's guilt, and no longer tax-deductible guilt. For their face creases, these people are more than happy to blow seven hundred and fifty bucks a throw on collagen shots that only last a month, but they're embarrassed, so they go all out on something like this to compensate. Some of the plastic boys are the biggest spenders of all. I see that Gary Tearston and Stephen Genender *both* have tables."

"Well, for sure you ought to know all about guilt, Robert." Pete Rivkin looked at his friend slyly. "Sometimes I think you invented it. But you may have a point. Do you know that at the Hillcrest Country Club you have to show that you give at least five percent of your income to charity every year if you want your membership to stay current? In Palm Beach, you can't get into the Country Club until you've given away a million bucks minimum."

"That's unbelievable," Jane said. "In England charity's more or less a dirty word. A bottle of sherry to the village fête maybe, and the odd check to the Distressed Gentlefolk on the there-but-for-the-Grace-of-God principle, maybe something for animals—but nothing like the scale of this. I think everybody feels that because we've got a welfare state, individuals don't have to bother, and that it's a bit patronizing to give people money."

Pete nodded. "To some extent it's a racial thing. You gentiles aren't as guilty as us. God knows why not. And in this town you're not as rich. You won't see many WASPs from the California Club or the Los Angeles Country Club here. This is the Hillcrest and Beverly Hills Tennis Club crowd." He chuckled wickedly as he peered around the room.

It was also, thought Jane, the older crowd. Hard-line film people, lots of "faces," the hotshot agents, the older, more established rock stars like Rod Stewart, the easy-listening boys like Neil Diamond and Barry Manilow, and a retinue of "service" people—the doctors, the dentists, the P.R.s, the interior designers. They were the sort of people Jackie Collins wrote about, souped-up crinkly-wrinkly golden oldies, kept in a sort of "undead" suspended animation by their tummy lifts, fat-suction treatments, and their Morey Parks rhinoplasties—their minds pickled by dry martinis; their psyches expanded, quieted, stimulated by "substances"; their anxious bodies subjected endlessly to "immunological" and other bogus diets and a steady inflow of the latest vitamin combos and trace-element flavors-of-the-month.

It was a million miles from Melrose and La Brea here, although most of these people could find their way to the City or Tommy Tang's, and it was light-years away from the young club scene where the new L.A. bubbled and simmered. This was the Chasens/Bistro Garden/Jimmy's crowd who wore Galanos "gowns" from Amen, and little "creations" from Scaasi and Ungaro. They had their blackheads removed at Georgette Klinger and by Jolanta Widuch, they were massaged by Bella

Kruper, and their hair was styled at Elizabeth Arden and Emil Riley. Their handbags were by Hermès, Gucci, and Giorgio; their handguns were Bijan; and their sheets were from Pratesi.

These women had a very simple objective in life: to be size six. This meant dieting, of course, but it did *not* mean buying the diet book that was highest on the *New York Times* Best Seller List. Oh dear, no! Instead it meant long consultations with Hermien Lee, and even longer and more expensive ones with endocrinologists, who could be relied on to obscure the basic message that people got fat by eating too much and exercising too little. And it meant excursions to the fat farms or "spas" like the Palm-Aire or the Bonaventure in Florida or the Greenhouse in Texas, where one could cheerfully spend three thousand dollars a week to buy somebody else's will-power. Not that daily-bread exercise was totally ignored; they had places for that, too, like Walter Rohzen's and Robert Carreiro's, galaxies away from the sweaty honesty of Body Express, where the new generation went.

These people's morals were by Mammon, their minds by the way, and their children by almost anyone at all.

"Who are they all?" Jane turned to Pete Rivkin.

Pete Rivkin laughed. All around the room he could see the effect she was having. In a way it was her first time "out" and he had chosen this ball carefully. She was getting maximum exposure to the "old" Hollywood—all the studios had tables, all the top agencies, most of the "now" indie production companies. She wanted to know who they were. They all knew exactly who *she* was. In itself that was the measure of Pete Rivkin's phenomenal star-building success.

"Well, let's see if I can pick out the *heavy* artillery. Right. That one over there is Fran Stark, Ray Stark's wife. She can make or break you socially in this town. Behind her is Mrs. Johnny—Joanna—Carson, stronger than ever since the divorce. You wouldn't want to be on the wrong side of her if you wanted to give your money away in style. The couple standing by the next table are relative newcomers. The pretty one on the left is Victoria McMahon, Ed's wife. The one with the jewels is Marianne Rogers. Kenny's lady. They're both pretty hot right now. It ain't no court of St. James, but it's all we got."

The flashbulbs were going off at more or less everyone. Whom did you shoot at a Century City charity ball? The Charlton Heston/Gregory Peck/Kirk Douglas perennials were obvious but safe. Or the gray eminences of the social scene like the Haymans, who owned Giorgio, or the bizarrely named but socially shit-hot Contessa Cohn—they were more adventurous but perhaps just a little obscure. It was rare to find that delicious combination of novelty and fame. But from the point of view of the hungry photographers they merged deliciously in Jane.

George Christy was shepherding the new *Hollywood Reporter* photographer through the social snake pit. From the veteran gossip columnist there was nothing he wouldn't learn. "Well, hello there, Pete. Congratulations! Biggest ever, eh? And *this* is the reason. My word. All my *best* clichés aren't good enough. You are *so* beautiful." He reached for Jane's hand with the ease of the socially self-confident. His columns in the new-look *Reporter* and in state-of-the-style *Interview* were the very last word on Hollywood. Eat your heart out, *W* and *Vanity Fair*. "I can't say I ever watch TV, but you know, I did last week. Simply *had* to see what everyone was talking about. And now I know. Well, well, well, isn't this fun?"

George Christy peered out optimistically at the same old world through his thick, rose-colored spectacles, immunized against déjà vu, absolutely certain that everything was bright and beautiful, all creatures great, not small. He turned to the photographer. "Now you be sure and get half a dozen good ones of Ms. Cummin. All you'll have to do is point the camera and shoot. I don't think even *I* could take a bad picture of her."

Christy's practiced eyes scanned the table, searching for the angle, the new face in town, the musical-chairs relationship, the hot deal brewing. Around Rivkin things tended to happen, just as Jane Cummin had "happened."

Shifting uncomfortably in his seat, his piercing, intelligent eyes and off hand good looks proclaiming his indifference to both the Christy charm and the Christy influence, Robert

Foley caught the Christy eye. It was immediately apparent that he was the "story."

George Christy flicked around the table. "I think I know all your friends, Pete. Hello, Laddie. Gene, Gilda. Richard, Paula." He nodded happily at each. "Now, wait a minute, there's a face I don't know." He lunged out an impossible-to-turn-down hand at Robert Foley. "George Christy," he said.

Robert lifted one unwilling buttock an inch from his seat.

"Oh, George," Pete Rivkin said, "this is my great friend, Dr. Robert Foley. Robert runs a free clinic down in Watts and raises a bundle of money for Live Aid. Right now he's my number-one guy. He asked me to see Jane for a part in *Nights* and the rest, as they say, is history."

"Oh, my, my! How fabulous! Isn't that just wonderful? Have you two known each other long?" George Christy slid into gear. No one could extract a secret so fast, no truth serum so painlessly.

But in mid-interrogation Robert Foley had had enough. The band had begun to play, and the claustrophobia was closing in. It was a good moment to spirit Jane away.

"Listen, Pete. You handle the P.R., okay. I'll take Jane away for a dance." He held out his hand to her, and she rose thankfully to take it.

In a few seconds—surrounded by cowboys and Cleopatras, Pattons and policemen, murderers and Moseses—they were to all intents and purposes alone on the crowded dance floor.

He looked down at her and smiled. "Well, what do you think of the American dream?"

"I like *your* dream, Robert." She nuzzled in close as all around the tongues hurried to work, and the necks shifted like angle-poise lamps.

The tap on her shoulder was much too hard to be friendly.

"Hello, soap-opera star. How does it feel to be the toast of the town? For a minute or two."

Jane twisted as her heart began to pound.

Julie's face, teeth bared, eyes narrowed, was alive with hatred. She stood foursquare, hands on commodious hips, her mammoth breasts spilling out of the little-girl chiffon dress.

"Ohmigod," said Jane. "Malice in Wonderland."

Julie's head shot back at the unexpected speed of the counterattack. It had been an ambush. Surprise had been on Julie's side. Jane wasn't supposed to have organized her defenses so fast.

Julie reached around behind her and produced her partner like a conjuror the rabbit from the hat.

An Italian soccer player? Jane thought. A cha-cha merchant at a dance palace? A father's nightmare, a raw teenager's most potent fantasy. He looked like an oil slick off the Louisiana coast. You could have picked your teeth with the points of his soft leather boots, played chopsticks on the perfect ivory of his even teeth, lived like a queen forever off the melted-down bullion from the multiple medallions that would be nestling beneath the frilly dress shirt.

"This is Antoine," Julie said. "I expect you'll be wanting to fuck him." She laughed nastily.

"Listen, Julie, it's you they call the British Open. Not me."

Robert Foley could hardly believe his ears or his eyes. He looked askance at Jane. Her cheeks were flushed, her eyes sparkling. And who *was* this terrible apparition with her cheap gigolo?

Robert moved fast. Taking Jane in his arms, he swept her away into the safety of the crowd, leaving the woman who looked like a Christmas decoration to splutter her fury and indignation.

"What was *that* all about?"

"*That* was Julie Bennett."

"*The* Julie Bennett?"

"*The* Julie Bennett. She's not my greatest fan."

"Nor you hers, I gather."

They both laughed, but Jane didn't say any more.

"How did you come across her? What did you do to upset each other?"

"Oh, it's a long story. Boring," Jane lied. Julie had torn up her good mood like a wet tissue. "Listen, Robert, I have to go to the loo. Shall I meet you back at the table?" She just needed a minute or two to put herself back together.

There was something so safe about the ladies' room; it was

a sort of conspirator's command center. In it, one could feel that at least half of humanity was on your side.

The big, cheerful girl with the jolly laugh said, "Hi. You're Jane Cummin, aren't you? I'm Wendy Stark. I must just say I think your show is wonderful. Such a relief to have people wearing the right clothes and living in the right houses. I was beginning to think I'd got it all wrong. Did you hear that, Candy? You ought to get Aaron to upgrade the 'Dysentery' lot. Give 'em all gold American Express cards at least, even if he can't bring himself to send them platinum. At the moment they're trucking along on green."

The round-eyed, faunlike Candy Spelling, with the look of semipermanent surprise quite common to her species, had to agree. "Just what I'm always saying. They should make me a consultant to the show. There's absolutely *nothing* I don't know about spending money."

The ice-cold wind knifed into the room, cooling the laughter, freezing the good time.

"Ah, Jane. I thought it was you, slinking off to the loo. I couldn't bear to leave without saying good-bye *properly*."

Julie Bennett ignored both Candy Spelling and Wendy Stark, both of whom she knew slightly. All her heavy guns were trained on Jane.

"Oh, you shouldn't have bothered, Julie. I can say good-bye to you anytime."

"Have you heard from Billy?" Julie's usually huge eyes were gimlet small as they gleamed and flashed.

"No, but I read that he was a big success in New York. Sell-out exhibition. Everybody wild about his paintings. Do you remember all those rude things you used to say about them, Julie? Amazing how wrong one can be, isn't it? And to think you have a reputation for knowing about art."

The direct hit lit up Julie's face like the billboard at Marmont and the Strip. She tried to regain the initiative, but she was reeling from the blow.

"So he walked out on you." Julie spat out her statement.

"*Did* he? I thought it was *you* he walked out on. He told me he could take just about everything, but that the 'bedroom duties' made him 'toss his cookies.' I wonder what he meant by that?"

Candy Spelling and Wendy Stark, eyes on stalks, ears flapping, didn't wonder. Wendy let out a loud guffaw of uncontrolled delight. When you'd hung around the Pigott-Brown/Rupert Deen London scene, there was *nothing* you enjoyed so much as thoroughly bad behavior.

"He never said that. *He never said that*. He was a lousy fuck. He couldn't fuck his way out of a paper bag." Julie's face was puce.

"Well, you ought to know, Julie. You're the one with all the practice. After all, you've been paying for lessons for years. Is 'Antoine' your new instructor? He looks as if he's got a reasonably strong stomach. For sure he'll be needing it."

"How dare you speak to me like that? How dare you. You . . . you cheap whore. You little piece of shit . . ." She raised her hand to strike, but, quick as a flash, Jane caught it in a vicelike grip.

"Good-bye, Julie. It was 'good-bye' you came in here to say to me, wasn't it? You know, Julie, you're beginning to lose your timing, and that's bad news for any comic." Jane dropped Julie's hand as if it were contaminated and walked determinedly to the door.

Over her shoulder the barely coherent babble spluttered and splashed against her ears.

"Destroy you . . . tomorrow . . . I swear . . . you're finished . . . do you hear . . . do you *hear*?"

TWENTY-ONE

ROBERT FOLEY HAD HAD SOME BAD DAYS IN HIS life, but this was the worst.

On the table in front of him the four pictures seared their appalling message into his brain.

On the other side of the desk, dressed for some extraordinarily appropriate reason in head-to-toe black Givenchy, sat the best-selling authoress in America.

"It took me ages to pick the best ones," said Julie in chatty, conversational style. "But I think I've got a representative selection. What is it everyone says? 'I don't know much about photography, but I know what I like.'"

Robert Foley's face had collapsed like an avalanche in the Alps. Although he was sitting down, his whole body had crumpled, crushed by the enormity of what the photos meant. Despite the air-conditioning he had begun to sweat.

Julie was knocking on the gates of Nirvana. "Are you fond of ice cream?" she asked with the innocence of an asp.

Robert Foley's fist, already clenched, the knuckles snow white, crashed down hard against the desktop. "Shut up! *Shut up!*"

"I only asked," said Julie Bennett pleasantly.

"Where did you get these?" he whispered.

"From Jane's girlfriend."

The lie was the truth. The photographs said so.

Robert Foley fought to make sense of it. Jane was making

love to a girl, was being made love to by a girl, in the most extreme way imaginable. This was no chaste kiss between young girlfriends. This was hot, searing, steamy sex, pornography so hard that it could cut diamonds. Jane? His Jane? Sweet, gentle, funny, sensible, beautiful Jane? It defied belief. "This isn't Jane," he said with all the conviction of a psychopath in the confessional.

"Oh, *isn't* it? Silly me. It looked so like her. And that other girls looks *so* like the Lucy Masterson she used to work for. Well, what a relief, because I'm going to spread them around a bit. I think they're just wonderful, and if it isn't Jane then so much the better."

"*No!*"

Julie Bennett tried to save every last nuance of the scene for memory. The idiot was straighter than a line between two points. She knew he wouldn't be able to cope with happy snaps of the true-blue action. He'd close their relationship down faster than Salt Lake City would close a branch of Plato's Retreat.

"Why are you showing me these . . . terrible things?"

"Oh, I thought you had a right to know. We Americans are huge on that, aren't we? Responsible choices, and freedom of information, everything public and aboveboard?" Because you stared into her eyes last night, and billed and cooed at her like a teenager at the homecoming queen. Because she looked at you as if the solar system shone from your puckered shy ventricle, and because she held on tight to your shiny dinner jacket and crammed her cunt against your twitching dick, you fucking loser wanker piece of cheap shit. And because I want to cause her pain. Pain and angst, and heartache and humiliation, to pay everyone back for the desperate life I've lived so long.

Robert's voice was quiet, resigned. "What are you going to do with them?"

Julie treated his question as if it were an honest inquiry, the picture editor at *Cosmo* asking politely where the photographer was going to place the pix.

"Ah, what a good question. Bit strong for *Hustler*, don't you think? And yet the really gamy magazines haven't got the circulation, have they? And they're so *good*. I wonder if Jane signed a model release? Perhaps they deserve private circulation. Sort of limited-edition collector's item for the opinion makers of the town—Rona, and Barbara, and Dan Galvin at ABS—he's a broad-minded, regular sort of guy—oh, and your host last night, Pete Rivkin. He certainly has the 'right to know,' doesn't he? Maybe he could use a few of them as publicity stills for the *Beverly Hills Nights* P.R. Should play great in Peoria—if the broadcasting-standards boys and girls have that retinitis pigmentosa we raised so much loot for last night."

There was only one other question, the one Americans just loved to ask.

"Why?" he murmured.

"My word, Dr. Foley, I thought that *doctors* always knew the answers to questions like that. Every time I open a magazine or turn on the television there's a brilliant 'scientist' telling me why I do the things I do. They seldom seem to *agree*, but that doesn't seem to matter. Well, let's see. Perhaps it was a bad birth experience, or my 'inferiority complex,' or a problem with the collective unconscious, if one wants to duck a little of the responsibility. I suppose the Electra deal is a little unfashionable now, with Freud under attack, but I imagine we should entertain the possibility that this is all about wanting to fuck my father . . ."

Her words died away in her throat, and the roaring sensation filled up her ears. She could feel the blood rushing around her body. Her heart was thumping, and her spine was jelly, and suddenly it wasn't fun anymore.

Through the swirling mists the doctor's eyes were piercing into her. And the room was revolving like a spinning top.

THE INTERCOM CRACKLED WITH STATIC BUT THERE WAS NO mistaking the enthusiasm of Jane's welcome. "Terrific. You got away early. Hurry in."

Robert Foley's face was a death mask, as the big gates swung open at the touch of the invisible button.

Shock and horror: the words were news-headline hyperbole, but they painted the best picture of the chaos inside him. The irresistible force had collided with the immovable object and something had to give: his image of the sweet beauty who was longing to see him, or the vision of lesbian lust. There wasn't room for the two of them in the same mind, certainly not in his—that pristine, empty shrine to iced charity and otherworldly goodness.

But there was another emotion, absolutely undeniable in the heart that was just learning to love—jealousy. He had given himself to Jane. He had allowed her to pluck him from Grace—that prickly pedestal, whose comfortless perch at least separated him from the need to feel the feelings that the masses felt. And now he was repaid by this.

The girl he had chosen to love loved someone else. Someone called Lucy Masterson. There was another spine-chilling possibility. What if she didn't love Lucy Masterson at all? What if the photographs pictured not love but lust, or worse still, not lust but lucre?

The anger boiled within him now. How dare she? How did she dare to love him when she had done these things with a woman? What else lay beneath the carpet of her past, if the turned-up edge revealed this secret? And what of Julie—the billowing book queen with her acid tongue and her awful threats. Where did she fit into the devil's jigsaw? Was she, too, a homosexual, wreaking a fiendish vengeance on a faithless lover, or a feared and hated rival?

Julie had told him nothing. Less than an hour before she had staggered from his office looking as if she were about to have a coronary. He had never seen such an abrupt change of mood, and all in answer to his question, "Why?" But that was then and this was now. In seconds he would be face to face with Jane.

He stalked past the vast acacia tree, through the cobbled courtyard, and in his heart his temper fought with the things his intellect told him he should feel. This was Jane's tragedy more than his. If Julie Bennett did what she had promised to do, the rocket of Jane's orbiting career was about to destruct in a publicity maelstrom of cosmic proportions. Then she would need the quiet understanding of the man she loved. And the way he felt right now, there was no way he could provide it.

The carved oak door was open, and he stormed into the airy hallway. Jane rushed across the tiles to greet him, flinging herself into his arms, not noticing the thunder on his face. He pushed her roughly away and caught the incomprehension in her eyes.

They were in his hand. All four of them. Hot and horrid, with their ghastly message.

Robert Foley thrust them at her, cruelly, callously, willing the pain that now she would feel, the pain she had made *him* feel.

Jane looked down. At the hatred. At the wickedness. "Oh, God!" she said.

"Why didn't you tell me, Jane? I had a right to know. Surely to God I had a right to know."

He heard the echo of Julie Bennett's mocking words.

Jane turned away, shaking her head from side to side, as if to clear away the cobwebs of the nightmare.

She looked back at him, at his stricken, indignant face. For a second it seemed she would speak. She opened her mouth. To deny the undeniable? To excuse the inexcusable? To explain the inexplicable?

But he cut her off. He didn't want her words. He wanted his. Robert Foley began to shake with the indignation of the righteous. "How dare you do this to me, Jane? How dare you cover up your squalid past? It's bad enough you use my friends to make your career, but how can you pretend to love me when you have all these . . . disgusting secrets? I trusted you, and you repay me like this. What else is there for me to know about? What other nasty little surprises do you have for me . . . ?"

His eyes blazed their fury.

So did hers.

"Why don't you go fuck yourself, Robert Foley," she said.

"What?"

"I said, go fuck yourself, Mr. Squeaky Clean. You ought to know how. I taught you how to do it."

Robert Foley took one step back as the unexpected reaction exploded in his face.

"Jane!" he said, not knowing any longer what on earth he meant by that. Somehow the scene had been rewritten. In his scenario anger had played first. Then contrition and abject apology (hers). Last, as an optional ending, the plot had called for magnanimous forgiveness.

"Don't 'Jane' me, you pompous, posturing little arsehole. How dare you come mincing into my house full of pride and prejudice, lecturing me without even asking what it's all about? You know the trouble with you, Robert Foley? You think you're a good deed in a naughty world, and that everybody ought to treat you like the second coming. Well, here's some hot news. You're history. Get the *hell* out of my house, and get the *fuck* out of my life."

"Oh dear," said Robert Foley, as he backed away toward the front door.

All the anger was gone now, and the thing that was left was not a comfortable thing at all.

It was the blinding realization that Jane was absolutely right.

JANE EXPLODED INTO THE STUDIO LIKE A HEAT-SEEKING MIS-sile searching for its target.

There she was—queen of the flesh jungle, her pert rump toward the door, bending down low over the inevitable camera.

Jane hardly had time to orient herself. The door had been wide open and she was crouched low on the crest of her own adrenaline wave, speeding in toward her destination.

Lucy half turned to check out the crashing commotion, as somebody shouted "Hey!" and someone else said, "Can I help you, lady?" But she was too slow. Jane's Nike-sneakered foot arched upward in drop-kick mode and zapped into the right buttock of Lucy Masterson's ass, sending her reeling across the room.

For a millisecond or two it looked like she would keep her balance as she staggered forward from the force of the blow.

But the strobe unit lead had other ideas. So did the upturned edge of the powder-pink background paper, taped to the floor a yard in front of the naked male model. Suddenly Lucy had lift-off. She twisted into the air as she tried in vain to avoid the obstacles and then, quite literally, she was going down.

The centerfold for *Boy* magazine, his hard already going soft, watched in horror as Lucy Masterson's face zoomed in toward his crotch. His avoiding action was way too slow. Wham, bam, and thank you, sir, she was into him, and with a mighty squeal of shock and pain he floated into the chaos of whirling, swirling, falling limbs.

Jane stood back to catch her revenge. The twenty-minute drive from the top of Benedict had been an age of anger and frustration. The tears of rage had all but blinded her as she had burned past the Beverly Hills Hotel and taken rubber off the radials on the right down Doheny. Lucy Masterson had ruined her twice. She had blown her lover out of her life and pushed her career to the brink of the cliff. She had it coming.

Jane could feel the glorious tingle all up and down her leg. That had been contact. It had been just the right discharge of pent-up emotion, far better than a lifetime of est and Esalen and Insight. Lucy Masterson lay where she had fallen, the look of terminal surprise painted all over her face. The blast-off from nowhere had been one thing, the searing pain in her butt another, but the most remarkable thing of all was lying up against her mouth.

Jane looked at her, and suddenly humor flooded into the vacuum left by the fury. Her face softened into a smile.

"Wow, Lucy, I didn't know dick was your bag." She began to laugh.

So, eventually, did Lucy. She lay there just a bit longer than necessary. "What's a girl supposed to do with a thing like this? Smoke it?"

The model was shrinking fast, so fast that both Jane and Lucy began to wonder if it would disappear altogether, sucked back into the body cavity as it sought to escape the scorn. He scrambled to his feet, said, "Well, really!" and, with a petulant shake of his long blond curls, ran for the dressing room like a ferret for its hole.

Jane strolled over to Lucy, still laughing, and extended a conciliatory hand. There was something about the girl. She was unique. Jane couldn't judge her by the standards of the world.

Lucy allowed Jane to pull her up, the rueful smile all over her face, as she rubbed her rump. "I guess I had that coming," she said.

"Did you sell those photographs, Lucy?" The accusation was back in Jane's voice.

The shock on Lucy's face was genuine. "No *way*! Did they show up? Somebody stole them from my room, and I'm pretty sure I know who it was."

"Somebody gave them to my boyfriend. Nice trick, wouldn't you say? Who took them?"

"Julie Bennett. I'm ninety-nine percent sure. She took me for lunch, and she was in the apartment alone first. When I got back later, they were gone."

Julie. Julie. Always Julie. Jane's heart was thumping again. Of course that was true. Julie, who would apparently stop at nothing to destroy her. God! Where would they turn up next? With Rivkin? With the cosmetics companies? With the network?

"Well, that's the end of me," said Jane simply. "You've blown me away. What the hell were you *doing*, Lucy? Christ, I was *unconscious*."

Lucy spread her hands out wide. "Listen, honey, what can I say? I was boozed, I was stoned, I was out of it, and I was into you. Really into you, you dig? The real crime was you being so beautiful. And I wanted to believe you were really loose. Julie said you were and there was a part of me that pretended you were just playing hard to get. I'm real sorry, but I guess that's no help." She screwed up her face. "And you're so famous now. Those pix must be dynamite. Why the *hell* did Bennett want them? She into you, too? Maybe she wanted to get rid of the boyfriend and leave it at that. You gotta go see her, straighten it all out."

"I can't talk to her, Lucy. She wants me dead. I can't tell you why. Only a shrink could. But she's crazed about flattening me. She's obsessed. She just keeps trying and trying.

Everything I do, every relationship I have, she wants to destroy."

"But can she *do* things like this? I mean, is it legal? Maybe the cops could help."

"I guess she can. It's not blackmail. She isn't asking for money."

"Yeah, she's just into distributing fine-art photography." Lucy brightened. "I suppose we could get her on breach of copyright."

Jane tried not to smile, and failed. "Hey, it's all very fine for you to laugh, but what are the Estée Lauder people going to say when they find out how their star relaxes after a hard day on the set?"

"You could always try the ice-cream companies."

Jane made a mock kick to the other side of Lucy's ass. "Listen, sweetheart, if you ever try and pull a trick like that again . . ."

"No chance, darling. No chance at all. I'm on a diet."

"*What!* Lucy!"

They were friends again, just like that. Jane had come to kill, and stayed to laugh, and she only had to look at Lucy to know why.

JANE SAT MOROSELY AT THE TINY COUNTER OF THE BODY EXpress snack bar and wondered what the hell she could do. The Rivkin office had been on the telephone all morning, and the answering service had been getting desperate because she wouldn't take the calls. "Urgent" had become "extremely urgent," and then some idiot had actually uttered the immortal words "matter of life or death." Soon cars would arrive as they tried to cut through the telephone barrier, and when Jane felt that was imminent, she had fled.

It was quite obvious what it all meant. The game was up. Rivkin had seen the photographs and Jane was about to become the shortest-lived star in the whole history of Hollywood. She would lose everything. All the contracts had morals clauses, which turned them into lavatory paper if Jane did anything to embarrass the sponsors or employers. The pictures would certainly do that. In a day or two she would be a pariah. It would be worse than that; she would be a joke, a dirty joke.

She had needed to get out, to have some time to herself. In her experience there was no better cure for anxiety than an hour and a half's workout at Body Express. The thrashing activity, the loud music, and the group pain made her forget most things.

There was a quarter of an hour to go before the advanced class, and Jane sipped pensively at the black coffee as she waited. The guy behind the bar looked as if somebody had poured formaldehyde into his brain. His eyes stared at Jane—unblinking, his head stock still, as he watched her with single-minded concentration. He was a typical L.A. waiter/actor/surfer, and he was winding himself up to speak his lines.

"You working right now?"

He didn't recognize her. That was fine. A few didn't.

Jane smiled a wan smile through the gloomy thoughts. "Not right now." Or ever again in this town. "What makes you think I'm an actress?" In Hollywood "working," as in "are you working right now?" meant actress.

"Well, I mean, you're real great looking. I mean *really* great looking. You gotta be an actress or model or something."

His face lit up as he let her see the southern California teeth. The blond hair looked nine parts hydrogen peroxide, with minimal streaking input from the sun. He *really* emphasized the "really."

Jane laughed. He was quite cute. "Well, thank you, sir."

She felt the color high up on her cheeks. In L.A., compliments were an art form. Great hair, neat eyes, wild mouth. It was the same with the smiles; you gave them and you got them everywhere—at the car wash, at the stop lights, on the freeway, in the movie lines, in the Beverly Center, and in Tower Records. Mostly they didn't mean a lot. They were just mutual stroking as the Los Angelenos practiced their sex appeal in the least dangerous way possible, safe from the organisms that now threatened all casual unions, and not as heavy as telephone sex. But somehow this young guy was saying exactly what she needed to hear.

She'd never really noticed him before. He had surfer's shoulders, a waspish waist, and upper arms muscled from swimming rather than sculpted at Gold's Gym. The T-shirt was plain white, and mercifully free of commercial messages. White linen trousers and a Swatch watch made up the rest of his statement. He looked very healthy, and very, very clean. Good enough, in fact, to eat.

"I've seen you in here before. Several times." His smile played around the corners of lips that would get chapped in the surf, the ones on which he would smooth the Neutrogena lip gloss, just after he'd touched up his nose with zinc oxide total sun block. What he meant was, "I know you. I've watched you. We go back at least a few days."

Jane just smiled back at him. Her expression and her silence telling him more than her words could. Keep going, beach boy. It was the perfect distraction—from all the things that had so suddenly gone wrong with her picture-perfect world. She could feel the pain recede like cold at the first touch of the sun's rays when it crept from behind a too-wide cloud.

"You're really awesome. You're really getting to me. You know that?"

Suddenly she was aware that she was all but naked. The Dance France leotard was barely legal, on probation. It clung to her body like a second skin, pink and perfect. Jane shifted on the plastic seat and watched the airhead with the angel's body thinking about the bits of her that moved.

It was her turn. "In this place I expect everyone attracts you." Jane smiled playfully as she jerked her thumb toward the big picture window through which the beginners' class could be seen—hard bodies hurting in kaleidoscope colors, dripping sweat.

He smiled back, stood just a bit straighter, and let her see it.

Jane felt her eyes sucked down. His erection thrust out against the linen trousers, proud, defiant, daring—confident of the effect it would have.

Jane felt the sweat break out all over and her lips go dry. Her tongue sneaked out against her will, and coated the dryness with saliva, before rushing away to hide, ashamed at its demonstrative lack of control. Swallowing would be nice. But swallowing was mysteriously impossible. She tried to look away. But where? To his face, to see the triumph there? Could she look at the clock, at her suddenly interesting feet, or the fascinating backs of her hands? Inside the pants it was moving and Jane knew with absolute certainty that it was she who was moving it. Her excitement could make things bigger. Her nipples were suddenly alive.

She tore her eyes away, to the face, the eyes, sheeted over with desire. A film of sweat basted his upper lip, parted from its partner by a centimenter to allow the escape of the faster-moving currents of breath. He was so brown, and healthy, and young and uncomplicated, a package of longing, beautifully wrapped like the finest present, the one she would tear open, eagerly, destructively, to get at the thing she so badly wanted.

Minutes ago they were aliens, two kids hanging around in the L.A. world—nice and clean and straightforward and looking for laughter, and the good times that kids looked for. Now they were almost lovers, speaking to each other through his blood, thrusting and throbbing into the part of him that he could watch her eyes want, and through her breasts, rising and falling so eloquently.

With so much talk there was no room for words. He reached down and touched himself—laying the flat of his palm against the contours, stretching the material across the tense skin, showing her its outline, all of its strength and promise, the things that it could do for her.

His voice was a whisper when he spoke. "Do you want it?"

Jane felt her mind stop. When it started again it was no longer hers. Would her lips work? Could she get the dry message to him?

"Yes," she whispered back.

She shivered her acquiescence. Her breasts strained against the inadequate material, her nipples reaching for him, as her whole body joined in the chorus, singing in unison of her desperate need. His body would be hard and tight and his sweat clean and lickable. He would push into her and fill her up. In the intensity of the present she would lose the past and forget the future, and he would buck and rear and moan and flow into her, dampening her with his sweet feed, cooling the fires of her lust with the liquid of his power.

His eyes darted away from her, as she watched the heaving of his chest.

"Come with me." His voice was husky.

She followed him quickly.

In the dressing room it was quiet and cool, and so dangerous, deliciously illicit for the impulsive act.

Jane looked around nervously and loved the guilt as it embraced with lust. There was no love here. She would simply use the brilliant body, a young and brand-new toy to play with and be played by.

He motioned to her. Toward the door marked MEN. He locked the door behind them and turned to face her. Panting, their breath fighting to escape and enter their suddenly inhospitable bodies, they both knew what must be done. Not the intimacy of kisses, no quiet, gentle declarations of attention and respect, because this was war. The timeless battle between young warriors greedy and anxious for the spoils of physical victory. They would rub and grind and fight for joy, and each would win, and each would have the ultimate prize.

Holding her eyes in his, he reached down. Jane could sense when it was in his hand—from the faraway look, from the little shudder that shook the powerful shoulders, and from the low moan that jumped from his lips.

In the cramped space she knelt before him—his back to the door, her bottom crushed against the cold porcelain. Huge and alive, it pushed against her cheek. Hot and glistening with his passion, it touched her hot lips, and then the glorious smell of him was in her nostrils.

He tasted so very good. She touched him gently at first, her tongue the explorer, resting nervously at the tip of him. Then, with the courage of need, she began to devour him, greedy, languid, stripped of all decency, of all pretension. With long, slow strokes she licked the moisture from him—without shame, without apology. Down toward the dark base, up again to the shining surface, down again to the fetid source of the wild aromas. Then, knowing him now, she opened her mouth wide to take him in. Her teeth the ally, she explored once more. The proud rearing tip of him her prisoner—then the whole length of him held tight in the wet softness of her mouth, thrusting to the edge of her throat, fighting back, determined to impose itself upon her.

He took her head in his hands as he forced himself into the mouth that longed only for what he, too, wanted. Delicious coercion. Jane loved it as he pushed firmly into her, merciless in his pursuit of pleasure, impervious to her own feelings or desires, as if her mouth existed only for him. His strong arms held her captive as his hips and buttocks pistoned against her head, and the blond forest rushed toward her and away again.

Jane reached up for him—her hands snaking out to touch the now soft, now solid muscles of his thighs and buttocks, drawing him into her, resisting as he pulled away.

She readied herself. The grip on her head from the straining strength beneath the palms of his hands grew more powerful, the stick that beat at her soft mouth more callously relentless. Her eyes strained upward to watch him as he approached the end of his journey. Head thrown back, lips parted, the golden hair wet with sweat as he prepared for the moment. What's your name, beautiful master? Are you called anything at all, you who will do this thing to my lips and teeth, to my throat? You who will unload all your pent-up want and need and desire into the mouth of a perfect stranger? She closed her eyes and tried to imagine the thing she would only feel, and would not see.

A low grumbling moan gurgled from the back of his lips. Wonderfully soon her essence would be wet with his sticky sweetness. Then he stopped, and both of them knew what his stopping meant. It was the end before the beginning.

Jane held him between her lips so that he was only just inside her. In front of him was the welcoming carpet of her tongue—prostrate, eagerly awaiting the blond nobody to whom she had so capriciously given her body.

She felt the shudder run through him, and then it was upon her—a glorious foaming fountain in her mouth, filling her, violating her, in the love bath that she loved, showering her with the glorious particles of lust.

He bent over her and communed with his orgasm. He was oblivious to her, interested only in the mouth that pleased him, the hostess that had so willingly accepted the most personal present of all. On and on it went, longer and more bountiful than either could have imagined.

And then it was out of her. Jane smiled up at him with the gratitude of passion. She reached out and touched the thing that had pleased her—holding it in her hand and marveling at the act that it could do. She knew him now. Not his name, or his family, or his religion, but by the wonder that was in her mouth, that would soon be elsewhere.

It was her turn. It was her time.

She watched him carefully as she touched her own body. Her hands smoothed over her breasts, reaching up to free them from the flimsy material that covered but did not restrain them. Naked to the waist now she let him watch—his eyes marveling at the wonder of her nipples, her entire geometry. He reached forward to touch them and inclined his head as he tried to tell her what he wanted. But Jane took his hand away. She wanted him to look until his eyes melted and his mind bubbled, and he was ready to do again to her what he had just done.

He watched her as she eased the pink leotard away, past the deep slash of her belly button, past the flat curve of her lower stomach, to the soft, downy field of wet desire, its awesome symmetry framing the pink perfection of the lips of love. Just beneath the pleasure source, at the top of her smooth, sloping thighs, she left the rumpled leotard. There—crumpled and sweat soaked—it stayed as a deliciously obscene underline to the blond haven above.

Now Jane reached down and touched herself. All the time she watched his face. Her forefinger meandered slowly through the damp meadow to the shy gates. For a second or two it lingered there—uncertain, seemingly insecure—then, gently it slipped inside.

She looked first at herself as her own finger moved luxuriantly within her and then up at him—smiling as she saw what she had done and what she had intended to do. If it was possible he was harder than before.

Jane's finger plunged deeper as she enjoyed the wonder on the face of her lover. He had never seen a body like hers playing with itself, enjoying itself, loving itself in front of him. Capriciously she withdrew the hidden finger and, reaching out, she traced the contours of his dry lips, wetting him with her love as he had soaked her with his.

Then she twisted around, and showed him her bottom—lifting it up shamelessly until it pushed against his hardness. The high buttocks thrust back at him, and she smiled wantonly over her shoulder without shame, without pride. Both hands against the thin walls of the cubicle, the firm flesh of her kneading against his hotness, daring him to do what he wanted to do. The small space was heavy now with the scent of love, a crucible for lust and the desperate delight of strangers.

Bending at the knee she lowered herself toward him, watching him over her shoulder. But he wanted it all. As Jane sank down, so did he, kneeling behind her in the blissfully small place.

He leaned in toward her with the tender reverence of the awed lover. Tentative at first, his lips sought the secret places, nervous lest they should touch her in some unseen spot where inhibition might live, becoming brave at the shuddering surrender to his anxious tongue.

Jane's moan was soft and low in the back of her throat at the foreign feeling. She held herself still. The shy invader must have the freedom to learn, to transform the strange into the familiar.

Long and hard now he lapped at her. Darting inside her, his tongue was strong and insistent—all of her was open to it, and all of it he used to please. Jane held on to herself. It was almost too much. Meteors of ecstasy winged in from the corners of the glorious solar system that was her body—from her tingling bottom, from her dripping thighs, from the besieged center of her world. But now she was fighting back—an alliance for mutual pleasure concluded with the enemy. She arched her strong back and pressed both hands together on the pipe of the cistern and thrust herself at the mouth that loved her.

Taken by surprise at the sudden and unexpected strength of the counterattack, he fell back willingly, the hunter hunted. Now his mouth was the victim, and Jane the aggressor. She ground her buttocks at him as he fought to breathe in the abundant wetness, pushing back with all her might to capture the tongue in the place where it so desperately wanted to be. It was a war that both could win, that both were winning. And, as always in the battle of love, it was not enough.

Jane felt it first. The emptiness that no tongue could ever fill. The overwhelming desire to be complete. In the maelstrom, quite suddenly, she stopped the frantic motion. In the lull of the truce both were still.

He breathed in deeply. She stretched upward, bowing her back, straightening her legs for what he would do now.

From his crouching position he stood, and she turned to face him, marveling at the wetness of his face and the splendor of his sweat-soaked body. They wore the ravages of love-making like medals, proud and defiant, the spoils of victory in the campaign whose climactic battle was still to be fought.

She smiled at him, in gratitude and in encouragement, and reached out both her hands to hold his strong waist. He did not smile. His face was alight with desire as his hungry eyes devoured her. With her right hand she held him as he moved in toward her, her hand guiding him to the place he longed to be. For a second she allowed it to hover at the brink as she searched his eyes for the evidence of his bliss. Hot and impatient it rested there, nuzzling her, moving uneasily at her entrance. Then she moved, too. And sensing it, he pushed forward. On the astral plane where pleasure lived, both lovers waited, helpless in the knowledge that this must go on, and that they could not freeze the drama in the glory of the moment.

The force of his movement shook her free of her little world. Impaled on him, she was in the air, thrust into space. The breath rushed from her chest and the groan spurted from her mouth as the terrible, wonderful thing ripped and roared in her pelvis. Her hands, slippery against the hot wet flesh, threatened to lose their grip but he caught her—a strong arm snaking out around her waist to lock her in the vice from which no escape was possible, and no escape was wanted. Posed deliciously between the hammer and the anvil, Jane's legs reached out for him, scrambling to trap the joy as they fought to imprison him within her and to give her the fulcrum against which she could push back.

She floated there, cocooned, gasping for breath, and she watched the straining, searing muscles that held her, defying gravity as they thrust her upward.

There was yelling in her heart and in her mind as Jane tried to fight back the orgasm. On and on this must go. But his eyes were the ally of the feeling in her body. "It's all right," they said. "Do it now, and I will do it too. With you. Always with you, wherever you may lead."

"Ohhhhh." Her voice sounded the warning, the apology, the plea.

"Yes," he murmured.

"Noooh." The helpless defiance in the face of the longed-for-inevitable.

The arrow shuddered in the middle of the target. In sleepy concentric rings the waves of shock rumbled outward, growing as they went, touching and caressing every millimeter of her body with their urgent strength, as if a hot stone had been dropped into the middle of a bubbling pool. Her legs rigid, she locked onto him, her hands buried deep in the wet hair at the back of his neck, as the life flowed out of him and into her. She could feel its magical surrender as, out of control, it spent its energy within her, and the thought of it rushed to greet the memory of the taste of him, and all against the majestic background music of the nerve-racking orgasm. Here on the hard plain of ecstasy she called to him, oblivious of who would hear, or who would care—the groaning despair of her shout mocking the bliss that had mothered it.

He staggered with the strain as the climax shook him, and his knees buckled as he twitched and shook within her. Jane felt him rock beneath her as he tried to hold her up. Slowly, jerkily he sank down, until, mercifully, Jane's buttocks rested on top of him. Deep inside her the last offerings were spent, and his head lolled forward onto her glistening chest as his lungs sucked for breath amid the shiny, sweet-smelling sweat of her breasts. She held him gently, cradled in her arms. This blond stranger, whose name she didn't know, but whose love was hot and warm within her.

Jane's sigh of satisfaction signaled the relief in her heart. Somehow this crazy exercise in freedom had strengthened her for the thing she must do. Now at last she was her own woman, and although they could take away the baubles and trinkets of her fame, they couldn't touch the body that the world would love, or the mind that would always respect itself.

TWENTY-TWO

JANE STRODE INTO THE COLLECTIVE NERVOUS breakdown that was Pete Rivkin's office with the arrogance of Joan of Arc marching toward the flames. There was a wild sense of anarchic liberation within her, and a mad, fiery courage flowed in her veins. The wrecked leotard, destroyed by her wanton lovemaking to the man with no name, was the symbol of her defiance. She was caked with sweat, grubby with passion, and licked by lust, and now at last she knew what she thought about everything and everyone. The world could go screw itself. Jane Cummin, cornered and at bay, was about to use her claws.

The secretary, her face flushed, leaped up as if she'd been shot as Jane crashed into the anteroom.

"Oh God, Ms. Cummin. Thank goodness you're here. Mr. Rivkin's been trying to reach you. He seems terribly upset."

There was a question, a hint of accusation, the touch of a threat all wrapped up together in her last sentence.

All morning the sleek offices of Rivkin Enterprizes had bubbled with nervous tension. The consensus along the grapevine was that it had all started with the big manila envelope delivered by special courier, addressed to God, and marked in magenta FOR YOUR EYES ONLY. Pete Rivkin, according to his ugliest and most garrulous secretary, had obeyed the instruction and opened the envelope in a closed office. That was when the bad vibes had begun.

Opinions differed as to his physical state when he emerged from the office a few seconds later. That he'd seen a ghost was one, not very imaginative, description. A rewrite man hanging around the outer office had done a bit better: "He looked as if he'd just given too much blood." All agreed about what had happened next.

"Get Jane Cummin on the phone. Right away. Find her, wherever she is. Okay? Understand?"

Next he had canceled a vital production meeting and an equally important script-approval session. To cap it all he had rescheduled a meet with Digger Murdoch and refused telephone calls from Swifty Lazar, Sly Stallone, and Fran Stark. Whatever was wrong was big bananas. About that there was absolutely no question at all.

Inside his office Pete Rivkin had wrestled with his personal demons. From the soft leather of his desk top the photographs stared up at him—Jane's dreamy, sleepy, languid face mocking him. Jane Cummin, star of his hit series, and also of pornographic pictures that had curdled his blood.

The note had been businesslike. Julie Bennett was about to distribute copies of the photographs to everyone who was anyone in America. She just wanted him to be top of the list, because of his "interest" in the "porno queen."

The home truths had been unavoidable. If Bennett did what she had threatened, *Beverly Hills Nights* might not survive it. Jane certainly wouldn't. He had buried his head in his hands as he had tried to comprehend the horror of it all. It was hardly possible. Jane a lesbian, perhaps even a hooker? He could have never believed it if the evidence hadn't stared him in the face.

Jane shot past the flushed secretary and aimed herself at the door of Pete Rivkin's office. She didn't know what she would say, didn't even know what she thought, but boy did she know what she felt. That would be *more* than enough.

His haunted face flicked up to find hers as she opened the door of his office. The messages were all there—coded into the face she had come to love and respect. Relief at seeing her, accusation, anger, disgust, disbelief, overwhelming sorrow. Never for one second had she doubted that he would have the photographs by now. And there they were. A little packet of human nastiness polluting the surface of his desk.

"Jane!"

She walked right up to him, proud, arrogant, the armor of her self-respect effortlessly warding off the slings and arrows of his accusation.

"Listen to me, Pete," she commanded coldly, imperiously, the icy determination of her clipped syllables ensuring that she would be obeyed.

"I was unconscious when those photographs were taken. The other girl put something in my drink. But I *was* making love to her before that."

Pete Rivkin opened his mouth, but the words wouldn't come. All morning he had planned the speech. The sense of betrayal was so strong that all he had wanted was revenge, and the words he had rehearsed had been intended to sear Jane's soul. Now, confronted by the magnificence of her presence, they had been effortlessly wiped from the blackboard of his memory.

Jane hadn't finished. "I don't know what you're going to do about all this." The haughtiness was all over her voice. "But I sure as hell know what you ought to do."

Rivkin's brain was coming back on track. This wasn't his script, but it would have to do.

"Jane, for Chrissakes we're in terrible trouble here. What the *hell* are you trying to do to me? I mean, who cares you're into chicks, but these photographs can sink *Nights*. This Bennett cunt's screwed your career, but she's got me by the balls, too. If these photographs get to Galvin's desk I'm yesterday's hamburger meat." His eyes went mean. "If you want to turn yourself into a dessert plate on your own time, that's your business, but if some weirdo's gonna circulate the photographic evidence of it, then by God it's mine."

"Oh, shut *up*, Pete, and *think*." She threw a sweat-stained arm, long and beautiful, toward the ceiling in a gesture of dismissal. "Talking dirty isn't going to solve this problem."

He watched her, his hypnotized eyes inches from the crotch covered only by the barest strip of material from the high-cut leotard. God, she was amazing. Totally and completely irresistible.

He was calming down. In the face of such determination there was suddenly a light at the end of the tunnel, the realization that the nightmare could end.

"Jane, what the *hell* are we going to do? Why is Julie Bennett *doing* this? I didn't know she was a psychopath. What's she got *against* you? Is it some jealousy thing?"

Again Jane brushed away his questions with a sweep of her hand.

"Listen, she can't get away with this. Even if it's not technically blackmail, it's an evil thing she's trying to do. She has a high profile. Morton Janklow's her agent, and Crown publishes her books. They'd go ape if they found out she'd tried to pull a stunt like this. And what about her readers, and the book clubs, and the TV rights? With your power in the Industry you could probably sink her mini-series all on your own. At least cut the money in half. If she went through with it, she'd lose her reputation and a fortune at the same time. I think she ought to realize that. I think someone ought to tell her. I think *you* ought to tell her. If she hears it from a big shot like you, and you put some top spin on it, she might climb down. You just got to try, Pete. For your own sake. For the sake of *Nights*."

And, of course, for her, too.

But strangely she didn't care about that, and it was not caring that made her so very strong. Right now her glittering future in the material world was small print in the story of her life. What mattered desperately was that Julie Bennett should be stopped.

She towered over Pete Rivkin, the power of her purpose washing over him like waves over a stony beach. She bathed him in her determination and soaked him with the strength of her desire. She could feel the mighty change in herself. Now she could move mountains and it felt wonderful. If before she had been content to be a passenger on the tide of life, she was one no more. Instead she was arbiter of her own Destiny, and never again would she allow others to control her fate. With the nuclear weapon of her incredibly forceful personality she would obliterate any obstacle that stood in her way.

"It might work," he said, allowing the beginnings of a smile to invade the corners of his mouth.

Jane felt the wild joy in her heart. "You can do it, Pete. Go off like a firework. Don't lose your temper. Use it."

Yes, that was it. Temper, judiciously applied with force, had a way of melting opposition. He had been using the combination for years to devastating effect.

Already the engine of his moral outrage was revving up. This bloated scribbler with her dirty blackmailing habits was trying to torpedo his star and his series. You couldn't turn on your TV without losing yourself in her mammary land. You couldn't struggle into a supermarket without risking burial beneath the mounds of her breathless books. On every talk show he had ever watched, she was flogging the things as if she had never heard of dead horses, her brassy, ball-breaking pseudo-bitchery droning on like road drills on an eardrum. Well, the cat woman had met her nemesis, her lion tamer.

Pete Rivkin picked up the telephone. His eyes were on Jane's as he spoke. "Get me Julie Bennett in Palm Springs," he said.

She sounded pleased to hear from him. "Mr. Rivkin. I'm glad you called. So you got my little package? Looks like you'll be auditioning for a part in your nice new series, doesn't it?"

Pete Rivkin's voice was splintered glass. "Listen, fuck rat, and listen good. I'm only going to say this once. I've torn these pictures up, and I've forgotten about them. I literally can't remember them at all. Now if you ever do anything to remind me about them, ever, just once, do you know what I'm going to do? I'm going to call a press conference and tell everyone who will listen exactly what your role has been in all this. I'm going to run an ad in *Publishers Weekly* every week for a month exposing you, and another in the *New York Times* book section, and I'm going to write to every publishing house in America with a copy of the letter you sent to me with these photographs. And know this: It may have filtered through to that cesspool you call a mind that I have a certain amount of influence in the television business. I personally guarantee that I will call in every IOU I possess to get you blacklisted from the networks, and to make sure that every show in the country airs the details of this business. By the time I've finished with you, you'll be as desirable as a used condom on Miami Beach, and not even an Eskimo will buy a copy of that rancid trash you write. Do I make myself clear?"

"Oh," said Julie Bennett.

"I said, 'Do I make myself clear?'"

"It may be that I've miscalculated."

Pete Rivkin's cold fury singed the line. "Don't you ever, *ever*, miscalculate again."

"I understand what you're saying, Mr. Rivkin," said a chastened little girl.

It was as near as he'd get to a promise.

It had worked. Pete Rivkin let out a shuddering sigh.

Jane saw it all in his eyes, and the relief exploded within her. All at once she felt drained. Through the sheer naked force of her personality she had snatched triumph from the foul-smelling jaws of defeat. She tumbled down into the armchair, as Pete Rivkin stood up and walked around the desk toward her. He laid a hand on her bare shoulder.

When he spoke his voice was shaking. "In all of my life," he said, "I don't think I've ever met anyone I admire as much as you."

IN SOUTHERN CALIFORNIA, AT LEAST, THE ANNENBERGS WERE society's equivalent of the vicar's knickers and the bees knees all rolled into one. So desert high society had drooled for weeks over the engraved invitation to drinks at the famed Sunnylands estate—set unbelievably at the intersection between Frank Sinatra Drive and Bob Hope Drive—the place where the Reagans spent their New Year's Eves, where Nixon had retreated after his resignation, and which boasted probably the best private art collection in America.

Julie had been there before. But not since Walter Annenberg had bought his sister Mrs. Enid Haupt's collection of Impressionists to forge the most intriguing privately owned ensemble of modern French painting, including the famous Gauguin, *La Sieste*.

Julie Bennett sipped pensively at her champagne as she stared longingly at the painting. A Polynesian woman, her back to the artist, seemingly at ease on the hard red-ocher floorboards, wore an English straw hat with a polka-dot band. Facing Gaugin, a moon-faced woman stroked determinedly at some white material with an old steam iron. There were three other figures all facing in different directions, all doing absolutely nothing against a lush landscape of yellow and green.

The voice winged its way over Julie's shoulder and she recoiled immediately at the dreadful sound.

"Rather fine, no? Eighteen ninety-four, when Gaugin was getting a bit fed up with being poor. Must have been kicking himself for giving up the stock exchange."

The voice was perfect Eton. It came as a package with the smell of Royal Yacht that they all wore, and the oily self-confidence that, with so very little reason, they all effortlessly assumed. Julie looked at him as if he were a dog mess on a dinner table, and his eyes flickered their immediate interest at her obvious disdain. Englishmen wanted only to belong to the club that didn't want them; they were drawn genetically toward women who could give them a hard time. Well, this poodle faker with the art background had come to the right person. The sound of his drop-jawed nasal accent had put Julie straight back into an evil mood, and she was never far from that anyway.

"Dear, oh dear! Have you been watching poor Kenneth Clark's *Civilisation*, or do you get *Reader's Digest*?"

He laughed, a high-pitched, whinnying sound, delighted at the irreverence.

Julie looked him up and down. Turnbull and Asser cream silk shirt, blue-dotted tie, double-breasted lightweight suit—the jacket worn open, Gucci shoes—a brand that said he was a progressive.

"I'm afraid I know who you are. We all do in England, you know. You're Julie Bennett." He sounded rather proud of that, as if it proved he were not the insular sort. The intimation was that Julie Bennett would be mildly relieved that someone like him knew who she was. There was also the faintly surreal impression that he was giving her some useful information—that he was in a position to tell her her own name.

"Well, I don't know you," she said rudely. "Nor do I want to," was left hanging in the air.

"I'm Henry Bicester. I run the modern-paintings thing at Christie's." He beamed his pleasure at her. There, you common little woman. You might be rich and famous but you don't know how to behave, and the fact that your mother was some fake Balkan princess cut no ice at all in the bar at White's. Expatriate trash. He had spoken his *name*. The thing that counted. Now she should know that the Christie's business was actually superfluous, because of course he was an earl. That meant that his wife was a countess, his eldest son a viscount, and his two other sons were "honourables," although nobody would dream of calling them that. It also meant that his only daughter was called Lady Mary Wilmington, Wilmington being the family name. He watched Julie carefully to see if she had picked up the coded message. American romance writers made such a terrible hash of English titles, although technically this writer was of British stock.

"Oh, you're Lord Bicester, are you? I think you sold a couple of paintings for me a few years ago. Not very well, I seem to remember." Not bad. She'd got the "Lord" right. It was amazing how many people didn't realize that peers, viscounts, earls, and marquesses were all called "Lord" to their face. Only a duke was called "Duke," or if you were a servant, or an unmistakable social inferior, "Your Grace."

"Yes, I think the market was weak at the time. They went a little underestimate probably."

Julie's lip curled. That was a typical auction-house trick—to put in a high estimate of what the picture will sell for, to con the seller into using your firm, whisper to the trade over the grapevine what the reserve figure is, and give them a chance to rig the bidding among themselves. When the picture fails to sell and gets "bought in," you come up with an anonymous private buyer after the auction—actually a friend of yours—who would be prepared to "take the picture off the owner's hands" at about ten percent over the reserve. "I would recommend selling, Miss Bennett," he had said, "even though the price is a little disappointing. It doesn't do for a picture to fail at auction. You'd have to keep it for many years before trying again." Julie couldn't remember whether Bicester had spoken the lines himself, or whether one of his minions had. They all sounded the same anyway. They were upper-class used-car salesmen with the morals of Jack the Ripper.

"We hear a lot about your collection, you know. Very different from all this, but one imagines, almost as fine . . . in its way." He waved an effete hand around the room. In desperation, Julie Bennett's eyes followed it—anything to avoid having to look at the glistening, round patrician face with its shiny nonchin, rabbit eyes, and crinkly, pubic-textured hair.

The unadventurous Impressionists—safe as houses, daring as ditchwater—stared back at her. She rather liked the wall of black porous Mexican rock on which the better of them hung. That was a nice touch, and the William Haines' furniture was pleasantly understated—cream on beige on white, to avoid detracting from the main events. The boys were all there—a brace of standard Cézannes (apples and melons), the squiggly Van Gogh showing the women gathering the olives, and that star of a million picture postcards, Monet's *Les Coquelicots*, over the signed black-framed portraits of the royal family. Julie couldn't help noticing the handwriting on those. Philip and Charles—all but identical; Queen Elizabeth and the queen mother, a curiously similar *Elizabeth R*; and then the odd woman out—Princess Anne—the writing bold, no-nonsense rebellious, resembling the others not at all. Margaret Thatcher provided an unlikely juxtaposition to the left-wing royals who loathed her. Talkative as usual, her inscription read, *Walter and Lee—with every good wish to two wonderful people*.

The room was filling up now, the eager faces cascading in to mix with what they considered to be their social superiors. Julie smiled inwardly. It was a funny place, the desert. Palm Springs had a reputation for being grand—a bit like Hobe Sound, Newport, or Saratoga—but actually it wasn't like that at all. In fact it was all part of East Coast West Coast schizophrenia. In California they thought that fame and aristocracy were one and the same thing, whereas on the East Coast, where social structures were less crude, class lines were modeled more along European ones. But the funny thing was that, although Palm Springs was supposed to worship the gods and the goddesses of the movie screen, who had invented the place, very few stars or even starlets actually lived there. They had been there in the past, but they weren't there any longer —and one had to scratch around a bit among the Sonny Bonos, the Dinah Shores, and the Tony Curtises to come up with anybody who really fitted the title "star" at all.

"Julie, Henry—you know each other, of course. I'm glad you could come, Julie. Isn't Henry wonderful on the paintings? He's a houseguest, so he's had a chance to do all his homework."

Lee Annenberg was a small, bright-eyed, lively woman, clearly determined to have a good time. It was seldom that she threw a cocktail party like this but the Desert Museum was a favority charity and noblesse oblige.

"Listen, Julie, has Henry told you we've got Evan Koestler staying for the weekend? Well, it's terribly exciting, but you must have heard about this new painter he's discovered. You know—the one that everybody is raving about—Billy Bingham. Do you know I've commissioned him? I've never done it before. Have you? Walter thinks I'm quite mad, but he's humoring me. Anyway, I flew up to see him the other day. He's just moved back to the West Coast, and he's got this wonderful studio right down on Venice beach, where he's turning out these paintings that make you want to die, they're so beautiful. I'm absolutely thrilled about the whole thing. My own Bingham painting. Have you heard of him, Henry? Yes, you must have. What do you think of his work?"

Blood was rushing through Julie Bennett's ears like an express train. In front of her eyes lay a fine mist. Her plans for Jane had been sabotaged for the moment by the unpredictable Pete Rivkin, but there were still scores to be settled with Billy. Now it seemed that he had moved back within her sphere of influence. Of course there was no way that Lee Annenberg would know that Billy had been her lover. She liked to keep the house boys under wraps, and they were bored by desert socializing anyway.

"Oh, he's just the best," Henry replied. "No doubt about it. Evan really pulled off a coup there. Startlingly original use of color. Really very special. What do you think, Miss Bennett?" The English were purposefully slow to use first names, and there was a mild sneer in the "Miss."

Now Billy's success was confirmed by the English simp from Christie's in New York, and by Mrs. *TV Guide*, the ambassadress—both trumpeting the brilliance of her own pet toy boy as if *they* had invented him. The Billy Bingham who had walked out on her, who was now a star in the firmament, courted by people who hardly had the time of day for her. Billy Bingham, who had fancied Jane.

Jane. Again the funeral music roared in her ears. Jane would not go away. Jane survived the slings and arrows of Julie's most outrageous assaults and lived on to plague her, to insult her, to force her back to the time she tried so desperately to forget. Jane was a supernova, the beauty with the world at her feet. Jane had the powerful friends who could threaten even her own remarkable career.

The gall dripped on Julie Bennett's psyche. A woman scorned. A daughter abandoned. The fury of hellfire. Wild-eyed, she looked around her. She wanted to break something —to create a terrible scene. To throw the Chinese Tang figures into the shallow pool beneath the fifty-foot cupola where Rodin's Eve luxuriated among the papyrus and other plants.

With an effort she fought for control. She caught Barbara Sinatra's eyes. Then Leonard Firestone's. Then Daniel Galvin's. Slowly, the storm receded. She drank deep on the champagne and reached for another glass from a passing waiter. Her mind was no longer shrieking; it was beginning to work on what it must do.

"Did you say Evan Koestler was here, Lee? I'd just love to see him. Who knows, he may be able to get me one of these Binghams that everyone is raving about."

"Yes, he's here somewhere. I think I saw him out on the lawn a few moments ago."

The lawn at Sunnylands turned into the nine-hole golf course. A private golf course was far from unknown, but in the desert where water was at a premium it was something of a luxury. Evan would never be far from the luxuries of life.

Julie smiled graciously at her host. "Do excuse me. I think I'll go and find him. 'Bye Lord Bicester. Interesting to meet you."

Evan was where he was said to be—part of a group of people, presumably not the art lovers—who had spilled out onto the emerald grass. Julie approached stealthily from behind. "Hello, Evan," she said.

He swiveled around. There was something ominous in her tone. In the English accent.

"Ah, Julie Bennett," he replied neutrally. His mind would be trying to remember exactly how it had been left between them. Julie could have enlightened him. He had conned her, stolen her man, turned him into a star, and made a fortune in the process. As far as she was concerned there was absolutely no health in him. Her plan, however, dictated that he didn't know she felt like that.

"How lovely to see you in the desert again, Evan. So much has happened since last we met."

"Yes, our mutual friend has had a resounding success, as you must know."

He was so dapper, like a little toy soldier, all beautifully painted and sharp in the right places. He smelled like a glossy magazine that had taken too many ads for the scent manufacturers.

"He has indeed. He has indeed. I thought it was those of us who are of English extraction that are the experts at understatement, Evan." She smiled graciously.

He smiled back, wary.

"Yes, the bottom line is that I failed to smell the talent when it was right in front of my nose. That's the truth of the matter, isn't it, Evan?"

"We all have bad scenting days."

"It infuriates me, you know. I want to put it right."

"'Put it right'?"

"Yes, I want to buy some Binghams."

"Ah, I *see*." Evan's smile was genuine now. This he could understand. She wanted to catch up. It would cost her, but what was money compared to pride when you made Croesus look like a two-bit hustler playing the slots in Vegas?

He slipped into dealing mode, his neat eyebrows flicking up as he forced his eyes to go honest. "Well, dear me, Julie, if anybody deserves a Bingham it's you. No question about that. Such a pity that you fell out with each other. Such a pity. I'd have thought he'd have given you one, but you know how he is. Full of pride, and rather prickly . . . No, the problem is supply, I'm afraid. The show was a sell-out, and I'm just holding on and waiting for some more work. As you know, there's no hurrying *that* process." He watched her slyly. Would she fall for that one?

"Come on, Evan. Don't bullshit me. I've been in this game a long time. I'm Julie Bennett, remember. What have you got in the back room?"

"Oh, yes. Quite. The back room. Not a very great deal, I'm afraid, and a lot of what's there is really promised. You know, to *old* clients."

Julie heard the note of reproach. You should have used me before, rich scribbler, Evan was saying. You should have sent some of the royalties my way.

"How much are you charging?"

Evan stiffened. It was moving fast. He was going to get rid of a couple. Maybe three.

"One hundred thousand, but only to firm holders. Not to traders."

"Listen, darling, I've never sold anything in my life except a couple of fakes through Christie's, and the odd book. About fifteen million of those in hardback at around seventeen dollars and about forty million paperbacks at five bucks apiece. That's just America, of course." Julie found it necessary to do that sometimes. People occasionally had to be reminded just how rich she was.

Evan Koestler's calculator mind could do the sums. He had arrived at the figures, and he smiled. There was nothing that he appreciated more than telephone-number-size amounts of money—especially when the area codes were included.

"Were you looking for more than one?"

"Yes, I was."

"Well, to be totally truthful, there are one or two in the back room." He laughed charmingly, like a little boy caught out in a fib, a white lie, nothing serious.

"I'll take them all, Evan. Every single one."

"What?" He stared at her in disbelief.

"You heard, Evan. I said all of them."

He put up both hands. "Oh no, Julie. No. No. No way. We're talking forty pieces here, and I have clients to satisfy."

"I'll take all forty at one hundred thousand each."

"Ah!" Evan said it again. "Ah." Four million dollars. That would give him better than a chance at the duchess of Alba's paintings. They had been offered to him only a few days before—a miraculous Goya, a delicious Velázquez. He had had to decline for cash-flow reasons, but the four million would enable him to make the buy of the decade—if anything could be as good as the Billy Bingham coup.

"If you agree you can have my check right here. This minute, against your receipt and written promise to send me forty Bingham paintings as soon as they can be delivered to my agent."

All his life Evan Koestler had been a fast mover. He had never moved so fast as he did now. His little hand shot out and captured Julie Bennett's.

"Done. Dealt," he said.

Together they had walked back into the big room, through the desert crème de la crème, and nobody had liked to object, although everyone had wondered what the best-selling authoress was up to, when she had written a check to Evan Koestler, using as her table the smooth contours of a 1960 Jean Arp bronze.

"YOU SURE WE'RE ALL FIXED UP AT THE DOOR? LOOKS LIKE you need a passport down here." Lucy Masterson peered out of the stretch limo suspiciously at the unwelcoming streetscape of West L.A.

"No problem. Tom Cruise telephoned Helena this afternoon. The doorman has my name. Even if he screwed up we could probably finesse it. One or two people recognize me in this town, you know, Lucy."

There was a gentle rebuke in there somewhere. The myth was that you had to know Helena Kallianiotes to get into her otherwise impregnable nightclub. But it was the exceptions that proved the rule to be true. Jane's face was so unbelievably "now" that she would sail through the door on a cloud of cloying congratulation, demonstrating that in this town friendship was instant, not percolated.

Sunset had wound down into Silver Lake and still they headed east. Jane kicked up her legs onto the bucket seat in front and breathed in deeply, inhaling the rank night air of the steamy L.A. suburbs. She'd never been to Helena's before, and it was one more feather in the cap of stardom, one more badge to wear on the sleeve that would prove to the world that she was now a card-carrying member of the Hollywood heavy-hitter brigade. At Helena's on a Friday night the crowd would be divided into the watchers and the watched, and it was simply a fact that Jane would be in the latter category.

"How the hell did that broad get everyone to cream down here? Wasn't she a belly dancer or something?"

Jane laughed. "Helena was the butch hitchhiker in *Five Easy Pieces* with Nicholson. He started her off, really. At the opening-night party here he gave Anjelica Huston a baby elephant for her birthday. I wonder what the hell she did with that."

"I guess Nicholson could start a nightclub up my ass."

"For sure. Small, exclusive, lots of ambience. And it could get real crowded if the gawkers and gapers moved in!"

Lucy laughed. "Yeah, that place Lou Adler had that they all used to hang out at—the room above the Roxy they called 'On the Rox'—that was a pretty good hole. They had art deco matchboxes in there that said 'Living well is the best revenge.' Wasn't my idea of living well. Even the roaches looked like they were slummin'."

"Well, for a long time this place didn't even have a booze license."

"They'd better have some of Helena's hitchhiker friends,

or I'm history. Wonder if that Demi Moore'll be there. Yeah, she'd do me just fine."

"You'd have to peel her off Estevez."

"I'm relyin' on you for the diversion, sweetheart. Now that you're free you gotta spread yourself around."

Jane sighed. It was true. She was free, and sometimes she wondered about freedom. There was a gaping hole in her heart where Robert Foley had been, but she hadn't tried to contact him—nor he her. A part of her regretted her furious response to his callous reaction to the photographs, but endless nights of thought and intellectualization had blurred the edges of fact, and now she didn't really know what had happened, why it happened, what was right, what was wrong.

To a man like him the photographs must have been the most terrible shock. But where had been his compassion, his goodness, the ability to forgive and understand that she imagined to be the cornerstone of his personality? He had stormed into her house and treated her as if her guilt were a foregone conclusion. And in the face of his prejudice she had recoiled from protesting her innocence, and then recoiled from him. Now, and a thousand times since, she wondered if she had done the right thing. She could write him a letter perhaps, explaining what had happened, with another from Lucy corroborating it. But her pride hadn't let her, and as the days turned into weeks, it became more and more impossible. Sometimes she could rationalize it, that Robert Foley was not the man for her. He was a prig and a prude, lost in his Victorian moralizing and his selfish pursuit of a perfection in which the milk of human kindness was sadly lacking, always crying for the bleeding crowd but unable to understand the weakness of one mere mortal. She was young, and wild, riding the tiger of a stupendous success, and a man like him wouldn't be able to cope with it. She didn't need a father figure, long on wisdom and short on joy, lost in a love affair with the poverty and pain of which she would never be a part. What she needed was youth and fun, and life and irresponsibility . . . and Robert Foley's hard, austere body crushing down on hers beneath the hot sheets in the calm canyon. That was the problem. The intellect said one thing, and her emotions another.

"This it?"

"I think so."

It didn't look like the most important nightclub in Los Angeles. An off-white stucco shoebox, with no sign, rose drearily above a nondescript row of storefronts. The parking lot, however, was no longer a mugger's paradise. It was thick with limos, burly chauffeurs, muscled "minders," and high-end cars. Every now and again one of them would belch out a group of Helena's hopefuls, distinguishable from the "regulars" by their nervous gestures and flushed, anxious faces as they worried and fretted over whether they would pass the door test. One nod, and admission to the milk and honey of Canaan. A shake of the head and unceremonious ejection into the wasteland.

"Wait for us here, Louie. Okay?"

"Okay, Miss Cummin. I'll be right over there by the street lamp."

At the door a desperate, sweating man in cowboy boots was trying to explain to the doorman that he was someone they ought to know. "Listen, did you see *Trance* with Bill Hurt? I wrote the script for that movie. Is Bill in there tonight? He'd sign me in. Maybe I could go in and get him. Right?"

"Mr. Hurt isn't here this evening."

The man brightened at the news.

"Well, that's too bad, because he's a real close friend of mine. We go back a long way. He said I should come down here and talk to Helena. She here?"

Helena's nicotine-stained, gravelly voice cut into the night air. "Listen, darling. If I don't know you then you don't get in. It's quite simple. And I'm telling you—I don't know you."

"But Bill—"

"Isn't here. Now, if you want to come along with Mr. Hurt then he can introduce you to me, and then I'll 'know' you, and then you can come in. So let's take a rain check on it, okay?"

The girl hanging on the writer's arm was beginning to let go.

Failing to get into Helena's, where every dance was a career move, was failure with a capital *F*, and L.A. wasn't big on failure. It could be contagious. Which was why the doorway at Helena's was filled with a force field of neurosis.

Jane didn't have to speak.

"Oh, Ms. Cummin," said the doorman with due deference. "Mr. Cruise telephoned about you: It's an honor to have you visit our club. Helena, this is Ms. Cummin."

"Hi, Jane. Come on in. Tom said you'd be coming. Glad you showed. Hope you can stand a crush. It's gotten out of control in there."

Helena was fine-looking rather than beautiful—and with a lived-in look that hinted at late nights and speedy company.

Jane and Lucy drifted into the cavernous club, all minimalistic haute tech, with peach-pink walls and a billowing gray material draped across the ceilings. They passed through a crowded bar, and then a huge crammed dance floor to a cramped restaurant area where thirty tables were separated from the dancers by see-through screens.

The crowd parted for them, and on every side the little whisperings of recognition told the tale. Jane Cummin was vast.

Jane felt the adrenaline surge through her. This was why the famous came to places like this. It was one thing to see the movie grosses, read the contracts, lap up the good reviews, but this was where you *felt* the fame—among your peers: the raw touch of it, the jealousy shining in their eyes, the gratitude as some of your glory rubbed off on them.

"Do you see who I see?" said Lucy.

Jane saw. At the table a few feet in front of them was Billy Bingham.

Their eyes locked together as he rose to his feet.

"Jane!"

There was no time to think about what she felt, as her memory rewound to find the appropriate frame. It was her guts speaking when she spoke.

"Hi, Billy. I thought you were going to rescue me from the wicked city. Decided to slay the art world rather than the dragon?"

She was quite pleased to see him, but there was no spark at

all of the things there used to be, simply the desire to enact a playful revenge.

Billy, however, looked devastated, knocked sideways, his normal sulky cool shredded. Outwardly he appeared the same —jeans, T-shirt, Dexter boots—but he seemed cleaner, somehow more polished.

He actually stammered as he spoke. "Jane. God, you look wonderful. Amazing. Con-congratulations on your success."

"Yes, L.A. was pretty good to me in the end. Lucky I didn't count on you. I'd still be hanging out at the Marmont and you'd be stuck with some gigantic check. About an eighth of a painting, at least."

She smiled to let him off the hook, but his haunted face said he'd like to hang on the hook a while longer.

"I'm sorry . . . I just had to . . . you know, the art thing." He splayed out his hands.

"Listen, forget it. I was only joking. We both did okay. You remember big, bad Lucy? Well, you were right about her. All she wanted was my body." God, could she joke about it already? Sometimes she surprised herself.

Billy lifted a hand to acknowledge Lucy. So much had changed. But some feelings had stayed the same. He still disliked the bleached-blond bomber. And he still wanted Jane.

The girl by his side shifted around rudely, her eyes stabbing. Billy turned to her. "Oh, this is Cathy. She does P.R. for Columbia. Jane. Lucy."

The girl softened a bit. At least she'd been acknowledged. Jane might be a rival, but she was a famous one. "I like your show," she said.

"Thanks." Jane's smile flickered over her like a passing searchlight. "So you're back in town, or just visiting?"

Billy looked down. "Yeah, I came back. I gotta studio in Venice. New York was too cold and dirty." He half laughed.

"That's great. I must come down and see it sometime."

"Oh, yeah, Jane. You do that. How about tomorrow for lunch?" There was eagerness in his voice.

No way, Billy Bingham. Young, ambitious, moody Billy. Once you walked on me. Never again.

"No, I can't tomorrow. Or any day the next couple of

weeks. I'm snowed under at the studio. Give me a ring some-time. It'd be great to get together."

She gave no telephone number, and Billy knew she'd be ex-directory. In Beverly Hills the phonebook was thin as a Piaget watch. For a second he wondered whether or not to ask for it. Something in her eyes told him not to risk it.

The guy who bumbled up to them didn't look like much but he *was* a lot, and he was going to be very much more. The smart-aleck smirker had a receding hairline and a Nixonian stubble.

"Hi, Bruce!" Jane sounded delighted. *Nights* had long since surpassed *Moonlighting*, but Bruce Willis didn't mind, because *he* was huge—locked in with Tri-Star, signed by Mo-town, with a five-million-buck wine-cooler endorsement con-tract with Seagram's, recently renewed.

"You gotta dance with me, dream girl. I'm gonna break your leg," said the lopsided grin.

It was the offer that nobody would refuse.

Billy Bingham sank down into his chair. In front of him, the over-grilled swordfish kept uneasy company with the glass of Perrier. His eyes followed Jane onto the dance floor.

Lucy sat down jauntily in an empty seat and smiled en-couragingly at Cathy from P.R. "I like your dress," she said.

"Thank you. I didn't catch your name."

"Lucy Masterson. I take beautiful photographs of beautiful girls like you. You shouldn't be in P.R.—you should have P.R. done on you." She made it sound like an exotic perver-sion.

"Lucy takes porno pictures," said Billy Bingham.

"Seen anything of Julie Bennett lately, Billy?" Lucy fired back. She turned to Cathy. "Billy used to 'work' for Julie Bennett before he became famous."

"Oh, did you, Billy? You never told me that. What did you do for her? I thought she was a writer."

"Personal assistant, weren't you, Billy?"

The implication was unmistakable. He was her catamite, that wonderful Greek word for a "boy kept for unnatural pur-poses."

Billy's face darkened.

"The plot thickens," said Cathy carefully. "What sort of personal assisting did you do for Julie Bennett?"

"Maybe you'd better ask her sister. She's dancing with Bruce Willis over there."

The throbbing nightclub seemed suddenly silent.

"*What* did you say?" Lucy Masterson's jaw had dropped wide open.

"You heard what I said," said Billy Bingham.

PART FIVE

TOMORROW IS ANOTHER DAY

"Do you give a damn now?" whispered Scarlett.

Rhett Butler didn't answer. He picked her up, sweeping her into the air, and his strong arms crushed the breath from her trembling body.

"I've always loved you, Scarlett," he said.

Julie Bennett, *Tomorrow Is Another Day*

TWENTY-THREE

From Julie Bennett's bath she could see the mountain. It was very important in Southern California to have a tub with a view. In the rest of America, bedrooms, and especially bathrooms, were considered to be private places where exciting, secret things happened. And even the houses on the ocean in places like Palm Beach had few bedroom views of the sea. If you could see out, then it was at least conceivable that some Peeping Tom would be able to see in, and in a country that regarded sex as more important even than cleanliness or godliness, there could be no worse thing than that. Julie Bennett, however, was born English, and the English harbored no such taboos. Sex was a very lowly rated pastime there, certainly below gardening, royal-family watching, and dogs. If some entrepreneur wanted to climb up the mountain to see her naked, then such initiative and effort probably deserved to be rewarded.

Like the ocean, the mountain was never the same from one day to the next, from one minute to the next. The light show was always changing the colors melding and diverging and recombining in an ever mobile kaleidoscope.

Julie lay back in the bubbles and waited for the water jets to start up again, as she peered happily out through the vast picture window extending from the side of the pink marble bath. All around her the marble extended in a flat, two-foot-deep surround, so that everything one needed for a bath was within easy reach: huge jars of bath oils—Opium, Chloé, and the green pine essence from Penhaligon's in London; a big rough loofah from Fortnum's; and a Staffordshire dish overflowing with soaps—Dior, Floris, and Roger Gallet. There was a pile of crisp face towels from the White House in Bond Street, the initials JB sewn in understated Oxford blue.

Over to the right, just far enough away so as to avoid being splashed but still within reach, was the control panel for the sounds and the visuals. When she got tired of the mountain she could choose from a hundred-odd satellite channels on the wall-mounted Sony twenty-inch XBR monitor screen, or flick into the eight-channel piped stereo that could reach every room in the huge house.

The water-jet-timer cut in and the hard streams rushed out from their multiple sockets to pick and pluck at Julie's relaxed body. Around her neck the Opium bubbles danced, shooting off the delicious scent to compete for attention with all the other sensations. Baths like this were so decadent, and the glass of pale pink Pol Roger 1976 rosé champagne certainly struck no discordant note—except that it was warming up. Damn! Julie reached out petulantly and emptied it unceremoniously into the bubbles. About fifteen bucks' worth. Maybe more. She reached out for the silver Asprey's ice-bucket and poured another glass. Twelve noon, and she ought to be writing—not swilling champagne, listening to Mozart, and planning the destruction of a brilliant career.

She picked up the white cordless and punched the 212 long-distance number. This wouldn't take long.

"Julie Bennett. You're sure they've all arrived? You've counted them and checked them over? Forty Binghams. You're quite sure? Good! I'll be in touch."

She slammed the telephone down as she reached for her Louis Vuitton address book. She dabbed quickly at her hands with a towel, flicked the book open under *C*, snatched up the telephone, dialed another New York number.

"I want to speak to Henry Bicester, please. Julie Bennett calling."

No point using the title. Even the girl at Christie's would probably think "earl" for a first name. It was three o'clock

Eastern time. The English upper classes would have struggled back from their liquid lunch by now and be tidying up before they slipped away from "work."

"Miss Bennett. How nice! How can I help you?"

Julie heard the condescension. The Henry Bicesters of this world never really recovered from the dissipation of the family fortune and the dreadful necessity of having to work. They had all chosen the most gentlemanly profession they could find—the smooth, silky world of fine-art auctioneering—but at the bottom line they were salesmen, hawking paintings for a cut. They would themselves happily admit that, the ability to call a spade a spade being one of the qualities such people affected, but they never wholly came to terms with it. Hence the patronization. Julie Bennett might be able to buy Bicester a million times over, and certanly might put a lot of business his firm's way, but in a lifetime of Sundays she would never, ever, be his equal—and it would be as well for her to realize it.

"How was your weekend?"

"Fun. Frances loves to get out of New York, and old Annenberg has a pretty good cellar and didn't hold back."

A man like Bicester would go anywhere for some good shooting and some '61 claret. At the Annenbergs the main attraction would have been the wine. No upper-class Englishman would have been seen dead on a golf course—golf being an exclusively middle-class game.

"Did you tell me you ran the modern-paintings side at Christie's?"

"Yup. I do the really modern stuff. After nineteen forty-five, really. The contemporary sales. French Impressionists are somebody else."

"Could you sell Billy Bingham's work?"

"Well, I don't really see why not. We haven't done so yet, of course. He's only just been invented. But, yes—there should be quite a demand in fact. Yes, we'd rather like to sell a Billy Bingham." He was warming to the idea. It should be worth some P.R. points. "Did you buy one at the opening and then regret it when you got it home? If so, I'm sure the cleverest thing to do would be to send it back to Evan Koestler and let him find you something else."

Bicester's desire to make a sale didn't blind him to the undesirability of giving someone like Julie Bennett a bum steer. For a Julie Bennett an Evan Koestler would probably even give her her money back.

"No. I want to do it through Christie's."

"Fine, well drop it in sometime, and I'll have a look at it and give you an idea of what we might get."

"Actually, it isn't just one painting. It's forty paintings." Julie reached for the champagne. This was rather fun.

"Oh, dear, no, Miss Bennett. That would be a disastrous thing to do." The patrician voice was suddenly suspicious. "How on *earth* did you get hold of *forty* Billy Binghams? They're very tightly held."

"I got them from Koestler. I bought up the whole of his back room. You can check with him if you like. In fact I wish you would. I took possession of the paintings early this morning. I could have them round at your offices by this evening if you like."

The fifteenth earl of Bicester—the family motto, "Never at a loss"—was now having trouble discovering words. "But why would you buy forty paintings and then want to sell forty paintings? . . . I'm not quite sure that I understand what this is all about."

"I'm quite serious. It's very simple. I have forty Billy Binghams and I am asking you to sell them for me at auction. That is what you do, isn't it? You *are* an auction house, aren't you?" Was this all too hot for Bicester and Christie's to handle? Where was the famed British phlegm?

Bicester straightened himself up inside as he picked up on the rebuke. "Yes, of course we *could* sell them for you. No question about that. But it would be quite the wrong thing to do to sell them all at once. A sale like that would knock the stuffing right out of the market. Destroy the price at a stroke. You'd be lucky to get peanuts for them."

"Yes, that's right. They'd go for next to nothing."

"But you must have paid a lot of money for them. At least

fifty thousand each, I would suspect, from what I've heard about recent prices."

"One hundred thousand each, as a matter of fact."

"Well, there you are. That's my point. You wouldn't get a fraction of that if you unloaded them all at one go. If for some reason you don't want to go back to Koestler, you'd have to sell them very carefully, over a long period of time, and just hope that the market could take it, and that he remains fashionable." Bicester had regained his stride. He had made the mistake of overestimating the intelligence of this woman. Clearly, despite her collection, she had picked up absolutely nothing at all about the art game. Some dealer or other must have had fun bleeding her white.

He plowed on. "What I'm trying to explain, Miss Bennett, is that with a new artist like Bingham the price is really an artificial one. The dealer is able to set the price by keeping a careful control on supply and demand. If he does that well he can manipulate the price gently upwards, as he builds the artist. It's all based on trust. The buyers trust the dealer to maintain the value of their investment. If you unload a whole load of stuff onto the market at once, then the price drops like a stone and the holders who have paid fifty thousand start to panic, and *they* try to unload. It's just like a run on a bank. When confidence goes, everything goes." Bicester thought he'd put that rather well.

"I know all that stuff," said Julie Bennett curtly, positioning her magnificent rump to receive the attentions of a particularly cunningly placed water jet. "Will you sell them, or shall I ring Sotheby's?"

The mention of the dreaded rival concentrated Bicester's mind wonderfully. "Ah. Well, yes we could. We could do that for you." He paused. "But you'd lose a fortune, and destroy the artist, and possibly the dealer, too." At least she couldn't say she hadn't been warned.

"And that's exactly what I want to do," said Julie simply.

IN THE BAR OF THE CARLYLE EVAN KOESTLER'S PERRIER tasted strangely threatening. There was no reason at all for that. After all, the sun was high in the sky and his reputation, bank balance, and everything else that mattered were tucked right in next to it, basking in the reflected warmth. In fact, he couldn't remember when things had been better. It wasn't at all like an Englishman to go for the amateur dramatics, but Bicester had sounded like some raincoat man out of a Le Carré novel—cloaks, daggers, and muttered innuendoes. The Carlyle bar was hardly the run-of-the-mill venue for the exchange of dark secrets, but that was what he had been told he would be getting. God, secrets were so unpleasant. Evan couldn't even bear to be surprised on his birthday.

Bicester rushed in, on time, looking flushed. He ordered a dry martini as he sat down, and he plunked a copy of the *Financial Times* on the bar. It's color matched the pink on his cheeks.

"Hi, Evan."

Evan just watched him. His little belly was all knotted up. This was quite ridiculous. What the hell was the matter with the telephone?

"You've got big trouble, Evan. The biggest. Julie Bennett says you sold her forty Binghams. She was on the telephone late last night asking Christie's to sell the lot at our next modern sale." Anything after lunch was "late last night" to the Henry Bicesters of this world.

He looked at Evan Koestler slyly as he downed half the martini. Bombshells didn't come any bigger than this.

"What?" said Evan.

"Did you let her have forty Binghams without a nonresale undertaking?" Bicester's question was the most potent affirmation that the whole dreadful business was true.

"She can't do that," Evan's voice rose.

"If you haven't got a contract, and she's got the pictures, she can do whatever she fucking well likes."

Bicester took out the second half of the drink and motioned to the bartender for another. He wasn't drinking to soothe the stress; this was par for his pre-luncheon course. "Can you make it with Boodle's, this time?" Clubland always laughed like hell about the fact that the smart St. James Club's name had ended up on a gin bottle. That was impossibly down market, but actually the gin itself was rather good. In England it was always green-bottled Gordon's for martinis, but the problem in America was that the export Gordon's was significantly sweeter. Boodle's made the best drink. Tanqueray was supposedly the chic gin on this side of the Atlantic, but it was out of the question in the West End.

"But you won't sell them for her, will you, Henry? Knowing what it would do to me, and my artist."

Henry Bicester looked straight ahead. He had anticipated this bit. Auction houses couldn't afford to fall out with dealers who provided the most important part of their custom. Peddlers of paintings, except when they were eating at each other's throats, stuck together closer than copulating dogs.

"Well, it's a rather tricky one, Evan. That's why I rang you the moment this madwoman got hold of me. Thought maybe you'd be able to dissuade her. After all, she's going to take a financial bath if she goes ahead with her crazy scheme. But the way she tells it, that seems perfectly acceptable to her. The point is if *we* don't sell them, then somebody else will. The chaps at Sotheby's would sell their own grandmothers if they had the faintest idea who they were. If we do the deed, then at least we can all work together and try to prevent total disaster. God knows how."

Evan wondered where all his blood had gone. Bennett was going to do it. Christie's was going to do it. "It can't be done."

"I'm afraid it can, Evan. Will someone tell me, in simple words so I can understand, why it is that Julie Bennett wants to ruin you and Billy Bingham and doesn't mind about losing the best part of four million dollars in the process? Frankly, I can't think of anything at all that would be worth losing the best part of four million."

Henry Bicester shook his head. Four million dollars would buy fifty thousand acres of Scotland with several three-hundred-brace-a-day grouse moors, a mile or two of salmon on the Spey, the best stalking in Invernesshire. It would buy a grade-two listed gem in a Nash terrace off Regent's Park, three or four hundred acres in Wiltshire with high pheasants, a trout stream, and prize-winning pedigree Guernseys on the home farm. There would be no more of this nonsense about working for a living—just lots of sport in the bar at White's and a knee-trembling spade girl for the afternoons to make up for poor Frances's deficiencies—a girl who wouldn't complain about his performance, or rather the lack of it, and who might catch him a sharp one or two across the buttocks with the Swaine, Adeney and Briggs riding crop, and let him put on her knickers and high heels for a laugh in front of the looking glass as he sucked back the after lunch kümmel-on-the-rocks that she would keep for him in the refrigerator of the Bayswater flat that he'd have helped her finance.

Evan Koestler had broken every rule in his own book. A lifetime of experience had counted for nothing when the novelist queen had waved her mighty check. He had outsmarted her once, and he had underestimated her as a result. Now he would pay with everything, with literally *everything*. And he had even known the facts; Bingham had been the Bennett lover, and he had walked out on her, leaving all the motives for revenge in place. Evan, unbelievably, had handed her the ammunition on a plate. Why? The answer was easy. Bicester had just provided it. No one in the ridiculous, money-oriented world in which they lived could believe that anybody else was prepared to lose vast sums of loot for something so unsalable as revenge. It was on that fundamental miscalculation that he had foundered.

"When are you selling the pictures, Henry?" His voice was hollow.

"My people want to put them up as soon as possible. Tack them on to the end of next week's sale. You know, print up a cheap addendum to the catalogue. No presale publicity. Perhaps no one will notice."

"Pah!"

Bicester nodded. Yes, that was a pious hope. "What will you do, Evan? Buy them back yourself?"

"For four million, and me the only buyer in the room? The price would still drop like a stone and I'd end up bailing Julie Bennett out, and throwing good money after bad. And I don't have four million. Do you?" A few days ago he had had Julie Bennett's money, but already it was sitting in the Banco Central in Seville in the duchess of Alba's account, in exchange for the paintings he had just *had* to have, paintings that would take years to turn back into cash.

Bicester wondered about a third martini. It was a very bad business, but he was feeling rather good. There was something so stimulating about the misfortunes of others. The Germans even had a word for it: *schadenfreude*, delight in the misfortune of one's friends.

"Do you fancy a spot of lunch, Evan? I'm meeting Leo Castelli and Tom Armstrong at Les Pleiades. Can't get enough of their lamb stew. You're more than welcome to join us."

"No. No. I think not, Henry." Evan stood up, the movement doing his color no good at all. Beneath the tan he was gray. "I've got to get back to the gallery. Make some calls."

He was still there, but Henry Bicester got the distinct impression that actually he had already gone.

"Thanks for letting me know about all this," said the apparently disembodied specter in a vacant voice, as it walked unsteadily toward the door that led out to Madison Avenue.

ON THE TWIN PRINCIPLES THAT NOTHING SUCCEEDED LIKE EXcess, and the weird biblical prophecy that unto them that hath . . . , people were now bending over backward to give Robert Foley money. Pete Rivkin had started the golden ball rolling but now it had its own momentum. He had spread the cash around like fertilizer and the major crop—much to his surprise—had been a line of hard-hearted society matrons eager to give him more. On paper that was all very fine, but in practice it created all sorts of problems for Foley. For a start it separated him from the only method he knew to reduce his chronic free-floating guilt. To cure the poor with his own hands was hardly cost effective now. Somebody had to administer the projects and oversee the builders as the new wings sprouted, decide whether the American whole-body scanner was a better bet than the European one, and deal with City Hall on the zoning. Then there was a formidable business of coping with the inflow of funds. There was a time and a tide in the affairs of men, and the new trend should be milked for all it was worth before some fickle follower of fashion called a halt to the whole business and moved the bored plutocrats on to the next "in" charity. Robert Foley had been around L.A. long enough to know that nothing was hot forever. So the shiny dinner jacket had acquired an almost surreal glow as it polished the chairs and withstood the groping fingers at endless galas and interminable private dinners—and the transcendental gloom that the whole process conjured up sat on his head like a dark cloud.

Twice a week, however, there was respite from this misery, and a glorious pain of a different kind. On Tuesdays and on Thursdays, in the middle of prime time, Robert Foley did what the rest of America did. He sat down to watch *Beverly Hills Nights*—or rather Jane Cummin, its star. If it was possible, he loved her more now—as her unavailability concentrated his longing and distance fanned his desire. In the dim light of his ancient Magnavox, Robert Foley was once again bewitched by her charm, squirming as she squirmed in the arms of her small-screen lovers, holding his breath as the events of the plot threatened her, rejoicing in her triumphs, plunged into the depths by her failures. It was love, of course. Even he could recognize it now. Somehow it had taken the distance to show him that.

She would have forgotten him. He was an unimportant stepping-stone on her pathway to the stars. Nor did he blame her. She deserved so much more than his crippled, attenuated personality with its vile conflicts and its peculiar obsessions. At her moment of need he had failed her—allowing his petty jealousy to produce a reaction as trivial and mean as it was cruel and insensitive. She had done the right thing and left him. Now he hadn't the gall to try to reenter her world. Thank God Rivkin had contained the damage. It was the only bright spot in the tragedy of his lost love.

In the back of the limo that the Stones had sent for him, Robert Foley tried for the umpteenth time to exorcise the ghosts. It had been billed as a small, intimate Bel-Air party and so, in a way, it was. Sixty for dinner. Six tables. Leona Stone had flown in Bruce Sutka from Palm Beach to do the little party, and for once he had played it traditional. His briefing had been straightforward: Nobody was to know about Leona's most recent facelift. That had dictated a color scheme of peach pink. The valet parkers spirited the gaunt, tortured figure of Robert Foley, shining in his slippery suit, into a pale pastel paradise. The Stone mock Tudor wouldn't have looked half genuine in the home counties but, sitting self-satisfied on four and a half acres of prime-cut Bel-Air, it had a potent statement to make, and every one of the guests could hear it murmur the phrase "ten million bucks" over and over again. If you added in the rather obvious Impressionists and deducted, say, twenty percent for fakes, then you arrived at nearer fifteen million, not counting stocks, Calvin Stone's mighty income, or the beach house at the Colony that they used on the weekends. It wasn't Palm Beach/ Hobe Sound rich, but for the West Coast it would do.

Leona Stone—dressed head to toe in Valentino, the designer of the minute—came at Robert Foley like a vampire bat. She was passably good looking, and at fifty much admired in Hollywood for hanging on to Stone for the best part of twenty-five years. It was unremarkable, in a town where money screamed rather than merely talked, that nobody wondered why she hadn't junked the psychotoxic old fool within a week or two of marriage.

"Robert, Robert," she shrilled, wincing slightly at the state of his tuxedo. "How marvelous. You're right on time. I know you medical people make a specialty of being late. Come on in, darling, and have some champagne. Now, you know you've got to make a little speech, don't you, darling? Later on."

Robert muttered his acquiescence as he shifted backward to avoid the enthusiastic spray that showered from the pendulous lips. She was telling him not to get too drunk and blow the speech. She needn't have worried. In the Hollywood of the eighties, in the Material World, there were very few who could afford to get drunk anymore, especially at an event like this. Everything could and would be used against you and, most important of all, the need to get drunk would be interpreted as a sign that you were pretending you didn't care. That it was merely a *pretense* would be obvious. Why else would you be out there playing the game?

"Now, let me think. Where have we put you? Oh, I know. You're at the Aaron and Candy Spelling table. Next to Sherry Lansing, I think. Yes, I'm sure that's right. We'll all be sitting down in a minute or two."

She twirled away, a white tornado, to uproot couples and reorganize groups like some manic gardener.

Robert Foley looked around gloomily. The tables were scattered about on the candlelit patio and the champagne was being served on the green baize lawn beyond. Even he, far from a connoisseur of such things, had to admit it had been rather well done. The tables were covered with dark pink cloths over which a lighter pink chintz had been thrown, the top cloth consisting of a mass of intertwined pale-peach-colored roses. The centerpiece of each table was a huge bowl of roses, whose colors mimicked those of the material on which they sat. All around the central flowers were tiny candelabra, the lampshades and their tassels pink yet again and echoing the peach-rose motif. The entrance to the patio was lined by twelve large dogwood trees in full bloom, and throughout the entire ground floor of the house enormous crystal vases of dogwood branches were scattered on every available surface, including the dark mahogany of the twin Steinway pianos— the ones the Stones used occasionally to embarrass their friends with inexpert duets.

"Dinner is served," said the butler—a ludicrous figure of fun in a Court of Versailles servant's outfit.

Everyone moved quickly to obey, well aware that if the food was going to live up to the décor and the Dom Pérignon 1982 champagne, then split-second timing would have to be observed. Some had already taken a peek at the handwritten menus when they had been investigating their placements. The first course would be lobster bisque, and that needed to be piping hot.

Robert sat down first. To his right was some classy-looking charity commissar he didn't know. To his left Sherry Lansing —one-time model, former studio boss at Universal, now running her own production company—had not yet arrived.

Robert Foley turned toward his right and plucked an opening line for his strictly limited repertoire. "What beautiful flowers," he managed without any enthusiasm at all.

At which point somebody did the thing that always maddened him. Hands covered his eyes from behind. Now he had to guess who the hell it was.

Then Robert Foley felt the electric current switch on inside him. It zipped through his body in a tingling madness. His heart lightened.

She bent down low to his ear, still holding his eyes in delicious darkness as the smell of her wafted toward him. Low, her lips near to him, she whispered her message.

"I love you, Robert Foley, and I'm taking you back."

TWENTY-FOUR

EVAN KOESTLER PACED THE THICKLY CARPETED floor of his office. This was what execution felt like. You stood upon the platform and the crowd stared at you, watching, mouths hanging open, to see how you would die. Would you go like a gentleman—a quip on the lips, some potent aphorism that people would quote after you had gone? "They all said I could make an artist—I wanted to prove I could break one, too." Good-bye, Evan. Or would you put up an unseemly struggle? Everyone always hoped for that—the frantic attempt to bark the executioner's shin, to sow just a little nastiness in return for the ultimate unpleasantness that was being perpetrated on you.

He stopped walking and sat down behind his desk. There were two basic options. He could walk away gracefully, to Venice perhaps, for a month or two of bellinis and boys at the Cipriani, and later emigrate to Europe, leaving his reputation behind to be murdered. That way he would keep what he'd got. It would be a life of physical ease, but of psychological torture. He would still be Evan Koestler, but he would no longer be singular, special, or even significant. Or he could fight, risking not only his reputation but his financial independence as well. If he gambled all to win against the odds and the odds did him in, then he could look forward to a lonely, impoverished old age, trading insults with the wallpaper until death released him. But at least that way there was hope.

Evan scribbled frantically on the blotter in front of him, the Santos ballpoint scurrying this way and that as he tried to make the sums add up.

He could borrow four million dollars. The lease on the gallery would be security, together with his own collection, and a few bonds here, and some stocks there. He could just about raise the money to buy the pictures back himself and maintain the price. If he did it with enough aplomb, the art world might forgive him. It might just conceivably be interpreted as a gesture of considerable strength, the dealer who had the nerve to put his money where his mouth was. It would be a potent statement of his belief in Bingham, and just possibly his clients would be persuaded to hold the line and not cash in their chips onto a trembling market. But it would take only a few waverers to ruin him. Four million would be scraping the barrel; if any more Binghams were flushed out onto the market by the Bennett selling spree, then the price of Binghams would drop like Humpty Dumpty, with Evan's reputation and net worth tumbling after. Julie Bennett would have ravished his career.

Whichever way he looked at it, the scales were balanced. He needed some other factor to make the difference—and somewhere, out there, he felt there was one, but he couldn't for the life of him think what it was.

Then, quite suddenly, he knew.

It was called Billy Bingham. The beautiful boy who would kill for his art. The lean, hard body and the moody, hungry eyes that wanted more than life itself the thing that Evan had given him—the thing that was now threatened. Billy Bingham had given him the greatest success of his life so far, but Billy had never parted with himself. Somebody else had his affections—the blue-eyed girl called Jane who had exploded from nowhere to become the most famous face in America. From a thousand gestures, hundreds of unguarded comments, from the work itself, which often used images of the superstar, Evan could tell that Jane's influence was still strong within him. But if he mortgaged himself to go for broke, then Billy would belong to him, because Evan would hold the beating heart of his future in the palm of his hand.

Billy would have to make sacrifices in return, because Evan would be the hero who saved him a second time. No, it wouldn't be too much to ask—hardly enough, really—to insist that Billy Bingham become his lover.

BILLY BINGHAM SLOUCHED ACROSS THE WEST BEACH CAFÉ and made it to the corner table. It seemed the late lunchers were all looking at him, but not the way they had looked two weeks ago. Then the art groupies who frequented the place had stared, and he had received a sort of quizzical respect from the card-carrying creators who now had to admit that this parvenu was making far more than they were. Mostly they had been pretty friendly, but then bikers like Billy Al Bengston and desert rats like Ed Ruscha were pretty friendly people. Even heavy hitters like Bob Graham, whose cavernous Venice studio/foundry was even bigger than Billy's and whose stretched limo was bigger than *anybody's*, would greet him now. But for how much longer?

The word was out, all over America. It had even made *Entertainment Tonight*, and *New York* magazine had covered the delightful, delicious scandal in depth. Hell hath no fury like a woman scorned, allied to the money-can't-buy-you-happiness-but-it-can-sure-help-to-spread-some-pain theme, was wonderful stuff. The book queen that America loved was about to blow four big ones on sinking the career of her former lover. The phoniness of the smart art market was about to be exposed for the millionth time; a dozen art fortunes were in jeopardy. With bated breath, the public waited for the denouement of the real-life soap. Would there be tears and public recriminations? Would there be violence? After all, when careers were snuffed out and pride took a fall, could one not expect drastic actions, especially among art people who were known to care deeply about very nearly everything? And would the pain shoot out, or inward? Would there be murder or suicide, as the rich and famous came down to the level of everyone else and let it all hang out for a breathless America?

Billy sat down and flicked open the magazine he had bought. Maybe it hadn't been such a good idea coming here.

But on the other hand it was four thirty in the afternoon, and he had purposefully missed the trendy lunch and the even trendier dinner. He ordered a Bas Armagnac Croix de Salles 1918 at a cool fifty bucks a glass, and stared blankly at the pages of *Artforum* as he waited for it.

"Good luck on Tuesday," said the waiter as he put down the glass.

Billy looked at him bleakly. No, this hadn't been a good idea. He went over it again, looking for fresh angles, for the escape hatch in the solid wrought-iron hull. He reached for the glass. The thick caramel-colored spirit seared the back of his throat, taking away his breath as it was supposed to do, and for a brief moment gave him something else to think about.

It had been over a week now since Evan had called, and already the options were narrowing fast. At first there had just been the facts. Bare, unpleasant, unadorned. Julie Bennett was going to sink him, and she had the guns and the ammunition to do it. She was also, incidentally, going to sink Evan Koestler at the same time. Evan had presented it as a fait accompli. In vain had Billy searched for alternatives.

"Can't you buy the pictures in, Evan?"

"I haven't got that kind of money."

"Can't you borrow it?"

"No way."

"You mean there's absolutely nothing that anyone can do?"

"That's about it, I'm afraid."

But somehow, even then, Billy had known that Evan Koestler had been positioning himself for some deal or other. He had sounded anxious and negative, but he hadn't sounded destroyed.

"But what about the money you got from her? Can't you use that to buy them back?"

"It's gone, Billy. I could get it back but it would take time, and there is no time."

"But what about my share? You could use that."

"It's not available, Billy. The terms of our contract dictate that I render you half-yearly statements. I don't owe you that money for another six months, and I can't get it till then. It's unfortunate. It's a disaster, but that's the way it is."

He had sounded almost pleased. Then Evan had rung off and Billy's agony had been strung out for four days.

He tried to get Evan on the telephone, but Koestler had been as unavailable as a studio head to a cheap starlet who was trying to land him with a paternity suit. He had paced the studio, the beach, the combat zone of the after-dark Venice streets like a zombie. The life that had only just begun was ended. The rocket ride to the stars had apparently been a cheap, restricted-ticket round trip. In a town where everyone was used to fast careers, he was about to make *The Guinness Book of Records* as the speediest yet.

The gnawing pain had eaten away at him. Without art and the recognition of his genius, there was no movement, no motion, just rust and decay. In desperation and fury he had considered killing himself—and Julie Bennett. But what did that achieve, except empty revenge followed by nothingness? Either way his dream would die and his glory would fade. He had clung to the hope that Evan Koestler would find a way to save them both. But Billy's calls went unanswered, and daily, in the news rags and the scandal sheets, he read his obituary. The sale was approaching, and he was about to be obliterated as if he had never been.

But now everything had changed. He remembered the morning's conversation clearly.

"Billy? Evan." The voice had sounded conciliatory, penitent, excited. "Sorry I haven't been able to get back to you, but there's been a lot going on and I wanted to wait until I had some hard news."

Billy's heart had all but stopped.

"Listen, I think I might have found a way to get hold of the money I'd need to go for broke in the sale room and support the price."

"Oh God, Evan, that's wonderful." Billy's heart was sprinting back.

"But it hasn't been easy. I've mortgaged everything, literally everything. I'm risking my whole world, my future, to try to save you, Billy."

There had been a break in Billy's voice when he had spoken. "Evan, if you do this thing for me I will never forget it.

Ever. You name your price. I mean . . . I'm just so grateful. . . ."

"Yes, there is something I would want from you in return, Billy."

Billy had said nothing. A sixth sense whispered to him what was coming.

"I want you to come up to New York—right now, today—and I want you to move in with me. You and me. Together. Just the two of us."

Evan's meaning had been perfectly clear. The pause had lasted forever.

"Or you won't help me," Billy had said at last.

"Or I won't help you."

"You know I'm not gay."

"That's not my problem. It's yours."

"Can I have some time to think?"

"You can have till six o'clock—West Coast time."

Billly reached for the Armagnac and finished it in one gulp. He motioned for another. He looked at his watch. The half hour had slipped away. Five o'clock.

He stared around as if looking for inspiration. The formidably good taste of the modern décor laughed back at him, gray on white on beige—the color coming only from the up-to-the-second artwork on the walls. Frank Stella. Chuck Arnoldi. Ed Moses. Served him right for hanging out in a restaurant frequented by artists. What would he do? There was an hour to go.

One thing was quite certain. It had been an all-or-nothing offer. No pussyfooting. No bargaining. His body in exchange for his art, for the world's recognition. It wouldn't be the first time that such a deal had been struck and surely it wouldn't be the last. But his mind stopped every time he tried to think about it.

Luckily the brandy was in there now. Smoothing the passages. Dulling the edges. He picked up the big balloon glass and swirled the thick liquid around, watching it cling to the walls, smelling its mind-melting aroma.

Billy stood up. He dropped some bills on the table. Five

thirty. It would take ten minutes to make it back to the studio. Maybe just a bit more.

At five to six, the pictures stared down at him, huge, mocking his dilemma. We are just color and paint, and canvas and shapes—but you who made us are powerless to resist us, they seemed to say.

Billy walked among them in the soft light of the early evening. They would always look like this, but they would not be the same. Their *meaning* would be different. Their significance would be changed irrevocably by what he would do, or fail to do now. His telephone call could destroy their meaning, or it could make them live again. For now they sat all alone in the limbo that a woman's hatred had created for them—waiting to be rescued, waiting to be condemned.

Six o'clock. Billy's hand reached out for the telephone. He punched numbers.

"Hello, Evan," he said.

YOU DIDN'T NEED A KNIFE TO CUT THROUGH THE ATMOSPHERE in the Christie's sale room. More like a chain saw. It was thick with excitement, the drama dripping off the walls as the art world waited eagerly for the assassination. New York had been longing for this and now New York was going to get it.

On paper it was a run-of-the-mill affair, a low-key contemporary sale with no special invitations, no tickets. The sale so far had been nothing exceptional—a second-rate Stella, a couple of third-rate Pollocks, otherwise a Motherwell or two, quite a good Don Judd, and a passable Warhol. Of the hotter, lower-priced items, the Blum Helman stable had played best. C.Z. Whitmore of Palm Beach had picked up a couple of Donald Sultans, and the gallery itself had moved in on an Ellsworth Kelly sent in by some Dallas oilman whose friends had never been impressed by it and who'd needed the money since oil had slipped from grace.

Henry Bicester straightened his old Etonian tie and peered round the room grandly. He rather fancied himself at this—his Anderson and Sheppard suit immaculately cut around the shoulders, the red-dotted handkerchief thrust untidily into the breast pocket, his New and Lingwood shirt with subdued, narrow white-and-navy-blue stripes. His proud Aryan face thrust toward the contents of his sale room, cold and authoritarian.

"And now, ladies and gentlemen, a rather unusual group of lots for sale. B. Bingham. Lot number three hundred and twelve. What am I bid?"

Billy Bingham sat looking straight ahead, wondering if it had been at all wise to come. The last few days had been the eternal damnation of hellfire, with first the devil's pact, and then the waiting, the one worse than the other. He had made the dreadful bargain with Evan and even now he could feel the dread that the hungry eyes had squeezed from his body. He had never been with a man.

Now to get his own way he would have to allow Evan Koestler to get his, and every fiber of his being revolted against the fact. He had made one proviso. The relationship was totally, exclusively dependent on Evan's being successful at maintaining his price and his reputation. Trying and failing would not be enough, even though that was the deal that Evan attempted to strike. At the end of the Christie's sale, if all went well, then he would sign the lease deal on his body. Now his fate hung in the balance—on one side fame, fortune, and sexual servitude of the basest kind, and on the other the poverty and the anonymity, the failure and the freedom.

Across the room, Julie Bennett watched him. He wouldn't look at her, but then she had expected that. It made it all the better, because it meant they were all reacting to the shots she called, and in the whole of her life Julie Bennett liked that best of all. She felt the triumph bubbling through her. Not long now and her expensive ex-lover would be a cheap one again. Even if it cost the best part of a book, it was a small price to pay. Billy Bingham would be destroyed. Jane's lover would be obliterated.

She shifted in her seat and stared at Bicester. "Get on with it," she hissed under her breath.

Over to the right of her sat Evan. She'd never seen anybody so tense. His reputation was about to be broken up in front of his eyes, and the greedy eyes of the whole New York art world, and stuffed in great, big, indigestible chunks down his throat. Wasn't the world a wonderful place?

Evan stared at the auctioneer in desperation. This was the longest of long shots, but it was the only chance. The reserves on the paintings were set at eighty thousand. He personally would bid against the reserve but there were four or five of his stooges scattered around the room who would enter the race to give the illusion of a hotly contested competition. Bicester, too, would pretend to be accepting bids from the rest of the room until he reached the reserve figure. That was standard practice in the sale room. The problem was that this was New York and everyone knew who everyone else was. Anybody who knew a collage from a still life would be able to recognize that the bids from the floor were phony, all working in concert with Evan. If the other big dealers, the museums, and the private collectors working through their usual front men sat on their hands, then the world would know that the market for Billy Binghams was nonexistent and that the price was about as real as Astroturf.

The murmuring background noise had reached fever-pitch levels. Nobody seemed to be talking but everyone was mumbling—like a crowd scene in a play. What were they all saying, Evan wondered. Cheese? Abracadabra? Soda water bottle?

"Can I have a little quiet in the room please." The earl of Bicester barked his command and was instantly obeyed, thanks to the English accent and the supercilious curl of his tongue. He looked down at the book in front of him.

"I have fifty thousand bid. Fifty thousand for it. Do I hear fifty-five? Fifty-five thousand. At the back. Sixty thousand. Against you, sir. Sixty-five thousand I am bid."

His head ducked up and down, and then from side to side in the funny stylized fashion that auctioneers employed. It was like handwriting; no one had precisely the same way of doing it, but it wasn't at all the way the uninitiated would have conducted an auction.

Evan looked around. Pretending to be entering the bidding for the first time, he waved his catalogue in the imperceptible gesture that in the art world was the equivalent of firing a starting pistol. Bicester caught the shy movement instantly.

"In the front seventy thousand I am bid. And seventy-five." His eyes zipped back to Evan. "And seventy-five, and eighty and eighty-five."

Evan paused. God in his heaven, where were the others? He was on his own. Bidding against himself for art that was about to be worthless. Should he stop now and run screaming from the room? If he did that, it would mean exile in a Tuscan villa to wait for the grim reaper, with good wine, decent food, and the odd Italian boy from the village. He looked over at Billy, set in aspic, to the right of the room.

"Against you, sir. Eighty-five I am bid." Bicester looked down at the book. They were over the reserve. The bidding action was on the floor now.

"A hundred thousand," said Evan. Again the room began to hum. Evan Koestler was going for it, and against all odds. The outsiders hadn't come in. Evan was on his own.

"Against you at the back of the room. Against you, sir, I am bid a hundred thousand for it. Any more? One hundred thousand dollars."

Bicester waved the little hammer in the air and brought it down, making a short, sharp tap on the polished mahogany of his lectern. "Sold to Koestler. A hundred thousand dollars." It was the custom to use the names of the dealers.

"And now lot three hundred and thirteen. I have fifty thousand for it. Who will bid fifty-five? Fifty-five?"

The green-coated floorman was against the side wall, pointing up at the vast Bingham canvas so that the room could see what was being sold. The smaller lots were brought in by hand and held up beneath the lectern, but paintings the size of Billy's were scattered all around the room.

Like a child mesmerized by the writhing of an advancing cobra, Evan Koestler looked across the room at Julie Bennett. She was winning, feeding off his lifeblood, and he was paying her to do it. He had just paid her a hundred thousand dollars minus the sale-room commission for the privilege of strangling his reputation. He had staked his all on the rest of the world coming into the auction, and it looked as if he had lost.

Billy was panicking. He could sense that the plan wasn't working. The paintings—his beautiful paintings, the ones they had fought to buy a few short weeks ago—were lepers in the swimming pool.

Julie twisted around in her seat and beamed at the room. Thank you all, her expression seemed to say. Thank you for making me so happy and my enemies so sad. What wonderful people you all are to be on my side.

"Fifty-five. And sixty-five and seventy . . . and five . . . and eighty and five . . . and ninety . . . and five. A hundred thousand dollars. Do I hear more? I have a hundred thousand in the front."

Evan's prayer climbed skyward. It was almost his for another one hundred thousand. The gavel hovered in the air as Bicester rehearsed the words "sold to Koestler." But then, quite suddenly, the aristocratic head jerked up.

"And ten. A hundred and ten thousand I am bid at the back of the room."

Julie Bennett, Evan Koestler, Billy Bingham, and the rest of the New York art world twirled around to find the newcomer. Who had bid? Who the *hell* was it? It was not a Koestler plant.

Evan was nearly on his feet as his wild eyes scanned the thronging crowd.

Bicester's words cut into his consciousness. "I am bid one hundred and ten thousand dollars. Against you in the front, sir."

Evan waved frantically behind his back. His eyes didn't leave the back of the room, searching the sea of faces for the identity of the bidder.

"A hundred and twenty."

Please God, let him come again.

There! He saw it. The incline of the head over to the left. Evan's heart stopped. No. *No! Yes.* It was Don Marron of the Museum of Modern Art. MOMA had just bid a hundred and twenty for a Billy Bingham.

Evan swiveled around again to face the front. In a moment of inspired genius he waited.

"A hundred and forty to the left of me. Against you, sir, at the back."

Evan saw that one, too. Christopher Matlow, sitting next to C.Z. Whitmore and bidding for him. Whitmore, perhaps the richest serious collector in the world aside from the Gettys and their museum, was in the thick of the bidding. Against MOMA.

"Hundred and fifty to my right." And the Pace Gallery, bidding for a client.

"And sixty, and seventy and eighty..." And Knoedler, and Irving Blum, and Whitmore again.

The sun rose in Billy Bingham's heart as it set in Julie Bennett's. He had survived, and, even as he sat there, on the uncomfortable upright chair that the grander auction houses like to inflict upon their customers, survival was metamorphosing into triumph.

"Two hundred and twenty... and thirty... any more... at the back... any more?" *Bang!* "Sold to Museum of Modern Art. Two hundred and thirty thousand dollars!"

For a second or two there was a pandemonium as the information sank into three hundred skulls. Thirty-eight lots to go. And MOMA had just paid two thirty, and Whitmore the underbidder, the Pace dropping out in the high hundreds.

The hard core of the art market was in the room. But outside, littered about on Park and Madison, were hundreds of their colleagues—people who for one reason or another hadn't bothered to show. They would regret it, and the insiders would make sure that they did, because they were missing the opportunity of a lifetime. Those who had the power to make the bids could strike into the window of opportunity at the expense of their absent friends, and of their less powerful neighbors who had attended the sale but hadn't gotten permission from bosses or partners to spend heavily, who hadn't bothered to line up the bank financing. People like Whitmore, who didn't have to think about money, would clean up now, secure in the knowledge that every painting that found its way into his collection would be underwritten by the very fact of its prestigious presence there. And he could always move on a few to friends—like the Saatchis, or to Rupert Murdoch, whom he was attempting to initiate into the wonderous world of high-powered collecting.

Julie Bennett shook her head, stunned. She watched first Billy, then Evan, then the glistening cutaway chin of Henry Bicester. She was on the verge of making a fortune and it felt like the end of the world. The art freaks had blown a collective gasket, and what had been planned as an execution had been transformed into a coronation. Billy Bingham and Evan Koestler would be bigger than ever before, unstoppable now —floating on clouds of glory while they dumped on her. She stood up. She had to get out. But there seemed to be a magnet on her seat. She sat down again hard as the next lot came up.

The bids were coming in like machine-gun fire, fast and furious as the prices of the Binghams flowed on the surf of optimism, excitement, and surprise.

Before it had begun it was all over. In thirty of the strangest minutes in art history, forty Billy Binghams had gone for a phenomenal eight million dollars. Julie Bennett had made a profit of four million and watched her former lover ascend to the right hand of God the Father Almighty. Around her they were actually clapping—in a Christie's sale room. It had never been done before.

The single crowd divided into one around Billy Bingham and another surrounding Evan Koestler. Occasionally bits would break off from the one group and filter across to the other. Around Julie there was nothing but wide-open space. Although she was a financial winner, she was perceived as the loser. She had tried to obliterate the two men who were now the stars of the art firmament, and as the fickle trendsetters tried to hitch themselves to the latest bandwagon, the first thing they did was to spurn the woman who had tried to destroy them. It would have gone the other way, of course, but it hadn't, and that was all that mattered.

Billy Bingham felt the power and the glory flow through him. Never had he imagined it could be like this. It was better than an orgasm, better than the wild joy of creation. The fingers that plucked at his sleeve and the voices that showered him with praise were the evidence of that reality. His face shone with the realization that he was at the target, that his body was the arrow quivering, shivering in the center of the bull's-eye. He needed no one now. Not even Evan, who had made it all possible. Especially Evan. To give him the good-bye kiss in front of all these people would be the most potent signal of all that he had arrived where he wanted to be.

Evan fought to cut his way through the crowd. He was back, bigger, bigger by far than before, and everyone in the room knew it. Evan had demonstrated courage and belief and steadfastness of purpose that the art world had not realized existed in its midst, and on the victor the spoils of victory were being heaped high. But Evan had another goal, another prize to claim. Billy Bingham, the most famous artist in the world this minute, would sleep with him tonight.

He came up behind Billy, and he reached out to touch his coat, to call attention to the fact that he had arrived to stake his claim, to collect on the Mephistophelian pact.

Billy Bingham sprang around, and his hand whiplashed out to sweep Evan's hand away from him. "Take your filthy hands off me! Do you hear? Don't ever touch me again!" Billy shouted the words.

Evan sprang back, as the crowd erupted into a chorus of "ooohs" and "aahs." It was almost too much for them all. There had already been enough to fuel the scandal mill for months, and now this.

Koestler had been publicly humiliated by the artist whose reputation he had just saved, and in a way that allowed the most tantalizing of speculations.

Leaving an astounded, deflated Evan Koestler in his foaming wake, Billy powered through the ecstatic crowd toward Julie Bennett.

Eyeball to eyeball they stood together.

"Thank you, Julie. Thank you from the bottom of my heart," Billy's voice throbbed with hatred. "You have shown the world my genius. Now know this. Every day, every minute, for the rest of my life, I will look for ways to do you harm. And one fine day—I promise—I will destroy you as you have tried, and failed, to destroy me."

He pushed past her, oblivious to the raging sea of spectators—the crowd of witnesses. Oblivious, too, to the parchment white that sheeted Julie Bennett's usually round and ruddy face.

But it was she who had the last word. "You're just a silly little boy, Billy Bingham," she hissed. "A stupid child." Then at his retreating back she screamed the words, "You destroy me? Over my dead body!"

TWENTY-FIVE

LEONARD FIRESTONE WAS IN THE SAND TRAP. BOB Hope was tight up against a fan palm, and President Ford was hooked, way out on the fairway of the neighboring hole. Daniel Galvin III, however, was slap bang in the middle of the main drag with a simple seven approach shot to the fifth green of the Thunderbird course.

In a way that summed up Daniel Galvin's life so far—right on target, the going apparently easy, positioned to win. In corporate America Daniel Galvin was a megastar, and in other places too: board of trustees of the L.A. County Art Museum, charter member of the elite and powerful L.A. Community Committee, member of the board of governors of the Performing Arts Council of the Music Center, and board member of the Coca-Cola Company, Bank of America, and the General Telephone Company of California.

He swaggered toward his ball and addressed it like a board meeting, with considerable aplomb and a liberal sprinkling of pomposity. He swung the iron. The backswing just a bit too fast, the downstroke dangerously wristy for a ten handicap player, he slid under the ball. Spinning like a top toward the right from the slice, it sailed toward the pale blue sky, caught the breeze, and at seventy-five yards—bored with its flight— it dropped like a stone into the immaculate sand of the bunker.

Which was a metaphor for Daniel Galvin's predicament, because today he was a worried man.

He had long since been fed up with the money. There was far too much of that, and after a while it got to be a bore—all those decisions about managing it, the tax problems, too many houses to live in, endless servants wanting orders. But power was another matter altogether. That was a commodity that he couldn't get enough of, and he had never met anybody who could—the sublime feeling of knowing that you mattered, that when you shouted *jump* the air was full of people, important people with jumpers of their own.

At ABS he had as much power as he could want, both as CEO and largest shareholder. But because it was a network, the political influence he could wield was enormous. It was one thing to peddle shampoo and quite another to sell prime-time nightly news. On that he could get as much slice as he had achieved on his bunkered ball. Ostensibly you gave the facts straight. But which facts did you choose to display and which to hide? Of course it wasn't a full-time, hands-on business. There was a vice president in charge of that. But that particular VP was merely a finely tuned telepathic receiver who had been selected exclusively for his deference to Daniel Galvin III. So the mighty lined up at the Galvin door, and he wouldn't have it any other way.

But now his cozy world was threatened. ABS had been trailing in the ratings and the Emmys, but in the musical chairs among the networks there was nothing particularly unusual about that. Next year, with the profits of *Beverly Hills Nights* coming in, things would look better. If there *was* a next year. Daniel Galvin had never approved of opportunists in the business world. A stately, magisterial progress of patricians up through the ranks of the corporation was his ideal. He therefore didn't approve at all of the maverick corporate raider with the powerful backers who was trying to take over his company. At first the business community had scoffed at David's attempt to fell the mighty Goliath, but the attack had been mounted with considerable skill and, as a result of judicious buying in the open market, and well-timed press releases, the ABS stock, weak before the bid approach on the lower profits, had now taken off into the stratosphere. Already the big shareholders—the insurance companies, the pension funds, and the unit trusts—were wavering in their loyalty to their soul brothers, the present board of directors under Daniel Galvin.

It began to look like there was a real possibility that Daniel Galvin would lose the battle. He had tried all the standard defenses—a green-mail payment to the raiders for the share stake they had built up, the so-called poison pill in which the company took on extra debt to make itself less digestible to predators, and a few less orthodox methods. All had failed. Now there seemed to Galvin's far-from-uncanny mind only one way to prevail. ABS would have to increase its profits and its share of the Nielsens, and it would have to do so fast. But how? There was only one thing that everybody knew—and that was that nobody knew what the public wanted.

There was some good-natured ribbing on the fairway.

"Well, Dan, my people tell me it's early retirement for you. Think of the golf you'll be able to play. Should be good for a couple of strokes off your handicap." President Ford could get away with a joke like that. Not many could.

The fine cloud of powdered sand leaped into the air as Daniel Galvin blasted it with a nine iron. Everything moved but the ball. It sat there. Mocking him.

"What you need, Dan," said Leonard Firestone, "is some good news from the ratings. Can't argue with success."

"Yeah," growled Galvin. Firestone should stick to property. Firestone had brought Gerry Ford to Thunderbird and the two friends lived next door to each other on the thirteenth fairway, with the house that had belonged to Ginger Roger's mother as a dormitory for the secret servicemen. Now they were partners in a one-hundred-fifty-million-dollar development.

"I like these mini-series things, but you know they don't go on long enough. What I'd like to see is one that goes on for a couple of weeks every night for two hours. Then you could see it all, get involved but not be kept hanging on forever, like with a series. Sort of more like a midi-series, or even a maxi-series." Gerry Ford was the sort of guy who didn't mind admitting that he watched junk television, and further, that he enjoyed it.

Daniel Galvin turned slowly to look at the ex-president.

What a wonderful idea. The American people had made the biggest mistake of their collective lives when they had preferred Jimmy Carter to this one—the man who had exorcised the ghosts of Watergate and slipped the backbone into American foreign policy with the *Mayaguez*. A mighty midi-series. The biggest stars, the best book, a fortune on P.R., millions on locations. It could be a winner. It *would* be a winner, if handled correctly.

"And Dan ought to sign up Julie Bennett's latest book. Julie's right there, halfway up the mountain, scribbling all day. You know her, don't you, Dan? She's a big contributor to the Desert Museum, and to Bob's cultural thing, and Barbara Sinatra's abused children. She's a bit prickly, but she's all right, and the kids swear by her novels. So does Betty."

Bob Hope pitched in. "I heard she's just done an amazing thing. Bought up the rights to all the characters in *Gone With the Wind* from the Margaret Mitchell estate. She's writing the sequel. Calling it *Tomorrow Is Another Day*. Should be worth a few bucks at the box office. Book One didn't do so badly." He cackled the famous Bob Hope laugh.

But Daniel Galvin III wasn't laughing at all.

Scarlett O'Hara rides again in the biggest production in the history of television. ABS would never have to do another thing. The profits would be up in the stratosphere.

How soon could he decently get off this golf course?

In the Julie Bennett hate cocoon any distraction was welcome. Jane was everywhere—woven into the fabric of America. She stared from the magazine covers, shone from the Sony screens, and her silky voice caressed the airwaves on Owen Spann and Michael Jackson. Julie Bennett, who always maintained that media was the plural of mediocre, nevertheless watched, read, and listened to everything, and Jane's success was the bitterest of pills. The fame was one thing, but the money could buy power and independence and safety. That was what really hurt. Jane Cummin—the advertisers' dream, with an income bigger than hers. Sometimes she had steeled herself to read the ads, her eyes all puckered up with pain and rage. Jane Cummin, the mysterious English girl with the deliciously shady past. The P.R. people had made a big thing out of it. Who is Jane? What is she? The implication was that she was some fantastical creation who had floated down from a far-off planetary system to sow her loveliness in the fields of America. Against the blank background of mystery, fantasy could roam free. No longer English, she belonged to the world. Jane Cummin was an idea. An idea that had pushed Julie Bennett to the brink of insanity.

All her dark plans had been sabotaged. By Billy Bingham —erstwhile toy boy and now the artistic superhero of his generation. By Evan Koestler, who had stolen him away, saved him as he teetered on the abyss, and then been discarded for his faith like an empty beer can on a beach in summer. And most of all, of course, by the little sister, by her father's child, the symbol of his treachery. By the daughter of the hated mother who had destroyed him, who had driven him to the black despair and desperate death.

At least the Daniel Galvin invitation to a tennis party provided some other focus for her mind. That and the *Gone With the Wind* coup. Julie Bennett cheered up a bit at the thought of that. Finding a plot for an unwritten book was always something that worried authors. Where would the idea spring from? Would it spring at all? What if imagination's well had run dry? She had picked the book up one day and read the front and the back pages—the two most important of any novel. From the back page the last sentence of the book had leaped at her.

Tomorrow Is Another Day. At once she had known what the next year's work would be. Negotiations with the Margaret Mitchell estate had been protracted, but the hard cash had speeded them up. Three and a half million for the right to tell the world about the rest of Scarlett O'Hara's and Rhett Butler's lives. It was cheap at that price. The moment the ink had been dry on the contract she had set to work and in forty days had hammered out an in-depth synopsis of twenty-five thousand words. Now she was polishing it, before laying it on Morton Janklow, the New York superagent who would turn it into a hard/soft guarantee that would bring tears of envy to the eyes of every author in the land.

Daniel Galvin? Daniel Galvin III, wasn't it? That was a funny business—all that one-ing and two-ing and three-ing as America tried to play the title game. In a few hundred years there would probably be Daniel Galvin the Tenth. Oh, well. Everyone had to start somewhere, and three quarters of the titles in England had been created since 1900. The beerage, they called them, since brewing beer and contributing to the Conservative party kitty was the preferred way of buying one's gentility.

What did she know about him? Not a lot. The Fords had brought him to lunch a little while ago, but she hadn't had much chance to talk to him. She *did* know that he ran ABS as a one-man puppeteer. She knew also that recently ABS had become a target. The raider/arbitrageur whose name she could never remember had built up a stake and was bad-mouthing the far-from-brilliant Galvin profit record—and the shareholders were wavering as their mouths watered over the paper profits the gunslinger's bid had brought. Still, the Galvins of this world didn't throw in their chips without a fight, and chips Galvin had in abundant profusion. His house at Thunderbird Cove was apparently a Steve Chase masterpiece, according to *Architectural Digest*. It would be fun to peek inside.

Julie relaxed on the expensive leather of the Rolls' back seat. On either side, the self-satisfied country clubs stared back at her, a bit like the castles that dotted medieval Europe as the plutocrats of America retreated from the rape and pillage and crime into impregnable fortresses where they could lead their rarefied lives in peace. Why else would they choose to shut themselves up in these manmade islands of exclusivity? The thought of it made her blood run cold. One unwise night in the bar, with a few innermost thoughts exposed as the martinis unwound inhibition, and you died your social death in the luxury prison you had hoped to live in for the rest of your life. Every time you were caught cheating at golf, every time your husband got too friendly with the waitress, every time you forgot to draw the bedroom drapes on the little perversion that was the only way your husband could get it up— the next morning you might as well call the realtor. Each club had its own characteristics—Thunderbird and the Vintage Club WASP-ish as hell; Morningside and Rancho Mirage Country Club wall-to-wall nouveau riche; the best golf and tennis at La Quinta; the best clubhouse, Ironwood.

Julie Bennett flexed her powerful legs and peered at them without enthusiasm. Women's tennis gear didn't flatter her. The pleated skirt looked a bit like the frill on a ham bone, and her stocky frame had the word *squat* playing on the edge of everyone's lips. Still, it was a functional body, and it knew its way around a tennis court. José Higueras—number seven on the Association of Tennis Professionals' list and the part-time pro at LaQuinta Hotel Tennis Club—saw to that. Two or three times a week he would drop by after nightfall and put Julie through the ropes on the floodlit North/South court. As a result her swing was smooth, her positioning was excellent, and above all her eye never left the ball. So Daniel Galvin III had better watch out.

She swept through the gates of Thunderbird—stopping only for the security ritual, the equivalent of nodding to the altar before you sat down in church.

At the gates it was the same again, and then she was in the vast courtyard of the Galvin house.

Julie was impressed with the compound. Steve Chase was good. The desert had been brought inside the house and tall cacti poked up like totem poles, next to mature fan and royal palms. The square geometry of the buildings merged perfectly with the landscape, the natural color of the stone in harmony with the beige of the hill that towered over the house. They passed the pool, its mauve tiles the exact shade of the twilight sky, with its massive sculpted stone chairs and tables, merging utility with the beauty of their form.

Daniel Galvin jumped up from the table at which he had been sitting. "Julie Bennett," he boomed. "How very good of you to come." His handshake was professionally hearty.

"I love your house."

"Well, thank you. We like it." He looked at her warily "It's a great pleasure to meet you properly at last. That was a marvelous lunch you gave, but somehow we never really got a chance to talk."

Where were the other guests? Julie wondered.

Clearly something of a mind reader, Galvin replied, "To be totally frank with you, Julie, I have asked you here because there is something I want to discuss with you. But I know that you like a game of tennis, and so do I. So if it's okay with you I thought we might play a set or two and then get to the business afterward. It's just us, I'm afraid. Never been a great fan of doubles."

"Sounds good."

Julie looked him up and down. She meant it. It did sound good. Playing endless tennis with a pro was one thing; a bit of healthy competition was another. Galvin looked like he'd be a safe player, a big, slow man who wouldn't take too many chances. That would make him a good opponent, because she liked to take her chances whenever she could. What did he want to discuss with her? It was unusual not to go through Mort if it was business, and Galvin would know that he represented her.

The chauffeur had brought her racquets in from the car.

"Well, let's get to it. The sun's cooling down now. Best of three?"

"Fine."

He led her toward the court. "What time do you like to play best?"

"Oh, I usually wait till the sun's gone completely. But this is fine."

"Busy on a book right now? The kids love your stuff. I only get to read balance sheets and business memos that the girls make up for me. Can't remember when I last chose my own reading." He seemed rather proud about that.

"Yes, I've always got something brewing."

Julie was cagey. It was an old dealer's trick. She would pick up the background information before the meeting started. There would be more fishing trips on the tennis court when the guard was supposed to be down. By the end of the first set she'd have a shrewd idea of what it was he wanted.

"Anything in particular?"

"Not really."

He peered at the stone wall of her defense as he loped

easily by her side. They all said Bennett was a tough cookie. They all were right.

Soon they were on the immaculate court, very well maintained, the rim of the net Foreign Legion white, the surface the rust-colored red of the typical desert court.

"Rough or smooth?" Galvin twirled the racquet.

"Rough."

"It is."

The knock-up was deadly serious. These two were real competitors, in life, in everything. Probing for weaknesses, hiding strengths, they hit the ball straight at each other, down the middle of the court. When it was clear that no valuable secrets were to be revealed, both agreed to start.

"Ready when you are," said Julie.

"Fine."

Julie reached up with her left hand—straight not stiff—and pushed the ball into the air above her left shoulder. Her hip beneath it, she reached up to the full extension of arm and racquet and hammered at the ball, using her body weight to direct it toward its destination. She put everything into the serve—an all-or-nothing gamble for success, aiming at the far-righthand corner of Galvin's court. She was on target. The powerful first serve snaked over the net and Galvin's forehand didn't even come close.

"Ah," he grunted as the ace swept by his outstretched arm.

Fifteen-love.

Another one. This time missing his reaching backhand by inches.

Thirty-love. Julie was hot.

Now two double faults as Julie's aggressive first serve caught the tip of the net, and both her second serves, failing to play for safety, missed the target by a foot apiece.

Erratic. That figured, Galvin thought. If he could keep the ball in play then she would make mistakes. She would beat herself. People who played against his solid, rather unimaginative game often did. It was true in business, too. In a deal she would make lightning decisions, some good, some bad.

Thirty-all, and still no rallies.

This time the service got through and so did the return. Her backhand looked very solid. She had positioned herself well, which was more than half the battle, and she didn't skimp on the follow-through. Body sideways on, feet well balanced. The ball snaked over the net toward his forehand. Back to her forehand. She returned it, a little late on the hit. The ball was high, and running into the net, he was able to tuck it away quite firmly an inch or two inside the baseline of her backhand court.

Thirty-forty.

The next service was an express train. Slap-bang at him. No time to run. The ball landed foursquare on the white line and kicked up toward his chest where it struck him hard, without his racquet having a chance to get anywhere near it.

"Deuce," said Julie Bennett with determination.

Galvin cursed inwardly. Two aces and a direct hit. Humiliating. And he *hated* being humiliated. He would buy her project for peanuts. She might be able to serve, but he'd murder her in a deal. He forced himself to concentrate, to watch the ball before it even left her hand. He moved back a bit toward the baseline. Clearly she believed in giving the first serve all she had, and the second one not much less—the high-risk, high-reward approach.

He shortened his backswing and returned it safely. For a minute or two they played a Chris Evert baseline game, with great long loping forehands and backhands, probing each other's positioning and testing their consistency. It was Julie who went for the drop. A Galvin forehand cross had fallen a bit short, and he was on his heels at the back of the court. The drop worked and Galvin ran for it, like a cold battle tank starting up in the early morning fog of the German plain. The ball had all but stopped moving by the time he reached it. But he couldn't stop. On and on he went until the net stopped him. Quite suddenly. He almost toppled over it.

"Fuck," he said quite loudly.

"My advantage," said Julie.

Again he managed to return the bulletlike serve—to her suspect forehand, to his safe backhand, to her smooth backhand, to his steady forehand. The sweat stood out on his brow.

She was storming the net, and he had time for the lob. Up

and up it went—high over her head as she turned to scurry back to the baseline. In by an inch, but she was under the bounce, her forehand reaching up for the smash. The ball streaked past him, clearly in. It was not even in the same county as his racquet face.

"Game," said Julie Bennett smugly.

Screw you, thought Daniel Galvin III.

And so the battle had raged: flashy, wristy Julie with her cannonball serves, her double faults and her topspins, with her wild smashes into the net and beyond the baseline, and her cunning drop shots that always infuriated her less mobile, more straightforward opponent; big, safe, dependable Daniel Galvin who could count his double faults on the fingers of one hand and whose seldom-needed second serve was a carbon copy of his first. The tortoise played the hare, the rapier dueled the saber, the thoroughbred raced the cart horse. Julie Bennett had won.

In the fifty-foot drawing room with its mountain views and its rather good Schieles, Klees, and Kandinskys, Galvin pretended not to mind as he offered the sweat-soaked Julie a cold drink.

"I think I'll have a scotch."

It was her dealing drink.

Galvin laughed. It was his, too.

The fact that both had lost a few pounds' worth of water and that the last thing that either needed was dyhydrating alcohol didn't seem to matter. The game had been the thing. Now the thing was the business. Galvin had wanted to win too badly once the game had started to give away any clues about what he was after.

"Ice and soda?"

"Water. No ice."

"God, you English. Masochists!"

He sat down opposite her and wondered how to play it.

"Word is you bought the rights to a *Gone With the Wind* sequel."

"Yes, I suppose that's no big secret, although it isn't in the trades yet."

"I think it's a wonderful idea."

"For a book?" She was onto him.

"For a book and a TV series."

"An ABS series."

"That sort of thing." He laughed. Nervously.

"You ought to talk to Morton Janklow about that."

The cards-on-the-table thing usually worked pretty well. He took a deep breath.

"Listen, Julie, I know you have a hotshot agent, and I have a whole office full of development people at ABS, but the point is I want to buy the small-screen rights for the *Gone With the Wind* sequel. Expanded mini-series. Vast budget. State-of-the-art director. Hottest writer in town. The works. The thing gets made because I *am* the green light at ABS. I'm not talking option money, I'm talking rights. Half on signature. Half on first day of principal shooting."

"How much? I'm not cheap, you know."

"Two million dollars."

"Five."

"Three and a half."

"Done."

Julie drank deep on the scotch. She looked up at the mountain. Whence came her help? Forget it. She had helped herself. Never got three and a half for a TV movie before. Nobody had. She'd only paid three and half to the Mitchell estate. Now that was even and the book—hard and soft— would flow through to her bottom line for nothing.

Absentmindedly she asked, "Who gets to star?"

"Christ, I don't know. Whoever is right for the part, I guess."

"Suppose it's not very important."

But Julie Bennett was quite wrong about that. It was to become ridiculously, disgustingly, grotesquely important, and it was going to turn her world upside down.

"EVERYTHING'S PERFECT, ISN'T IT?" ROBERT FOLEY TWISTED the brandy glass between long fingers and let out a sigh of the deepest satisfaction.

"Wow, from you, that's something." Jane's face broke

open in a broad smile. Robert Foley seldom said things like that. He didn't believe in devaluing the currency of sincerity.

She twirled her fingers into his hand. "Yes, it is perfect. Better than perfect."

It was a magic moment. They were dining in a wonderful restaurant that nobody, with the gorgeous exception of Shari Belafonti-Harper, had ever heard of—Mon Grenier, tucked away from the world in Encino but with the best strawberry and Grand Marnier desserts in the world. It was the sort of occasion on which things tended to happen. The very best things.

Robert turned to look at her. "I love you, Jane."

"Tell me why." She smiled like a naughty child. It was difficult for Robert to say those kinds of words, and she wanted so very many more.

He laughed. "Oh, you want chapter and verse?"

"Certainly I do."

"Well, because you're very beautiful, and obscenely attractive, of course . . . and because I like the way you look when you're asleep, and the smell of you . . ."

"Mmm, Robert, this is wild. More. More."

"And of course I love your strength—that you don't give a damn unless someone gives a damn about you, and your optimism, and cheerfulness, and the fact that your mouth always looks moist and . . ."

She leaned in toward him, the wet lips he loved brushing tenderly against his.

"If you don't look out I'll tell you what I like about you." She murmured the husky threat, so that he could feel her breath, strawberry sweet, against his cheek.

"Jane!"

"Yes."

She moved back an inch or two and let the adoration flow toward him, her heart singing in her chest as she saw its reflection in his eyes.

"Jane . . . I don't know how to say this. . . . Jane . . ."

"Telephone call for you, Ms. Cummin." The waiter's voice was quite firm. In L.A. telephone calls took precedence over everything.

"You're not serious?"

Robert's incredulous laugh backed up her question.

"Yes. Mr. Pete Rivkin. Very urgent. I can plug the phone in at your table." The waiter was determined. This was the Valley where half the studios were. Rivkin phone calls were accepted, even by stars like Jane Cummin. It would be blasphemy not to take it.

Jane turned toward Robert to see if the moment was still there. It was.

"Wait!" her voice was sharp as her eyes threatened the unwelcome messenger.

"What were you going to say, Robert?"

"Maybe you should take Rivkin's call. Did you tell him you were going to be here?"

"No *way*! He must have called every restaurant in town. Armies of raw-fingered secretaries tapping it out to find me."

"So this is what our life will be like together. I can just see it on our honeymoon—the yacht, the stars, flying fishes in the moonlight, and Pete Rivkin long distance on the radio telephone."

"What? Robert! Honeymoon?"

"Yes, that was my question."

"Ms. Cummin, Mr. Rivkin has waited a long time." The waiter couldn't bear it any longer. There was nothing on earth that these two could be discussing that would possibly rank with the importance of a Rivkin telephone conversation. He thrust the receiver at her like a baton in a relay race.

Pete Rivkin's voice was burbling down the line. "Is there anybody there? Don't leave me hanging on here. For Chrissakes, somebody answer this goddamn phone . . ."

"Pete. Stop panicking, for God's sake. It's me. Trying to have a quiet dinner. What on earth do you want?" The exasperation was mock resignation and she didn't mean one ounce of it, because something wonderful was happening, the most wonderful thing in her life so far.

"Oh, Jane. Thank *God* I got you. Do you know how hard I've tried to find you. . . . Listen, sweetheart, something *incredible* has happened . . ."

"I know, I *know*!" She squeezed Robert's hand as the excitement bubbled within her.

"What do you mean, 'you know'? You can't possibly know. I've only just heard myself . . ."

"Go on, Pete. I'm talking about something else."

Pete Rivkin paused. Was she drunk? Unlikely but possible. The hell with it. He couldn't keep this in a second longer.

"ABS wants you to play Scarlett O'Hara in a sequel to *Gone With the Wind*. I'm producing and directing. Isn't it fucking fantastic? Can you believe it?"

Jane heard the words, but she was thinking of the other ones. Of Robert's.

"Yes," she said. "Yes!"

Robert Foley grasped at it.

"You'll marry me?" It was half said, half mouthed.

"So you'll do it?" Pete Rivkin babbled into the telephone. "They'll pay you very nearly anything. It's going to be a huge mini-series, on for days, and we can shoot it in the hiatus from *Nights* . . ."

"Yes, I'll marry you."

"What? Christ, Jane, what the hell's going down? Are you hearing what I'm saying . . ."

Jane laughed, her happiness exploding into the music of the sound. "Oh, Pete, Pete. Yes, I hear you and yes it's great and yes, of course, I accept, but do you know you've caught me at a bad time? Do you know that? You've caught me at the most important moment of my life."

She put the telephone down on the table—the line still open—and she melted into Robert's arms.

He wrapped her tight in him, crushing her close in the embrace that no man would put asunder, and from the rust-red tablecloth the sounds of the demented chipmunk crackled and squeaked as the background to their bliss.

" . . . Fuck's going on . . . *Gone With the Wind* . . . Scarlett . . . biggest thing's ever happened to me . . . what the hell . . . stoned or something?"

TWENTY-SIX

JANE BOUNDED INTO THE ROOM LIKE A GAZELLE ON amphetamine. Pete Rivkin was fussing about in the large ante-room, quite obviously waiting for her.

"*There* you are. Thank God. Listen, Galvin's in my office right now. Don't say a thing, okay? Just 'yes' and 'no' and 'three bags full.' Whatever he says, don't disagree. We can iron out the details later. You and me. Trust me."

Jane looked at him suspiciously. If he was a cat then the roof was hot. This was not at all like Peter Rivkin, the icicle man she had come to know. Was Galvin *that* much of an ogre?

"Listen, Pete, today anything goes. If you got favors you want from me, now's your time. Robert proposed to me last night. *Despite* your valiant attempts to screw it up."

Rivkin took a step back. He had the look of a man who couldn't take much more sensory stimulation, but who realized that some sort of response was de rigueur. "And you accepted?"

"Certainly I accepted."

"Well, that's wonderful, Jane. I'm so happy for both of you . . ." His voice trailed off. "I guess you'll still be able to do the *Gone With the Wind* thing . . ."

Jane patted his hand reassuringly. Clearly Pete Rivkin had things on his mind. "Okay, Pete, calm down. Calm down. Do you think we ought to find you a Valium?" She laughed. Rivkin would eat a hedgehog before he ate one of those.

She took him firmly by the hand. "Come on, let's go face the lion in his den. Don't worry, I'll protect you."

Galvin rose to his feet as they entered the room. He held out an affable hand. "Jane Cummin. What a very great pleasure. On behalf of ABS let me take this opportunity to thank you for all the wonderful work you've done on *Nights*. Sit down, Rivkin. Do please sit down, Ms. Cummin."

He surrendered himself to the leather of the chair on which Pete Rivkin usually sat. Daniel Galvin III had taken over his office like the Soviet Union a Warsaw Pact nation, and the smell of raw power steamed from his every pore.

"Well, I guess Rivkin's given you the bare bones of the *Gone With the Wind* thing. Frankly, we're very excited about this project at ABS. *I'm* very excited about it." There was no doubt in the Galvin mind, or anywhere else, that his excitement and ABS's were one and the same thing.

"Yes, the situation is that we have obtained the rights to the motion-picture sequel to Margaret Mitchell's novel, and we're now formally in preproduction of *Tomorrow Is Another Day*." He beamed at Jane, waiting for her audience reaction.

Jane, remembering her anteroom promise to Pete, said nothing.

Galvin was only mildly put out by the lack of response. He went on. "And, as you know, you are to be our Scarlett. Let me say, right away, that there was never any question of anyone but you playing this part. Rather different from the first time around, eh? You're blond, and Scarlett was a brunette, but times change, and you're a star. And Mr. Rivkin will be your David O. Rhett Butler, I'm told, is as yet an unknown quantity, although there is a Robert De Niro lobby, and, I think, a Robert Redford one. So we come to the question of your fee. I gather you don't have an agent. Is that wise?"

"I've never needed one. *Nights* is all I've done, and I trust Pete to do what's fair."

"Good. I think you're very sensible. In this life you have to know what you want and be satisfied when you get it. Agents tell you what to want, and that's ridiculous. Only you can know that. Well, let's not beat about the bush. I'm going to give you my very best offer, and because I believe you've been fair with us I'm going to be fair with you. Two million dollars. Half on signature. Half on first day of principal photography. If you'd had William Morris or ICA batting for you, my first offer would have been half that."

"I accept," said Jane, keeping it short. What would she *pay* to play Scarlett?

"Great. Wonderful. Then we have a deal. That wasn't hard, was it, Rivkin? Christ Almighty, you Hollywood boys could do with a bit less bullshit and a bit more dealing. Think of the money you'd save on all those lunches." He sat back in the chair and surveyed his formidable girth. "Rivkin should have all the paperwork next door. So we won't waste much more time. Get on with the show. That's the thing, isn't it?"

But he had to squeeze a few more drops out of it. After all, this was quite an occasion. This was *his* production. For years and years he had laughed at New York corporate executives who had "gone Hollywood," but now he could see the attraction of it, like the buzz of offering a girl who looked like Jane Cummin two million bucks. And the glorious *subservience* of all the Industry players. They made a fine art of sycophancy. He could do with a bit more of that in New York.

"Yes, I'm very pleased with this whole deal. It's really my baby, you know. I found the project—the Julie Bennett book —bought it, picked you and Rivkin for the package, and not just because we have you under contract . . ."

"What did you say?" said Jane.

Galvin's monologue petered out. Like an oil tanker in the Gulf, it took him time to stop. He wasn't used to interruption, but something about Jane's tone of voice demanded an immediate answer to her question. "I was saying that I had been the prime mover . . ."

"It's a Julie Bennett project?"

Pete Rivkin's leg prodded into Jane's below the table.

"Well, yes and no. It's an ABS project now. *My* project. We own the motion-picture rights. I think Bennett has script approval, for what it's worth, doesn't she, Rivkin?"

He seemed irritated that the conversation had moved from the general to the particular. Men like Galvin were never very fond of particulars. There were little people in back rooms whose job it was to make entrepreneurial dreams come true. He was a broad-brush-strokes person. "Why do you ask? Don't like her books or something? Can't say I've read any. She's a touchy so-and-so, but she plays a mean game of tennis and drinks scotch afterward."

Pete Rivkin's eyes were beseeching her not to blow it. He needn't have worried. She wasn't going to.

"Does she know I'm playing Scarlett?"

"Christ, I don't know. Is it released, Rivkin? Does she know? Does anyone know? I suppose I've told a few people."

Pete Rivkin's voice was pitched a little higher than usual. "I don't think we've told her. Don't think she asked." He looked at Jane meaningfully as he said with emphasis, "The contract she signed didn't give her casting approval."

"Does that answer your question?" Galvin stood up. "Well, I've got a plane to catch and work to do. Can't sit around all day going through the small print. Wish I could afford the luxury. It would be better for my arteries." He beamed patronizingly at Pete Rivkin and warmly at Jane. "The very best of luck, Jane, if I can call you that. Break a leg, as they say in the theater. I think you can make my show the best thing that's ever happened on television."

And then he was gone.

Pete Rivkin talked fast. "I didn't tell you about Julie on purpose, Jane. Don't be cross. There's nothing on God's earth she can do about it. I've checked through the contract with a magnifying glass. And we'll keep her away from you on the set. No problem. I just didn't want you to blow the best thing that's ever happened to us. I can't tell you what the production budget is on this one. But you can tell from what they're paying you. It's bigger than the biggest. ABS is going for bust. The show needs you. Without you it can't begin to break even."

For a second or two Jane looked at him. She hadn't believed that it was possible to get any better inside her heart, inside her head. But it had. Because she had just been handed on a plate the thing she had long desired—her sister's head.

* * *

EVAN KOESTLER STARED HARD AT THE LETTER, WHICH WAS
the only thing on his great big brown leather desk. He read it
again, and again, and once again.

> To Evan Koestler,
> This letter is to inform you that our dealer relationship
> is terminated. Those pictures that you already have in
> your possession are yours to dispose of in terms of our
> former agreement. All my work-in-progress and the
> many canvases I have at my studio in Venice are now
> mine to do with as I wish, no part of any sale price
> owing to you.
>
> > Billy Bingham

Evan tried to still his shaking hand and to make sense of
the electric surge inside his brain. It was unbelievable. The
language. No "Dear Evan." No "kind regards" or even "sin-
cerely yours." The treachery. The sheer, unadulterated treachery. Evan had invented him. Evan had saved him. Evan had
showered the treasures of the world on his damnable head,
and now this.

It had been bad enough after the sale. At the sweet moment
of triumph the cup of victory had been swept rudely from his
hands. The whole world had been ready to cheer for him, but
after Billy's astonishing and unforgivable outburst, they had
smirked instead. The main story—on the wires, in the papers,
across the networks—had been the remarkable triumph of the
Evan Koestler prodigy, but in the drawing rooms, in the bedrooms of the plutocracy, in the places where it *really* mattered,
there was only one topic of conversation. Evan's own phenomenal invention had opened wide the door of his closet.

The money had almost made up for it. Now the money was
being sprayed at him, an even though they laughed at his little
"secret," the buyers had lined up to back his artistic judgment.
The Billy Bingham dealership was a license to print dollar
bills, and the golden fallout permeated through to the other

artists in his stable, enabling him to mark up their pictures faster than the price of bread in the Weimar Republic. So Evan had put a brave face on the public humiliation. Billy Bingham might have rubbed his nose in the gutter, but at least he hadn't pulled the dealership.

Now he had. Evan held his head in his hands and felt the pumping of the blood in his temples. Was there anything he could do? Legally, there was not much. When the relationship of trust between dealer and artist fell apart, lawyers couldn't put it back together. Possibly, just possibly, he could demand his fifty percent cut of all the pictures that Bingham had painted up to this date. But how many were there and how could he recognize them? How could he know when one had been sold, and to whom, and for how much? The only people who would profit from that line of approach would be the lawyers. Evan would blow his cool chasing the sales, scrambling pathetically after an artist who no longer wanted him, an artist who had publicly humiliated him before the whole wide world. It wouldn't take the tongues long to get to work. Hell hath no fury like a dealer scorned.

Which left the other option, the one Evan had only used once before, in the very early days when risk was the name of the game, and the desire to get on the murky, muck-ridden bottom rungs of the ladder had been stronger by far than the desire for food, drink, and personal safety.

He had kept in touch with Guiliano over the years—a card at Christmas, a case of good wine on his birthday, a rather charming religious scene from the eighteenth-century Italian school on a wedding anniversary. He had remained at arm's length of course, but there had always been a short note of thanks, keeping the lines of communication open for that rainy day when favors could be exchanged, when the rough could be made mysteriously smooth, when problems could be induced to melt away.

Billy Bingham had just made a mistake, perhaps the biggest mistake of his life so far. And it was far from impossible that he would never get a chance to make a mistake again.

With trembling fingers Evan Koestler reached for the telephone. The number was nowhere else but in his mind.

"Evan Koestler calling for Salvatore Guiliano," he said.

It was a minute or two before he was through. The voice at the other end was cautious, careful. For a minute or two they talked—of family, of the New Jersey weather, of neutral things. Then Evan took the plunge.

"Salvatore. I have a big problem. I am calling to ask for your help. A man has done a terrible thing to me. Have you heard of an artist called Billy Bingham . . . ?"

Evan's question was not answered directly.

Guiliano's voice was businesslike. "And you want me to point out forcibly the error of his ways."

For a minute or two the oblique conversation continued. Nothing spelled out as innuendo disguised the brutal reality of the transaction.

It was almost as an afterthought that Evan added, "It would be most appreciated if Bingham were to believe that this 'message' was coming from someone called Julie Bennett. I would be eternally in your debt, Salvatore . . ."

JULIE BENNETT ZOOMED ALONG THE CORRIDOR OF THE RIVKIN office building as if it had been built especially for her. The warm glow of anticipation was already coursing through her. Hollywood baiting was always fun. Every year or so, when the networks greedily bought the rights to her books, she would steam into town and drive them all to drink.

The preproduction script meeting in the desert had been an appetite-whetting apéritif for the main event. There had been tears in the scriptwriter's eyes as Julie's tongue had assaulted the first draft, and all around the room lips had fought to stay buttoned as the scarcely vieled insults had ripped and torn at the air. The word had been quite clear: Don't irritate Julie Bennett, take it all, turn the other cheek. Anybody who answers back is history at ABS.

"I just never *saw* it as a comedy. Nobody mentioned it to me. So you must forgive me for my surprise. But if we're *aiming* for laughs, maybe we should go the whole hog and actually *have* a few. This parody stuff is too subtle." Sarcasm was supposed to be the lowest form of wit, but irony with hypocrisy was the English national vice, and Julie had majored in it.

Now it was time for a rematch and Julie was practicing some armor-piercing insults that would slip through the Hollywood thick skins like an alarm bell through beauty sleep.

There should be some fun on the casting front, too. On all her mini-series she had approval of that. Sometimes it was the best part of all. Such marvelous fun to sabotage up-and-coming careers. For weeks she'd read in the trades that this one or that one was up for a part in the latest Julie Bennett blockbuster. Their eager little faces would pout and pose on the talk shows as they coyly let slip that they were in the running, and Julie would file it away for later use. Dreamicide in the city of dreams. It was better than murder. The producers would plead and the directors would fume, but she would be unmovable behind the impregnable fortress of the Janklow contract, flinging down barbed missiles from the ramparts at the impotent army below.

Not that she'd used Janklow this time. She even felt a tiny bit guilty about that. After all, agents' commissions were supposed to be an all-or-nothing business. But somehow she felt that this time she had done all the work—she'd had the idea, bought the rights, peddled them personally to Galvin. Why shouldn't she save the fifteen percent, just this once? It was worth more than five hundred thousand.

She punched angrily at the button of the elevator, eagerly awaiting the opportunity to sow a little unhappiness. Rivkin especially had better watch out. There was an old score to be settled.

"I've come to see Rivkin," she said rudely to the secretary, "and the 'writers.'"

"I'll see if *Mr.* Rivkin is available. Whom shall I say it is?"

Julie Bennett raised her eyes to the ceiling. The secretaries in this town all seemed to suffer from presenile dementia. Maybe it was a slow virus communicated by the typewriter ribbons. "Julie Bennett," she said.

"Oh, Miss Bennett, I didn't know you were you," the girl giggled in her impressed confusion.

Julie Bennett's eyes murdered the misplaced mirth.

Chastened, the secretary flicked the button of the intercom. "Mr. Rivkin, I have Julie Bennett here for you."

"Tell her to wait!"

Julie Bennett exploded. "Tell the asshole that my time is money, and just because everyone in this stinking town is addicted to wanking it doesn't mean that the rest of the world is hooked on it." She shouted the words, so that they would carry through the intercom to Rivkin. Then she turned on her heel and strode purposefully toward the closed door of the Rivkin office.

"You can't go in there," shouted the secretary.

"Go suck a lollipop, airhead," said Julie over her shoulder.

She flung open the door and made with the speech as she opened it. "Listen, Rivkin, I don't wait for anyone in this town. My meter's running and if you give me any shit, then Dan Galvin . . ."

Her eyes collided with Jane.

"Hello, Julie," she said.

It was an ambush. And she'd walked slap-bang into it.

Rivkin was behind the desk, Jane, in the armchair opposite him, turned to face the door.

Words died in Julie's mouth. "What the *hell* are you doing here?" she managed at last.

Jane just smiled at her.

Pete Rivkin broke the silence. His voice was still and calm but there was a wicked triumph in it. "I thought it appropriate that you should meet our star. Jane has been signed to play Scarlett," he said simply.

They were both watching her now, the way small children watched a fly whose wings they had just removed.

"What? What d'you mean?"

Again nothing but the satisfied smiles.

"Listen, you two birdbrains, can't you read? I have casting approval, and the day the porno queen gets to fart in my series is the day they bury me."

For a marvelous moment she saw a window of opportunity. Could these fools have made the most elementary mistake of all, not reading the contract? If so, then this was going to be better than she had dreamed possible, as their hope dashed to the ground on the spikes of the small print.

"You don't have casting approval. You have first-draft script approval, which shall not reasonably be withheld—otherwise you don't have a thing."

"If this is some kind of bad joke . . ."

"The joke's on you, Julie. At long last. They're paying me two million to play Scarlett in the teleplay based on your book. How much did you get?" Jane's voice sang her joy. The slate was being wiped clean.

Julie's eyes, wide with alarm and the beginnings of bitter despair, ran all around the room. In her gut she could feel it slipping away. Mort hadn't done the contract. She hadn't put the deal through him. Somebody, somewhere had botched it. *She* had.

Rivkin was reaching forward onto his desk. There was a bit of paper in his hand. A contract.

"Have a look yourself. I can't see anything about casting appro. Neither can my lawyers. It is your signature, isn't it?"

But Julie didn't want to look; she didn't want to see. She wanted only to maim and kill these people who tormented her, whatever the cost.

She stood in the middle of the room and pulsed with rage. "I'll get you for this. I promise. I swear. I'll wreck this show. I'll ruin you all. Do you hear? *Do you hear?*"

"Try to do that and you'll ruin yourself. Get the *hell* out of my office." Pete Rivkin's voice matched her anger syllable for syllable. "Or I'll have security come up here and *throw* you out."

Julie Bennett backed toward the door as the room swam through the mist of her tears. All the time Jane's smile of satisfaction burned into her.

"Good-bye, Julie," Jane said sweetly. "I have a feeling I won't be seeing you again."

On the other side of the closed door, Julie Bennett's mind howled its defiance.

"Oh yes, you will. Oh yes, you will," it screamed. "And the world will be seeing more of you, Jane. No matter what it costs. The world will see much more of you than it ever dreamed of seeing . . . or ever wanted to see."

BILLY BINGHAM'S SPIRITS SOARED WITH THE SETTING SUN. Long and lean now, the shadows licked at the beach, and the hot sand trickled deliciously between his toes. All around him the world was changing—slipping from daring day to nervous night.

An hour or two before, bikers and hikers, skaters and psychers had painted the eyes of onlookers in kaleidoscope colors, and talked to their imaginations with Walkman mime shows, brash body language, and all the subterranean counterculture sensations there were to be found on the very limit of the fault line where the land lived in constant peril at the edge of the sea. It had been a magic world of tall-assed girls with copper-toned piston legs and Day-Glo smiles—pouting promise and sexy sleek—as they wafted by on a smirk and a daydream. In this voyeur's paradise there were deep-V crotches and sweat-soaked see-throughs, lip-glossed lovelies, and tall dark strangers, slick ebony muscles, and slack, sloppy morals all set against the ghetto-blasting, roller-skate-roaring raunchiness of the California wet dream.

But now, already, the subtle shift toward the twilight zone was transforming the beach. The ghosts were coming out to play, and the citizens of the sunlight had disappeared. It was the turn of the creatures of the night, and soon the beach would be awash with creeps crazy for coke rocks; stoned sex fiends lusting for knife-point unions against stucco walls; sixties children time-warped from the "me generation" waging one-man wars against the crafty conservatism of the eighties.

Billy smiled to himself as the specters began to creep from the shady alleyways to inherit the heat-lapped darkness. Such a very short time ago he had nothing to fear from these people. In his smelly biker's jacket and the oil-painted Levi's, the aroma of poverty had clung to him then and the hollow-eyed night people had sniffed it. Then he had been immune from danger as he had walked among them, but now . . . well, now it was a different world.

He bent down and let the dirty sand filter through his fingers as he felt the delicious touch of danger. He was only about a hundred yards from the safety of the vast studio, with its steel doors, iron grilles, and computerized Westec alarm system, but he was out here now in the no-man's-land with the nobodies and anything could happen. Could they sense it? That he was the ultimate "have" in the domain of the "have-nots"?

Billy walked slowly toward the fortress that symbolized his princely position in the material world, and his mind flashed back over the rocky road that had led to the power and the glory. The last month or two had been the best of all—from the glorious moment in the Christie's sale room when he had secured his stupendous reputation and defeated his former lover to the day last week when he had finally blown Evan Koestler away forever.

He had held back from dropping Evan, until it had become apparent that he needed him no more. The Annenberg commission had opened the West Coast floodgates, and the New Yorkers had laid siege to him, approaching him directly in their fevered attempts to get hold of his work. He could sell infinitely more than he could produce, and at current rates it would take him a year or two to catch up on demand. To pay Evan fifty percent of his income was nothing but criminal stupidity. So he had hit him with the ultimate Dear John. Evan deserved it all.

Anticipating events, he had shrewdly begun to store paintings in the Venice studio rather than shipping them directly to Evan's gallery on Madison. Maybe forty paintings were stashed in there now. At present rates—not allowing for the inevitable price hikes—he had stockpiled more than eight million bucks' worth of spare art. Four million dollars for the price of a letter. Four million that Evan Koestler would never see.

Then, there were the sisters. The extraordinary, all-preoccupying sisters. One hot from Heaven with the angel's body and the serene soul. The other helter-skelter from Hades with the hatred of the world burning in her heart. One he wanted. One he loathed. One he would have. The other he would destroy. His money and his power would pave the way for the realization of his ambitions.

The heavy steel door clanged shut behind him and Billy felt the blanket of safety descend on him. It was cool in here. Cool and friendly and welcoming in its contrast with the horrors of the combat zone outside. He sighed and leaned back contentedly against the door. This was the way he liked it—not tucked away in the pretty security of Carmel, or in the patrolled privacy of Bel-Air, but here, on the brink, where the raw, rough smells of the lowlife could creep and crawl onto his canvases, making them alive, vibrant, throbbing with the reality that only contact could create.

He walked along the corridor to the studio space, and the canvases stared down at him like indifferent children at an indulgent parent. God, how very much he loved them. They filled him with the purest joy, because they were his seed. They would go out into the world, and they would be planted in the far corners of the country, of the globe even, and they would produce their harvest of fame, recognition, money, and success. Each one would repay the love he had invested in it a thousandfold with the wonderful love of strangers—of dealers, and megarich art groupies, of taste arbiters, and fashion fakirs—all united in their adoration of the artist.

He slumped down in a big armchair and the wave of tiredness crashed over him. He had been up all night working, and even with the dawn he had been unable to sleep. He had a painting to finish. So he had stayed awake until an hour or two ago, when he had taken to the sidewalks and the cafés, and the sand.

He was beginning to drift. His eyelids were heavy.

Through the light fog of near sleep Billy heard the noise—a sharp crack, the sound of something falling. Then silence. He lay back—quite still—in the womblike chair as his senses wandered back together. He didn't open his eyes. There were so many things in the studio that could have made that noise—the taut canvases, their frames expanding and contracting in time with the thermostat of the air-conditioning system, brushes, tubes of paint, ladders stacked precariously against slippery white walls.

For a second or two he hovered there, wondering whether to wake or not to wake.

Down, down he went once more into a wonderful dream. Evan and Julie danced like performing bears to the sharp crack of his whip, and the world cheered and Jane squeezed his hand and whispered, "I love you, Billy Bingham, for all the wonderful things you have made."

In the pitch blackness the voice was quite definite. "Wake up, Mr. Bingham," it said.

A hard hand was on his shoulder.

But the voice was polite, almost apologetic, although the accent didn't jell with the tones. Brooklyn? The Bronx?

The flashlight was shining directly in his eyes, and he tried to sit up as sleep merged into wakefulness.

The hand on his chest stopped him. "Lie still, Mr. Bingham," said the calm voice.

"What the hell . . ."

"Are you right-handed, Mr. Bingham?"

He was wide awake now, and the fingers of fear were on his skin at last.

"Yes, I mean, what do you want? Do you want some money?" He squirmed to test the strength of the hands that held him.

"Don't move, Mr. Bingham, or you're wasted. Okay?"

The flashlight moved an inch or two, picking out the shape of the gun barrel that hovered an inch from his eyes.

Billy felt the freezing touch of panic. "Listen, there's some cash in the drawer over there. And . . . I guess this watch is worth . . ."

"We don't want no money. This is business. That's all."

"What do you mean? What do you want?" The fright was all over his voice, making the words sticky and the breath brittle.

"The message is that Julie Bennett wanted this."

"For fuck's sake, wanted what? What are you going to do?"

"Wanted us to burn your pictures and screw up your hand."

"*No!*"

The terror had him by the throat now. It was all around

him, in his guts and in his heart, drifting through his whole body, touching him with its icy fingers.

"Listen, listen, I've got money. I mean really a lot. I could pay anything. More than you dreamed . . ."

The tape blanketed his mouth as the steel trap closed around his right wrist.

"Okay, torch the canvases. We'll take care of the other bit."

He was screaming but there was only gurgling in his throat. He kicked out with his legs, but the ropelike arms that held him moved not an inch. And his arm—his right arm—was being dragged away from his body, flattened like pasta on some hard surface.

Dear God, no! Not his right hand. The fingers that held the brush.

It hurt in his soul. There was a sound borne of the ultimate horror, an awful splintering, crashing, crushing noise that ripped at his essence and scrambled his brain. Again and again and again his silent scream communed with it, until the two were one, merging in the unholy alliance that signaled the murder of his future and the assassination of his dreams.

TWENTY-SEVEN

POOLSIDE IN BENEDICT CANYON, LUCY MASTERSON sipped on the ice-cold martini and laughed out loud at the lonely sky, as John Cougar Mellencamp—soft and creamy on KROQ—gave her the lowdown on his hometown. She was thinking of Jane. Brilliant, beautiful Jane with the larger-than-life-size heart, who could forgive and forget and keep her as a friend when she had every reason to bury her. Jane, who had finally gotten even with the mad sister who hated her.

At that very moment she would be rubbing Julie's nose in the glorious mess she had created for herself. It was the first day of principal photography, and just over the hills, down in the Valley studio-land, Scarlett O'Hara would be sipping mint julep on the mocked-up veranda at Tara. And out on the edge somewhere, lost in a sea of grips and boom microphones, cranes and tall lights, would be the fuming, furious, impotent Julie Bennett attempting in vain to exercise her "script approval." It was a wonderful vision—the criminal prostrate at the feet of the victim. Jane would be riding her star into glory, placed there by the very person who dreamed only of her destruction.

From the moment Billy Bingham had let slip in Helena's that Jane and Julie were sisters, it had all fallen into place. It explained a lot, but Lucy had kept it to herself. Jane must have had her reasons for wanting the relationship to be secret.

One day she would volunteer the information. Until that time Lucy was happy to keep her mouth shut.

She reached for the cold martini. It was generous of Jane to let her use the house while she was shooting. Later Lucy would wander down to the court and whack a few balls into the net, or maybe just order up lunch before anesthetizing herself with some MTV. Decisions. Decisions. It was tough as hell at the top.

The warbling of the telephone cut into her thoughts. Was it the house phone or the one from Michael Landon's old estate down below the road? Sometimes it was difficult to tell. In the quiet canyons sound traveled as fast as bad news.

Lucy pulled herself up languidly and meandered lazily toward the cabana. One of the lines was ringing. She pushed the flashing red button. "Yeah?"

"Jane?" The voice was sharp, full of tension, urgent.

"Nope. She ain't here. She's workin'. Any message?"

"Christ! No." A pause: "Who are you?"

"It's Lucy Masterson. I'm a friend of Jane's. Who *is* this?"

"Oh, Lucy, it's Billy Bingham. Listen . . ." He could hardly speak.

"What's going down, Billy? You sound freeze-dried."

"Yeah. Listen, Lucy. I'm sorry . . . I need to find . . . Julie Bennett. In the desert they said she was in L.A., maybe shooting some movie with Jane. I don't know . . ."

"Billy, are you okay? You sound ill." His words were slurred, but there was no mistaking the determination that was propping them up.

"Lucy! Julie Bennett. Please!"

"Well, I think she's over at the Universal lot. Jane's shooting a Pete Rivkin TV thing there. Julie's got something to do with it, an' I know she's goin' to be there today because Jane was laughing about it last night."

The whirring of the line said Billy Bingham had gone.

Wow! Money and fame didn't sound as if they agreed with Billy Bingham. Lucy wondered what he needed Julie Bennett for. Who knew? You could become addicted to the weirdest things. For sure that piece of flesh would be an acquired taste.

The right-hand buzzer was alight, the intercom to the front gate. Lucy pressed it irritably. "Who is it?"

"Special messenger with urgent parcel for Ms. Jane Cummin."

Lucy flicked the switch that opened the gates and mooched back toward the house. In this town everything was urgent. It was probably an invitation to some social climber's dinner party.

The courier ambled across the courtyard, not knowing that his "hi there" smile was falling on stony ground. "Sign here, please. Hey, you gotta great tan." Lucy gave him a "drop dead" look as she flicked the pencil across the book.

She took the parcel. Brown manila. Noted the words. UR-GENT. FOR JANE CUMMIN. OPEN IMMEDIATELY.

That sounded pretty insistent. It was probably better to take a look. If it *was* important, she could always reach Jane at the studio. She ripped at the envelope as the chastened messenger retreated.

It looked like photographs, P.R. shots probably. For Lucy, looking at pix of Jane was always a pleasure.

But there was no pleasure at all in looking at *these* pictures.

There was only horror, and fear, and terror for her friend, and the dreadful danger that had engulfed Jane once again.

WHEN ROBERT FOLEY'S BEAT-UP CHEVY ROARED DOWN THE approach road to 3000 Benedict Canyon Drive, Lucy Masterson was standing in the open gateway. It had been thirty agonizing minutes since she'd phoned him.

She ran toward the opening window of the car. "Robert, thank God you're here. Listen, she's done it again."

Lucy fumbled at the envelope, grabbing for the note. "There's a letter. Saying she's going to distribute the photographs and she doesn't give a damn what Rivkin does. She's going to start at the set today. Hand them out to everyone on the series. Right in front of Jane. And she's called a press conference for this evening at the Bel Age. She's going to do it, Robert. The crazy bitch is going to do it!"

Robert Foley's haggard face stared back at her. "The same

photographs?" There was accusation in there with the question. Jane had forgiven Lucy. Robert Foley couldn't.

"Yes." Lucy flicked her eyes away from his.

"Show me the note."

Julie's big, round, flamboyant hand meant what it said. There was no mistaking the angry determination of the words. Jane as Scarlett had been the last straw. Julie didn't care anymore—about the books and the money and the acclamation. Nothing mattered any longer but the terrible revenge she must have on the beautiful girl who would be his wife.

His haunted eyes sought Lucy's once again. "Why, Lucy? In God's name, why?"

"I don't know. I don't *know*! She's crazy. She needs a doctor. We've got to do something."

"Get in. Do you know where she is?"

"Yes. She's somewhere on the Universal lot. Over in the Valley. We could make it in twenty minutes, maybe."

Robert Foley crunched the gears and turned the car in the narrow driveway. "If we get there in time, maybe we can stop it. Maybe Pete can stop it, like he did before." The Chevy screeched out onto Benedict and powered up toward Mulholland.

"How could she do a thing like this? It's just *incredible*. To her own sister!"

"What did you say?" At the Mulholland light, he turned to look at her.

Lucy stared back at him, at first not understanding what she had let slip. "God, yes. You didn't know either, I guess. Jane and Julie are sisters. Billy Bingham told me. For some weird reason, neither of them wanted anyone to know."

Robert Foley's mind was suddenly, inexplicably, on red alert. It was a brain-fusing revelation. But somehow it was even more than that. The feelings in his gut, the strange wrenching at his heart, was way ahead of the intellect's power to understand.

"Jane Cummin and Julie Bennett are sisters?" He wanted to get it right. "They can't be." Somehow forbidding it was necessary, even though it didn't help.

"Yes, they are. Bingham said so, and I believe him. He

lived with Julie, and I can't stand him, but he's not the type to make up a thing like that. Perhaps it makes things easier to understand. I mean, some family thing that would explain all the hatred."

"Both English. Julie Bennett's father was an actor . . . I think I read . . ."

Robert Foley's mind was screeching now, singing the impossible descant with a voice that had lost all control. Too fast. Too slow. Too loud. Too soft.

"And her mother some European princess. Yugoslavia? Albania?" said Lucy.

"No!"

Robert Foley's shout reverberated throughout the ancient car and sent Lucy's racing heart into overdrive.

Behind them the driver leaned heavily on the horn. The lights had changed.

"Hold on, Robert," said Lucy nervously. "Don't lose it now." They had to get there. Had to *do* something. It was funny how she could get people wrong. She'd imagined he was the coolest seed in the center of the cucumber.

But Robert's foot was on the accelerator, and his mouth had closed down around the dreadful shout and was now a jagged scar across his face.

Because now he knew. He knew what it was all about. What the whole dreadful business was all about.

Two heinous crimes were about to be committed. One against nature. One against God.

LIKE A WOUNDED ANIMAL, BILLY BINGHAM MOVED PAINFULLY toward his objective.

He had lost everything, but he had to hang on to his senses, for just a little bit longer, until it didn't matter anymore.

Strapped across his chest, wrapped in the bloody bandage, his useless hand screamed its unending messages at his brain. At the emergency room in Santa Monica they had been visibly shocked, and in the whiteness of the young resident's face as he had probed the carnage Billy had read the writing on the wall of his artistic future.

"I don't know if we can save this hand."

All his dreams, his ambitions, and his longings would be sliced from him.

Amputation. But in the absence of a future there was still purpose, the glorious single-minded purpose that alone could revenge the murder of his soul. And it was the contemplation of that, not the Percodan, that he was using to quell his pain.

In his nostrils was the acrid smell of his burning art. In his ears there was still the reverberating sound of his bones breaking. In his memory, written in blood, was a woman's name. The name that had come from behind the flashlight.

Julie Bennett.

The art-loving producer at Universal had been only too pleased to provide the studio pass for the art hero. But it was so difficult to fight back the waves of nausea and the unconsciousness that threatened to sabotage his mission. It was so hard to stay upright as he lurched drunkenly beneath the burning heat of the midday sun. Thank God for the thing that he could feel beneath the clenched fingers of his left hand . . . the firm, ribbed butt of the gun.

THE WORDS THAT ROBERT FOLEY HAD UTTERED FELT AS IF they didn't belong to him; his voice and his mind had been taken over by a far more powerful being.

On the edge of the *Tomorrow* set, he shuddered with the exertion of his quarter-mile sprint across the vast studio lot and with the terrible realization that after all the years he would now finally be forced to make his choice.

He could see it all, as he craned his neck above the crowd. Jane, standing proud on the wooden porch of Tara, the close-up camera groveling at her beauty, capturing the look of shocked surprise as she stared down at her tormentor.

Julie Bennett was a few feet in front of her and below her, and her arm was raised high, holding the envelope like a dagger. There and then Julie was about to expose her, to throw the terrible evidence among the crew who worshiped Jane, so that she could watch the shame in the eyes of the gentle girl she longed to destroy.

Now, at the sound of his voice, startled by its spine-chilling urgency, she paused.

On the set there was silence.

A movie more mighty—more real—than any ever filmed was gripping the imagination of everyone.

Robert Foley shoved his way toward his objective. Nobody tried to stop him. No one was able or willing to stand in the way of a man whose face defined fury and whose purpose looked like destiny.

Julie Bennett had reached the foot of the stage and now she turned like a cornered jungle animal, the leopard at bay, claws open, her ripe, red lips stripped away from her teeth. Her smile was a grimace, twisted and cruel, as she hissed the words.

"I want you all to see . . . what I have here."

Her shaking hand reached inside the envelope.

The crowd surrounded her now. Nobody spoke. All action had stopped in the face of naked emotions too powerful to resist.

Robert Foley stepped into the silent circle, as if through the gates of hell. Unflinching, he walked toward her, and his voice was soft now.

"Julie, listen to me," he said.

Above them, Jane watched the drama unfold. She stood rooted to the spot, unable to think or feel as the blood drained from her and the nightmare unfolded before her eyes. In slow motion the photograph was emerging from the envelope. Julie had made her terrible decision. She was prepared to destroy everything to achieve her mad, evil objective. But Robert was there. And behind him, melted by the heat, her big breasts heaving with exhaustion, stood Lucy Masterson. Jane was a spectator to her own fate, but even then she felt there was something else that she should remember. Someone else was here, but with no reason.

"I don't want to listen. To you or anyone. I just want . . ."

"You *must* listen to me—before you destroy yourself, and your flesh and blood."

Robert Foley's voice was quiet as the hurricane's eye. "I was a priest. Before I became a doctor, I was a priest."

Sudden doubt hovered above Julie Bennett.

Jane's hand flew to her mouth. A priest! Robert Foley a priest. The air whistled from her lungs and the adrenaline surge tide shook her body. A priest! A vow of celibacy. The renunciation of the flesh. Robert Foley. Robert Foley in her arms. She recalled his desperate scream that afternoon in Benedict Canyon, as he betrayed his promise and flooded her yearning body with the life he had vowed never to give. Yes, there *had* been another lover. The lover that went by the name of God.

"But you're a doctor," said Julie Bennett, uncertain at last. The awesome feeling built within her that this man—who stood before her, so haunted, so impossible to ignore—knew something she must hear.

"Yes, but I *was* a priest."

Robert Foley's face was haggard with the enormity of what he must do. He tried to hold on to himself, to force from his lips the story he should not tell. There would be no going back from this act, the passing on of God's own secret. He would forsake his Master anew. He would reveal the words he had received in that confessional so many years ago.

He spoke slowly, carefully, and with the terrible intensity of the damned.

"I was a Roman Catholic priest in London many years ago. One day a woman doctor, an obstetrician, came to see me to confess. She was in torment because of something she had done. She was your doctor, Julie—and your mother's doctor, too. When you were so very ill. When they thought you were going to die."

Julie stared at him in horror—mesmerized—as he brought the ghosts to life. In the depths of her body she felt the memory of an ancient and specific pain, a pain that felt like death.

From the portico, from the distant astral plane where her soul was, Jane listened, numbed by the drama that was unfolding before her.

Pete Rivkin moved to Foley's right hand, an impotent spectator. Daniel Galvin III, inexplicably silenced at last by the drama, stood dumbstruck at his side.

Robert Foley's voice was strained. The words dragged

from him, forced from his mouth, the pain flickering over his face like the candles of a burning altar.

"You were unconscious—all but dead—as she performed the Caesarean section, and everyone thought that the baby was dead, too. But it wasn't, Julie. By some miracle the baby lived. Your baby. Your own baby."

"No!" Julie's denial sprang from her. She had no baby. She had no womb. In the barren desert, her life had been spent in gruesome celebration of her infertility.

"My baby died," she pleaded, her voice small, like that of a little girl.

"At the moment the baby was born the doctor was told there was trouble with your mother's birth. It had been completely free of complications, but for some reason nobody ever understood, the child was stillborn. You, who didn't want your daughter, who had conceived her in anger and jealousy, had the live baby. Your mother and father, desperate for another child, had the dead one."

Breath hissed from between Julie Bennett's teeth.

Above them Jane's eyes widened as her heart pounded.

"The doctor switched the babies. You were told that yours had died. But your mother's child was *your* child, Julie. Jane was never your sister. She is your daughter."

Robert Foley stood up straight. He had betrayed God to save the woman he loved.

A strangled cry rose from the cold heart of Julie Bennett. Conceived in her icy depths, it rushed upward to be free of her.

Jane saw the sudden movement on the periphery of her vision.

Billy Bingham.

Billy alone had not understood the meaning of the strange words he'd heard. He had only seen the object of desire, floating, coming, going on the tide of uncertain vision. He swayed and staggered, and he tried to remember the hate that would make him do the thing that he must do. Yes, she had destroyed his beautiful paintings and turned his hand to pulp so that he could never be what he *had* to be, become what he had to become. He laughed out loud at the ridiculous enormity of it all. How could she be so evil? He lurched forward into the limelight and stood in front of the monster and dried her scream in her throat as Julie Bennett's wild eyes saw her nemesis. With his good hand he pulled the gleaming gun from his pocket and he pushed it gently against her pillow-size breast.

Billy Bingham squeezed the trigger.

The roar of the gun and the belch of blood broke the spell that bound the audience. Daniel Galvin moved first, launching his massive frame across the intervening space at Billy. But Billy had been hanging by broken fingertips to the precipice of consciousness, and now that he had seen the blood spurt from the monster he could let go at last. He fell, dropping, diving into a glorious oblivion amid Daniel Galvin's flailing limbs.

The sound of the second shot was muffled, its noise lost in the cushion of heavy bodies. And nobody really noticed the fine flecks of bright red blood that had appeared, as if by magic, on Billy Bingham's unconscious lips.

Julie Bennett had staggered back with the force of the original bullet, and now a silly smile of recognition, fear, and supplication wrestled with shock for control of her face.

"Billy?" she said, her useless question hanging in the air, shaken by the reverberating sound of the shot.

Robert Foley sprang toward her, one arm behind her head, the other around her waist as he lowered her willing limbs to the ground. She sat there, quite still, watching him, her eyes flicking backward and forward to him, and to the blood. There was so much of it, the crimson spreading out to conquer the white of the tentlike caftan, deep and rich and red.

But her mind was already going back to the words she had heard, trying to put them in order, to understand the extraordinary thing that she had been told. Immediately the horror was flooding back.

"Jane? Not Daddy's girl? Mine? My baby?"

Tears mingled now with the blood, flowing silently from her, coursing quietly, as the crimes she had committed hovered above her restless soul.

She looked up at Robert Foley, but he wasn't there anymore. Instead her head was cradled in different arms.

The arms of her daughter.

"Jane? Jane! Dear God . . . what . . . have I done?"

Tenderly, Jane rocked her, bobbing gently with impossible emotion of the raging sea of feelings.

"Oh, Julie. Julie. If only we had known . . ."

But twin hammers had struck Julie Bennett's eyes, fragmenting them with a glassy stillness.

"Jane . . . forgive . . ."

Jane crushed her close to her breast, and Julie's lifeblood flowed against the heart it had mothered.

"It's all right now. We're together now," Jane murmured.

EPILOGUE

JANE WALKED SLOWLY TO THE EDGE OF THE CLIFF. IT was so quiet here, high above the sparkling city, all wrapped up in the scented night. The dry wind was blowing softly, touching her cheek like the breath of a lover, as it traveled through the starlit sky on its endless journey from the desert to the sea.

Above her the moon was solid in the heavens, painting the ocean beyond the distant hills, and before her, lost in its own mad importance, silent and shimmering, lay the city of the angels that had captured her heart. Down there in the glittering pleasure dome, the neon paradise of maybe and might-have-been, a real-life drama was unfolding. Her mother was fighting for the life that Billy Bingham had all but destroyed.

Mother. The word seemed so strange, shorn of meaning in the emotional maelstrom that had engulfed her. But at the same time it spoke directly to her blood, shouted its meaning in the depths of her heart. The mind-numbing fact that had wrenched itself from Robert's lips had dissolved all the hatred and the desire for revenge in the simple warmth of daughter's love.

Jane's sigh merged with the jasmine-laden night air, as her eyes roamed over the jewel-studded carpet that was Los Angeles. Somehow the gleaming lights comforted her. "We know all about sorrow, about life and death, and hurting hearts," they seemed to say. She wiped the tears from her eyes and allowed the sad smile to play around her lips. Yes, L.A. knew all about emotional dramas. It may not have invented them, but it had discovered how to turn them into fame and fortune. Even poor Julie would have appreciated that.

Below her the car climbed the canyon road toward the house, and she knew it was Robert. At once the emotions collided, as her longing to lose herself in his arms fought with her unwillingness to hear the message he would bring.

She turned and inclined her head to one side, listening intently for the sound of tires on gravel.

And then, there he was, striding through the brightly lit house and across the terrace toward her.

Jane searched his face for the truth as he hurried nearer, but then she could wait no longer. She ran to him, her arms reaching for the lover she would marry, and she buried herself in the comfort of his strength.

"Darling, oh, my darling," she murmured.

He held her tight to him, crushed against his chest, his fingers caressing her hair, rubbing gently against the soft skin of her neck.

"I love you, Jane. I love you so very much."

She lifted her eyes to his, and her soul went out to the haunted man who had learned at long last to love.

He looked down at her, and his hand moved to smooth away her tears.

His voice was quiet. "Billy's dead."

The pain danced across her face, but it didn't wipe away the question in her expression. "Julie?"

"We won't know for a while."

Jane tore her eyes away from his, and once more they sought the twinkling lights of Los Angeles—the silent, seductive city, scene of all her triumphs and her wild despair. Out there Julie was battling for her life.

And she might live. Her mother might really live.

She held Robert more closely—for comfort, for strength, and because she loved him so desperately—as together they gazed upward at the dark enigma that was the velvet sky.

About the Author

PAT BOOTH is the author of the novels *Palm Beach,
Sparklers*, and *Big Apple*. Formerly a high-fashion
model in London, she is an established photojournal-
ist with three one-woman shows to her credit and has
published several books on photography: *Making
Faces, Self-Portrait*, and *Master Photographers*. Pat
Booth lives with her husband, Dr. Garth Wood, and
their two children in Palm Beach and London.

*Now that you know
how hot Pat Booth can be,
read her #1 bestseller*

Palm Beach

Town of the super-rich,
the super-spoiled,
the super-ruthless.

Land of sun-drenched sex and champagne-drenched parties...where status and power are pursued relentlessly.

All her life, beautiful but poor aerobics instructor Lisa Starr has dreamed of making a splash in Palm Beach. Now she's got her chance.

She will be helped by the aging queen of Palm Beach society, Marjorie Donahue. She will be loved by the handsome, charismatic Senator Bob Stansfield. She will be hated by the selfish, mysterious Jo-Anne Duke. And she will show them all that money and power are no match for the fierce determination of a smart, tough woman from the other side of the bridge.